Belizean Pedicure

An Ezekiel Novel

D Malone McMillan

3/16

This manuscript is a work of fiction. Any resemblance to any person, living or dead, is purely coincidental. No part of this book may be reproduced or transmitted in any form or means, electronic or mechanical, including photocopying, recording, or by any information storage and retrieval system without permission in writing from the author.

ISBN: 978-0-692-64882-7
Printed in the United States of America 2016

Panem et cirenses

Gentle my Rose with fragile heart
Rough façade but cover frail
Of tender heart unwalled now held

"When we read the creation story we run the risk of imagining that God was a magician, with a magic wand which is able to do everything. But it is not so. He created beings and let them develop according to internal laws which He gave everyone, so they would develop, so they would reach maturity."

Pope Francis (2014)

"It vexes me when they would constrain science by the authority of the Scriptures, and yet do not consider themselves bound to answer reason and experiment."

Galileo Galilei (A long ass time ago)

PROLOGUE

"Truth nor justice is a derivative of the opinion of the majority. Like the sum of two integers, justice and truth remain a constant, unswayed by the whimsical fancies of public opinion." It seems odd to be quoting the lyrical musings of a raving lunatic, imaginary friend, or mythical Incan god, whichever the hell Hobo might in truth be. Regardless of his origin, mental health or physical state, my time with Hobo taught me a few truths, not the least of which being our Creators gave us free will yet, paradoxically, we seem destined to always follow the most tragic of paths. For nearly four years, I haven't dreamed. Well, sure I've dreamed, but the ordinary garden variety; not those with the feel and substantive weight of reality. Hobo, my mysterious ethereal vagrant, remains absent. Some days I wonder if he ever really existed or was just perhaps another fanciful ghost of that bizarre long night's apocalyptic vision. Time erodes memory as well as the certainty the vision was anything more than a crazy Jack and Ambien fueled dream.

The current reality, although not without its fair share of unsightly blemishes, is infinitely better than my apocalyptic vision. The sitting President is most certainly horrific, absent any sustainable foreign policy strategy. We have an imperial leader who willingly brought our country to the brink of class and race warfare with its resultant economic disaster for the sole purpose of furthering his agenda and popularity. Rumors swirl regarding the President's ties to the radical elements of the Muslim community. Yet his popularity grows among the liberal elites and naive youth of our country. It is the participation trophy generation after all that is coming to age. Even so, we will most likely survive this President's tenure at the helm and without a shred of substantive evidence of a sinister conspiracy…just colossal arrogance and stupidity. At least we can hope it is with ignorance and not deviant intent in which the President so brazenly acts. Burdened with $19 trillion (and climbing) in debt, the President chips away at the Constitution with Executive Orders like a drunken sailor on shore leave.

Hillary will likely follow. It is her turn and I hear and she is in alleged possession of a vagina. So that. Although a self-avowed Socialist is giving her a run for her money in securing the Democratic nomination. Never thought I would see the day Joe McCarthy's prophecy would be fulfilled. All the Republican candidates are spraying live, automatic fire within the conservative tent. They are foolishly ensnared with conservative social issues instead of focusing on what is important at the federal level...fiscal conservatism. Who cares if two gays get married? Maybe it is just nature's subtle stratagem to control the exploding surface population by reducing the birthrate. Illegal immigration will resolve itself if you empty the welfare rolls, forcing the lazy, otherwise able, entitled Americans to take jobs to eat or buy crack. Abortion? Why the hell is that issue even a federal conversation? Hell, it's a complicated question but murder, if that is what it is, is not even a federal offense. For certain, Republicans need to get the hell out of our bedrooms. Three is a crowd. Perhaps the first woman President can outperform the first president of color. There is hope, at least, and not just the brand of hope from well-written, superbly-delivered speeches. And with hope, anyone can find happiness...even Ruth.

On a micro level, my reality (while not perfect, relative to the vision) is spectacular. Ruth, my free-spirited sister, is rebellious, heavily-tatted, pierced, and a single mom to two bratty children; one destined to play nose tackle in the NFL. Fortunately, her sexual endeavors are restrained and restricted to some semblance of privacy and without the benefit of compensation. Mom lives with Esther, my oldest sister, and is growing older and crotchetier by the minute, thus torturing Esther's husband, Morris, on an hourly basis. Rose, my lovely bride, miraculously remains at my side in spite of my completely inadequate explanation of her missing pink panties.

GENESIS

So God created human beings in his own image, in the image of God he created them; male and female he created them.

Iquique, Chile; April 1, 2014: A deadly earthquake with a moment magnitude of 8.2 struck 90 kilometers of the coast of Iquique today at 10:46 PM local time. The quake was preceded by a number of moderate to large shocks and was followed by a large number of moderate to very large aftershocks, including a M7.7 event on 3 April. The massive earthquake triggered a tsunami reaching heights of over two meters hitting the coastline of Chile.

Alongside Global News

CHAPTER ONE

It was early afternoon and the Belizean sun was hot despite the season. Ardy stumbled over to Ruth's lounge chair with a frozen margarita, spilling half the contents on to his severely sunburnt arms and legs before he emptied the remainder onto her flat, well-tanned belly. Ruth didn't budge, other than to pull her shades down and eye Ardy with well-earned suspicion. Most of the frozen concoction rolled off her but for a small pool that remained trapped in her pierced belly button. Ardy pulled himself up to his knees, planted his face in her stomach, and started licking the drink off her belly. Ruth was undisturbed by his salacious behavior but Rose being Rose leapt from her chair, positioned herself behind Ardy, and delivered a rather forceful kick to his nuts.

Ardy is that friend. You know, the one your wife loathes with every cell in her being yet grudgingly tolerates therefore requiring reciprocation for the half-dozen or so of her friends you similarly loathe. Mathematically I have found the ratio to be 3:1 for the best of wives; that is to say, for every three of the wife's annoying, self-entitled, pretentious, loud-mouthed, judgmental, back-stabbing girlfriends, the husband is allowed one creepy male acquaintance. Seems all together fair.

My buddy Ardy has a rather unfortunate appearance, strongly resembling Elmer Fudd. A strange cosmic coincidence exists regarding my friends and their likenesses to cartoon characters. Ardy is quite short, a bit heavy, and completely bald. His fashion sense is likewise unfortunate, preferring Hawaiian shirts, jean shorts, and Jesus sandals. Given my current beer-to-exercise ratio and time's relentless passage, I am in no place to be judgmental. We are no doubt in far too many ways birds of a similar feather. Perhaps lacking in classic good looks, Ardy is harmless and generally a nice guy, but a bit of a creepy, old pervert. Rose would likely argue more than a bit.

"Zeke, will you please remind me why you invited this cretin?" Rose asked me.

I pointed to her friends, Ivy and Keara, both passed out on their lounge chairs with visible drool rolling down their faces. "Those residing in glass houses should restrain from throwing projectiles." Rose was a catch - she allowed a 2:1 ratio.

A longtime friend, Ardy predated my lovely wife Rose, and had been there for me when I needed a friend. He had always possessed an insatiable crush on my younger sister Ruth and, quite frankly, Ruth had not exactly discouraged him even though, thank God, she had zero romantic or sexual interest in him. I am fairly certain Ardy would have married Ruth. I am positive carnal knowledge of my sister was high on his bucket list. Now he lay face down and semiconscious at Ruth's feet in a puddle of a toxic mixture of his urine and rapidly thawing margarita.

"Now what the hell am I supposed to do with him?" I asked Rose, thinking perhaps she had overreacted a touch. Corporal punishment was not Politically Correct anymore and a forceful nut shot clearly rose to that weighty level. Couldn't she have just placed him in time out to consider his actions?

Rose tossed a brightly colored beach towel over Ardy, more to camouflage his presence than to protect him from the brutal Central American sun. "Let him sleep it off."

Ruth's full lips formed into an exaggerated pout as she leaned over and peered at Ardy lying at her feet. "Now who's gonna buy me drinks?"

"Your fiancé?" Rose suggested, full well knowing that would never happen. Regrettably for Rose, she remained the only sober person in our group. Her patience was understandably wearing thin, a frequent condition of anyone in my presence for extended periods. We were in Belize for the improbable event of Ruth's nuptials. Her fiancé was out reef fishing with our close friends. Rose nodded her head side to side in disgust. "Damn bunch of alcoholics."

I corrected her; "We're drunks, Hun. Alcoholics regularly attend meetings."

Rose pointed her middle finger in my direction and headed for the swim-up pool bar to grab herself a drink. Sobriety is overrated. Ruth called after Rose while shaking her empty tumbler; "I still need a frozen margarita." Ruth received a wiggling four-finger salute from Rose.

"What the hell is that supposed to mean?" Ruth asked me.

"A full flock of birds," I explained.

"Huh?"

"She ain't bringing you a drink," I loosely translated the vulgar gesture.

Ruth nudged Ardy with her multi-colored painted toes in an unsuccessful attempt to rouse him from his alcohol and Rose enabled slumber. To label Ruth unconventional would be a severe understatement. She bended to no one's rules, even when it came to pedicures and nail polish selection.

The charter boat with Mario (Ruth's fiancé) and the boys pulled up to the resort's dock. Ruth had shared her body with the strangest of bedfellows over the years, but Mario took the cake in an entirely different flavor. Previously an HR Vice-President with Austin's old firm, he had managed to land a lucrative position with NBC in New York. Of Italian descent, Mario was about Ruth's age, an average-looking Joe with thick, jet-black, receding hair. He was soft-spoken, highly intelligent, well-educated, un-tattooed, teetotaler, and devoutly Mormon. Mario was Betty Crocker vanilla. Ruth had never tasted vanilla, and, as such, vanilla was an exotic flavor and a perfect match for Ruth.

Mom, a devout life-long Southern Baptist, remained skeptical until Mario assured her the Mormon doctrine included the entire unabridged Baptist Bible. Mom, like most of us good Baptist, considered the King James version of His word as The source document. Mario wisely omitted the latter day addendum from Joe Smith. Edits to King James were the work of the devil. Mario also gave sincere assurances he was not into the polygamy scene. "One wife at a time is handful enough," he explained. Boy was he likely to get a lesson on "handful" with Ruth.

He was a widower with two grown kids and, by all accounts, a kind, gentle, non-judgmental man. Mom reasoned even God would not object to the mixed marriage given, hands down, he was the best catch Ruth had ever landed. Deathly frightened of water, Mom had remained stateside for Ruth's wedding. Raised on a farm full of ponds, swamps and streams, she inexplicably never learned to swim like so many other rural farm kids. Go figure. She bathed in only a half inch of water to avoid the unlikely, yet highly probable, drowning hazard. No way was Mom going to surround herself with water, even if to witness the modern day miracle of Ruth's nuptials. She was not getting any younger. I dreaded the thought of losing her...again. Mario's family, a bit more judgmental than Mario, hadn't made the trip, but instead planned a Mormon ceremony in Utah when the happy couple returned stateside. That should make for an interesting occasion.

Ruth dipped her toes into the thawing margarita goo and pressed them under Ardy's nose. Ardy initially dodged her efforts to rouse him. The soft, sensual touch of her brightly colored toes fully restored Ardy's consciousness summoning his perverse obsession with feet and he started sucking the sticky urine-tainted goo off her toes. Mario walked up, leaned down, kissed Ruth and pointed to Ardy, still attached to Ruth's toes. "Belizean pedicure?" he asked, ambiguously.

Rose returned from the swim-up bar, handed Ruth her drink, kissed Mario on his offered cheek, and kicked Ardy in the nuts for the second time. Somehow I expected it would not be the last. "Creep."

Dinner was scheduled for 9:00 PM at Fido's in San Pedro. This gave us all several hours to nap and freshen up. We were to meet on the resort's dock at 8:30 to catch the water taxi to town. San Pedro is a small fishing village on Ambergris Caye - which translates roughly into Whale Shit Small Island. The island is largely undeveloped and has a very primitive infrastructure. The main road is dirt and, in the rainy season, typically a giant puddle of mud, virtually indistinguishable from the remainder of the landscape. The real highway is the Caribbean Sea between the beach and the barrier reef located about 500 meters off shore.

As is the peculiar habit of my aberrant family, we gathered on the resort's dock slightly prior to the appointed meeting time. Being punctual even when punctuality was completely irrelevant was our somewhat bizarre obsession. One of which, at least. Frank and Annie Ruth, absent for much of the day, joined us. Frank was my requisite creepy, wildly eccentric, but good-hearted uncle. A career Army man, he served numerous tours in Korea and Vietnam while married to a lesbian Puerto-Rican. The marriage ended shortly after his Army career. Our great country discharges its cannon fodder in times of peace in order for some elected official or another to piss away the resultant savings on one useless pet project or another that lines the pockets of favored relatives, friends and/or donors. Frank's lesbian wife grew increasingly frustrated by the severe hardships of full-time penis dodging. Now Frank lived in a trailer on the family compound in Southern Georgia. Annie Ruth was a remarkably spry lesbian centenarian. Perhaps lesbians were drawn to Frank's bizarre aura. She regularly crashed funerals to secure new friends as the old ones expiration dates came due at an ever steepening logarithmic rate. She passed herself off as a distant relative. She was not, yet our family adopted her.

Frank, wearing wrinkly-butt-cheek exposing jean shorts, a tank top, and combat boots contrasted sharply with Annie Ruth in a print polyester Sunday dress, low heels, and heavy stockings. "You look nice," I said to Annie Ruth, demonstrating a clever derivative of Albert's genius. She was over 100 years old after all. At that age, beauty lies with the beholder and is subject to the inalienable forces of relativity.

"Thanks," Frank replied. I'm uncertain if he was trying to be funny or if he was just wildly delusional.

"Where the hell you been hiding all day?" I asked Frank.

15

"Pretty takes more time," he replied, without a trace of a smile.

Ardy stumbled out, last to the dock, betraying his clear failure of prudent down time utilization. He had at least showered and changed into a fresh Hawaiian-style shirt; this one with a Tabasco bottle motif, unbuttoned deeply, displaying much of his rotund, albeit hairless chest.

The sea lay calm inside the barrier reef, but the resultant wakes from the heavy boat traffic made for a bit of a rough ride. Ardy, hanging off the stern, blasted chunks less than five minutes into the boat trip thus feeding the remnants of his alcohol-soaked lunch mixed with an afternoon snack of complimentary cocktail nuts to the nocturnal (as frequently assured by many daytime tour guides) bull sharks. He wiped his face with an offered towel, smiled and said, "puke and rally."

Frank yelled over the engine noise, "Varsity Blues." Frank possessed an impressive mental library of movie and book quotes and often repeated them as if they were his personal real-life stories. He also took great joy in calling others out when they used a quote without giving proper credit. For this quote, I wasn't too sure the movie wasn't Friday Night Lights. Those two movies were interchangeable in my head, much like Space Cowboys and Armageddon. I think movie producers cheat off each other's papers.

Rose gave me an evil look, "Awesome, just frigging awesome."

Fido's is on the beach in downtown (a term loosely used) San Pedro. The well-worn, large-plank wood floor is covered by a giant teepee-like structure of native woods and palm fronds. It's a large, open-air bar and grill and a popular night spot for tourists, expats, and locals alike. Dress in San Pedro is well south of mere casual. Bathing attire is perfectly acceptable, and I would have seriously doubted any establishment ever turned anyone away for something as mundane as a dress code violation. Large caliber automatic weapon…maybe. We had a large group of about ten...maybe more if I had stopped and counted. Ardy, at the back of the group, stumbled and wiped at the puke on his Hawaiian shirt. Just as we found a table on the outside deck with a view of the sea, the bouncer intercepted Ardy on the rough hewn steps leading up from the beach.

"Sorry, man, bar is full." The bouncer said, putting a heavy duty flashlight on Ardy's chest.

Ardy protested, "Those are my friends. I'm with them." He pointed toward us seated just a few feet away on the deck, as he unsuccessfully attempted to push his way past the bouncer. A young couple from Ohio walked by and into the bar.

"Sorry my friend, like I said, full up. Maybe some other time. Perhaps, the second Tuesday of next week. It's our special topless asshole night. Drinks are free for assholes and you will fit right in." A group of six Canadians walked past, the men shirtless and the women with bikini tops displaying southern-leaning, overexposed breasts. Time is such a relentless bitch.

"But you let them in. I'm a tax-paying, flag-waving American; I know my rights." Four older, chunky guys wearing Red Sox jerseys walked past Ardy, bumping into him as they squeezed by to get into the bar.

"Listen, friend, if you must know, you are in violation of our strict jacket and tie dress code." A couple of midgets holding hands and dressed like girl scouts walked between the two, followed by an entire party of gay, flamboyantly dressed men.

I got up to go save Ardy. Rose yanked me down to the table. "Don't make me kick you in the nuts." I really needed to work on her violent tendencies.

A vile-looking stray dog began licking at Ardy's sandals where a bit of Ardy's regurgitated lunch had lodged. The dog had a serious overbite with a couple teeth missing. No doubt of some random mixture of breed, it appeared to be an unlikely cross between a Chihuahua and a German Shepard. Essentially bald, except a few random tufts of grayish hair, the dog was absent both an eye and a leg. The remains of the missing eye was just a grotesque empty socket. The right hind leg appeared to have been ripped off just above the knee joint. Clearly a male, the dog had unnaturally massive balls. Ardy nudged the dog away with his leg. The dog barred his teeth, growled, and resumed licking again. Ardy kicked the dog with force. The crowd at the bar, attracted by the commotion, booed as the dog whimpered off. Ardy continued making his case with the bouncer without success, oblivious to the dog's stealthy return. The dog lifted his right stump, unleashing an impressive stream of urine onto Ardy's leg. The crowd applauded as Ardy retreated out toward the beach into the night, squawking a stream of profanity-laced oaths, momentarily defeated.

Rose laughed uncontrollably, "Tripod just pissed on your friend."

"Don't you feel a little bad for him?" I asked Rose.

"The dog or Ardy? 'Cause Ardy, he was sucking on your little sister's toes." I just shrugged.

A couple of margaritas later, my concern for Ardy, if not completely forgotten, was seriously diminished. Fresh fried snapper, crab, lobster, coleslaw, plantains and french fries arrived at the table. Nothing is as mouthwateringly savory as truly fresh seafood. A live band started playing southern rock cover songs: Tucker, Wet Willie, Allman brothers, .38 Special, White Witch, and Cowboy, and, of course, no southern rock playlist would be complete without Skynyrd. There is something uniquely ironic to hear a cover band that likely has never set foot in the States singing of their sweet home in Alabama.

Giuseppe, Rose's baby brother, kept the drinks flowing. He had made a killing importing pirated goods from China and had generously offered to pick up tonight's tab which included Mario's indulgence. At least six deep into bottled water (priced the same as the local brew), Mario sat at the head of the table. Ruth provocatively danced on the table's top. We sat by the rail where there was a narrow column supporting the thatched roof. Ruth disturbingly seemed much practiced at the ancient sensual art of utilizing a vertical pole while dancing. The chunky Sox fans, impressed by her talents and paucity of clothing, came by and tossed Belizean dollar bills in her general direction. "Making it rain" was discounted on the island given the favorable exchange rate of $2 BZ to $1 US. Mario just offered a brilliant "that's-my-girl" smile. I liked Mario, but for the life of me I could not comprehend their obvious mutual attraction. He was perhaps the most conservative man on the planet and the complete polar opposite of my near-naked sister currently circumnavigating the pole in an inverted position.

Ivy grabbed the 16-year-old bus boy's ass as he walked by. Rose's best friend, Ivy, was about her age and not a bad-looking sort. She had beautiful blue eyes, a sizable rack, and long blonde hair…although I seriously doubted the carpet matched the drapes. I had not been, nor wished to be, made privy to that personal detail. I value my nuts. Our well-bosomed waitress spilled the entirety of the next round down Ivy's blouse. "Gringa."

Mario belted out Frank Sinatra tunes on karaoke during the band's frequent breaks which were required to maintain the appropriate level of island buzz. Our neighbor Sam accompanied Mario's performance with a very demonstrative air guitar with Sam's wife, Flo, joining them on air drums, all off-beat but enthusiastic. Giuseppe took orders for counterfeit NFL jerseys from the Canadian guys at the adjacent table while subsequently working a deal with the bar's owner to import Saranac beer. Keara arm-wrestled the midget pair simultaneously, one on each arm, for 20 Belizean dollars. My sister Esther, stone-cold sober, sat quietly by Morris nursing his first and only Cuba Libre, uncomfortably observing the surrounding madness. Austin solicited fishing tips from a group of locals who were likely guiding him to an ambush in order to kidnap him for ransom or, in lieu of suitable ransom, a bit of sadistic pleasure. Annie Ruth and Frank entered the wet t-shirt contest, later placing first and second, respectively. Larry smoked Cuban cigars by himself on the rail, looking out to sea. Rose was threatening to beat the Red Sox fans single-handedly with a full bottle of Belikin beer if they didn't immediately concede the Yankees were the bomb.

The bar closed at 4:00 AM and, as water taxi service had long since been suspended, we just moved the party out to the adjacent beach. The midgets, Canadians, waitress, former Sox fans (Rose is very persuasive), and bartender all joined us in the sand. Giuseppe had tipped nicely and the waitress brought a cheap but still unopened handle of tequila. Ivy inquired as to why the bus boy didn't come join us. The waitress gave Ivy an extra-long pull of tequila, holding back her chin until the tequila splashed down her face. "That's my baby brother, punta." Someone started a fire. I dozed off and when I woke, the fire was down and the sun was up.

It was early, and only a few locals were out and about. We began strolling down the beach toward the dock for the water taxi. Rose pointed to a large, fleshy object about twenty yards out, partially covered in the sand. "What the hell is that…a beached manatee?" she asked. As we approached, a naked human form lying face down took shape, partially camouflaged by the sand and washed-up turtle grass. An American flag stood planted in its ass, gently fluttering in the persistent onshore breeze. Crude lettering and graffiti covered the man's back resembling those on a bathroom stall at a truck stop frequented by men seeking other men for knowledge of the carnal variety. Someone had artfully drawn a Mohawk on his bald head with a pink sharpie. The stray dog, Tripod as Rose predictably called him, hovered over the man's head, blocking the view of his face with his unnaturally massive balls. "Is Tripod tea-bagging him?" Rose asked.

"Is that man alive?" I asked, thinking that to be the more compelling question. The naked man answered in the affirmative with a groan as he swatted feebly at Tripod. The dog responded by raising his stump, discharging a dark yellow stream into his face. The man, fully awake now, punched at Tripod, managing to cuff its ear with considerable force. Sadly I was more concerned with the state of the dog's hydration level. The man turned in the sand to get off his belly and onto his knees, the dog returned and attacked his exposed ball sack with considerable gusto. The man tried to stand, but the weight of Tripod attached to his mangled intimates knocked him to his ass, breaking the flag's pole off in his rectum in the process. I grimaced in empathetic pain.

"The damn dog is biting my balls!" Ardy cried, as we all recognized the sad figure to be.

"That's gonna leave a serious mark," I thought to myself, wondering just how modern the health care system was on the island.

Tripod mercifully released Ardy's nuts and scampered down the beach. Ardy sat cross-legged rubbing the sand out of his eyes using his sand- and blood-covered hands, while bleeding rather freely from both ends. His face flashed recognition and he mustered a smile. "Anybody got a beer?"

Babylon, Persia; April, 2016: The leader of The Brothers of Islam (BOI), Muhammad Bayii released a video where he is shown beheading Ron Pahlavi. Ron was the nephew of Reza Pahlavi, the former Shah of Iran. Bayii's, a former Sunni cleric from Iraq, rise to power and his ability to bring the Shi'a and Sunni factions of Islam under one tent has been a growing concern of many Western countries. Bayii, in a rambling statement, accused Pahlavi of treason against the Islamic State in "failing to complete his mission." It is unclear as to the "mission" Bayii referenced.

In a remarkable twist, Bayii claimed the deposed Shah, a Shi'a Muslim, was murdered by the "Great Satan" after meeting with him in Iraq in 1980 to discuss a plan that would return the Shah to power and unite the branches of Islam. Bayii also attributed the deaths of two of Pahlavi's children to "the evil schemes of the Great Satan." The deaths of the Shah's son Ali-Razi and his daughter Leila were ruled as suicides. Bayii threatened further retribution against unnamed members of Ron Pahlavi's cell for their continued failure to "exercise the will of Allah." Pahlavi, with the billionaire kingmaker George Smith, an unnamed Mexican Cartel financier, along with several other unnamed influential associates were rumored to be involved in a 2008 conspiracy surrounding the Presidential election. No charges were ever filed. State Department and White House representatives declined to comment.

Alongside Global News

CHAPTER TWO

Of Mayan descent, Juan was short in stature with a flat nose, jet-black hair, and dark skin from his heritage and deepened by his chosen occupation. He met us at the dock at 1:15 PM - only 15 minutes late - which in island time translates to at least 15 minutes early. Hangovers were our common thread, except for Ruth's fiancée Mario, of course. I loved him, but seriously wanted to knock the silly 'I don't have a hangover' grin off his face. No one had heard from Ardy since we abandoned him to the local police earlier that morning for medical treatment. "Foster, snorkeling party of ten?" Juan asked, as he tied the line to the dock's cleat.

Mario answered, "One short, but that would be us."

"Then please come aboard." Juan smiled broadly exposing a gold capped front tooth and waved us aboard.

Our crew slowly and deliberately began to get on board, given blinding headaches, churning bellies and the unstable platform. As we began to get situated, Juan asked, "Is that our missing guest?" Juan pointed to Ardy waddling down the dock, his mobility severely hampered by a large plastic garbage bag filled with ice and duct-taped around his mid-section.

"You're frigging kidding me," Rose said. "He is not with us. Just go."

Ruth looked at Rose and frowned. "No, Juan. Espere, por favor. El es mi amigo loco."

Belize is the only country in Central America where English is the official language, having been colonized by the Brits as British Honduras in the mid-1800s. Even so, much of the population were native Spanish speakers along with Belizean Kriol and some even more bizarre hybrid of Spanish and Kriol. With all the various ethnic backgrounds, even the English could be a bit challenging to comprehend. And adding to the equation the

23

copious alcohol consumption (the normal state on the island) by the speaker and/or the listener did not improve comprehension.

"You speak Spanish?" I asked Ruth.

"Claro que si," she answered.

"How is that?" After Ruth's practiced pole performance the evening prior, the revelation she could speak Spanish fluently created a disconcerting déjà vu moment.

Rose asked, "What's up with the twenty questions? The girl can speak Spanish. Is that a problem for you?"

Yeah, I thought. And she can pole dance. What other mysteries might my sister hold? Ardy stepped on board in obvious pain. Mario asked, "You sure snorkeling is a good idea, buddy?"

"Wouldn't miss it, and besides," Ardy shook a pill bottle, "awesome drugs. I can't even feel the stitches in my nut sack." He dry swallowed a handful of the pills. "Any beer on board, Paco?"

"It's Juan, gringo. And yes, but not until after snorkeling."

"Fuck that, I'm parched." Ardy grabbed a beer out of the cooler. "Damn Paco, your English is pretty good for a Mexican."

Juan smiled a cold smile, "Beso mi culo, bobo."

"Gracias," Ardy returned Juan's smile. Ruth laughed. I loved to hear her laugh. Ruth lived life at full speed and without the benefit of a safety net. I was frightened for her at times, as she took great risk without any hesitation or consideration of the possible, and quite frankly, likely unfavorable consequences.

Hol Chan Marine Park is a twenty minute boat road from the resort. The park is located at a cut in the barrier reef in about thirty feet of water. The water is crystal clear, in varying shades of green and blue, dictated by the composition of the ocean floor. The cloudless sky seemed to magically melt into the sea on the cusp of the horizon. Ardy passed out five minutes into the boat ride, lying flat on his back with the ice pack situated on his nuts. He looked like shit. Ardy had made a half-assed but woefully unsuccessful attempt to remove his pink-Sharpie Mohawk only to succeed in turning his bald dome a pale shade of pink. Likewise, the sodomy-themed graffiti on his torso was smeared but still clearly visible.

He had giant welts all over his body and his face from mosquito bites, and his severely sunburnt skin, where not covered by the graffiti, was a bright, fire-engine red. Ivy started cutting the duct tape securing Ardy's ice bag with a dive knife she inexplicably had strapped to her calf. Rose noticed Ivy and asked, puzzled (as we all were), "What the hell, Ivy?" I was uncertain if Rose's line of questioning was directed toward Ivy's weapon or its current utilization…both equally unnerving.

"Ruth wants a peek at his mangled nut sack." Ruth nodded her assent. "Truth is, I'm kind of curious just how much damage Tripod inflicted." Ardy didn't budge. Ivy sliced his swim trunks open after removing the ice bag. "Ahhh, shit. You can't see his balls for the freaking bandage," Ivy said, perversely disappointed. She positioned the knife under the bandage in order to continue cutting it away when Rose thankfully intervened.

"It's a good thing. Do you honestly want to see Ardy's balls? He might wake up and think you want to blow him."

"Gross, Rose!" Ivy exclaimed, immediately stopping her ill-conceived task.

Rose added, "And you can never un-see something like that. Let's just let that sleeping dog lie."

From within the boat's center console, barking erupted. Juan opened the storage locker and a three-legged mutt jumped out into Ruth's lap. "It's Tripod," Ruth laughed.

"Senorita, el nombre di me perro es Senor Feliz." Switching to English for us all to understand, "He is a most sensitive animal and gets very angry when you mention his missing leg." Juan whispered the last part of the sentence. Meanwhile, Mr. Happy, aka Tripod, was rooting around aggressively in Ardy's crotch as he remained passed out.

Ivy asked Juan, "Might Tripod prefer penis by chance?" Senor Feliz barred his broken teeth and growled at Ivy before returning his attention to Ardy's crotch. None of us dared move the dog off of Ardy, subscribing to the adage of never taking a favored bone from a dog. Ardy remained motionless, woefully oblivious to his canine sexual assault, as the boat slowed, approaching the reef.

"So tell me," Giuseppe asked Juan, "how did Tri..." (Tripod offered Giuseppe a brief guttural growl before returning to his favored mission) "...Senor Feliz lose his leg?"

"He fell overboard one day...er, night...at Shark Ray Alley, and a bull shark took it from him." The Captain moved to the bow of the boat and attached a line to the buoy moored to the bottom. About a dozen boats, over a hundred snorkelers and half again as many divers were in the water. A couple of smallish nurse sharks ventured close to the boat. Ivy squealed loudly. Austin pointed out the nurse sharks were basically oversized catfish. The squeal was, however, of sufficient volume to wake Ardy from his drug- and alcohol-induced slumber to the sight of his one-eyed tormentor tearing at his bandaged nuts. Ardy matched the pitch and volume of Ivy's squeal while grabbing Tripod gruffly by the neck and flinging him overboard. "Senor. If you would not like to swim to shore, you will be now retrieving my precious," Juan said softly.

Ardy was unmoved by Juan's gentle tone, but the machete stationed at his nuts was suitably convincing. Ardy jumped overboard, squealing loudly again as the saltwater found his recent wounds. Tripod immediately swam up to his unlikely rescuer and started licking Ardy on the face. Ardy, unappreciative of the physical display of emotion, purposely dunked Tripod under the surf. As Ardy lifted him above his head to hand to Juan in the boat, Tripod predictably released an impressive stream of urine onto Ardy's upturned face. For a relatively small dog, he had one massive bladder. Ardy rinsed the piss off with saltwater and climbed back in the boat wordlessly as the rest of us jumped overboard in snorkeling gear.

Juan joined us and gave us a guided tour of the amazing reef, leaving Ardy unattended on the boat with Tripod. Juan clapped his hands underwater to gain our attention when he spotted something of interest. Sea turtles, moray eels, nurse sharks, sergeant majors, grouper, and jacks cruised the clear water around the reef, along with a handful of other colorful tropical fish that looked strangely out of place in their own environment rather than inside an aquarium. The sea was clear and the visibility amazing. After some forty minutes, we swam back to the boat. Ardy had used the time to selfishly kill the remaining beer on board and swallow a couple more pain pills. Based on Tripod's extraordinary calm nature, I highly suspected he had fed the dog a couple of beer-chased pain pills, as well.

Our next snorkel stop, Shark Ray Alley, was only a ten minute boat ride from the marine park. Juan informed us that local fishermen had used this area to stop and clean their day's catch for many years, tossing the bloody remains overboard. After some time, sharks and rays began to hang out for an easy meal, and now swarmed any boat that entered the area. Rose approached Juan at the boat's stern where he was preparing a plastic chum container by slicing up about a gallon of fresh sardines into a fetid mixture of bloody, odorous fish parts. They chatted in conspiratorial tones too quiet to make out the conversation. Juan's face lit up as he nodded in agreement, and Rose returned to her seat with a frighteningly devilish grin.

Juan removed the line attached to the buoy and began the short trip over to the Alley. He had us all gear up and advised the best time to interact with the sharks and rays was when he first pulled up and set anchor. Ardy planned to remain on board, as the saltwater irritated his wounds. As Juan slowed the boat, about a dozen nurse sharks ranging from three to seven feet were already trailing the boat along with several rays, some of which possessed impressive five- to six-foot wing spans. Perfectly clear, the blue water made it easy to see the sandy bottom only about eight foot below.

We were all geared up, and Juan asked Ardy to move to the bow and prepare to toss the anchor over on his order. Ardy gingerly moved to the bow, secured the anchor in one hand and the rope in the other. He faced out to sea while his swim trunks flapped in the wind, exposing a bit more of his ass than I cared to see. Rose stealthily moved up behind him and attached a hand towel filled with chum to a loop in his split swim trunks. This can't be good, I thought. The Captain suddenly reversed engines and, as intended, tossed Ardy into the shallow water. The sharks immediately surrounded him and completely covered him from view. A large male nurse shark rooted the others away and began aggressively tearing at the chum bag affixed to Ardy's injured ass. In the process, the shark briefly held Ardy underwater, face down with his swim trunks parted by Ivy's cut. Tripod seemed genuinely concerned for Ardy and stood on the bow barking relentlessly. The rest of us were hysterically laughing although, in retrospect, we should have at this point been offering some semblance of physical assistance or, at a minimum, passive concern. With her head playfully cocked to one side, Ruth asked, "Is that shark humping or eating him? I really can't tell." Mercifully, the chum quickly exhausted, and the shark released Ardy to the surface. Ardy, gasping for breath, eyed Rose with suspicion, but wisely refrained from comment. He managed to climb back on board, unaided.

"Beer me, bitches."

Rose responded, "Love to, but some asshole drank it all."

Ardy opted for a couple more pain pills chased with the only remaining beverage on board, bottled, or more precisely bagged, water. He had to be approaching life-threatening overdose levels but, then again, there are fates worse than death. And being sexually violated by a nurse shark shortly after having a flag stick broken off in one's rectum and subsequently having one's balls eaten off by a one-eyed-three-legged-mutt might just make that lofty cut. Juan eyed Ardy suspiciously as Senor Feliz laid uncharacteristically lifeless on the Captain's chair. Ardy positioned himself on the boat's bow far away from Juan and was shortly fast asleep or, more accurately, unconscious.

The ride back was mostly uneventful until we approached the resort's dock. Senor Feliz remained lifeless, and Ardy still held his position perilously close to the bow of the boat. Juan, clearly a seasoned captain, killed the boat's engines just as we hit a large wake at a 45-degree angle from a passing water taxi. Ardy slid off the bow into the sea. Instantly awake, he squealed again as his wounds opened, and he began bleeding rather freely. Ardy started swimming for the beach, only about 60 yards away. A large shark immediately took notice.

"Senor Ardy, please return to the boat at once."

"Screw that. I'll swim to shore," Ardy said, noticing the nearby shark. "It's just another one of those giant catfish."

"Suit yourself, Senor, but you gringos really need to learn how to better identify your shark species. That one there..." he explained, pointing to the massive, shadowy object circling Ardy, "...ain't no catfish. That tiburon, mi amigo, is a bull shark." The shark stopped circling and slowly swam up to Ardy from the rear. Undoubtedly with thoughts of Tripod's gnawed off leg, Ardy thrashed about madly in an attempt to return to the boat but made precious little progress. The bull shark gently nudged Ardy's leg. Ardy squealed. Tripod came to life and started barking incessantly. The shark gingerly approached Ardy again and took a test bite out of his upper calf. Ardy squealed and lost consciousness. Ivy retrieved her dive knife from its sheath, placed it in her teeth, and dove overboard in a rather remarkable Tarzan impression. The force of the water knocked the knife out of Ivy's mouth breaking her two front teeth in the process and strongly suggesting Tarzan's TV knife was constructed of a more pliant material than steel. The shark swam away, displeased with Ardy's offered cuisine. Tripod jumped overboard carrying a life vest in his mouth, while Ivy swam back to the boat unaided. Tripod swam up to the lifeless Ardy, gently bit him on the ear, and barked ferociously. Before anyone else offered assistance, Ardy regained consciousness, grabbed the offered vest, and returned to the boat. He lifted Tripod up to Juan's outreached arms. Tripod yet again unleashed a stream of urine into Ardy's upturned face. Their relationship was moving swiftly toward codependence. Either that or Tripod had a pee fetish.

Babylon, Persia; April, 2016: The Brothers of Islam (BOI) announced today the annexation of the United Arab Emirates into the Islamic Nation of Modern Persia. UAE joins Iraq, Iran, Turkey, Afghanistan, Qatar, Syria, and Pakistan in the newly minted, oil-rich nation ruled by theocracy and under Sharia Law. In a televised speech broadcast from the Hanging Gardens of Babylon, Mohammed Ghazi welcomed the Muslims of UAE "back into the warm bosom of Islam." Ghazi, as he has in the other assembled nations, immediately nationalized all privately-held property, publicly executed secular leaders, and gave non-Muslims 24 hours to exit the country with a stern warning to leave with only the "shirts on your backs."

A White House spokesperson, declining to comment on the BOI's history of beheadings, described the event "as a shining example of democracy at work. A peaceful transition of power to a duly-elected government."

Ghazi further stated, "We will not rest until we welcome all nations into the warm bosom of our Islamic Nation." Ghazi outright dismissed rumored plans to utilize the nuclear weapons arsenal acquired from Pakistan. "The infidel western nations will crumble from within into smaller and smaller morsels at the feet of Allah and beg the one true God to be a servant of our Great Islamic Nation."

Alongside Global News

CHAPTER THREE

The sun breaks early in Belize, warmly illuminating the emerald sea lapping against the white, sandy beach framed against the closely-abutting, green vegetation. Demonstrating one of God's countless miracles, nine--oops, eight (too soon, Pluto?)--planets orbit this star and we occupy the only Goldilocks one among the lot. In about twelve hours, God would perform a second miracle of this day as we were scheduled to witness the unlikely event of Ruth's nuptials. Rose made coffee, and we watched from our condo's balcony as the island woke from its evening slumber. A steady stream of beater bicycles rode by, transporting resort workers to their day's tasks, choosing the narrow beach path in lieu of the dirt and pothole-ridden road fronting the resort. Workers raked the beach, distributed lounge chair pads, and erected umbrellas, their shirts already ringed with perspiration. Smartly-uniformed maids made their way into the resort, preparing to stave off the creeping chaos beget by the self-absorbed guests. Tourists in brightly colored running shoes, determined to stay fit while in paradise, dodged the bicycles, sharing the narrow beach path. Fishermen pulled to the docks, picking up their morning charters to harvest the ocean's bounties or, at least, fatten their meager purses. A large iguana posed on a sizable piece of beached coral underneath a palm tree, its fronds fluttering in the gentle breeze. And there was Ardy, floating on a kid's blow-up raft in the middle of the resort's main pool, naked save a baseball cap and his mangled and blood-encrusted bandages.

"I should go retrieve him before security rolls his ass," I said to Rose.

"Don't you dare. Besides, it appears he is resting comfortably, and Ardy, of all people, needs his beauty sleep. I expect he suffered another long night at the island clinic. Twenty more stitches to add to his collection."

31

"Truth. At least this time he had Ivy as company. Did she find a dentist?"

"Hell no, but they give away pain pills at the clinic like candy. She will stay for today's wedding and leave tomorrow." I couldn't wait to see the wedding pictures. Epic.

My sister Esther and her husband Morris were sharing our two-bedroom condo, and they joined us on the balcony. Esther noticed Ardy floating in the pool and said, "Zeke, brother, you have some bizarre friends."

Ruth and Mario, returning from an early morning stroll, caught sight of Ardy. Ruth, fully clothed for a change, jumped into the pool, performing an impressive cannonball just inches from Ardy's float, waking him abruptly from his slumber. Ruth climbed on his naked back, and Ardy carried Ruth out of the pool on his shoulders. "And sister," Rose rightfully noted.

**

Rose's brother Giuseppe is an entrepreneur, certified lifeguard, international Saranac Beer ambassador, licensed paramedic, motivational speaker, grill master, importer of Chinese unlicensed goods, adjunct law professor, web designer, free-lance photographer, apothecary, paralegal, renowned juggler, dive master, fire eater, underwear model, notary public, and internet card-carrying ordained pastor and, as such, the officiate at Ruth's wedding. Rumor has it he is certified to perform brain surgery in certain South American countries, as well. He, like most of the crew, was pregaming at Cowboy's, the pool bar at the resort. The wedding was not scheduled to begin for another 90 minutes.

My creepy uncle Frank volunteered to photographically document the nuptials and showed up with a massive VHS video tape recorder and a Polaroid camera with extra film stored in his camouflaged fanny pack. Frank, along with his archaic equipment, belonged in a museum. He was wearing his signature inappropriately short shorts but with a buttoned-down, starched and brilliantly white shirt. He wore a wide black polyester tie with a white emblem, imploring us to not forget the Vietnam POWs and MIAs. The tie was perfectly aligned in the center of his shirt featuring a precise military gig line and was secured in place with a Confederate flag tie pin. Annie Ruth dressed, as always, in a conservative polyester print dress. She had unfortunately surrendered the thick hosiery to the island's oppressive heat. One-hundred-year-old legs, replete with large, dark clusters of blue spider veins, are a sight best left unseen. My buddies Austin and Larry sat on the swim-up side of the bar in bathing suits, smoking Cuban cigars and exchanging fishing lies with some of the resort's other guests. It appeared they had taken the resort casual dress recommendation for the wedding to its most liberal interpretation. Flo had Sam on a short leash after the crazy night at Fido's. She was rightfully concerned some of our brand of crazy might rub off on her impressionable husband. The two of them had made themselves pretty scarce.

The midgets sat on the bar and were chatting with Keara and drinking Belikin draft beer. Ruth had been rather generous with her wedding invitations the last several alcohol-inspired days, and the midgets fittingly sensed a good time. Today, the two of them were dressed as medieval court jesters down to their pointy-toed shoes. Nothing like embracing a stereotype to remove its sting. Conversely, Rose's friend Keara, a very statuesque (standing well over 6'2"), long dark-haired native Alaskan, was dressed conservatively. It made for an interesting contrast. The midgets were a married couple originally from Atlanta but currently residing in Tokyo. They both graduated from Georgia Tech with computer engineering degrees and moved to Japan to work for Sony. They owned a home on Ambergris Caye and worked from the island as much as possible, explaining the Japanese were ultra-conservative in the work place and drove them "bat-shit crazy." Here they could let their "midget freak flag fly."

Keara asked, "Do you prefer the term midget over little people?"

They replied in unison, more or less talking over each other, "I don't give a shit what you call us. It means the same thing. We proudly embrace who we are, and nothing you call us that means we are short little assholes will hurt our feelings. We don't care what you call us, just call us." Linus took a long pull of his beer and added for clarification, "...when there is a party."

"I'll drink to that," Keara toasted. "What do you guys do for Sony?"

"Can't tell you much about it, but it is a ground-breaking, virtual reality technology that seamlessly melds the real world with the digital world and will no doubt revolutionize the gaming industry."

The midgets had my full attention but quickly changed the subject. I remained a bit fuzzy regarding my past and unsure which memories were real and which just a dream. I hadn't had any crazy dreams in a long time, and Hobo - if he ever existed - had not made an appearance in a long time either. My mental state was as healthy as it had been in years but, on occasion, I had these intense déjà vu moments. The mention of virtual reality was one of those times. I pinched myself, literally; it was my crude method to validate I was not dreaming, as the entire scene, including Ruth's unlikely nuptials to Mario, had a surreal feel.

Ruth, of course, had also invited Juan, and he brought Senor Feliz along as his plus one. Ardy was as customary in a Hawaiian shirt, but today he added white linen pants held up with a pull string. Ivy opted for a skimpy bathing suit top and ultra-short skirt, hoping the 16-year-old bus boy would be present and suitably impressed with her ample breasts and long, tanned legs to distract his attention from the missing front teeth. Where there are ample tatas, there is always hope.

A newspaper reporter arrived from the San Pedro weekly newspaper to interview Ardy regarding his shark attack. In spite of the abundance of sharks, shark attacks were pretty rare on the island. She was young, thin, short, dark-skinned, and in possession of both a vagina and a pulse. Ardy stood, unnaturally erect, and made a futile attempt to suck in his gut. He was visibly drooling. Tripod, annoyed with the attention Ardy was giving the reporter, barred his broken teeth at her and was unceremoniously brushed aside by Ardy using his uninjured leg. "So, please Mister Ardy, tell me about the shark attack. You must have been terribly frightened, yes?" the reporter asked. It would notably be the only "yes" directed towards Ardy she would ever utter. Frank got up from his bar stool and started videotaping the interview with the lens cap still securely affixed to the lens.

"Not really. My faith in God carried me through," Ardy responded with considerable bluster, omitting his adolescent girl-like squeals, subsequent fainting spell, and unlikely rescue by his perpetually agitated, three-legged tormentor. Should anyone's life warrant the abandonment in their faith in the goodness of God, at least since Job, Ardy's streak of luck might just make the cut... And we were only in the early innings of a long ugly game. Rose rolled her eyes. Without the benefit of speech, Tripod displayed his displeasure by lifting his stump, soiling Ardy's white linen pants with yet another truly epic stream of piss. Unrequited love smarts. Rose laughed. Ardy kicked. Senor Feliz attacked. The reporter retreated. Ardy tried unsuccessfully to shake the dog loose, transferring too much of his weight to the injured leg, causing him to fall to the concrete floor. Tripod took the opportunity to change tactics and moved to attack his favored target, Ardy's balls. Ardy's linen pants were loose-fitting and Tripod only managed to grasp white linen instead of the targeted mangled meat. Ardy scrambled to his feet, abandoning his pants, now attached to Tripod's jagged teeth. Ardy fled toward the beach as fast as his injuries would allow, and Tripod gave impressive three-legged chase. We all moved outside to follow the show. The other resort guests gathered along the pool's edge, many with digital cameras, to give witness and record the surreal spectacle of a chubby, bald-headed man attired in a brightly colored Hawaiian shirt and what appeared to be a bloody, soiled diaper being chased by a demon-possessed, three-legged, one-eyed, mutt. This was truly paradise. Ardy headed for the sea, which proved to be yet another tactical error in a seemingly infinite series. Of late, Ardy was a favored play thing of the more malevolent aligned gods. Tripod followed Ardy into the warm, tropical waters, demonstrating a rather speedy, if not stylish, three-legged dog paddle. "That demon can swim!" Ardy yelled, followed by frantic cries for help. "Ayudame, por favor." Ardy was still a bit confused on the official language of Belize. Ardy had memorized a few key Spanish phrases in case of an emergency and began to utter them all. "Donde esta el bano?" "Neccesito uno mas cervaza por favor." And, ever the optimist, "Muestreme sus tetas."

Ivy, in a moment of compassion apparently absent from the rest of us, accurately noted, "Somebody should really go help him."

Rose asked, "Your legs broken, too?'

"I would help, but I'm not wearing any panties," she whispered loudly, pointing at the offending uncovered location.

"What were you thinking, Ivy? That's a seriously short skirt."

"Well, you wouldn't wear a mask to a party if you wanted to be kissed, would you?" Ivy inquired.

Frank adeptly maneuvered the video camera in an attempt to document Ivy's self-confessed lack of undergarments. "Sweet Potato Queen. I just love Ivy Conner Browne!" Rose rolled her eyes. Ivy wantonly parted her legs. Frank leered. Like I said...great wedding pictures.

Tripod caught up to Ardy and attached himself to Ardy's Hawaiian shirt with his remaining teeth. Ardy unbuttoned and surrendered the shirt to his attacker, buying himself a few more moments. The reporter returned with a camera and was snapping away, documenting the bizarre attack. Stories of shark attacks were rare, but photos of a three-legged dog attacking a tourist in the ocean would be pure gold. She saw a front page byline. Nearby in a boat, a familiar-looking group of men wearing gaily colored shirts maneuvered their vessel to rescue Ardy who had ventured thirty yards offshore to escape Tripod's jealous rage. Ardy was bleeding, injured and exhausted, and the men struggled to get him on board. One of the men heroically jumped overboard and pushed on Ardy's bare ass as the others pulled. The sea and Tripod had worked to dislodge his bandages. The resort guests along the pool erupted in applause. I was uncertain if the applause was for the rescue or the afternoon's performance. "We will be here all week, folks," I responded to the applause.

"Isn't that the group of gay guys from Fido's?" Rose asked. I shrugged as the boat headed out to sea with Ardy. Giuseppe ordered a round for everyone. Rose sent Ivy back to her room to change for the wedding and to don the appropriate undergarments. Juan waded out to retrieve Senor Feliz. The reporter smiled. Frank removed the camera's lens cover. Annie Ruth farted. Yes, Virginia, this was paradise.

***

Mario looked dapper in his all white tuxedo and was flashing an equally brilliant smile. He was seemingly beside himself as the appointed hour had arrived, and Ruth had yet to bolt. The only concession he had made to casual in his formal attire was the white flip-flops. He was standing erect underneath a wicker arch that was decorated with white streamers and red roses. A steel drum band played island tunes while the crowd gathered in the white folding chairs arranged on the beach in a semi-circle facing the sea. Many of the resort guests gathered nearby, anxiously anticipating something more than just another mundane, tropical wedding ceremony. We were almost certain not to disappoint.

Rose, Esther and Ivy were Ruth's official bridesmaids or matrons, if you will, all dressed in flowing white, ankle-length, cotton dresses. Ruth asked Annie Ruth to serve as the honorary "Grand Matron" at the last minute. Annie Ruth happily agreed. She was more accustomed to attending funerals than participating in weddings. She was in her polyester print dress, still sans hosiery.

Ardy was to be Mario's best man, but he was currently AWOL and presumably dead. Austin stood in for Ardy with his swim trunks, flip-flops and a tuxedo t-shirt while holding a plastic cup of draft beer. Larry sat in the front row, shirtless and in his swim trunks, using his cell phone to stream the video back to the States for Mom and Ruth's kids to watch. Giuseppe, the event's officiate, was appropriately wearing black shorts and a short-sleeved black t-shirt with a white priest's collar. Juan had dressed Senor Feliz for the occasion in a white-cotton tuxedo doggie sweater. Sam and Flo sat discreetly in the back row, positioned to make a hasty exit on the ceremony's conclusion or an emergency retreat should things get out of hand.

Everyone was present absent the bride and, well, Ardy. I had been instructed to wait off to the side of the ceremony on the adjacent beach for Ruth, as it was my privilege to walk her down the sandy aisle. I pinched myself hard again to make sure I was not dreaming. Time passed. A pair of Jesus birds walked on the water. A giant ray swam by. Mario was getting nervous, thinking perhaps Ruth had a last-minute change of heart and bailed or perhaps found a less appealing offer...I still didn't get his attraction, nor Ruth's, for that matter. I knew of no other couple more divergent in virtually every aspect than these two. Mario wiped perspiration off his brow and scanned the sea and the beach anxiously. None of us were privy to her planned entry route and manner. Annie Ruth surrendered to gravity and took a seat. Time is an ally of nature. She is patient and all things yield to her will in the end.

Finally a boat approached the beach from the south with a water skier in tow. It was Ruth. She had adopted island time. She skied up to the beach and expertly stepped out of her ski onto the sand wearing an all-white, daringly tiny bikini with a veil streaming in the wind behind her. The breeze caught her veil as she turned to waive goodbye to the boat's captain, and it flew off into the sea. Tripod dashed in the water and quickly retrieved it. Ruth affixed the sea-water-logged veil in her hair and kissed my offered cheek before pulling the veil over her face, covering her remarkable emerald green eyes. The remainder of her lithe, heavily tatted and pierced body was on display. A male resort guest wolf whistled. Tripod growled. No other guest deigned to risk Tripod's wrath. Tripod overcompensates for his size with ferocity and determination. I escorted Ruth down the sandy path while the strains of "Here Comes the Bride" played on the steel drums. Tripod happily brought up our rear escorting Frank documenting the event with his VHS camera.

"Who gives this woman in marriage?" Giuseppe asked. A traditional wedding ceremony question yet one I was totally unprepared to answer. This, after all, was far from a traditional wedding. We were winging it here...no rehearsal, no script...free form all the way. She was my sister, not my daughter. Dad had passed. I wanted to say something funny, as most certainly the bizarre setting called for humor. But I said the only thing that came to mind.

"No man can give what is not his. The Creators give us life and free will, and Ruth gives herself of her own choosing."

Rose looked at me like I was crazy and mouthed, "WTF?" I just shrugged and started to turn to take my seat, but as I did, I noticed a tattoo on Ruth's shapely tanned back. I had never consciously seen the tattoo, but it appeared remarkably familiar. The tattoo was of four animals surrounding the name Viracocha. I knew that name. It was the mythical Incan creator deity. I sat, a bit overcome and confused by the fierce déjà vu moment.

Before I knew it, Giuseppe was pronouncing the couple "Mr. Mario and Ms. Ruth name to be determined later." Additional negotiation was required on that front. Ruth reasoned there were three of them with the last name of Foster and just one of him. She had logic on her side, if not tradition. A rapidly approaching boat from the south stopped just a few meters directly in front of the ceremony, sending a tsunami over the sea wall. Just as Mario removed Ruth's veil to kiss her for the first time as man and wife, the men in the boat unceremoniously rolled naked Ardy into the ocean in perfect frame for Frank's VHS camera. Like I said…great wedding pictures.

Rose uncharacteristically teared up. I wasn't sure if it was from laughter or emotion, but I ventured to think laughter. I was wrong. Rose was genuinely happy for Ruth. "This is the third happiest day of my life," she said.

"Ah, that is so sweet. Our marriage being the first, of course. What would be the second?"

Rose looked at me like I said something completely outrageous. "No, honey, our marriage is the second. Witnessing the Yankees World Series win in game six against the vile Phillies is the first."

Silly me.

Dubai, UAE; May 2016: An undisclosed high ranking Pentagon source released documents purporting to show the President purchased a $5 million beach villa in Dubai. No US President has ever retired outside the continental United Sates. White House representatives declined comment regarding the purchase. According to UAE property records, the house was recently purchased by a Saudi law firm representing an unnamed client. The villa sits on a prime seaside location. The adjacent property is owned by George Smith, the billionaire "kingmaker" and longtime associate of the President.

Alongside Global News

Washington DC; May 2016: The Pentagon announced the resignation of two top Navy officers today. Both Admirals declined to comment on their resignations. In the past twelve months, more than fifty high ranking military officers have "retired" or "resigned" without any comment. A Pentagon spokesperson acknowledged this was an unprecedented number of retiring senior officers but had no further comment. The White House spokesperson declined comment when asked if the resignations had anything to do with the leaked documents regarding the President's new home in Dubai.

Alongside Global News

CHAPTER FOUR

No surprise here. Hangovers again ruled the day. I slept late but Rose remained snuggled in bed, snoring away until after normal lunchtime. Pretty much everything after the wedding was a giant blur. Esther and Morris were off fishing this morning on the inner lagoon, and I was sitting alone on the balcony drinking an overpriced Coke Light, nursing my throbbing head. We were scheduled to meet Juan for another snorkeling trip out to Shark Ray Alley in less than an hour. I doubted Rose was going to make today's trip. In a bikini on the adjacent balcony, Ivy used a straw to sip coffee though her missing teeth. I rightfully assumed she had overslept and missed the ferry this morning back to the mainland to catch her flight. Flo dragged Sam onto the first ferry off the island after the wedding. The remainder of our crew was currently out of sight except Ardy. He was at the swim-up pool bar drinking beer. I couldn't imagine the pool water being healthy for his stitches. A virulent brew of naturally occurring bacteria swimming in tributaries of small children's and large drunk's urine. Apparently the toxic combination of alcohol and pain pills had significantly clouded his judgment. Ardy was usually a very bright, hardworking, caring and logical (except when it comes to young women) man that typically exercised sound judgment. I couldn't fathom the depths of his bizarre behavior, but he appeared destined for further calamity.

Rose joined me on the balcony wearing one of my t-shirts, a frown, and nothing else. She is stunning, even with bed head, last night's makeup, and a grumpy face. "What's wrong, Baby?" I asked.

"The damn maid woke me up."

"That is some serious real world problem, Baby. The lady coming to clean up our mess woke you at a quarter after one. What a bitch! Shall I order her drawn and quartered for her heinous offense? On your command, Love, I shall have her earthly remains scattered to the four corners of the earth." She waved four fingers at me and returned inside to grab a cup of coffee.

Giuseppe's condo was directly above ours. He leaned over the rail. "You have an extra swimsuit?" he asked. "Frigging Ivy sliced mine in two last night. The crazy bitch reenacted Ardy's sexual encounter with the nurse shark. Damn near cut my balls off."

Ivy smiled and nodded unapologetically. "That happened," she said proudly.

"Did you just pack one?" I asked.

"Yeah. I just brought a carry on gym bag of clothes with me."

"Dude. You rock," I said, admiringly.

Rose returned with her coffee, the sleep brushed out of her hair, if not her eyes. She overheard the last of our conversation and disagreed with my assessment. "Really, Giuseppe, a gym bag for a seven-night trip. Do we even have the same mother?" Giuseppe didn't answer and just shrugged, puzzled as to why he should have packed a larger suitcase. Hard to believe they were related. Rose brought three extra-large suitcases.

"I would offer you one but it would swallow your skinny ass," I replied to Giuseppe.

Rose offered, "I have a black bikini. You can wear the bottoms. It will just look like a speedo."

Giuseppe wisely declined her generous offer. "Yeah…No thanks, I'll just wear a pair of dirty shorts."

The midgets, Lucy and Linus (doubtfully their real names but the ones offered), joined Ivy on her and Keara's balcony, both in their underwear. For the first time this morning, Rose noticed Ivy and her face immediately registered shock that Ivy was still in Belize; then something south of moral outrage when she noticed the midgets lounging on the balcony in their drawers. "What the hell, Ivy?"

"I overslept, Rose. Chill." Rose, God love her, tended to see a set of facts in their worst possible light. For instance, Ivy's previous pantyless comment combined with the presence of the near-naked midgets in Ivy's condo enjoying morning coffee equaled one freaky-ass orgy. I admit it was a possibility, but unlikely, even for a drunken and horny Ivy. And the midgets, while self-described as flyers of the freak flag, seemed a bit above this moral snap judgment, if only a tiny bit. Pun not intended. And Keara…no freaking way. The most likely probability, and the one I chose to believe, is the Peanuts pairing just passed out on the couch from near fatal levels of alcohol consumption. They were half my size and drank twice as much. There had to be consequences.

Giuseppe joined us on our balcony. One floor below, Austin and Larry, came out to their balcony. Austin called up, "I have the mother of all hangovers. I think I am passing on the snorkel trip today."

"Amen," Larry added. He was a man of few words. Giuseppe nodded this was a good idea. Ivy nor the midgets were scheduled to go, but agreed canceling the trip to be the appropriate course of action. The newlyweds Ruth and Mario were playing chess today. It was my innocent delusion. Ardy was talking up some drunk chick at the pool bar while she tossed back tropical drinks, interrupted only by frequent drags on a long, thin cigarette. His opinion was not consulted.

Giuseppe met Juan at the dock, paid and tipped him for the scheduled trip. Trading in pirated Chinese goods was quite the lucrative operation. Juan and Senor Feliz, having some free time on their hands, joined us at the pool bar where we had adjourned to from our respective balconies. Spotting Ardy, Tripod jumped into the pool and swam over to occupy the partially submerged bar stool adjacent to Ardy, resting both front paws on the bar. An inordinate number of resort workers were about gardening, sweeping, testing and cleaning the pool, but none gave notice or protest of the mangy dog's presence in the pool.

I cornered Lucy and Linus on the pool deck adjacent and overlooking the bar's swim-up stools. The midgets did not pack an overnight bag. Both were barefoot and still wearing the court jester pants and wife beater undershirts, having ditched the remainder of the costume. Disturbingly, I noticed Lucy was braless. Clearly a full grown woman, an attractive one no less, I couldn't help thinking of her as an innocent child. Overhearing their conversation about their work on an advanced virtual reality game program brought on another fierce déjà vu moment. I wanted to hear more. I ordered a round of Lighthouse from Wendy, the Belizean bartender, as she passed by. It's the locally brewed bitch beer but a good icebreaker after a night of hard drinking.

"So Linus, what can you tell me about your project with Sony? It sounds fascinating."

"Not much, really. It's cutting-edge shit, man, and as such, propriety," Linus said. "You know the drill…I could tell you, but then I'd have to kill you."

"I see. I was just curious. My neighbor's kid told me about two guys from MIT and their Augmented Reality project. I guess that is way ahead of you guys."

In spite of his initial comment, both Linus and Lucy suddenly became eager to share, and they filled me in on their project for the next twenty minutes. Georgia Tech grads are notoriously jealous of the attention MIT gets. It was crazy scary stuff. The project, not the unwarranted adolescent jealousy. That was just human nature. The project, much like Augmented Reality, blended the real world with the cyber world. The midgets' project utilized real world social media pages and news sites to drive a story-based game. The user picked from a number of initial scenarios: save the world, destroy the world, run for president, get laid, get rich, vanquish a rival, create a world from scratch, or jump into history at any point in time. The user, aptly called the Creator, inputted the game through a fictional character of his choosing, much like creating a fake profile on Facebook.

45

"In easy mode," Lucy explained, "the Creator can directly influence one other cast member's behaviors, but the goal is to get others to do your bidding through influence. Each cast member has free will. You can influence but cannot otherwise direct." The scary twist is all the cast members of the game were unwittingly played by real world people, and the game was even updated based on the contents of their social media pages and real current or historical events.

"Seems like a serious violation of privacy using real social media pages, don't you think?" I asked.

"Truthfully, it's not just social media pages. The game takes input from every application on their devices and every website the user visits. That is what makes the game feel so real and allows for it to take infinite directions and have infinite outcomes that feel unique and very personal to the user. And besides, the real social media pages are only used in a single direction, upstream to the game. The feedback from the Creator goes downstream to a cloud-based server that, using a fancy proprietary algorithm, decides how the cast member responds. The owner of the real page never sees the input from the game user."

"Still, kind of sounds like you guys may be crossing the Rubicon," I noted. There are some boundaries best left untested, some lines left uncrossed.

Ivy waded into the pool and took the vacant stool beside Tripod. She placed her ID, room key, and pain pills into the quart Ziploc bag on the bar already containing Ardy's and proceeded to order lunch, a frozen margarita with a straw. The clinic liberally dispensed narcotics, but then again, looking at the severity of their collective wounds, one shouldn't be judgmental. You never really know someone's story.

Ardy's new friend continued slamming the free booze, only now interrupted by the occasional bite of hamburger, as well as the frequent drag on her lipstick-stained cigarette. From a distance, and perhaps in the dark, she was not bad looking; but up close, in the harsh brightness of the tropical sun, it was pretty evident she was missing the proper equipment, or at least was not originally issued the equipment, to be considered a woman. Ardy was regrettably laser focused on the tranny's massive and nearly exposed boobs and missed the rather large hands, hint of facial hair and Adam's apple. In all fairness to Ardy, they were nice tits be they original factory issued or after market.

Assuming the mantle of protector of Ardy, Ivy nudged him and whispered urgently, "Dude she's..." she tilted her margarita toward the tranny "...a he." Ardy was unfortunately at the point of no return and ignored Ivy. Then again, perhaps he was deluding himself, or maybe it was just one of those any-port-in-a-storm moments. The lethal mixture of narcotics and alcohol likely clouded his judgment and vision, severely short-circuiting his normal decision-making process. The tranny took another large bite of the hamburger and, lubricated by Ardy's alcohol generosity, hurled copious amounts of tropical-colored fluid, peppered by lumpy chunks of partially digested burger, onto the bar. The tranny daintily wiped its face with a tiny cocktail napkin, took another pull on its tropical drink, and resumed eating the undigested portion of its lunch. Surely, I thought, that would do the trick for Ardy. "Really, Ardy...it's a dude, and a gross one at that," Ivy abandoned the hushed tones and implored Ardy with her eyes to see the monumental error of his ways before enduring yet another embarrassing event on this trip.

"Don't be a cock-blocker," Ardy whispered to Ivy.

Tripod started to growl.

"I'm just saying...there are two cocks in this kitchen," Ivy nodded her head toward the tranny's crotch. Aerosmith's Dude (Looks Like a Lady) streamed out of the Sony 3-disc changer set up on the bar. I spewed beer out of my nose. Wendy, visibly annoyed at the abuse of alcohol, quietly wiped my mess up. Meanwhile, Bruce...errrrr...Caitlyn Jenner was giving an interview exclusively to E-TV regarding his/her transition on a television hanging above the bar. "Are you effing kidding me?" Ivy continued on her mission to out Ardy's friend. "Look at the signs, Man! They're literally everywhere!" The Gods were making a concerted effort to insure Ardy was making an informed decision.

"Don't be such a hater," Ardy said and turned his attention back to the tranny who was now finished with lunch.

The tranny reached over, kissed Ardy on the cheek, and said, "Thanks, Love. Time for my beauty rest." The tranny rose to leave. Ardy stood and grabbed her elbow to stop her. He had invested too much time and alcohol to just let he/she sashay away unmolested. Tripod seized Ardy by the seat of his swim shorts and began growling fiercely through his closed teeth. Tripod was not one to share his favorite bone. Ardy swatted at Tripod, but he maintained his grip.

"Would you like some company?" Ardy asked, still painfully unaware as to the true nature of his intended mark.

"Sure, Sugar, but my lovin' don't come free."

Ardy looked at the tranny, puzzled. Ardy, although not the most handsome and/or charming sort, had not stooped to having to rent his love by the hour. He/She shrugged and began to walk away. Still confused, Ardy tried to follow, but Tripod had a firm grasp on his swim trunks displaying remarkable strength and tenacity given his diminutive stature. Ardy, lustlorn, awkwardly abandoned his trunks to Tripod's determined grip. Ardy, now naked save his bandages, followed the tranny to the pool's edge. Ardy and Tripod reached the tranny simultaneously as it began climbing out of the pool. Tripod launched himself and latched onto the tranny's crotch, spilling out the tranny's rather impressive manhood from its bikini bottom. The tranny fell to the ground, yelling a stream of creative obscenities. Ardy tripped over the tranny and landed on top of it with Tripod wedged between the two, aggressively attacking the tranny's balls. Ardy tried to stand, but his feet could not gain sufficient purchase on the slick pool deck and fell back on top of the two struggling combatants. Wiggling on top of the pair trying to gain footing, Ardy gave the unfortunate illusion he was attempting carnal knowledge with one or perhaps both of the unlikely combatants. Linus noted, "Now that, my friend…" he nodded toward the bizarre wrestling match, "…is letting your freak flag fly." Lucy nodded in wide-eyed agreement. We clicked beer bottles in a universal salute.

Four strong hands lifted Ardy off the tranny, aggressively pulled his hands behind him and secured them with a nylon zip tie. Four more did the same with the tranny. Mercifully, the resort workers wrapped a towel around both Ardy and the tranny. Tripod continued to nip at the tranny's ankles, unimpeded by the resort staff. "Sir, you are under arrest for soliciting a known prostitute, as well as attempting a sexual act with an animal…you sick fuck. Do you have any identification?"

"What kind of gardeners are you?" Ardy asked, now even more confused.

"Undercover vice-officers, you imbecile. What is it with you gringos coming here to our island thinking you can do anything you want and get away with it? You have no respect for our women, our children, even our dogs, for Christo's sake. Please present some identification, Sir."

The tranny was being led away by two of the other undercover cops. Tripod gave enthusiastic chase. Ivy, ever helpful, grabbed Ardy's plastic bag from the bar containing his ID and handed it to the cop. The officer pulled Ardy's ID out, along with the three bottles of narcotics. "Do the contents of this bag belong to you, Sir?" Ardy nodded yes. "You are also under arrest for the possession with intent to distribute narcotics."

Linus looked at me. "Dude…you have some freaky-ass friends." Lucy nodded in wide-eyed agreement. We once again clicked beer bottles.

***

Once just a quaint fishing village, San Pedro now primarily depended on the gringo tourist trade for its economic health. (It's also positioned conveniently in the middle of a major drug smuggling route.) The resort's security staff intervened on Ardy's behalf, explaining to the local police chief the cost of providing Ardy healthcare for his wounds and the real risk an American tourist might die in their custody easily overshadowed the solicitation charge. The island clinic, at the behest of security, provided the police with copies of the prescriptions for the narcotics, clearing Ardy of the drug charges. Not much could be done with the bestiality complaint but note the dog, in spite of Ardy's apparent amorous movements, was unharmed, and the dog's owner was not filing charges. Fortunately, one look at Ardy's festering wounds, and the police didn't argue further releasing Ardy the morning after his arrest.

Resort security lent me a golf cart to retrieve the newly-pardoned man, and I took the bumpy, unnamed dirt road - more of a path, really - into town. The village was small and, as with the rest of the island, the infrastructure quite primitive. Three roads, two of them dirt, ran north and south, aptly called Front, Middle, and Back by tourists and expats. The yellow and green two-story police station was on Middle. "You look nice," I lied to Ardy. He looked like dog shit and grimaced in obvious misery as he climbed into the cart.

"You have my pills?" I shook my head no. "Bastards didn't give them back to me. They threw me in a holding cell without a cot or air-conditioning. I lay on the nasty concrete floor all night in a corner, trying to go unnoticed. I had to shit in a cut off plastic milk jug. I need a fucking beer." I stopped at a small, improvised bar in someone's front yard just south of the golf cart bridge across the narrow San Pedro River that divides the island. Ardy ordered six Belikins. I paid the man.

"Meet any new friends?"

"Fuck you."

"Easy, Asshole. I just got you out of prison and bought you cold beer." I know he was having a bad day, er, trip, but it was mostly of his own doing. He smelled like shit, actually worse than shit. He smelled of rotting flesh, and I was a bit concerned he would shortly be joining Tripod as an amputee. Even so, if he weren't a lifelong friend, I would have gladly ditched his putrid smelling ass on the side of the road.

"Two scary mother fuckers in the cell with me," he finally answered after draining the first beer. "One white and one black. They looked American but spoke to each other mostly in Spanish, and the black guy called the white guy by some Mexican name."

"Paco?" I suggested, jokingly.

"Nah…some nickname like you hear in the movies all the time associated with drug cartels. El Frio something or other." I hit a pothole. Ardy spilled his beer and cursed loudly. Ardy had my undivided attention as I was overwhelmed with yet another strong sense of déjà vu. I pulled to the side of the path and killed the cart's engine.

"What was his name, Ardy?"

"I don't know. Why do you even care? Just get me home. I have some more pills at the condo."

"It's important to me, Ardy. Think."

"Frio Loco, maybe," Ardy replied, taking another swig.

"You certain?"

"Hell, no. I didn't know there was going to be a damn test."

"Think," I encouraged Ardy. I wasn't really sure myself why his name was important to me, but something told me it was vital.

"You're kinda freaking me out, Zeke. Loco…Lobo…something like that."

"Which one, Ardy?"

"Lobo…his name was Frio Lobo. Now get me home."

"What were they talking about?" I remained on the side of the path thinking I could get him to best focus prior to another overdose of pain pills. A cart drove by much too fast and splashed mud from the path all over Ardy.

Stoically wiping the mud from the throat of his beer, he continued, "I told you it was mostly in Spanish."

51

"Mostly. That implies they spoke English, as well. What did they say?"

Ardy looked at me like I was nuts, but he had heard more than perhaps he realized as he continued, "Best I could gather, the white dude was some kind of money man for some Central American assholes."

"And the black dude?"

"Do I look like Colombo?"

"No, you look like Elmer Fudd after Bugs Bunny took a giant shit on him. Now what else do you remember?"

"You're freaking me out, Zeke. I just want to swallow some pain pills and take a nap in my nice, clean bed."

"You can walk your ass back to the condo." Ardy started to get out of the golf cart taking his beers. I grabbed the beers. Ardy took one step on his injured leg and fell into a mud puddle. "Want to rethink that option?" He pulled himself onto his knees alongside the cart. I handed him a fresh beer.

He took a long pull. "Help me back in the cart."

"Soon as you tell me more about what you heard."

Ardy finished his beer and reached for another before continuing, "The black guy was from Dallas…I think." Ardy took another pull on his beer and wiped his face with a marginally clean spot on the tail of his shirt. "All tatted up. Really cool-ass panther on his arm. One of those burnt-in tattoos that raise the skin. I remember it 'cause I have never seen that type of tattoo so detailed. Musta hurt like a bitch."

"And…"

"And, what? Jesus, man, I was scared to death of those guys and stayed as far away from them as I could." A cart came by and splashed more muddy water onto Ardy. He barely flinched. He tossed his empty bottle into the cart and held his hand out for another. "Funny thing…they didn't seem to like each other very much, either."

"They still in the jail when you left?"

"Nah. Got bailed out in the middle of the night. Whoever they are..." Ardy finished his beer "...the cops got jumpy as hell when their friends showed up. Now take me the hell to the condo before I kick your crazy ass."

Menlo Park, CA; May 2016: Facebook ("FB") members nationwide are outraged over reports that FB is experimenting with users' accounts posting fake "news stories" on members' pages in order to gauge the reaction of its members. This comes just months after several lawsuits were filed accusing FB of mining data from its messenger service as well as other applications on the user's device. Facebook spokesperson Shawn Parker categorically denied any "inappropriate" manipulation citing the FB user agreement.

Alongside Global News

La Paz, Bolivia; May 2016: A series of UFO sightings in and around the Lake Titicaca area beginning during the autumn equinox have created a sharp rise in suicides among the indigenous population. Bolivian officials from the Ministry of Rural Development and Agriculture and the Ministry of Health and Sports issued a joint release dismissing the sightings as "mass hysteria" and further noting the suicide rate has not significantly changed.

 Local witnesses describe the sightings as "glowing blue spheres and bright white and rainbow-colored objects." Other locals, as well as tourists, and a noted amateur archeologist and author have reported hearing rhythmic music and witnessing visions of stars emanating from the famed "Gate of the Gods" located near the lake.

A Bolivian Government spokesperson dismissed the phenomena as a "combination of wishful thinking, excessive alcohol consumption, and publicity stunt."

Alongside Global News

CHAPTER FIVE

Having seen the initial round of the marathon chess match to its successful conclusion, the unlikely newlywed couple joined us on the dock for our final day's adventure. No word on the victor, but Mario looked exhausted which was unfortunate given today's grueling tour. We were headed to the Lamanai Mayan Ruins on the mainland. It's a one-hour boat ride, followed by a one-hour bus ride over tangential portions of the Pan American highway, and then finally, another one-hour boat ride up a narrow, winding river. On extended journey's arrival it is, of course, an imperative to climb the 200-plus near-vertical steps of the temple ruins. "Dude, you look gassed," I said to Mario.

He shrugged. "I really don't get the whole polygamy scene."

"Yeah, that would be a lot of chess for one man to handle," I said to Mario. Rose punched me in the arm.

Ruth kneed me playfully in the nuts. "Leave him be," she whispered in my ear. "He has to get up for another round tonight."

I screwed my face up in disgust. "TMI, dear sister." Mario looked at me puzzled, but just shrugged again. Ruth looked radiant. Chess play was good for her.

The tour boat pulled up to the resort dock, as usual, on island time. Ardy had clearly adjusted to the island's slower pace and sauntered down the dock to jump on after the rest of our crew had already boarded and found seats. Rose, noticing Ardy, added unwarranted editorial comment, "Fuck me."

I grabbed a seat close to Mario. He was a devout Mormon. I mean, the man didn't even drink coffee for God's sake. I knew a little about Mormonism but wanted to pick Mario's brain as the "Latter" in Latter Day Saints intrigued the hell out of me, and the last few days of déjà vu happenings had renewed my interest in religion. Although I am a non-practicing Baptist, I nevertheless have a keen interest in religions and in the nature of God. I mean, just who is this guy, and to what purpose did He create us? So many of modern civilization's religions stake passionate claim to the same tiny geographic area as their birthright and owe their genesis to a similar narrow span of time. Many of those religions carry remarkably consistent belief systems, even as they have slaughtered each other over the centuries for the smallest of deviations. Then there was this Church of Latter Day Saints. Their Bible had an addendum written much later and far distant from the birthplace of most modern religions.

Ardy laid his head in Ruth's lap as the boat pulled away from the dock. Ruth softly rubbed his peeling dome. Rose rolled her eyes. They were going to get stuck in the back of her eye sockets one day. The midgets cracked an early beer. Frank sipped from a flask. Annie Ruth found the shade of the boat's tarp and an available ear beside Giuseppe. Austin and Larry lit cigars at the stern of the boat. Ivy stripped her bathing suit cover up off and positioned herself on the bow for maximum sun exposure.

"So just when did this Joe Smith fellow write the book of Mormon?" I asked Mario.

"Joseph Smith didn't write the book," Mario noted.

"Now I'm confused. Then who wrote it?" I really kind of felt this fellow was more a modern day huckster than prophet. Then again I am certain the same was said about Peter, Paul and Mary. No wait…that was a pop band from the sixties.

Mario explained, "Smith translated the book from a set of gold plates he was led to by an angel called Moroni in the early 1800s…hence the title the 'Church of Latter Day Saints'."
Everyone downwind of Ardy shifted seats. He smelled of rotting flesh. The Captain, to a collective groan, motioned everyone back to their original seats in order to balance the boat.

"So where are these plates now?" I asked.

Mario smiled and shrugged. "No one knows. Smith returned the plates to the prophet Moroni after he translated them."

"Did anyone else see this alien or the golden plates?"

"Angel, you mean…and yup, the Three Witnesses saw the angel and the gold plates."

"So let me get this right. Smith and these 'Witnesses' saw this human form that represented himself as an angel of God?" I asked to clarify.

Mario smiled and nodded. He was a highly intelligent and well educated man with a strong sense of faith. Those can be difficult paths to straddle.

"Any of these 'Witnesses' happen to be relatives or drinking buddies?"

Mario frowned. I may have been approaching Mormon heresy. "Some were relatives, yes, but that does not discount the story."

Maybe a tiny bit, I thought, but what do I know? Religion was about blind faith in something unseen. The Christian Bible had a few holes of its own in its provenance. Mormons would argue a living God wouldn't have suddenly stopped talking to his followers 2,000 years ago. Valid point, I thought, and moved on.

"How did this angel get there?"

"A pillar of light descended upon him."

The boat passed a small fishing shack in the water, seemingly on the cusp of the sea and sky, before chasing into a tiny gap in the mangroves. For the next fifteen minutes, the boat followed a narrow, winding channel in the mangroves at an impossibly high rate of speed. I assumed the captain knew these waters well or perhaps was just solidly in the grips of a fanatical death wish. Had another boat been traveling in the opposite direction, there would have been a catastrophic collision. Talk was impossible, as it became necessary to hold on for dear life. Except Ardy. He tumbled to the boat's deck, breaking open the oozing stitches on his leg from the shark attack. A putrid mixture of blood and pus leaked onto the boat's deck. He remained prone. Ruth put her bare feet on him and rubbed his back gently. She seemed to have no limits to her compassion. Ardy moaned with pleasure. Rose rolled her eyes. The Captain cursed. The boat slowed.

"How does Brigham Young fit in?"

57

"Smith was God's chosen first living prophet. Young was the second, and he led the Mormon community from New York to Salt Lake."

"Is there still a living prophet that chats up the angels?"

"Yes, through an unbroken chain from Smith. The current prophet is Thomas Monson."

"So how does being a Mormon differ from a Baptist?" I asked Mario.

"Structurally, the two religions are quite similar. We take the King James Version of the Bible as the true word of God. We believe in salvation through Jesus, just as you do. We believe in baptism by full-body immersion, as well. The big difference is that we added the Book of Mormon and believe God's word is not just a static 1800-year-old book. Apostles and Prophets live today that speak to God and for God. We also are a bit more mystical than you stuffed shirt Baptists believing in laying on of the hands, heavenly inspired visions, speaking in tongues, healing, and all that jazz." Mario did jazz fingers for comedic visual effect. "We also take the Bible a bit more seriously. We don't drink alcohol for instance." Mario pointed at my beer as a completely unnecessary visual aid. I started to point out his recent bride was quite capable of drinking me under the table while suspended from a vertical pole, but wisely left it alone.

"Do you know how to tell the difference between a Baptist and a Methodist?" I asked Mario, grabbing a fresh beer from the cooler. He started to answer me, missing the line was the preamble to an old joke. I interrupted him before he ruined my punch line, "The Methodists say hello when they see each other in the liquor store." Mario gave me a courtesy chuckle and shook his head.

Ruth nudged Ardy with her toes to get him up. Rose rolled her eyes. Annie Ruth dozed off on Giuseppe's shoulder. Giuseppe wiped her drool with his sleeve. Frank laid his head in Ivy's lap. Ivy unceremoniously tossed Frank onto the deck.

"You planning on converting?" Mario asked me.

"Nah…just trying to figure this God fellow out. He is a mystery to me."

"You don't believe in God?"

"Nothing further from the truth. I absolutely believe in God, but I just don't understand him or just why a perfect being would have bothered to create such a flawed creation. Rose tells me I am supposed to surrender the mysteries of his origin to faith. I'm Irish, though. Unlike the French, we as a people struggle with surrender." Mario genuinely chuckled and we sat in silence for a moment.

"How about heaven?" Mario asked.

"My high school physics teacher taught me that although energy may change its current form, it is indestructible. I believe we are energy, and as such, yes, I think we are something after this fragile shell expires. What shape that something becomes…I remain utterly clueless."

"So I will take that as a yes on the heaven question. Do you believe in heavenly reward for your earthly deeds?"

"You know, I think we are accountable, but I would like to think that the present is something greater than just an insignificant preamble."

I went on to tell Mario about Reverend Bob. Bob was one of the few Baptist preachers I completely trusted. I was a pill in my teens searching for God. I exasperated the hell out of my parents, most preachers, and every Sunday school teacher, peppering them with unresolvable questions. Bob never tired of my questions nor belittled them. I believe he was honest, often answering that he had no answer or there was not an answer and that I simply must have faith. Of course, I then asked for an explanation of faith. There is a gorge in North Georgia that crosses the Tallulah River aptly named the Tallulah Gorge. In 1970, the 65-year-old Carl Wallenda, father of the famous flying Wallendas, widely promoted that he planned to cross the gorge on a tight wire whilst pushing a wheelbarrow. Bob explained, "Belief is standing on the canyon's edge and saying that you believe the stunt man can safely traverse the canyon. Now faith," he explained, "is getting in that wheelbarrow. Faith is blind and complete trust in things unknown to us, unprovable, and beyond our control."

Perhaps Bob's greatest lesson was explaining the simple concept of risk versus reward. Bob explained the risk of having no faith and choosing not to accept Christ as our Savior, "An eternity in a fiery pit," as a serious bummer. And I think we all could agree that was a significant downside. Conversely, there is no real risk in living a godly life. Religion is good for the propagation of civilization as it gives society a set of rules and encourages order over chaos. The Big Ten 'thou shalt' and 'shalt nots' make for a relatively concise, efficient and primitive legal system. The upside, of course, is our eternal heavenly reward. I always questioned our Christian religion's vision of heaven as one giant perpetual church service. Something besides nonstop praying and singing might appeal more to the younger set in the masses. Think gigantic sports bar with thousands of massive HD screens with free beer and wings served by a half-naked hot staff and nonstop sports action where your team always wins. Now that is a heaven we can all get behind. Certainly heaven is advantage Islam. Those guys have the whole multiple virgin thing going for them. Perhaps this explains the recent explosion of Islam. Pun intended.

The boat broke through the narrow channel to a small lagoon on the Northern River and abruptly slowed, coasting up to a rickety dock. We had arrived at Bomba village. The village is a primitive, tiny fishing community of less than fifty people, without the benefit of electricity or a diverse gene pool. A malnourished, mangy dog met us on the dock and, seeing an easy meal, took an instant interest in Ardy's injured leg. Frank helped Annie Ruth down the narrow dock. A small dugout canoe rested on the bank. Ivy and Ardy posed for a picture in the boat with the uninvited mutt. Frank snapped a Polaroid and started shaking the film. The village was a collection of small, unpainted wooden huts with villagers hocking hand-carved tourist goods made of native hardwoods. One of the huts had a tin-roofed porch where the tour company offered refreshments: banana bread, fresh fruits, orange juice, coffee and water. I made my way to the bathroom - another small hut with two stalls covered partially with swinging doors and two outdoor urinals exposed in all but one direction. Ardy swatted at the dog as he was trying to piss. The dog growled. I had seen this movie before and it did not end well. An old woman, bent from decades of hard labor and child bearing, approached Ardy and knocked the dog away with her walking stick. The dog scampered away barking. She was barefoot, as black as coal, and wearing a shapeless, brown garment. Her enormous, sagging breasts were visible through the large arm holes in the garment. The crone motioned a crooked finger tipped with a long, yellowing-cracked nail toward Ardy and wordlessly motioned for him to follow her. She turned and walked toward one of the wooden huts, pulling a canvas flap over the opening. Ardy surprisingly followed.

After refreshments, the green school bus stood ready to take us on our next leg of the journey. The crew queued up and began to board. Ardy was still absent. I exited the bus and entered the small, dark hut. It was filled with the acrid smoke of marijuana mixed with other both pleasing and pungent odors of an indeterminable nature. So thick the smoke and absent direct light, it was impossible to see until my eyes finally adjusted. The scene was disquieting. Ardy lay prone on the straw-covered floor, completely naked with his bandages removed. A coati (a coon-like animal) was leashed to a small table in the corner. The crone was smearing some dark, noxious mud over his entire body. I noticed disturbingly he was enjoying the mud massage.

"What the hell, Ardy?" He just smiled. "Dude, the bus is about to leave." I motioned for him to get up and leave.

The ancient crone frowned and waved me out, mumbling, "The troubled man be staying with me. He be here on your way back. Now be gone with you and your little devils." The coati barred his teeth and hissed. Ardy nodded his agreement. I left. He was a grown man, after all.

We left the village and Ardy in our considerable dust as we began the middle leg of the journey to the Mayan ruins. The Bomba Road and later the Northern Highway were but a series of potholes, occasionally interrupted by small patches of pavement. The driver piloted the ungainly bus by making suicidal dashes on the rare, small areas of available smooth surface. School buses are designed for transporting school-aged children along city streets at moderate rates of speed. The narrow vinyl seats did little to soften the sway of the harsh speed, direction changes and inevitable violent pothole collisions. Along with the driver, the tour company had engaged a second guide to accompany us on the bus. The two of them competed for our attention, trying to spill an uninterrupted narration of a relatively unimpressive landscape. The natives still practiced slash and burn agriculture, and the smoke from the jungle fires filled the bus, mixing with the dust from the road providing for a tangible, gritty taste of Belize. The rear guide pointed out mahogany, rosewood, cashew and stinking toe trees. The front guide and driver opted for the more exciting fare and pointed out monkeys, Toucans, crocodiles, and jaguars, unseen to everyone but his imaginative eyes.

"So where is Ardy?" Ivy turned in her seat and asked, suddenly realizing he was missing.

I explained he was receiving medical treatment from the village's medical professional. Ivy laughed.

Rose rolled her eyes and added, "And somewhere a village is missing their idiot."

We passed a group of small children dressed in identical uniforms. The driver slowed for the kids but still covered them in our dust. A malnourished horse looked on from the adjacent field as a large, dark-skinned woman chopped at the relentless jungle, using a large machete to clear unwanted growth from the horse's pasture. Both guides explained that Belize had a very good education system. Attendance and uniforms were mandatory for all kids. Shortly we passed the un-air-conditioned, single-story school building. The kids waived. This far up the road, the houses were a bit sturdier, and some appeared to have electricity. Large plastic or metal cisterns for water collection were a feature of almost every structure. A few homes had satellite dishes, none had cars.

Frank plopped down beside Ivy in the seat in front of us. He offered Ivy a pull from his flask. She accepted and, after cleaning the top with her swimsuit cover, awkwardly tilted the flask back avoiding contact with her lips and broken teeth. Drops of the sour-smelling liquid dripped down her mouth onto the front of her overexposed chest. Frank was wearing his ass-cheek displaying, cut-off jean shorts and a tight t-shirt over his scrawny torso. His ever-present Vietnam-era combat boots were on his feet, and a red bandanna was tied around his head. A camo fanny pack was belted around his waist. He excitedly offered his assistance to dry Ivy's chest with his bandana. Frank's voice was like gravel from an endless parade of cigarettes and coffee. Ivy declined his assistance and motioned for another pull on Frank's flask. It was a mistake to underestimate this man's intelligence in spite of his poor diction, bizarre fashion sense and deficient education obtainment. And when it came to younger women, he was like a dog chasing a car. I am not sure what he expected to accomplish if he ever caught one. "First taste is on the house. Second one...now that'll cost you," Frank explained, withholding his flask.

"I'll bite, creepy, old dude. What will it cost me?" Ivy responded.

Frank pondered his options for a moment, thinking, and "Should I bite the bumper or the tire?" Rose glared. Frank, after weighing a proper response, "I reckon a peek at those lovely tatas of yours ought to do it." Rose slapped Frank on the back of his head. He dropped the flask, spilling its remaining contents on the vinyl seat.

"Apparently two villages are missing their idiots." Frank was nonplussed. Ivy inexplicably felt sorry for Frank and pulled her bikini top down, briefly freeing both breasts before

63

reholstering them. Frank's face grew fire engine red. Rose said, "Make that three missing idiots."

Frank pulled yet another flask from his pack and offered it to Ivy. She drained half of it before returning the flask. Frank handed the half-empty flask back to Ivy while simultaneously readying his Polaroid camera. "All yours, honey. A good man honors his word." I think he was hoping for another peek show that he did not receive. Viewing, although only ever so briefly, a naked breast under eighty and pointing north inspired Frank to wax philosophically, "There's no doubt our Creator musta been a dude to have designed such a perfect form as a woman's tit."

"Thank you?" Ivy said, uncertain as to an appropriate response for such an inappropriate comment. But then again, Ivy had abandoned the high ground.

Rose rolled her eyes. Frank continued, "Crazy shit this is. We are such a trivial piece of even this universe and yet our Creator took the time to design a perfect tit. They provide both nourishment and pleasure in an attractive and convenient to-go container."

"Deep, Frank. I didn't know you were a philosopher," I muttered as sarcastically as I could muster.

Frank continued, unmoved by my sarcasm, "We humans are but a tiny electron, circling the nucleus of a single atom of the tiny scar on a flea on a dog's ass and yet...voila, a perfect tit." My sarcasm delivery techniques were in serious need of refinement.

The bus backed into a narrow, shaded lane next to the New River in the Orange Walk District, signaling the conclusion of the second leg of our journey. After a short nature break, we boarded an open thirty foot boat with twin Yamaha 250 engines. The guide from the bus joined us on the boat. The NASCAR-wannabe bus driver blessed with the superhero vision remained behind. Ivy wisely sought a seat away from Frank. The midgets flanked Keara like miniature bookends, exaggerating the relative size of all three. Giuseppe helped Annie Ruth on board. She found a spot next to him in the shade and promptly laid her head in his lap. Ruth stripped to her bikini, and she and Mario assumed a position near the bow in the direct tropical sunlight. Mario was wearing the tour website's recommended clothing: long sleeves, pants and wide-brimmed hat. Frank, still excited from his breast encounter, took a seat below Annie Ruth and openly stared up her dress. Any port - even an ancient one - in a storm, I guess.

The boat's Captain proved no less a daredevil, navigating the narrow river at break neck speeds with little consideration for possible oncoming traffic. The guide began his nonstop narration, pointing out the partially burnt-out compound of the former anti-virus king and alleged current raving lunatic, John McAfee. Rather unimpressive actually, just a handful of cottages on stilts. But then again, at the maniacal speed we were traveling, the damn place could have rivaled the Taj Mahal. The guide explained McAfee had fled Belize after he murdered his neighbor, Gregory Faulk, on Ambergris Caye in retaliation for poisoning his twenty-year-old girlfriend's vicious dogs. I hear McAfee has a different version of that story. I expect the truth lies somewhere in between, although I doubt McAfee's claim of complete innocence to the crime.

We passed a large community of Mennonites at a sharp bend in the river. This area appeared to be much more populated. The guide explained that of the 300,000 people in Belize, some 12,000 were Mennonites. About 2,000 Mennonites lived in this community known as Shipyard. They came to the country in 1959 and cultivated the majority of the country's produce and dairy products. My déja vu radar pinged. Certainly it seemed odd that some of the religions my Baptist upbringing taught me were borderline cults had produced some of the most industrious of people. On both sides of the river, the guide pointed out jungle resorts, some five-star, according to his story. From the perspective of the river, at least, I surmised the local star system was generously calibrated.

The river abruptly opened up onto a large lagoon, aptly named New River Lagoon. The Captain expertly navigated the boat to a large, well-maintained dock where we deboarded the boat and made our way to a picnic area. Included in the tour was lunch and, to my surprise, it was an excellent meal; grilled chicken, an assortment of fresh vegetables and fried plantains for dessert. And the beer was ice cold; always a plus. Frank expertly managed to reacquire Ivy's company, and together they chose to skip the solid selections and opted instead for a liquid lunch. Off the boat and away from the water, the atmosphere was more humid and brutally hot, absent the breeze. The guide, speaking directly to Ivy and Frank, warned us all that the ruins were a long walk, spread over some twelve acres and with no source of fresh water available. "It is very important to stay hydrated," he advised.

"Good advice, Captain," Frank replied as he fished two beers out of the cooler, placing one in his fanny pack. Ivy followed his lead, air toasting the guide. Frank expertly snapped a Polaroid of her cleavage as she bent to retrieve the beer.

"Consolation prize?" I asked. Frank aggressively shook the Polaroid and peeled off the developer. After appraising his work, he handed me the picture with an approving grunt. Rose snatched the picture from my hand and, without looking, tossed it into the trash receptacle.

Ivy retrieved the photograph, appraised its quality as suitable and returned it to Frank, "Whatever gets you through the night, creep." Rose rolled her eyes. Ivy slapped Frank's ass and motioned for him to follow. "Let's roll, Rambo. I got old shit to see besides your wrinkly ass."

"There are some 700 structures across over 900 acres at Lamanai," the guide explained as he took off down a gravel path toward the Mayan Ruins.

"I didn't sign up for this shit," Linus exclaimed rather loudly, trying to keep up with the brisk pace of the guide.

The guide slowed his pace a bit and continued, "But only about five percent of the buildings have been excavated." Sandwiched between Ruth and Mario, Annie Ruth brought up the rear without complaint. Sensible shoes or not, this may have been a bad idea for her. A group of Howler Monkeys greeted us as we walked up a series of stone steps into a large, grassy plaza fronted by a stone pyramid called the Jaguar Temple. "Lamanai," the guide explained, "translated from Mayan means submerged crocodile." He pointed out several crocodile reliefs carved into the limestone supporting his statement. The area had been occupied for over 3,000 years beginning 1500 B.C. Construction on the major structures had begun as early as 100 B.C.

A short distance further, we came on to a Pitz ball court. The court was shaped like a capital I. A narrow alley was open on both ends and flanked by stone walls. A large, circular stone occupied the center of the court. Pitz, explained the guide, was played by two opposing teams of two to four. The ball was likely struck by the player's hip. It appears to have been some strange hybrid of modern day volleyball, soccer and basketball. The game often had life-or-death consequences with some debate as to whether it was the loser or the winner that ultimately lost his head. Quite the unusual motivation technique if in fact it was the winner's fate. Then again, everything is relative. We tend to judge history from today's perspective, often mistakenly coloring the past with a modern palate. In a world where earthly life is suffering and misery, death and a promise of a glorious after-life might be quite appealing. Scientists, it seems, are humans and tend to ignore all data that does not support their favored theories. The most unusual item was the strange contents found in the court's central stone. In the 1970's, a compartment was discovered that contained several items, including miniature pottery in a pool of liquid mercury. The guide offered no explanation as to the mercury's purpose but noted similar discoveries of the toxic liquid metal in the tombs of the Egyptian Pharos.

The troop of monkeys followed high above us in the jungle canopy from the Jaguar Temple to the ball court, some using vines Tarzan-style to traverse from one tree to the next. One large, aggressive male, clearly the alpha, approached Ivy and tugged on her hand. "How cute," Ivy said as she reached down to pet him.

The monkey climbed into her arms. Apparently he thought her cute, as well, based on his sizable red rocket and the thrusting motion of his hips. Ivy tried to disengage him but he was a determined little fellow with a strong grip and a passionate sense of purpose. Frank managed to pry the monkey off of Ivy as the rest of us looked on in hysterical, but highly inappropriate, laughter. "No means no, you hairy little bastard," Ivy said, trying to make light of her sexual assault. The monkey retreated to the top of the ball court's stone walls. He was not accustomed to rejection apparently and took offense, chattering loudly. The other monkeys joined in with a chorus of angry grunts. In order to clearly demonstrate his displeasure, the would-be simian Romeo defecated into his hand and hurled the still steaming pile of shit toward Ivy. His practiced aim was true. The full gooey pile found Ivy's hair as she just managed to turn her face away before impact. "Shit," Ivy yelled.

"Yup," Frank replied.

"That wasn't a question, Asshole."

In spite of the insult, Frank surrendered his remaining beer in a futile attempt to wash the crap from her hair. The monkeys jumped up and down, chattering wildly in appreciation for the alpha's revenge. The guide advised a hasty retreat.

The excavated portion of the High Temple stands at a height of 108 feet, about ten stories, above the grounds. The steps are narrow, impossibly steep, and without the benefit of a handrail. Pre-OSHA period of civilization. One wonders how our ancestors managed to survive without a nanny-state's oversight from cradle to grave. Frank, in a mistaken effort to show his virility to Ivy, challenged the midgets to a race to the top of the pyramid-shaped structure. Linus flipped him off and took a seat on one of the wooden benches fronting the massive structure. Given the tools of the day, it was remarkable a primitive culture could build such an exacting structure and one that bore a remarkable likeness to other pyramids worlds away. Frank pestered Linus to the race. I suggested he challenge Keara. She agreed. Frank began running up the steep steps with half his ass cheeks exposed from this vantage point. Keara sipped from a water bottle in the shade. Frank reached the first plateau rather quickly but was clearly gassed. He paused and glanced down to see Keara still at the bottom. "You scared of an old man?" he yelled, with false bravado.

Mario and Ruth finally arrived at the bottom of the temple with Annie Ruth still alive and in tow. "Wait for me, Frank," Annie Ruth called up. She freed herself from Ruth and began walking up the bottom steps. Ruth grabbed her arm and asked Annie Ruth to join her on the shaded bench, explaining she was scared of heights and did not want to be left alone with the horny monkeys still prowling about. Annie Ruth, with a sense of purpose, reluctantly acquiesced.

After a brief pause and a glance to ensure Ivy was still watching, Frank began the second, even steeper leg of the journey, jogging up the first few steps. Keara remained at the bottom. After about ten steps, Frank paused and sat on one of the narrow steps. "I better go help him down," Keara said. Frank, on seeing Keara begin her trek up the steps, made a feeble attempt to continue the race but succeeded only in losing his footing and careening down the ancient steps, coming to awkward rest on the first plateau. Keara reached him quickly and pronounced him severely bruised, scratched and creepy but otherwise healthy. She carried him down the steps in a fireman carry, plopping him on the ground unceremoniously in the shade at Ivy's feet. She was a beast.

Rose looked at Frank and again rolled her eyes. He opened his eyes and grinned. His two front teeth were gone. "A matching pair of village idiots now," Rose noted.

The guide understandably cut our tour short, and we returned to the dock to board the waiting boat. Frank was bleeding from a thousand scratches. His left knee was swollen horribly, and he was bleeding from the empty sockets his teeth once called home. Keara assisted him back to the boat. Annie Ruth's thinning white hair was matted to her head, and she was visibly panting, although still without a single verbalized complaint. Ivy stopped in at the park's restroom and lathered up her hair with liquid soap from the dispenser, only to discover there was no running water to rinse it. She waded knee deep into the lagoon to wash the soapy shit from her hair. "Senorita...have we forgotten the translation of Lamanai...submerged crocodile?" The guide gently prodded Ivy's memory.

"Are you kidding me?" Ivy asked, still standing knee deep in the water.

"You better Belize it," he responded with the corny tourist slogan as he smiled broadly and pointed a few yards up the shore to a pair of partially submerged crocodiles. Ivy hastily retreated from the lake.

Frank angled for a seat by Ivy but Rose cut him off. "Don't you think she is a bit out of your league?" Rose asked.

"I like 'em young and tender," Frank openly leered at Ivy as she stripped to her swimsuit, leaned over the rail, and poured bottled water into her soapy hair.

"Why don't you just wait for Honey Boo Boo to come of age then?"

Frank thought for a moment and replied, "I do like my girls with a little meat on the bone."

"Ouch," Ivy responded with her index finger extended in Frank's face.

"Gross. Don't think I won't beat an old man in public," Rose said to Frank.

"Hangover," Frank shouted. "The good one, not those lame-ass sequels."

This time I rolled my eyes and found a seat away from the action next to Linus and Lucy. The Captain pulled away from the dock and sped toward a narrow opening in the dense jungle. Lucy pulled off her t-shirt. Frank wobbled to his feet and snapped a Polaroid. Linus backhanded him in the nuts. "Back off, freak." We passed a collection of small, thatched-roof, wooden huts surrounding a well-constructed house in a cleared section of the jungle on the north side of the river. There was a small, well-

70

maintained dock where several large black men were congregated, armed with assault rifles. Linus pointed. "A do-gooder, tree-hugging couple of lily-white school teachers from somewhere on the East Coast along with their teenage daughter moved to Belize about three years ago. You may have seen them on House Hunters International?"

"Oh, yeah. I love that show. Kinda weird they never change clothes, though. Feels a bit staged."

"You think?" Linus said sarcastically before continuing with his story. "The do-gooders set up that compound on the river as a school to teach the ignorant natives how to farm produce using hydroponics. I can't even imagine the colossal size of an ego required of someone that had never farmed a day in their life to think themselves capable of imparting wisdom to the locals on how to farm their own land," Linus said, shaking his head.

"How did that work out for them?" I asked.

"Well the husband, he drowned in the river." Linus added air quotes around "drowned." "The daughter, she just went missing. If I had to venture a guess, she was sold into the sex trade. But I am a pessimist by nature. Could be she volunteered for the gig. The farm, though, is a big success. It's a very well-run hydroponic farm now producing most of the marijuana used in the district."

"How about the mom? She still around?" I asked.

"Oh, yeah. She is. It turns out she taught the natives quite a bit about farming. And in spite of her missing family, she gets on quite nicely at the farm. I hear they call her Two-Liter Taylor."

"Huh?"

Lucy answered, "'Cause she can fit a two-liter bottle up her twat."

The return trip followed the same path. We docked in the Orange River district and re-boarded the school bus for the jarring ride back to Bomba. In spite of the rough ride, I managed a nap lying on Rose's shoulder. She nudged me awake as we arrived at the village.

71

Ardy greeted us as the bus pulled to a stop next to the small lagoon. He was high as a kite and wearing nothing but a leather loincloth. Otherwise, he looked great. His bite wounds, the visible ones at least, had nearly healed and looked more like scars than recent festering wounds. His skin was a rich brown, absent burn or welts from the bug bites. The sodomy-themed pink graffiti was no longer visible. His brain was fried, though. "Is it time to head to the ruins? Has the game started yet? Can I pet the monkey? The stars are pretty." He lifted his loin cloth, scratched his balls and walked in collapsing concentric circles guided by the crone's leashed pet coati before slamming into a palm tree and reversing course. The coati chattered loudly.

The crone walked up to me and grabbed my arm, forcing me to lean down where she whispered in my ear, "I be liking your friend Ardy. I think I might just be keeping him here as my pet." I pulled away from her. She laughed a long, toothless guttural laugh that conveyed no trace of humor. "I just be pulling your leg, pretty-eyed man. I don't want your boy. He too ugly for me." She motioned for me to come closer with an extended crooked finger with a long, yellow nail. For some reason, I could not resist. I pinched myself hard and squealed like a school girl from the pain. "What be wrong with you boy to go be hurting your pretty little self like that." She laughed again. My skin crawled. "Come here. I won't be hurting you. I have a message to give you from your boy Hobo." She pulled me down. Her grip was remarkably strong for an old woman. "For each reality, he say, there be as many other possibilities as there are stars in the sky." She pointed up to the sky. It was mid-day but millions of stars shone clearly in the sky. I pinched myself again. "You not be dreaming, boy." The stars disappeared. She placed a small, inordinately heavy package in the palm of my hand wrapped in dried tobacco leaves and securely fastened with twine woven from straw. "Be sure and give your friend Hobo this here for me." She reached up and kissed me on the lips, forcing her tongue into my mouth. "And this, as well." She walked away, laughing.

Rose punched me on the arm. It hurt like hell. I not be dreaming.

EZEKIEL

"But the children rebelled against me: They did not follow my decrees, they were not careful to keep my laws, of which I said, "Whoever obeys them will live by them," and they desecrated my Sabbaths. So I said I would pour out my wrath on them and spend my anger against them in the wilderness."

Ezekiel 20:21

"The path of the righteous man is beset on all sides by the inequities of the selfish and the tyranny of evil men. Blessed is he, who in the name of charity and good will, shepherds the weak through the valley of darkness, for he is truly his brother's keeper and the finder of lost children. And I will strike down upon thee with great vengeance and furious anger those who would attempt to poison and destroy my brothers. And you will know my name is the Lord when I lay my vengeance upon thee."

Ezekiel 25:17

Washington, D.C.; May 2016: The President signed an Executive Order today authorizing the State Department to use "all means necessary" to accelerate the immigration of 1 million Syrian refugees to the United States by the end of 2016. In a written statement, the President urged the governors Of Texas, Iowa, Utah, Idaho, Oklahoma, Nebraska, Nevada and Idaho to accept the orphans and children from this war torn country with all due compassion. White House representatives declined further comment and no details were released.

Texas Governor Bush was outraged, calling the Executive Order unlawful and a "cheap political trick" to buy votes and create chaos and unrest in GOP states. Bush promised immediate legal action.

Alongside Global News

CHAPTER SIX

Perhaps the greatest Lacrosse player of all time, Jim Brown played for Syracuse University. I hear he wasn't a slouch at football, either. And it was from that great institution of liberal higher learning Rose's baby sister, Dixie, was graduating with a very expensive four year degree in Physical Education. Dixie, much like the rest of Rose's siblings, was blessed with beauty, intelligence, and no small measure of athletic ability. Originally a premed student, PE proved a more suitable discipline, better facilitating six years of government and parental funded partying, along with starter husband exploration and testing. Dixie, not unlike the majority of her peers, enjoyed a good party and Syracuse consistently topped the list for best schools to pursue said endeavor. According to my best calculations, she should be able to pay back her student loans sometime just before her 157th birthday…Assuming, that is, she secured an adequate secondary and tertiary employment to supplement her modest teacher's salary.

I sat with Rose's Second Act family in the Manley Field House, anxiously awaiting the first of the two individual graduation ceremonies to end. Unfortunately, the torturous event had yet to even begin. Some 800 kids, mostly the privileged offspring of white families, were graduating with four, five, and six year degrees in some aspect of education at today's event after five, seven, and eight years of school. It was from this well-tended crop that our future generations would acquire the basics: math, spelling, English, history, and the evils of conservative thought. Inclusion, it seems, was paradoxically a key aspect of liberal speak among this predominately lily white assemblage of future educators. Irony along with any conservative doctrine was absent any course syllabus.

Rose's family lives in upstate New York. Her Mom and Daddy work a large dairy farm that had been in her mother's family for three generations. Rose's birthfather went missing in action shortly after spawning his second child. He found himself ill-suited for the dairy farmer's tedious schedule and responsibilities. After completing first chores one morning, he never returned from his daily cigarette and numbers ticket run from the Italian butcher shop in the village. This was before state sanctioned numbers games when there were only family-owned lotteries. Daddy helped Mom raise Rose and her older brother since they were toddlers and, by almost every measure, had done a damn fine job. Although he could have done a tad better with obedience training and perhaps efficient packing tactics. He also fathered six more kids with Rose's mom. Free labor is pretty handy on a dairy farm. Dixie was the last of the brood, owing her existence to an alcohol fueled moment of passion that came when her Mom, mistakenly thinking herself beyond child bearing age, passed on getting out of bed to grab the diaphragm. They are both salt of the earth, hardworking, kind of people with big hearts and great intentions. But, like most working, middle-class, families, they had seriously strained wallets. Nevertheless, for their baby, they found a way to fulfill her dream of attending Syracuse University.

I was assigned to sit between Rose and her grandfather, appropriately nicknamed Brat. For an 80-year-old, he had a keen mind and an adolescent sense of humor. Rose did not fall too far from this tree and the two of them together spelled trouble in all caps. At long last the students began their procession into the hall, some eight hundred strong. Dixie stands just south of five foot and had generously bedazzled her cap to better facilitate locating her in the towering identically dressed masses. Brat was the first to spot the munchkin. He magically produced an air horn and gave three short, shrill blasts. Rose's mom had carefully frisked Brat for contraband before she left the house. Brat, as always, proved himself highly resourceful. Dixie turned, flashed a brilliant smile and waved. Rose giggled. Mom frowned. I confiscated the air horn.

Dr. Hollings III stood to give the invocation. I am but a simple public school educated Georgia boy, but I thought invocation was just a fancy word for opening prayer. And prayer, in my book, was a brief, one way chat with your God of choice thanking him for all the cool shit and then asking a favor or two. I also get the Christian prayer is not PC anymore but this was the first time I realized among the learned that God, him or herself, had fallen completely from favor. "Oh great and wonderful universe, we adore thee," Hollings began reading from a set of 3 x 5 index cards. The whole from the heart thing seemed more important to me than a carefully scripted, well-read prayer. I liked to believe my God agreed. If He was the being I hoped Him to be, He cared much more about the content and intent than the presentation and packaging value. My God was moved by Amazing Grace sung out of key, with passion and accompanied by an untrained, arthritic woman on an untuned and battered upright piano. A well-paid music director accompanied by a 50-piece orchestra, also compensated for their time, added no value. Then again, Hollings was pointedly not praying to my God. Nevertheless, I bowed my head like a proper Baptist during a prayer. The good Doctor continued, "You provide an endless bounty of wonders to nourish, pleasure and amaze us at every turn. We are thankful for your endless diversity. The fragrant flowers that provide such great beauty. The towering trees providing shade. The rivers and streams. The mountains and valleys. The tiniest of insect. The sand, the rain, the giant boulders. We thank the universe for all the people of color. Oh great universe, you bless us with a diversity of sexual orientations and we thank thee for the gays, lesbians, bisexuals, and transgendered, both pre- and post-op. Help us ensure we are inclusive of all the people of differing colors, sexual orientation, and beliefs into your bountiful blessing and great spirit. We love your rain, your snow, your wind..." Brat managed to wrestle the horn out of my hand and gave it a long pull before handing it back to me just before every eye turned to seek out the offender. Brat immediately assumed a well-practiced pose of innocence, pointed at me, and shrugged as if to say "can you believe this idiot?" Dr. Hollings rhythm was disrupted by the interruption. She began again, after the hissing stopped, from the beginning. Finally she concluded, "...I love the earth and it loves me." A solid seven minute prayer without a mention of any God. World record! I sent the Guinness peeps an e-mail.

Dr. Keating was up next. He was well north of sixty and had spent his entire career, like most educators, within the liberal confines of the hallowed omniscient walls of higher learning. Never once doing an honest day's work in the real world, Keating was supremely self-confident in the purity and superiority of his wisdom. Inexplicably, for such a man of keen intellect, he found it necessary to read his entire speech verbatim from 3 x 5 cards, as well. One would think after thirty years of delivering some derivative of this very speech, he would have his speech memorized. I'll spare you the entire speech, but the theme was inclusion and the essential mission for teachers to rid children of the false beliefs wrong thinking parents instilled in them. The masses are much too ignorant to think for themselves. While I might agree with the liberal assessment, I believe it a God-given right to be stupid when it comes to your own life. And I much prefer my own brand of stupidity over the government sanctioned variety. Dr. Keating espoused it is a teacher's duty to "the universe" to overcome parental influence on children. I found it amusing that inclusion of all beliefs really means inclusion of all liberal beliefs. Syracuse, not unlike most institutions of higher learning, preaches the importance of a diversity of thought, yet paradoxically insists upon lock step compliance in the singularity of liberal thought. I am reasonably certain white supremacist groups would not find a welcoming seat at the Syracuse table. Nor should they. Yet the Panthers were clearly in attendance. Several dozen graduation caps were emboldened with the black paw logo of the raciest organization. In spite of popular belief, racism is not an exclusive club of the old, white, southern, man.

Sadly, higher education, once the bastion of free thought, has morphed into the self-proclaimed citadel of politically correct thought at the expense of all other ideas. It is the cradle of liberal speak where all dissenting unpopular ideas are squelched, brow beaten, crushed, condemned, and worse yet, simply forbidden utterance. Strenuously arguing against evil thought has noble purpose. But to forbid the debate of unpopular ideas is a dangerous and slippery slope. At one time in our great history it was of popular opinion that blacks were an inferior race and not worthy of the same rights and protections as white Americans. Fortunately, a few brave souls stood to argue otherwise. In today's PC environment, that thought may have been forever crushed.

Two sharply dressed, young undergraduates appeared at the end of our row and wordlessly indicated for me to join them. I started to protest my innocence then immediately thought the better of it. No one was likely to believe the kind, gentle old man was the perpetrator of the juvenile interruption and, quite frankly, the folding chairs were crammed together very tightly, offering little room and no comfort. I really did not see much downside for being escorted out of the hall. What was the worst thing they could do to me? Make me sit through another ceremony?

After a stern, and completely unnecessary, admonishment not to return to the ceremony, the two quietly closed the hall doors behind them. I found a bench in the lobby and I rented an overpriced soda from the vending machine. I amused myself the next hour or so playing Scrabble on my Smart phone. The soda's return came due and I located a bathroom. Sage advice was once given that at forty, one should never trust a fart. I sat. To pass the time, I used the Sharpie in my jacket to pen radical thoughts never spoken at Syracuse on the wall of the stall. If I were to be accused of juvenile behavior, I might as well be guilty.

"A democracy is always temporary in nature; it simply cannot exist as a permanent form of government. A democracy will continue to exist up until the time that voters discover that they can vote themselves generous gifts from the public treasury. From that moment on, the majority always votes for the candidates who promise the most benefits from the public treasury, with the result that every democracy will finally collapse due to loose fiscal policy, which is always followed by a dictatorship."

Alexander Tyler

Some will argue Tyler did not pen this but it is of a more modern and anonymous origin, most likely from the anarchist group commonly known as the Tea Party; the political group that promotes such evil concepts as self-reliance, fiscal responsibility, and smaller government. Sort of like the pasty-skinned, powdered wigged framers of the Constitution envisioned. Regardless of its origin, the quote smacks of a truth the liberals that run our education system and our country unfortunately ignore…for now. In spite of what the Orwellian pigs would have us believe, "Truth nor justice is a derivative of the opinion of the majority."

Shuffling feet alerted me to the culmination of the graduation ceremony. I finished up my business and texted Rose in order to locate the family and our recent, rightfully proud grad. Graduation from a major university is a big deal even if fifty percent of what is taught is useless information and the other half liberal, group-think, bullshit packaged as higher learning.

Everyone was outside on the grass close to the entrance to the building. Dixie was surrounded by the family as I joined the group. She had just finished introducing the head of her academic program. Brat grabbed my elbow and said rather loudly, "that there lady…" he pointed to the well fed, sedentary, middle-aged woman wearing a black gown displaying three velvet stripes on each arm, "… has a doctorate degree in gym." Ironically, I seriously doubted the woman capable of leisurely strolling a 5K, much less running one. A lot of us old farts don't hear as well as we once did and we consequently speak louder than we recognize. Not the case for Brat. His hearing was damn near perfect. He frankly just didn't give a shit who heard him. "I don't talk evil about anyone to their back. When I have something ugly to say, I'll say it straight to their face," he once told me. Rose's mom suggested on more than a few occasions that Brat might consider just keeping his trap shut and opinions to himself. Brat would counter "stupid people do stupid stuff." It would be wrong to withhold his wisdom for the sake of injured feelings.

"Excuse me, Sir, but my PhD is in Physical Education...not gym," Dixie's academic head said, clearly not amused with Brat's comment.

"A distinction Madam...excuse me...Doctor, without a difference," Brat responded, bowing gracefully at the waist in mock deference, revealing a white lie. He claimed arthritic pain severely limited his flexibility as the specific reason for replacing his entire shoe collection, all three pairs, with those that secured via Velcro. Dixie grabbed Brat's elbow and briskly lead him away. I laughed...apparently too hard and, with Brat safely removed, the ridiculed gym doctor focused her displeasure toward me.

"Why are you laughing? I suppose you have a doctorate degree in a more important field."

"No Doctor, Ma'am, I most certainly do not." I assumed my use of the double negative would serve to only further endure myself. "A PhD in gym makes perfect sense." I paused. She seemed confused as to the intended nature of my comment. We Southerners are most capable of delivering sharp insult smothered and covered in kind words and a smile. I continued hopefully to eradicate any confusion. "I simply cannot fathom a higher calling, and better use of time and scarce resources, than obtaining a doctorate degree in order to better teach our children and future leaders the proper play of Naismith's indoor diversion. The nation, nay, the universe, is a better place because of it. Your mama must be so proud." She extended her index finger aggressively into my face. Apparently decades of higher education leaving her unable to formulate adequate words to communicate her displeasure to us lesser beings.

Dixie hastily deposited Brat at a safe distance and returned to retrieve me. "Behave yourself, Zeke. I might want to come back here for graduate school."

"The universe certainly needs more highly educated gym teachers," I said. Dixie flashed her index finger in my face. I wondered if they offered a class on non-verbal vulgar communication techniques at Syracuse. Brat doubled over in laughter. Paradoxically Dixie, all damn near five foot of her, now teaches black high school kids in the Bronx how to play basketball. You can't make this shit up.

CHAPTER SEVEN

"Beer?"

"Check."

"Bait?"

"Check."

"More beer?"

"Check."

"You are aware it's nine in the morning?"

"But we are fishing."

"Valid point."

"Sunscreen?"

"Frigging eh, sunscreen."

Sam, his loving wife Flo, and their three rug rats lived directly across the street from our home in South Jacksonville Beach. They moved in during Christmas break the year the Mayan calendar suggested the gig was up for our planet. We became instant friends, almost as if I had known them for years. And I kind of did. I used to dream. And not just dreams, really, more like bizarre visions. These dreams had the weight and feel of reality. And not just for the brief twilight after waking. The dreams felt so real, I struggled distinguishing reality from fantasy when fully conscious and sober. Now I pinch the shit out of myself occasionally when I am uncertain if my reality is indeed real. Fortunately, those crazy intense dreams stopped. But for years, I thought I was nuts and, quite frankly the jury remains out on that scenario. Sam and his family were an integral part of my last dream nearly four years ago...even before I met them. Fortunately on this day, like many Saturdays, we were heading to the beach for a bit of surf fishing. It's not like we caught many fish but, like golf, fishing is damn fine excuse to drink beer before noon. That's how I roll.

"Hillary got this?" Sam asked, as he finished twisting his umbrella stand into the sand. I twisted the top of my Miller Lite and poured its refreshing cold contents into a red Solo cup, draining the last bit of froth from the bottle before tossing the empty back in the cooler.

"Likely," I finally responded.

"Really, that is all you have to say on this. I mean, you so accurately predicted McCain's victory in 2008. I just want to know who you pick this time so I can bet on the other guy."

I gave Sam a long, hard look without speaking. I didn't meet Sam until 2012 some four years after The President's first election. I didn't recall ever having a discussion with him on this, either. Even so, he was dead to right about my prediction. At the time, I could not imagine a scenario where our country would elect a virtual socialist to the presidency with questionable origins and an Islamic moniker. Boy, had I been wrong. The sheep not only elected the man, they reelected him to a second term in 2012. Both coast's population centers had overwhelmingly voted Democrat. Only the fly over states and Texas voted Republican anymore. I am not saying the Republicans have all the answers, as they clearly don't. They get way too wrapped up in social hot button issues that, quite frankly, our government should not even concern itself with. Government, especially at the Federal level, should stay the hell out of the bedroom. Our country was founded, and we have thrived, on the concept of a small federal government with the primary purpose of national security and the encouragement of free trade between the individual states and other countries. Now our country, at least the left and right coasts, believed in big government involved in every facet of our lives from educating our children, to determining the size of our fountain drinks, to dictating what doctor we could visit and the treatment that doctor would provide. The ignorant masses being ill-equipped to make educated decisions regarding their own lives, the highly educated liberals must choose for us all. That line of thinking scares the shit out of me. And it is not like the government has proven itself highly successful in the additional endeavors it has freely assigned itself. Do you really want to turn over the health care system to the same bunch of idiots that run the VA health care, the post office and Amtrak? I unfortunately did not see this trend changing in my lifetime. Free shit is a powerful campaign slogan. It seems the higher the educational attainment of our new breed of leaders the more blind they are to their ignorance. I continued staring blankly at Sam, trying to wrap my head around something that seemed a bit off kilter but unable to quite pinpoint the source of the imbalance.

"You okay there, Zeke?" Sam asked. I grunted, noncommittally.

Sam got up, baited his hooks, and waded into the surf to cast the sliced squid. A plus-sized, well-tanned, younger woman in the tiniest of thongs waddled by, pausing to make a rather uncomfortably close inspection of Sam's ass. Tattooed on her shoulder blades, cradled among the folds of back fat, were a pair of petite angel wings. Sam bumped into her as he abruptly turned, causing her to lose balance and fall face first into the surf. She struggled to stand. The incoming surf displaced her bikini bottom to around her knees, further complicating her ability to self-extricate from the ocean's grasp. In spite of the considerable comical quality, her oversized bare ass was a sight left better unseen. Sam fought to gain sufficient leverage in the retreating surf to assist and finally managed to wrap his arms around her considerable girth and help her to her feet. I furtively snapped a photo on my phone and posted it to Facebook. Sam was positioned behind her with his groin area tightly joined to her bare ass and both hands firmly grasping her remarkably undersized breasts. God has an adolescent boy's sense of humor. Sam apologized for his clumsiness. I laughed uncontrollably. She beat a wordless, hasty retreat north toward the pier. "What the hell?" Sam asked as he made his way back to his beach chair. I couldn't quit laughing long enough to attempt to make sarcastic comment. Sam managed without me. "All I know for sure is she is gonna need a bigger set of wings."

I closed my eyes. The warmth of the sun heated my skin pleasantly. The ocean breeze and rhythmic sound of the surf soon had me feeling drowsy. It was near dusk when I finally awoke. Sam was long gone. I had slept nearly all day. Knee deep in the surf directly in front of me was an oddly familiar shape. As he moved toward me, his unique odor reached me before my sleep addled eyes recognized him. It was the mysterious vagrant, Hobo.

Sam kicked my chair. "Wake your butt up, old man. It's the middle of the day."

***

I broke my arm in the queerest way. I am reclaiming that word. It means unusual and is by no means derogatory, unless one allows it to be. I am queer. No, not gay, I am unusual. Lifting a light piece of furniture, my radius bone snapped in two, with a distinct, sickening sound, easily equaling the volume of an M-80 exploding in a confined space. Perhaps I exaggerate; suffice it to say, it was an audible snap that featured a return of my partially digested lunch. It rarely tastes as good on the way out.

A few days after the cast was removed, I received the sad, but not unexpected, call that my Aunt Grace passed. She was of the last generation to suffer polio and Grace, hobbled by the disease, bore its stain with the remarkable grace of her namesake. Grace had given birth to four children, all boys; my cousins, two older, two younger. Like my father and many other salt-of-the-earth-southern-boys raised on the land during the Great Depression, Uncle Cotton was a very religious man. Those that have the least and suffer the most, tend to be the most faithful members of the flock. Perhaps intense suffering, social injustice, and the total dependence on unseen forces by necessity strengthen one's faith in a higher power. Without faith, there would be no hope, only suffering.

Cotton and Grace chose awkward, alliterative Old Testament Biblical names for their brood. Their youngest son, Abaddon, Don for short, was a bit troubled. (I held the most "troubled" honor in my family, closely followed by Ruth's more conventional brand.) In his late teens, he drank a few too many beers and managed to knock up a pretty, somewhat gullible, lass. Two years later, he had a few too many again, as was his obsessive nature (lather, rinse, repeat) and took her life in a boating accident. He was unharmed in the mishap, as us drunks often are, and so, miraculously, was his infant son spared. The infant, surviving the modern day Passover, matured to be a bit troubled, like his father. He worked as an LPN in a nursing home in Orlando. Here in Florida, God's waiting room, nursing home jobs were plentiful. He did his time changing the soiled diapers and bedclothes of the warehoused elderly while awaiting suitable opportunity to relieve them of their prescription pain meds. His dad, uncles, and grandparents lived about 20 minutes west and north in Ocala. No better people have walked this earth but seemingly there is always one destined to disappoint in every brood. I should know. I witnessed the disappointment in my own father's face. The grandson's seed fell uncomfortably close to the tree of the father. With his grandmother's elegant head propped on a silk pillow behind him, he explained to his uncle he would be unable to attend the funeral and join his cousins as a pallbearer. I assumed his honored role as pallbearer by default, bum arm and all. There are some requests you simply cannot refuse.

Only two of Grace's sons bore her grandchildren; the oldest Abraham (Abe) and the baby of the four, Don. Abe's sons were the other pallbearers. They were all young, strong bucks with thinning hair, cute, adoring wives, and each with a full litter of boys themselves. The Foster name would be passed on in Central Florida. Abe's only girl, Grace's beloved granddaughter, was a tiny thing; a surfer chick with deeply tanned skin, long blond hair, and no hint of makeup. She wore a plain, loose fitting sundress of appropriate length and flat sandals with no visible jewelry. Grace lived in a home of all boys and the granddaughter was her oldest son's last child and only girl. Grace could not have cherished her more.

My cousin Kenny, the owner of the miracle hiccup cure, came down to attend the funeral with his sister Georgie. Time is a relentless bitch to us all; even so, she had worked overtime on Kenny. His very best years were in high school where he was top of his class academically, star football player, and popular with the in-crowd. In a futile effort, I reasoned, to relive those good times, he continued to wear the same clothing and boyish hairstyle from his teens. In fact, Kenny's Facebook profile picture featured a black and white action shot, scanned from the yearbook, of himself tossing a football while dodging tacklers during a high school football game. The team was nicknamed the Dirty 30 as there were only thirty players that went out for the team. It was not a small school. This was soon after forced racial integration and the best athletes of both races could be found in the stands, in the parking lot, or at the pool hall.

Lest you judge the South too harshly, consider a few interesting facts. First, shortly after the Supreme Court ruled segregation illegal in the late 50's, many school districts, including ours, responded with Freedom of Choice plans. These plans allowed any kid to go to any school. There were several black kids that attended my school. I am sure it was not easy for them socially, but I never witnessed any physical abuse and very little overt verbal abuse. Perhaps they might tell a different story, but for the most part, we accepted the black kids like any other kids and they were judged on their own merits and not the color of their skin. Not to say the N word wasn't tossed out. But then again, don't we all tend to select the most powerful words from our vocabulary when we intend to injure? In the heat of the moment, I have called Rose a bitch. Rest assured, in spite of using the "B" word, I do not hate all women and in fact actually love that particular one, even though there are days I don't like her so much. Regardless, even if I hated a singular person and verbalized a hateful word to describe that individual, it in no way suggests I hate all people of similar race, sexual orientation, religion and/or gender. I paint with a small brush.

Ultimately, the Federal Courts ruled Freedom of Choice plans to be ineffective and began the long, arduous process of forcing full integration across the nation. Our Southern school district became fully integrated in 1969, amid a lot of jaw-flapping but no significant violence. Boston school districts were not fully integrated until a decade later and then only with violent protest. Yet it is us southerners that are labeled the ignorant racists. I have often remarked the difference between southern and northern whites regarding race can be explained as such. Southern whites, on occasion, speak of the entirety of the African-American race in disparaging terms while having multiple individual black close friends. Northerners, conversely, embrace the entirety of the race yet often have never so much as shared an individual meal with a person of color, much less shared a roof or a bed. Most certainly, I oversimplify and generalize a complex relationship.

Regrettably, the bitch (time) had padded 30 pounds to Kenny's diminutive frame in all the wrong places while cutting deep grooves in his once handsome face. Not that I could say much. The bitch had been less than kind to me, as well. She rarely discriminated. Time is the key ally of chaos, anarchy and decay. She even cast her evil spell in the virtual world eroding binary code in a challenging phenomenon known aptly as digital decay.

Kenny's sister Georgie was born late in her parents' life, a year or so after God saw fit to take my cousin and best friend, Paul. Six-year-olds are ill-equipped to deal with the death of a beloved playmate; nor are the parents of any child. It was an early and painful lesson in the inexplicable suffering of innocents; a lesson that I would never fully understand. Why does an all-powerful, all-just God allow the suffering of innocents? And please spare me the tired argument of original sin. Kenny's parents sought to replace the considerable void Paul's passing had left in their lives. Georgie was a beautiful and talented young lady. She sang and played the violin with remarkable skill. Utilizing this talent and her considerable beauty, she placed second in the Miss Alabama Pageant in her late teens. Pushing fifty, she remained a beautiful woman. A few extra lines, as would be expected, but no extra weight. Somehow she had found a way to cheat the bitch. Fortune was hers if only she could find a way to replicate and package the magic elixir.

Kenny was visibly annoyed Abe had asked me to fill in as pallbearer. Abe was the oldest of the cousins and we all looked up to him as a God. He gave us our first beer, showed us our first picture of a naked woman, and shared the intimate, if not somewhat inexact, details of sex with us. Even this late in our lives, Abe held an honored position among us cousins and, in all fairness, I would have likely been equally annoyed had the situation been reversed.

Cotton, my favorite uncle and Grace's husband, did not attend Grace's wake. He was suffering dementia and lived in the same nursing home as Grace had. On the day of the funeral, he sat carefully sandwiched between his sons on the front pew. Rail thin, he still possessed a full head of jet black hair. His boys had dressed him in jeans with a black turtleneck and loafers. He was a church going man and owned dozens of suits but had grown much too thin to fit in any of them. The boys had made a half-hearted attempt to shave him as well, but sprouts of stubble, both gray and black, marked his lined face. He was sobbing. Esther kneeled on the carpeted floor and embraced him. He was inconsolable. "I didn't know she was dying," he mumbled in a rare moment of clarity. "I let her go without saying good-bye." My eyes leaked. His sons began to weep with him. Their sons, standing in the pew behind them, rubbed their fathers' shoulders as they, too, fought back a tidal wave of emotions. The air grew thin. I gasped for air, holding back my own approaching sobs as a powerful moment of déjà vu swept over me, buckling me at the knees.

As much as I tease my sister about looking like Mom, I am a dead ringer for my dad. His name, Otsel, was as peculiar as my mom's (Wardine). He will likely never win father of the year, but God knows there have been far worse men that fathered children. Damned by faint praise. But it will have to suffice, as it's the best I have for the man. Mom argued dad didn't know any better. "That was how he was raised." I loved my Mom, but that's a lame ass excuse that needs to be discarded if there is to be any hope for future generations. As grown men, we must assume responsibility for our own actions. Possibly I judge Dad too severely and my children, in karmic harmony, will judge me similarly. My mom would certainly say so. Selectively recalling the bad memories and omitting the good was perhaps my imprudent stratagem to soften the blow of his death by painting him with harsh colors. There are many milestones in our lives' journey. One of the earliest is the somber loss of innocence the moment we realize our parents are fraught with the same human frailties that challenge us all. And then again, much further down the path, the day those frailties require the seismic melancholy shift to caretaker.

Cotton's moment of lucidity passed. He shook my hand and hugged me with remarkable strength. "Hello, Otsel. Where's Wardine?"

Grace was a small woman in the very best of health, but with age she had grown even smaller. Nevertheless, her coffin felt heavy. After the service, we carried her just a few steps in order to push the oak coffin into the hearse. I chose poorly and my newly mended wing was forced to carry the surprising weight. I made a mental note to switch sides at the graveyard. It was a short, dark ride in the bright Florida sun to the cemetery. The walk from the asphalt road to the cemetery plot was about fifty yards over uneven ground filled with the carved stone markers of generations passed. I made my way to the right side of the hearse in order to make use of my good arm. Unfortunately, the funeral director had us back out and my left arm faced the casket. The weight of the coffin over uneven ground was substantial. I misjudged the width of a gravestone and stumbled, causing the casket to tilt dangerously toward me. The grandson behind me tripped on the same stone and fell, releasing his share of the casket's weight. We managed to right the casket but the audible snap was unmistakable. I had re-fractured my arm. The pain was blinding, but this was not my day and I subsequently attempted to disguise my physical agony. We succeeded in placing the casket over the crypt without spilling out its beloved contents. My shirt was soaked through and I could feel the beads of perspiration rolling off my deeply wrinkled forehead. "You okay, little bro?" Esther asked. I shook her off, but could barely remain standing throughout the entire service.

Esther and Morris don't get out much. They both were retired and chose to spend their time in a carefully ordered life of chaos, spoiling their half dozen grandchildren. Esther mistook my near fainting episode as an emotional issue. Clearly seeing Cotton in this state was even more devastating than the loss of Grace and certainly a visible reminder of fates worse than death. I quietly explained to Esther that my distress was physical as I had likely broken my arm. I managed to wrestle off my suit jacket on the way back to the minivan. They roll in style. I sat in the front seat and Morris cranked up the AC seeing that my shirt was soaked through with sweat. The pain was excruciating and I was in imminent danger of losing consciousness and/or breakfast. Esther gingerly rolled up my sleeve and promptly fainted. My bone had not pierced the skin but was straining its design limits in an unnatural, grotesque manner. Morris, cool headed as always, searched the GPS for the closest hospital. My vision rapidly closed to singular dot.

I felt the faintest of pressure on my lips. A delicate hand gently stroked my head. Soft voices spoke in the background. A dullness surged through me and movement was difficult. I awoke in a strange and sterile place, attached with tubes to devices adjacent to my bedside and with my feet hanging uncomfortably off the end of the bed. Rose was at my side along with a large black nurse in pink surgical scrubs. A bowl of navel oranges rested on the table with a bright bow. A brightly painted figurine ceramic clown held balloons and a card. I pinched myself. There was no pain. I must be dreaming. I rolled to my side and pain from my arm caused me to lose control of my bladder. Yet as there was no warm, damp feeling, I concluded I must be dreaming. I felt between my legs and plastic tube snaked into the tip of my penis. I began to yank the offending tube out and the large black nurse grabbed my hand. "Not just yet, big boy. That's my job. You wouldn't want to take away all my fun now, would you?" She patted my penis like it was her pet Labradoodle. Rose laughed. I bet if the nurse was a hot, young thing, her response would have been significantly different. Why are nurses only hot in porn, I thought. I must be dreaming. I slept.

The bright morning Florida sun filtered through the shades. Through the drug-induced haze, I spotted Rose sleeping against the window in the reclining chair, partially covered in a hospital blanket featuring an assortment of zoo animals. A nurse came through the door and shoved a thermometer in my mouth while roughly attaching a cuff to my unbroken arm. The pieces were coming together. Rose farted and stirred. The nurse laughed. "Even hot chicks fart," she mumbled to no one. She left the room without further comment.

Rose came to my side. "What are you doing here?" I asked.

"You are here," she answered waving at the room.

"What am I doing here?" I asked. She explained. "Shit," I said looking down at my pink cast. "You pick out the color?" Pink was her favorite color but that was not my real concern.

"Nope. The closest hospital was a children's hospital. They kept you overnight as your blood pressure was all over the place." She turned away, trying to hide the concern on her face. Changing the subject she added, "Look, someone sent you balloons." Rose handed me the card. It was not sealed. Two tickets to Cirque du Soleil fell on the hospital blanket. There was no note.   The nurse returned. "Looks like you got your walking papers, honey." She removed the IV after snatching the tape from my arm. With one single, fluid motion she reached under the blanket and, without looking, unceremoniously jerked the catheter from my Labradoodle.

"Ouch!" I thought, but there was little pain. The drugs were good.

Rose got us a room at the Hilton Garden Inn nearby explaining we would travel back home the next day. By late afternoon, I was feeling pretty good, but I expect the Oxy may have played a part. We decided to make the 9 PM show at the Cirque, thinking, "What the hell? Free tickets were free tickets." At dinner, I chased the thin chicken soup Rose ordered for me with a couple Jack and diets I ordered for myself. I swallowed an extra Oxy to make certain the pain remained sufficiently at bay. Rose frowned.

We arrived at the Disney-themed strip mall containing the theater after a short ride. Rather unimpressive setting, I thought. Walt would not be pleased. We walked up thirty minutes before the doors opened and found an outdoor bar nearby to sit and continue my pregaming ritual. Rose was unamused. I snuck another Oxy. Rose is a NASCAR wannabe and during the ride over, she had jostled my arm and I was beginning to feel pain. Or maybe I was just rationalizing taking more drugs washed down by dark liquor.

We made our way into the theater amongst the Disney, Sea World, and Universal crowd. A uniformed usher guided us to our seats; front row center. Rose asked who I thought sent the tickets. I shrugged. Rational thought was beyond my current skill set. The house lights dimmed. Haunting music filled the auditorium and a live drum began to bang from somewhere off stage. A bizarre looking bald man, extraordinarily thin but absurdly well-muscled, entered the auditorium at the second level dressed in a wrestling singlet, exposing much of his lithe body and bent slightly at the waist. Four men with exaggerated girlish bearing, also bald, in white face outlined with a royal blue stripe pranced gaily behind the muscled man. More followed; a surreal procession of peculiar characters in strange, brightly-colored costume. An assortment of musical instruments were being played by some of the cast, creating a cacophony of seemingly random noise but with an underlying rhythm that seemed to convey a familiar pattern. Others marched as if on parade. A couple of clowns carried a collection of brightly colored boxes precariously stacked high on a stretcher. A young man, not much more than a boy, really, rode a brightly colored BMX style bicycle, performing tricks in the aisle, dangerously close to the audience. The well-muscled thin man leading the procession turned down the center aisle passing by our seats, pausing to wink at me as he climbed on the stage. He was without his flaming orange hair and beard, but his radiant crystal blue eyes were unmistakable and my face must have flashed some combination of shock and recognition.

"You know that man?" Rose asked.

How to hell to explain this? Rose, this version of Rose at least, had never met Hobo and I really wasn't sure he was anything but a figment of my overworked imagination combined with excessive alcohol and drug ingestion. I pinched the exposed skin above my pink cast. There was no pain, no real sensation at all. I wasn't sure if this was due to my state of overmedication or a false reality. I shrugged.

The lights dimmed. A spotlighted toy train crossed the enormous stage followed by the Hobo on a tiny bicycle. Brightly colored objects flew through the air in rhythmic, hypnotic patterns. A man walked diagonally across the stage, suspended in the air above the floor balancing on a taut wire carrying a brightly-painted, immodestly dressed, young woman. Another couple soared around the stage perimeter on a gigantic flowing red satin curtain. Four tiny pubescent Asian girls, wearing plastered smiles and matching green costumes tossed wooden objects in an impractical fashion attached to small cords while standing on each other in an equally impractical manner. A cannon of confetti filled the air amongst dozens of lithe bodies somersaulting across a void and up the vertical wall of a vacant building facade. The girlish men reappeared inexplicably from under the stage floor and assumed a prone position, painted heads resting in their hands, to view the spectacle. The music stopped briefly and, in the darkness, I could hear the sound of numerous bare feet running across the stage. The lights came back up as dozens of gymnasts sprinted across the stage, flying off trampolines buried in the floor performing incredible acrobatic feats coming dangerously to rest inches from the edge of the stage. Our seats were slightly below the stage and I was a bit unnerved that one of the acrobats would fly off the stage into our laps. No sooner the thought, the stage lights dimmed and a striking young blond acrobat with curly hair misjudged the edge by mere centimeters and landed square in my lap. I reached for her to break her fall or, as more likely, to instinctively protect myself from harm. Fortunately she was tiny and flexible and managed to not harm herself or me. With her arms wrapped around my neck, in an oddly familiar manner, she locked eyes briefly and smiled before kissing me lightly on the cheek and nimbly returning to the stage. The spotlight followed her across the floor, a whirlwind of grace and implausible movement: summersaults, flips, and finishing with a handstand, bending her legs over to the floor behind her perfectly shaped ass. Rose squeezed my hand and motioned for me to look in my lap where there was a single sheet of folded stationary. On it printed neatly in ink revealed by the flashes of ultraviolet stage light was an address and a single letter: "V".

"What the hell, Zeke?"

I shrugged.

***

One often hears that curiosity proved unfortunate to the domesticated feline. I was all for heading back to the hotel after the show. Rose, assuming the feline role, insisted we do a drive by the address on the stationary and dutifully inputted the address into the car's GPS. It was late, well past midnight, when we pulled into the Orange Grove Mobile Home Park, just north of Orlando. The park was subtly lit. The road was a bit narrow but well-maintained and crossed with frequent, bright yellow speed bumps. The grounds were well-manicured, featuring hibiscus and palm but nary a citrus tree of any variety. Orange, Palm, Sea, Lake…all popular misnomers in the sunshine state for real estate developments. Swamp, Retention Pond, Meth Lab, Crack House are often more accurate, but marginally less desirable names. Real estate agents and developers have a long history dealing in half-truths. Florida, after all, was home to Ponzi's swampland con. The homes in Orange Grove, though manufactured, seemed more permanent than mobile.

We made our way through the park, following well-marked addresses to the very back. There, a solitary mailbox with the target address fronted a narrow opening in a barbed wire fence hidden partially by a tall hedge row of flowering Hibiscus. A narrow road, really more two ruts in the sandy soil, led into an abandoned and overgrown orange grove. Were half-truths better than total falsehoods? I silently wondered. Much of this part of Florida was covered in orange groves until Walt, air conditioning, and a series of brutal winters came to central Florida. The path disappeared into a sharp corner, illuminated only by our headlights. The sight and sound of the skeletal trees scratching the sides of our car was a bit unnerving. A half mile down the path led to an ancient silver Windstream travel trailer modified with a lean-to addition fashioned of rusting corrugated sheet metal off to its left flank. The front yard was carefully manicured; smooth stone pebbles outlined with pieces of brain coral. There was light spilling out the screen door and a small man silhouetted by the light came to the door.

"I'm thinking slam this bitch in reverse," I said to Rose. She put the car in park and shut the engine off. "Not a good idea."

Rose shrugged and opened the car door. And I'm not the good listener.

Hobo rapped on my window. He was wearing nothing but a pink thong and Jesus sandals. "You getting out, Ezekiel?" Before I could respond, the blond acrobat from the show came to his side in pink booty shorts and matching jog bra. She had removed the theatrical make up unveiling a smooth alabaster face with delicate angles and crystal blue eyes. She was of similar size and build to Hobo with just the subtle differences in geometry that remind us our Creator is a dude or a lesbian. Looking, staring Rose would later say, I could not help but notice she was stunningly beautiful.

Rose joined them beside my still closed door with a "WTF" look on her face and her hands on her hips. Finally, Rose unnecessarily verbalized the words her posture so well communicated. "WTF, Zeke."

I opened the door. Hobo embraced Rose. "It's so good to formally meet you. Zeke has told me so much about you."

"He has, has he? Funny…" she said wriggling out of the awkward embrace "…I know nothing of you," elevating her left eyebrow as she glared at me. I shrugged. The acrobat's name was Aja. Pronounced like the continent Asia, she explained while extending her delicate hand. Rose retorted sarcastically, "I am Rose, pronounced like the flower." Hobo did not offer an explanation as to the relationship between him and Aja.

"Nice panties," I said to Hobo pointing to his pink thongs.

Aja responded, "Thanks."

A toddler's cry came from inside the trailer. Aja excused herself to investigate. Hobo invited us inside the sparsely furnished Windstream. The walls and ceiling were covered with newspaper clippings in dozens of different languages and some alphabets completely alien to me. The papers were in turn covered in varying geometric shapes and colored markers and connected with strings and dotted lines in a seemingly haphazard manner. In the center of the ceiling, within an isosceles triangle, free from clippings, a single word was spelled with letters clipped from magazines of varying font size and style like a ransom note from a made for TV movie in the 1980s -"SECESSION." Stacks of newspapers stood in the corner. The interior of the Windstream seemed unbelievably spacious and from a back room, Aja retuned with chubby, flaming red-headed toddlers, one on each hip, both hungrily suckling a small, pale, bared, flawless breast. Rose kicked me in the shin, causing me to squeal like a little girl from a mixture of pain and the embarrassment of getting busted. Both toddlers simultaneously released their assigned nipple and brought a chubby finger to their puffy lips, as if shushing me for disturbing their meal. I excused myself to use the bathroom.

The bathroom was without a door but a series of colored plastic beads hanging from its frame provided a modicum of privacy. Inside, the floor was covered in pink marble and featured an antique cast iron claw footed tub, dual vanities, a large walk-in shower, an antique porcelain toilet with the tank suspended on the wall above the bowl and a modern bidet. The walls and ceiling were likewise covered in newspaper clippings. In the moment, the only peculiar feature of the travel trailer's implausible bathroom was the bidet. I splashed my face with cool water and returned to the main room.

"You have a fucking bidet?" I asked Hobo, incredulously. Hobo's hygiene was not one of his strong points.

"Language, Ezekiel!" Hobo sternly admonished me. Aja sat on a pink bean bag chair in the corner where the twins continued their meal, seemingly undisturbed by my harsh language. Aja had covered her breasts with a pink blanket, likely sparing me from further punishing shin kicks and a future ass whipping. He continued, "Cleaning your bottom with TP will achieve a similar result to cleaning up ground-in crunchy-peanut-butter off a shag carpet."

***

Hobo kicked my beach chair. "Wake your butt up, old man; it's the middle of the day." Hobo stood uncomfortably close to me, silhouetted by the sun. I instinctively grabbed my right arm. There was no cast. "What is wrong with you, Ezekiel? You look like you have seen a ghost."

100

"No ghost, but do I see an asshole?" I asked Hobo about the circus, the clipping papered Windstream, the redheaded twins, and Aja.

He looked at me like I was the crazy one. "Dude. You do acid in the sixties?"

"I was a damn toddler in the sixties," I said, thinking that was a self-explanatory negative response to his question.

"Darn young to be dropping acid, Ezekiel. No wonder your elevator pauses mid-floor on occasion." Remembering a past lesson, I chose to not argue with crazy and just shrugged my shoulders in unconditional surrender. "You have something for me," Hobo stated with a certainty and an uncharacteristic urgency in his voice. At first I had no idea as to what he spoke of but Hobo pursed his lips and bent at the waist displaying a remarkable likeness to the old crone's pose in Belize.

"I do. It's at home."

Hobo wordlessly reached into my backpack and pulled out the tobacco leaf wrapped package from inside. I had no recollection of placing the object in my bag. He carefully removed the twine and unwrapped the object. It was a disc of some sort, about eight inches in diameter and it shimmered in the bright sun like pure gold. Suddenly, a thousand stars twinkled brightly against a black sky, even though it was mid-day.

Babylon, Persia; July 2016: Brothers of Islam and The New Black Panthers Party (NBPP) held a joint news conference today, announcing the signing of a Mutual Defense Treaty between the two "nations." A spokesperson for the Brothers of Islam, Mohammed Ghazi, promised its full resources in defense of the NBPP against their common enemy, the Zionists, and their Western Allies.

A spokesperson for the State Department characterized the announcement as "peculiar."

Alongside Global News

CHAPTER EIGHT

Frank was holding court, regaling the assembled extended family with Vietnam War stories; stories he very likely pilfered from the crop of Vietnam-era movies beginning with Coppola's ground breaking 1979 dark classic Apocalypse Now. "Some reporter asked me how I could shoot women and children. I answered...it's easy. You just don't lead 'em as much." No one laughed. Frank was career Army, the real deal, not some rear echelon poser, and had spent a significant amount of time "in the shit" on his numerous tours in both Vietnam and Korea. Perhaps too much time. But for whatever reason, he favored and retold stories stolen from movies as if they portrayed his own personal history. Perhaps the truth was too painful or too boring to recite or maybe Frank was just delusional and reality and fiction were no longer distinguishable. It happens.

We were at the family compound, hanging out by the vinyl, above ground pool, listening to Frank's alternate reality war stories while he burnt Bubba Burgers on the charcoal grill. The grill was, ironically, fashioned from a 55-gallon barrel of Agent Orange. It was Mom's 80th birthday celebration. Her kids, siblings, grandkids, along with some close friends were all assembled to wish her well. Mom's siblings lived on a ten-acre tract in Enigma in South Georgia. Five double-wide trailers encircled the pool and the property was bordered by a chain-link fence topped with razor wire. The pool had a large wooden deck for sunbathing. The grounds were covered with large granite stones and the occasional patch of dry grass. Otherwise, the compound was featureless, save the flag pole sporting a large US flag, a smaller version of the Stars and Bars of the Confederacy, and an even smaller Don't Tread on Me flag replete with coiled rattlesnake.

Frank, nonplussed by the lack of laughter and the uncomfortable body language, continued; "You know how I could tell the VC from the civilians?" I knew the answer. Frank was quoting from the movie Full Metal Jacket, yet I wisely remained silent, thinking perhaps Frank should pilfer lines from less popular movies. "If they run, they are VC." He smiled broadly and continued…"And if they stand still, they are well-disciplined VC."

I asked Frank, trying to call him out on his unadulterated plagiarism, "Frank, do you like the smell of Napalm in the morning?"

He assumed a Duval-like pose in Apocalypse Now, squatting on the beach, and replied missing, or perhaps ignoring, my attempt of sarcasm "I do. It smells…like victory."

Annie Ruth interrupted Frank. "A little less talk and a little more cooking, old man. You're burning my meat and I don't like old, dried-up meat."

"Pot, kettle, black," I muttered under my breath and guzzled the remainder of my beer.

"Ezekiel, are you crazy son, or just plain ole stupid? He is not using a pot, it's a grill." Annie Ruth chastised me. God should have taken this woman home decades ago. Yet here she remained, in possession of her teeth, most of her wits and, apparently, a keen sense of hearing.

Ruth rose from her lounge chair, retying her bikini top as she stood, but not before giving Frank a brief glimpse of her perky, tattooed breast. Ruth was early fifties but somehow, and not through clean living and exercise, maintained the body of a much, much younger woman. She cannon-balled into the pool, splashing water over the grilling meat and her husband of just a few months, Mormon Mario, laying on a float in black shorts and a long sleeved black t-shirt. Annie Ruth reached up and wiped the drool from Frank's mouth with a handkerchief in hand. Fortunately for Frank, Mom was inside enjoying the air-conditioning, visiting with her sisters, and missed Frank's decidedly unsuitable reaction to the brief glimpse of his niece's perky, tattooed breast. She did not cotton to this side of Frank. Ruth, Mom gave the obligatory "my child does nothing wrong" pass. Like most of Mom's siblings,

Frank was as good-hearted as they come. Also like most of her siblings, Frank was a bit peculiar. Rose would aggressively argue more than a bit, especially when it came to Frank. Not a criticism, just a fact. I mean, Jesus was peculiar and I sure as hell will not criticize any man willing to die in place of my sorry ass. Quite frankly, I would gladly nominate most of my aunts for sainthood were we of the Catholic faith. (Us Baptists need to start us our own hall of fame.) These women all quietly sacrificed much for others. Now Aunt Rudine...I guess I will just employ the Mom rule..."Don't say nothing unless you got something good to say."

"I see you still bleed gray," I said to Frank, motioning toward the Confederate flag.

The published truth is relative and dynamic with time, geography, and unfortunately, the politics of those who pen it. Napoleon characterized history "as a pack of lies agreed upon." Less notable a historic figure, Frank quoted the author Nelson DeMille who wrote "position determines perspective." As a frightening example for a brief moment let's speculate this century's antichrist managed to keep his ego in check and refrained from opening up a second front with the Ruskies. Damn fine chance Adolf and his evil doers would have won or at least not lost the second big war. Just how might history read had Adolf's henchmen penned the accounts of World War Two? Just speculating here but perhaps Adolf might have come across as a standup guy. The bastard might even have a bigger than life-like Greek monument dedicated to his memory.

Now one must forgive us ignorant Southerners as we tend to hold strong feelings regarding what we considered to be The War of Northern Aggression. It is a common misconception, promulgated by the liberal Northerners that the war was all about slavery. It was not. Lincoln's Emancipation Proclamation was late in the war and was just as much a ploy to reignite waning public support for a long, ugly war without a clear end in sight. His number one general was resting his hind quarters on the wrong side of the Potomac and needed serious motivation to reengage those stubborn Rebels. And for goodness sake, don't confuse Southerner pride with racism. Not many a redneck will attempt to defend slavery. It is wrong, it was wrong, and it will always be wrong. Slavery is pure evil. It did exist, it does exist, and it will always exist across virtually every continent affecting virtually every race of mankind. Sometimes the chains are iron, but just as effective and cruel are the economic and social chains that bind one man to another. Slavery existed on both sides of the Mason Dixon. Washington, Jefferson, Adams, Franklin, Madison, and most of the whole lot of our founding fathers owned slaves at one time or another. The South depended on cheap labor to farm and consequently held the largest portion of slaves. This was wrong. Regardless of the reason, there is no excuse for owning another living soul. It is evil. (And so, too, is the profiting from or utilization of goods and services produced by slave labor. Check your clothing and toy label before you climb on that high horse and look down on the South.)

"You're damn right I bleed gray," Frank replied.

Beginning with South Carolina, eleven Southern States seceded from the Union based on the principle of State's rights. South Carolina pointed to the Constitution, which specifically states "…that the powers not delegated to the United States by the Constitution, nor prohibited by it to the States, are reserved to the States…" It was the States' call to prohibit slavery, not the federal government's decision to make. Even the Democratic Party during their 1864 convention in Chicago agreed that Lincoln's actions were a disregard of the Constitution. Again, allowing slavery was a bad call and I am not for a minute defending the ownership of a human being. Nor am I one of the Southerners that refutes slavery as a catalyst for the secession. South Carolina, and most of the other seceding States, quoted the U.S. Declaration of Independence, "…the right of the people to abolish a Government when it becomes destructive to the ends for which it was instituted." Abe said hell to the no, not on my watch, and declared war on his own countrymen by declaring a naval blockade of all southern ports in 1861.

Lincoln began the war as much to preserve the Union and his legacy as to right the wrong of slavery. But, I merely suggest, at the great risk of heretical condemnation, a truly great diplomat could have, should have, would have fashioned a better solution to end this evil than directly contributing to the death of 600,000 Americans. This, to place in historical context, is more American deaths than the Revolutionary War, both World Wars, the pure lunacy of Vietnam, the often overlooked War of 1812, and the Korean Conflict, in sum! Perhaps economic benefits to farmers growing cotton without the benefit of slave labor and a heavy property tax on slaves would have been a sufficient catalyst to end the practice without so much damn bloodshed. I am just saying. I think there was a better way to get the job done than the massive amount of blood Lincoln's solution spilled. Some two percent of the American population perished as a direct result of Lincoln's brute force strategy. A bit more perspective…that would equal eight million dead Americans based on the current population. Yet, universally we hail Lincoln as the great president, even as his General unnecessarily burned a swath of civilian towns and farmland through Georgia on his infamous march to the sea.

We wage war by some archaic gentlemen's code where we delude ourselves that our actions are somehow civil and just. These rules forbid the slaughter of innocents yet history hails Sherman as a great war hero after he burnt crops, destroyed private homes, and impressed livestock, leaving countless thousands of innocents to die of hunger and exposure. A decade after 9/11, revisionist historians stood on the Senate floor condemning the CIA for water boarding terrorists with grandiose speeches of morality, justice, and integrity while simultaneously supporting the targeting and killing of suspected terrorists using drones from 25,000 feet, vaporizing the alleged terrorist and anyone unfortunate enough to be in their proximity. War is not civil nor is the suffering limited to the combatants. Let us never delude ourselves otherwise.

Even Mandela in South Africa accomplished the removal of Apartheid with much less bloodshed than the Kentucky born vampire slayer. Dr. King improved the civil rights of Blacks and again without 600,000 American's splayed on the battlefield and countless others left mutilated, impoverished, homeless, orphaned, and destitute. Not suggesting Lincoln was a bad guy. Merely saying just maybe a great man could have formulated a less bloody plan. Interestingly, the mere suggestion that Abe is not a bigger than life savior will likely get me labeled as a racist. It's the lefts go to argument to squelch opposing views. Anyone that disagrees with their "agreed upon lies" is racist or sexist or some dastardly aberration of both. Nevertheless, truth nor justice is a derivate of the opinion of the majority. Like the sum of two integers, justice and truth remain a constant, unswayed by the whimsical fancies of public opinion.

Frank lifted his stained wifebeater to wipe his sweaty brow and turned his back toward me, displaying a waving rendition of the Stars and Bars just above his ass crack. "You have a Confederate flag tramp stamp? Robert E. Lee just rolled over in his grave."

"Hmm!" Frank grunted and continued. "Damn Yankees seized his land holdings and made it into Arlington Cemetery. Yet the great general and patriot was not even buried at Arlington. His own damn land! That would be why the glorious son of a bitch rolled over in his grave."

Ruth climbed out of the pool onto the deck. Her bikini bottom slid down her wet ass, exposing much of her dragon tattoo disappearing into the crack of her shapely bottom. Frank was again mesmerized by Ruth's immodest skin display. Rose noticed Frank leering and tossed a football at his nuts from close quarters and at a severe pace with clear intent to do permanent damage to his manhood. Frank doubled over in pain, bumping the grill onto its side, spilling the meat and charcoal onto a small patch of dried grass. The charcoal ignited a small fire dangerously close to where Frank lay writhing in pain. Ruth squatted over Frank, pulling her bikini bottom aside and loosed a stream of urine onto the fire, successfully extinguishing the flames but not before Frank wiggled himself into the stream, smiling at his good fortune. Rose kicked him in the nuts. Annie Ruth gingerly wiped the pee off his face. Frank never stopped smiling. I helped Frank up to his feet, being sure to steer clear of his damp areas. He continued to smile at Ruth. I reminded Frank, "Creepy dude…for so many reasons…and she's your niece."

"That sister of yours would make a damn fine soldier…Adapt…Overcome…Improvise."

"Heartbreak Ridge," I mumbled at yet another pilfered quote.

CHAPTER NINE

It was inevitable. Ardy lost his job for foolishly mistaking a coworker's respectful friendliness toward her elders as an invitation to discreetly fondle her breasts. Ardy would unsuccessfully argue incidental contact but the flag had been thrown and the play was not reviewable. To further complicate Ardy's tenuous position, the 19-year-old, freckled-face girl's mom was Bridge partners with Ardy's long-suffering wife. Ardy unloaded the banker's box of personal belongings from his office in the driveway of his modest Florida rancher. He was formulating a plausible story to explain his sudden lack of employment and failed to initially notice the lawn was strewn with his personal belongings from inside the house. Ardy tried the door. It was locked and his key was inoperable. While continuing to fumble ineffectively with the lock, a black Ford Fusion pulled in behind Ardy's car blocking him in the driveway. Ardy kicked the door in frustration. "Son of a bitch, that hurt," he said to no one.

A small man, dressed in khakis, sensible loafers, a short-sleeved-white-button-down-shirt adorned with a red stripped clip-on tie stepped out of the car carrying a legal-sized manila envelope. Ardy turned and noticed him approaching from behind diagonally across Ardy's recently mowed St. Augustine grass lawn. "What new hell?" Ardy said in shocked disbelief.

"Ardy Duda?" The small man asked. Ardy nodded in the affirmative. "You have been served, Mr. Duda. Have a blessed day." The process server handed Ardy the envelope and beat a hasty retreat to the relative safety of his Fusion. He had been in this game long enough to know better than hang around to wait for his victim to fully comprehend the unpleasant nature of the visit. He was a small man, after all, and an attractive target for displaced anger.

Ardy dropped the banker's box, its contents spilling onto the already littered lawn. Limping around to the backyard, Ardy tried the side gate, only to find it securely locked, as well. He shook the gate. His French Bulldog, Spanks, barked and growled ferociously at his newly former master, despite its Lilliputian stature. He shook the gate aggressively and eyed it for a possible vertical assault. Ardy wisely abandoned that strategy. Ardy was vertically challenged and horizontally well-endowed. A less than desirable complement for scaling a privacy fence designed to handle considerably lesser loads. Sweat poured from his bald head in the hot Florida peninsula sun, drenching his white Hawaiian shirt. He leaned against the house, providing a modicum of shade and fished his cell phone from his pocket. Ardy dialed his son, hoping to secure an ally, only to find his company-owned cell was disabled. "Those bastards work fast," Ardy mumbled to no one while hurling his cell into the backyard in a failed attempt to hit Spanks. Spanks returned to barking while making a seriously deficient attempt to jump the fence and confront his attacker. Like most ankle biting dogs, Spanks was severely delusional. "Y tu Spanks, y tu?" Ardy yelled and kicked the fence in frustration breaking, unbeknownst to him at the time, six bones in his right foot. "Son of a bitch. That really hurt." Spanks increased the veracity of his barking.

Ardy reached for his wallet, the contents of which contained a company credit card, two tens, and three singles. Ardy smiled briefly, recalling the night prior's use of his singles in a young redhead's garter belt before remembering the severity of his current dilemma. His wife paid the bills and Ardy did not have access to their joint account. He recovered the envelope from the grass where he dropped it during his assault on the gate and retrieved its contents. The envelope contained divorce papers, an injunction requiring Ardy to stay two hundred yards from his wife, the alleged sexual assault victim and her extended family, a prepaid cell phone with only my number preprogramed, (Rose would later thank his wife for the favor) and a Greyhound bus ticket to Jacksonville, Florida. "How the hell she get this done so fast?" Ardy mumbled again to no one.

A noise from the front of the house interrupted his self-pity party. He breeched the corner of his house to see his company car, being loaded on the back of a Beach Wrecker flatbed. The wrecker driver smiled amicably and waved as he climbed into the cab of his truck. Ardy raised both his middle fingers in an angry, impulsive salute. The driver stopped the truck and exited the cab with a tire iron in hand. Ardy beat a hasty retreat on his impaired leg but was cornered by the locked gate and his lack of mobility. The driver whacked Ardy's right shin with the tire iron. Ardy folded onto the ground, whimpering from an unpleasant mixture of pain, embarrassment, self-loathing, and fear. The driver backed away. "Get a life, dude." It was not the end of a bad week for Ardy.

Ardy showed up at our front door two days later. He foolishly spent his $23 on two handles of Kentucky Gentleman rot-gut whiskey. He had not eaten or consumed anything otherwise, nor made use of a bath. His right leg from the knee down was wrapped in bubble wrap secured with duct tape. The visible half of his leg was several contrasting shades of purple. Rose took one look at Ardy and slammed the door behind her. I, being the merciful one in our relationship, grabbed a bottle of water, and a protein bar, and took it out to Ardy on the porch. He was lying in a fetal position on the stone pavers. I tossed my care package by his head. "Give me a minute with Rose, buddy." I shut the door behind me gently as to not waken the sleeping beast.

"Hell, no," Rose said quietly, but with a finality in her voice and body language.

"We can't turn him away, Rose. He is my friend and he looks like death."

"And the world will be minus one less cretin."

I spent the next twenty minutes making promises I could never keep that likely saved the cretin's life. I managed to negotiate a one night stay in our pool house. I walked back outside to let Ardy in. He wasn't going to be using the one night in the pool house. He was unconscious, lying in a toxic mixture of pus, puke, and pee. I called 911.

I waited in Mayo Clinic's emergency room for what seemed an eternity before the doctor came out. "You next of kin to Mr. Duda?" He asked.

"I expect the closest he has that will admit to it at least."

"Life partner?" The clearly gay doctor asked.

"Hell, no." I replied in disgust.

He straightened his posture and frowned. "You have a problem with homosexuality?"

"Nope," I answered truthfully. Could not give a shit less who you bone. I continued, "But really, even if I was so inclined, I would never suck that man's dick."

He thought for a minute and shrugged, "I see your point." He continued, "Give it about twenty minutes and check with reception for a room number. We are admitting your friend. He has several broken bones in his right leg and is severely dehydrated." He scribbled his cell on the back of his card and handed it to me before disappearing back into the bowels of the emergency room. I tossed the card. The receptionist laughed.

I found Ardy's room and walked in through the open door to see his disturbingly erect penis in Florence's hand. Florence was the medical technician weighing in at somewhere north of 250 pounds even without the benefit of the majority of her teeth. "You might, Mr. Ardy, think this all fun and games right about now, but just you give it a minute..." Florence pressed the catheter down Ardy's urethra into his bladder with one swift motion... "Until I press this tube down that baby snake of yours." Ardy squealed, instantly losing his erection. "Now, then." She patted Ardy's dick. "Looks just like a penis...only smaller."

Florence continued recording Ardy's vitals and setting up the room for its latest guest. Ardy sipped from a foam cup located on the adjacent bedside table spitting out the contents in disgust splashing Florence in the process. "This is fucking water!" Not sure Ardy fully appreciated his current environment and situation.

Florence jerked out the catheter. Ardy squealed. "Why the hell you go and do that?" Florence shrugged. She dutifully recorded the amount of urine collected and left the room, leaving the door open behind her.

"You might want to tone it down, Ardy," I advised. Ardy complied. "So, what is the verdict?" I asked Ardy.

"A half-dozen broken bones and a nasty staph infection in the foot. Might lose it." Ardy laughed. I noticed a bag of morphine hanging from his IV rack and better understood Ardy's cheery delusional state.

A very attractive, tall, thin, young nurse with a sizable rack walked into the room. She had her blond hair neatly pulled into a ponytail. Her skin was flawless and pale and her eyes a stunning royal blue. Ardy sucked his gut in. She smiled and gently touched Ardy's leg with a gloved hand, "Hello, Mr. Duda. I am Andrea. I will be your nurse for the day." Although she was fully clothed with only her arms bare in the loosely fitting scrubs, I expect she felt naked under Ardy's leer. She removed her hand and walked over to the laptop stationed by the door to review Ardy's chart. "Oh my," She said to no one. Andrea walked back over to Ardy and patted his hand in sympathy, despite his continued leer. "I'll be right back with some more drugs for you."

Dr. Garcia, Ardy's attending physician, walked into the room with her posse of four residents, all female, to Ardy's delight. It was like he died and almost went to heaven. "How are you feeling, Mr. Duda?" Garcia was of Cuban descent, a bit chunky, and stood somewhere under five foot tall. Despite that, something about her was exceedingly attractive. The residents were mostly nondescript but Ardy had zoned in on the singular cute one. She was of Indian descent, dark-skinned, tall, thin, with beautiful dark eyes out of a Disney animated movie. Ardy sucked in is gut when he noticed her smiling at him.

He held eye contact with the cute resident as he answered Dr. Garcia's question, "Much better but I need some more morphine."

"How would you describe your level of pain on a scale of one to ten?"

"Which answer will get me the most morphine?" Ardy smiled broadly, never losing eye contact with the cute resident. The resident giggled. Doctor Garcia did not and shot the resident a quick, wordless glance of obvious meaning. The resident immediately stifled her laughter. A residency at Mayo was a good gig. For some inexplicable reasons, young women find Ardy harmless and charming. I love the man but, in fact, he is neither.

Andrea returned with an armful of IV bags. She scanned Ardy's wrist and entered the drug cocktail information into the laptop after confirming Ardy's identity. "That was fast!" Ardy exclaimed, mistakenly thinking his morphine supply replenished.

"Antibiotics, Mr. Duda. Andrea can you please get Mr. Duda some Tylenol for his pain."

Ardy's face fell in disappointment. "Fuck!"

"Language, Mr. Duda. You are seriously ill. We have identified some six different infections along with your fractured bones and are still trying to categorize several more. Quite frankly, I am not certain how you are still alive. That said, keep this behavior up and I will not hesitate to transfer you to University Hospital."

Ardy looked over at me, "That a bad thing?"

I nodded my head in the affirmative and silently mouthed, "A very bad thing." Mayo is foremost a world renowned hospital, providing exceptional healthcare. Not to be overlooked are its creature comforts. It is modern and spotless with large, private rooms featuring Wi-Fi access, 40-inch flat-panel TVs, and a pull-out sofa for any guest of the patient. University is not any of those things and a glimpse into what we all face under Obama Care.

Andrea finished attaching the multitude of bags to the IV rack and produced a needle. "This one needs to go into your belly." Ardy's warning to behave was quickly forgotten. He took the opportunity to yank up his gown, exposing himself to the assembled female staff. He locked eyes on the cute resident who seemed paralyzed to look at anything but Ardy's exposed junk. The female audience aroused him and Ardy quickly became erect.

Dr. Garcia took the syringe from Andrea. "Allow me the honor." She literally punched the needle into Ardy's pudgy belly and yanked his gown down.

"Ouch," Ardy whimpered.

"Contemplate University, Asshole." Dr. Garcia and entourage left the room. I shook my head and followed the Doctor out of the room. I had enough of Ardy's madness for one day.

***

I convinced Rose to accompany me to the hospital the next afternoon to check on Ardy. We valet parked the car and took the elevator up to the fifth floor. "You have to be kidding me," Rose said just as the elevator doors opened. Ardy's exposed back side was framed by the two IV racks that he was wheeling down the polished hall. Rose jogged to the room to grab another gown. I walked up behind Ardy.

"Dude, your ass is hanging out in the breeze." I positioned myself behind him to block the rather unpleasant view from a couple of little girls walking down the hall to visit their grandmother. Ardy's saggy balls were hanging low enough to be on display below his hairy, white ass. A grown woman would be sickened by the view. It would likely change a 12-year-old girl for life. Ardy shrugged and continued lumbering down the hall. Rose mercifully caught up with us and hung the additional gown to cover his ass.

Andrea walked out of a patient's room. Ardy straightened and made a woefully deficient attempt to suck in his gut. "Hello, Mr. Duda. How are you feeling today?" She paused and gave Ardy a warm smile. She continued noticing the dual IV racks, each loaded with an assortment of IV bags and bottles, "You have a nice assortment of accessories, Mr. Duda."

Ardy smiled a creepy smile and said, while openly leering at her ample chest, "Nice rack, huh?"

Dr. Garcia walked by simultaneously. "University, Asshole."

Ardy's leg was booted and bandaged but was oozing, leaving a snail-like trail of green slime on the floor. Rose was wearing sandals and stepped in the slime. "Gross, dude."

Ardy laughed, lifted a leg up, and leaned forward into a flying pose, exposing his saggy balls. "I am a superhero. Snail man, I am." The two little girls visiting their ill grandmother stepped out of her room into the hall and witnessed the slow-moving, unnatural disaster that was Ardy. They began to quietly sob. Undoubtedly Ardy had just created two nuns or lesbians, or maybe, lesbian nuns. Florence grabbed one of Ardy's IV racks and his elbow and hurried him back to his room.

The room was filled with flowers, fruit baskets, balloons, candles, mobiles, puzzles and stuffed animals. "What the hell, Ardy?"

Ardy produced a pamphlet from the gift shop and tossed it over to me. "Frigging Obama Care is awesome. I got all this stuff for free."

Rose shook her head in disgust. "I've seen enough. The moron is alive. Can we go now?" Rose asked. Rose headed for Target to do some angry retail therapy that would likely do some serious damage to our credit card while I stayed with Ardy. Andrea came in and replenished Ardy's morphine supply, activating the bed alarm should he try to get out of bed while further impaired by the narcotic. Quickly, Ardy was asleep. I curled up on the sofa and started reading and shortly dozed off.

A piercing noise startled me awake as three women burst through the door. Ardy had tumbled out of bed while attempting to get up to pee. The women appeared to be members of the Cold War era, East German weight-lifting team. Ardy attempted to rise. The largest of the women, in a thick Eastern European accent, ordered Ardy to remain motionless. He wiggled. She pinned him down with a beefy arm across the chest. Ardy loosed an epic cloud of green fog. Dazed, she momentarily released her grip and Ardy squirmed to a sitting position. Apparently this is against strict hospital safety protocol. She slammed him back down to the tile floor, this time pinning him with her knee across his throat. Interesting safety protocol, I thought. Ardy's gown was up above his waist. His leg was oozing green slime and the entirety of the motley group was bathed in a malodorous visible fog of pungent green gas. Yet Ardy managed to retain his sense of humor. "Don't tase me, bro." The team maneuvered a heavy net under Ardy and proceeded to lift him and place him back into the bed. "Nicely done…" he hesitated searching for the right pronoun, settling on the politically correct but undescriptive"…ladies. But I still have to pee." The largest of the team, Gretchen, tossed Ardy the mostly empty urinal, splashing its pungent remains across Ardy's soiled gown and bed sheets. Ardy, nonplussed, lifted his gown and began peeing into the urinal. The three women began hysterically laughing, causing Ardy's penis to shrink further. The penis wears its heart on its sleeve.

Rose walked into the room just as one of the team commented to Gretchen in a not surprisingly deep voice, "I think your clit is larger than his dick."

Gretchen replied, "You wish." Rose walked out of the room. I followed.

I risked a return visit the next morning, finding Ardy navigating the busy hallway with Florence at his side, assisting with his dual IV racks. A tube snaked out his nose and was dripping green liquid into the pocket of his gown. Florence was attempting to attach a second gown to cover Ardy's exposed ass but Ardy was not cooperating. "Damn gown makes me look fat." Ardy explained to Florence.

"Damn, Mister Ardy…you are fat. Now put this here gown on to cover that lily white ass of yours or I am going to call HOPO."

"HOPO?" Ardy asked.

"The hospital popo Mister Ardy."

"You're making that shit up, Florence."

I began walking to Ardy's room. I wanted no part of this circus. Ardy continued down the corridor refusing to stop long enough for Florence to attach the gown to his back. He did though, pause at each open door to peek inside, hoping to witness a sponge bath of a comely young lass. Ardy complained to Florence, "This here ain't no striptease joint, Mr. Ardy. There ain't nothing but sick, old people in this place."

Ardy shuffled on to the next open door with Florence closely trailing him. Ardy yelled down the hall just as I was entering his room, "Zeke. Son of a bitch. It's that Frio Lobo asshole from Belize." Ardy was standing in front of the open door pointing into the room. Florence grabbed his elbow. Someone shut the door from inside as Ardy added excitedly, "and that black dude with the panther tattoo… I know his name now. Lobo called him Khalid." Ardy tried to pull away from Florence, dislodging his gown in the process. Ardy, naked and oozing goo from multiple orifices, tried the door but was tackled from behind by a large, muscular, black man carrying a radio in black cargo pants, black sneakers, and a black polo emblazoned with Mayo Security on the breast pocket and HOPO across the back. The IV racks crashed to the floor, partially spilling their contents. Ardy lost control of his bladder, adding to the toxic mess. Inexplicably, he fought against the Mayo muscle until the Olympic weight-lifting trio joined in and pinned him to the floor. Ardy was transferred to the psychiatric ward immediately and discharged later that same day. Obama Care did not cover psychiatric treatment.

Jacksonville, Florida; July 2016: United States Congresswoman from Florida's 5th district La

'Quisha White (D) held a joint news conference with The New Black Panther Party (NBPP) announcing the NBPP's planned construction of its "United States Southern Consulate" in Jacksonville. "We are honored the NBPP has chosen our fair city as its home and look forward to the positive presence the organization will bring to the African-American community here in North Florida." White also touted the NBPP would create over 500 high paying jobs for African-Americans to the Northside. The organization plans to utilize space in the Gateway Shopping Center until it completes construction of its new $100 million "Embassy" just south of Jacksonville International Airport.

Khalid Muhammad, the NBPP spokesperson, thanked Congresswoman White for assistance securing local and state tax credits as well as a federal grant. "The NBPP would have not located this vital mission in North Florida without Congresswoman's White invaluable vision, persistence, perseverance, and assistance." Muhammad stated in his speech to the largely African-American crowd, "Much like our brothers in Palestine, African-Americans are a people without a country. The NBPP Southern Embassy is but a solitary step in a long journey that will bring justice to our people and put an end to the African-American Diaspora."

Alongside Global News

CHAPTER TEN

Everything TPC Sawgrass Country Club is, Jax Beach Municipal course ain't. The fairways, a patchwork of sand, gravel, and weeds interspersed with sporadic patches of grass are aptly flanked by youth baseball and soccer fields, a vast school bus parking lot, section eight public housing, and a sewage treatment plant. The latter provides the appropriate aroma for my golf game and suitable cover for the Depends hackers that horde the morning tee times on the course. Situated a top several decades of festering refuse, heavy metals, indestructible plastics, indeterminate virulent chemical brew, and discarded bodies the course and neighboring youth recreational fields make good, if not somewhat discordant, use of otherwise wasted space. A severely errant first tee shot had been known, on more than one occasion, to disrupt an illicit business transaction in the neighboring hood. A concealed weapons permit was not mandatory to play the course but, nevertheless, a highly recommended optional accessory.

In the name of water conservation, the city-owned course only watered twice weekly. This, added to the frequent play by us hackers, reduced the putting greens to a similar surface as the fairways, only more closely mowed. The dress code, similar to the grass, was nonexistent. Cut-off shorts, flip-flops, and tank-tops were more prevalent than khaki pants and polos. The rules of golf were considered mere guidelines and, as such, improving one's lie was widely accepted and yelling in one's back swing highly anticipated. Cheap ass old farts walked for ten dollars in the summer afternoons and as often as not, the cash register was offline, making payment more on the honor system. The carts were inexplicably equipped with GPS as if exact distance mattered too much to anyone foolish enough to take this course seriously. The beer wenches were plentiful and appropriately scantily-attired serving the beer cold and the drinks strong. Had their beverage prices only been more reasonably priced, this course would have been my personal golf Nirvana. I loved it.

Ardy had yet again managed a miraculous recovery. I speculated he must be deep into his quota of nine lives or the Gods (or perhaps demons) just kept him around for pure entertainment value. A flock of migratory birds flew over our heads in the cloudless blue summer sky, casting a V-shaped shadow on the parched ground as Ardy and I approached the starter. George, the aforementioned starter, was a course relic. He was an ancient retired Navy Captain that took his task with more seriousness than appropriate. He represented order that was otherwise nonexistent. George advised us two others would be joining us on our "loop." He added, wiping the sweat off his brow with a white towel, "Looks like a couple…" I silently thought that "couple" was a bit redundant with "two" as he fumbled with his clipboard. He finally continued after locating the couple's names "… Mr. and Mrs. Mark Brunel." As was his nature, George didn't even crack a hint of a smile. Son of a bitch, I thought.

Ardy got excited… "The former Jags QB?"

I may have mentioned the Jax Beach muni-course ain't TPC Sawgrass. No self-respecting NFL QB, former or not, would play this course; sober, vertical, and willingly, at least. Then again, that train left the station when he played for the Jags. I was having another of those strange, intense déjà vu moments. I pinched myself. "Ouch," I yelped.

"What the hell, Zeke?" Ardy asked.

"Just making sure I wasn't dreaming."

Ardy looked at me like I was nuts.

Sure enough, Hobo and Aja joined us on the first tee. Hobo was in a black speedo and a pink mesh sleeveless muscle shirt. He had matching calf-length socks and a pair of traditional oxford Footjoys. Your typical yuppie golf attire, give or take a lightyear or two. Aja was stunning. She was dressed in a dangerously short white golf skirt and a skin tight white polo sans supporting undergarment. George didn't even raise an eyebrow as he checked their receipt before pointing at the tee box and declaring the tee box as ours. George wasn't much impressed with celebrity. Hell, George wasn't visibly moved by much of anything, except someone trying to start on the tenth hole without checking in with him first. George ruled the first tee box with an iron fist enforcing, without exception, the singular rule of importance to him…checking you off his list. A monkey, circus clown, Siamese twin, and a panda bear could play the course as a foursome, as long as George duly noted the cart number, driver's stated name on his clipboard, and verified payment through production of receipt when available. He had been known to send a would-be player back to the clubhouse for their receipt and subsequently admonish them for missing their tee time by two minutes.

Hobo did not deign to acknowledge us. Aja smiled and waved but remained mute. Hobo proceeded to place his pink ball atop a pink tee and address the ball with a pink-shafted driver. Ardy asked, "You know the color coordinated freak and that hot little piece of ass?" I nodded in the affirmative. Despite his Lilliputian size, Hobo crushed his drive some 300 yards out, close to the edge of the first green. He shot me a wry smile, but remained silent. Ardy and I both sliced our tee shots horribly, being certain to avoid the public housing parking lot and the physical danger a hook put in play off the first tee. A straight tee shot was not a reliable option. We both landed close to the ninth tee box.

Hobo finally commented, "One must control all the variables of the equation to achieve a successful outcome."

"Thanks, Captain Obvious."

Aja approached the red tees and bent at the waist to place her ball, exposing the lion's share of her ass. She was wearing the skimpiest of thongs, also pink. Not that I noticed. Ardy fell out of the cart on to the concrete cart path as he leaned over in order to obtain a better view. Aja wound the club around her lithe body, unleashing a lightning fast swing, propelling the golf ball over 250 yards. Ardy remained prone on the path where, from his low vantage point, he could admire the finer points of her game. Aja stepped over Ardy as she returned to the cart. Ardy smiled. "I love this frigging game." Aja birdied the hole. Hobo only managed a par. His short game proved less skillful than his ability off the tee. Ardy and I, after liberal lie improvements, salvaged bogies.

The second hole is a par five. The school bus parking lot flanks the left side of the fairway. The right side is guarded by a large Tilapia-filled retention pond and a ubiquitous flock of angry, self-entitled geese. The pond curves and intersects with the fairway about 260 yards from the white tees. With the prevailing onshore breeze, the water is in play, even for us hackers.

Hobo selected his pink-shafted five wood and ripped a perfect drive, just short of the water crossing. Ardy managed to control his lust and his slice and placed his drive just short of Hobo's, albeit with his driver. I uncharacteristically yanked the ball left into the parking lot and was rewarded with the sound of breaking glass. Hobo shrugged, "You played this course before." More a statement than a question. I re-teed and sliced one that managed to stay dry and in play but was encircled and guarded by the anti-social flock.

We drove up to the red tees. Much to Ardy's disappointment, Aja knelt daintily to place her ball, denying Ardy a second peek at her shapely ass. Ardy did not hide his disappointment. "Damn it all to hell. I hate this game." Aja's drive found its way between Ardy's and Hobo's. Ardy held the angry geese at bay, wielding his driver two-handed like a long sword, allowing me to access my shit-covered ball. I dropped a second ball, abandoning the defiled Noodle, and quickly struck it, managing to successfully clear the pond and land dead center of the fairway, just short of the elevated green. We drove up to join Hobo and Aja by their balls. Ardy was up next and he too managed a decent second shot, landing just past my ball.

Aja acknowledged his shot, "nice ball." Ardy laughed. It was scorching hot out and Aja's white shirt was soaked through, leaving little to the imagination. Although petite, her small breasts were clearly outlined and visible through her now translucent top.

Before she addressed her ball, she pulled her shirt up to wipe her forehead with the tail of the shirt exposing her impressive abs.

Ardy couldn't resist leering. He asked foolishly, "Can I just touch 'em?"

I am not sure if he meant her tits or abs, but Aja was not amused by either prospect. Hobo advised Ardy quietly but firmly in a tone only Hobo could master that seemed to be universally convincing; "Run." Seeing the look on Aja's face, Ardy wisely took Hobo's advice and headed back toward the tee box on foot. For a big man recently released from the hospital with multiple broken bones, he was remarkably fleet of foot. Aja took her time letting Ardy get about fifty yards down range before taking aim and flying her Titleist square into Ardy's retreating ass. The force, or perhaps the shock, of the ball knocked Ardy off his feet. He slid head first into the flock of geese and the ample shit piles they produced. The geese, perpetually annoyed, attacked the bald-headed intruder without mercy, pecking at his ears, fingers, eyes, and genitals. I power slid the cart into the geese with the intent of rescuing Ardy from his fowl attackers but instead sorely misjudged the turn, running over both of Ardy's legs.

"I fucking hate this game," Ardy yelled, as he attempted to gain his footing amongst the slick, shit-covered grass. Ardy finally managed to climb into the seat, covered in his own blood and a malodorous dark green sheen of geese shit. We outran the geese that seemed to have overlooked their God-given power of flight, choosing to waddle after us with remarkable speed. Aja was smiling broadly as we returned. Hobo seemed genuinely concerned. He bent at the waist to adjust his golf ball, pulling his speedos deep into the crack of his hairless ass. Although freckled, his ass was shapely and, under the right lighting conditions, easily mistaken for a young girl's.

"You can touch my ass, big boy," Hobo offered. Aja slapped his ass. Ardy in turn, foolishly interpreting her action as license, reached to slap Aja's. I gently nudged Ardy as Aja simultaneously side-stepped his grope, landing Ardy in the scum-covered pond. Hobo hit his ball, landing it dead center of the green. He tossed a bottle of hand soap from his golf bag into the pond behind Ardy as he drove off toward the green. Ardy took advantage of the soap and the water to wash the shit slime off his body but with only marginal results, as the shit slime was merely supplanted with pond scum.

I pointed toward the adjacent sewage treatment facility "not to rain on your parade, but…" Ardy shrugged and continued his ad-hoc bath. Hobo and Aja had parked their cart on the far bank and were pointing into the water and giggling. I assumed the source of the amusement to be Ardy. It was not Ardy…exactly. A four-foot survivor from the age of dinosaurs was stealthily approaching Ardy from his blind side and the dangerous scenario had activated their tickle boxes. Everyone has a different idea of comedy, but unless you just hated the poor guy, I'm not sure seeing him eaten by a gator should provide amusement. I held out my three wood to Ardy, "you really need to get out now." Fortunately my tone conveyed the urgency that was intended and Ardy grabbed the club. I pulled him safely to shore. I shook my head at Hobo.

"What's wrong?" Ardy asked.

I chose to ignore the alligator. "Another foursome is waiting on the tee box." Ardy shrugged and we continued our play. Hobo had a five foot putt left for par. His short game really sucked. Aja chipped in from off the green for eagle and was holding the flag. I had sank an unlikely twenty foot putt for par when my ball struck a rock and careened thirty degrees to the left and into the hole. I chose to disregard my ill-flighted ball hooked into the school bus windshield. (Guidelines…not rules.) Ardy was in-pocket, wisely choosing to take the remainder of the hole off to finish cleaning up back by the cart. I asked Hobo, "So, what's up?"

"If I miss this putt we will be all tied up," he answered.

"Am I dreaming?" I asked him. I seemed to only see Hobo in my dreams. My entire life, I had struggled distinguishing reality from dreams, but it has only been the last six years or so that Hobo had been a part of them. Whenever he is present, strange and unpleasant things seem to happen. I took his presence, real or imagined, as a bad omen, even though I kind of perversely enjoyed his company. I pointed at Aja just as he putted. "Is she even real?" I remembered I only had "met" Aja in my dreams at Cirque de Soleil and then later that night again at the impossibly cavernous Windstream she shared with Hobo. Hobo's putt slid under the hole and rolled past an equal distance from his original putt. Aja smiled and waved.

"Your problem, Ezekiel..." Hobo casually struck his putt, holing it for his bogie, "...is you continue to struggle grasping the immense elasticity of reality. That pretty little angel..." he pointed his putter at Aja "... is as real as anything. Your question should be, does she share the same reality as this you."

***

A flock of migratory birds flew over our heads in the cloudless blue summer sky, casting a V-shaped shadow on the white sand. An old man foolishly fed a flock of seagulls stale bread from his hand and was rewarded by a massive wave of aerial shit. Damn flying rats. A young mother played with her girls in the sand wearing a bikini better suited for one of her girls, exposing a large section of well-tanned but cellulite-filled butt cheek. "I said, beer me, bitch. You day-dreaming, old man? "Ardy asked. I fished a cold beer from the cooler at my side and wordlessly handed it to Ardy, who was sitting in a beach chair to my right with his injured leg in an air cast supported on a red wagon. "You been staring off into nothing for the past half-hour."

HOUSTON, Texas; August 2016: The long standing war between the Gulf Cartel and Los Zetas appears to have come to an end. A document obtained from Mexican federal law enforcement claimed that the Zetas and the Gulf Cartel had ended their quarrel and had joined forces under the Los Zetas banner. Los Zetas origin was as the security detail of a former Cartel boss and over time grew to become an independent criminal organization known for beheadings, mutilations and gory execution videos. The leaked document warns of an internal cleanup within the two organizations in order to bring about peace. "The Gulf Cartel and Zetas are present. We will not make any more mistakes and we will depurate from our ranks those that want to work with lies and abuses," the document states.

The series of conflicts, which has pitted the Mexican military, cartels, vigilantes, and police forces against one another, has had a devastating impact upon Mexico and the cartels' economic health. Frio Lobo, a mysterious American tied to the Los Zetas organization, has emerged as the leader of the Zetas.

A high-ranking, unidentified source within the Mexican government credits an individual within the Los Zetas identified only by his gang name Frio Lobo, with bringing the cartels and the Mexican government together. "Mexico, both the government and the Cartels, depend on trade with the United States for their economic wellbeing. It only makes sense that we act in a cooperative manner to seek out new ways to exploit that relationship."

Alongside Global News

CHAPTER ELEVEN

"How was your day, Love?" Rose asked as she aggressively navigated Turner Boulevard with one hand on the wheel, the other on her phone, and neither of her lovely brown eyes on the busy, six lane divided highway. She was exceeding the posted speed limit by 15 MPH and, as was her nature, holding the two second rule in contempt. We were in route to a fundraising event at The Jacksonville Baseball Grounds for Steve Denver. BJ, our neighbor's oldest kid, was in the back seat, oblivious to Rose's death-defying driving, playing video games of some sort on a portable device while listening to explicative-laced lyrics on his overpriced, celebrity endorsed, headphones.

Steve was the former Sheriff of some small town in Colorado. He was a very dark-skinned, large, black man with a full oversized head of short cropped hair, graying at the temples. Prior to his Colorado Sheriff gig, Steve served as an undercover agent with the FBI, leaving for reasons he never disclosed. A cursory assessment of Steve led one to deduce he was a tad slow and unimaginative. I believed this to be a practiced subterfuge, as he was neither. Steve was one of the most driven, intelligent, principled men I had ever met. He moved to Florida a decade or so earlier on the urgent insistence of his wife to secure employment without the requisite bullet resistant wardrobe. Initially he became an insurance investigator but quickly grew bored, frustrated, or some combination of the two and, over the protest of his lovely, long-suffering wife, joined the Jax Sheriff's Department. With his impressive resume, Steve started with the force as a Lieutenant in the Homicide Department. Given its demographics, it is no small wonder Jax is the murder capital of Florida. It sounds much worse than it really is. Most of Florida is a bunch of old farts. The standing joke is your parents live in Sarasota and their parents live in Naples. As one might presume, not many 90-year-olds off each other over drug deals gone bad. (A few short lived fist fights have broken out in the Villages over the occasional Viagra and available men shortages but rarely did the disturbances last very long or lead to gunplay.) And the earthly slice of hell, commonly known as Orlando, is chock full of rental minivans laden with young families that typically steer clear of committing homicidal acts, as well. Jax has the youngest average age population in Florida; it is also relatively poor, poorly-educated, and black. We do have drug deals gone bad. Consequently, business was good for Steve.

Steve was neither an impatient man nor one that rose easily to anger. Yet, the politics within the Sheriff's office tested his patience beyond its considerable limits. It was not so much that the office was corrupt. It was just layered in bureaucracy, inefficiency, and preferred to cover its own ass and promote feel good programs above solving and preventing crimes. You know, that shit we taxpayers pay them to do. He resigned his position, taking up the role as head of security for the Suns, the local AA baseball franchise. Steve had moonlighted with the Suns previously when he first moved to Jax. The pay was marginal but, as a side benefit, it included all the hotdogs, peanuts, and cotton candy he could eat. Steve could eat. And breaking up fights over foul balls, spilt draft beer, and jealous girlfriends rarely led to as much as a hospital visit. Now with the blessings of his wife (she, too, was appalled by the department's shenanigans), he began a campaign to toss the current sheriff and his unwieldy administration out.

Rose interned for the Suns during her season in hell...a.k.a attending law school. She had dreams that were quickly dashed on the harsh rocks of reality of being a sports agent. Apparently her beloved Yankees were "all set" with their representation needs. It was there she met Steve and introduced him to me for the second first time. Much of my long night's dream had blurred and dulled with time, not that it was ever crystal clear. Hobo had now reentered my life just as I had convinced myself he was but a curious fabrication of a long alcohol- and Ambien-fueled dream. Steve, in that long night's dream, was working as an insurance investigator and was my chief antagonist. As I recollect, it was due to his investigation of a staged home invasion gone bad and subsequent murder that had forced me into exile to avoid prosecution. I had no part in either. Okay, maybe a little part in the home invasion, but I was pretty certain I was kind-of-sort-of innocent, although, as I recall, there was some serious debate among dream Rose and myself as to the totality of my innocence, even on that account. Steve stuck out his oversize paw and smiled broadly. I instinctively withdrew my hand but, at the time, had no clear understanding of why he startled me. Rose, embarrassed by my obvious revulsion, tried to cover. "He can arrest you for being stupid."

"Thanks." I recovered quickly and extended my hand. I had grown accustomed to dealing with the subtleties and vagrancies of reality and quickly recognized this was one of them. Steve walked us over to meet the team owner's son and general manager, Pedro. Pedro was a very large, very white man in his late sixties. I had no idea how he got the nickname of Pedro. It sure as hell was not due to his physical appearance, ethnicity, or grasp of the Spanish language. The application of Occam's Razor suggesting the most likely answer is the correct one would intimate Pedro's given name is likely Peter and the nickname was given to differentiate him from another close family member with the same name. Nailed it!

It was dollar beer night, Thirsty Thursday, one of the more successful promotions the Suns (and just about every other minor league baseball team) employed to get butts in the seats. My personal favorite was the burrito roll, perhaps due to Rose and Giuseppe's gold-medal performance at a previous Thirsty Thursday, but I digress. The stadium was packed with half-dressed, barely-legal-drinking-age kids swilling cheap, lukewarm, draft-beer while parading up and down the stadium concourses to see and be seen. Thirsty Thursday was the "it" place for the broke-ass, drunk-ass, young ass, crowd. On this note I was batting a very respectful .333.

131

Pedro greeted us warmly, in his gruff, unintelligible voice, but was quickly interrupted by one of his staff. Sarah walked up. Guessing she was in her late twenties, she was dressed in a yellow Sun's polo, too tight, too short, ass cheek revealing, khaki shorts, and brightly colored sneakers. Her auburn hair was pulled back off her attractive, sweat-covered face. It gets brutally hot in Florida. Sarah leaned over to Pedro to privately communicate some issue or another, likely involving the overconsumption of alcohol; the dark side of cheap booze fueling raging hormones. He excused himself and spoke quietly to Sarah briefly before saying, rather loudly and for no apparent reason, "Sarah, you're getting fat. You need to start running and get in shape."

"Yo, fat ass I do run," Sarah shot back, matching his volume, with a look of confusion and anger on her face. Sarah wasn't fat and, relative to Pedro's impressive girth, Sarah was downright anorexic.

"Then run more," he retorted. Sarah sighed in disgust, turned and walked away, clearly pissed. I had never met Sarah, but something told me she would exact a pound of revenge for each ounce of Pedro's offense. Pedro was an old school white dude that had missed several memos from HR over the years. His dad, at 90 something, still took part in the day-to-day management of the franchise and had missed, or more likely chosen to ignore, even more HR memos. Perhaps he even wrote the HR policies. It really wasn't that long ago that the chasing of one's female help around the desk after consuming two or more martinis during office hours was considered the norm...or at least not completely aberrant behavior. The bar for a successful employee sexual harassment complaint was once set pretty damn high. Now commenting on the color of a female employee's blouse is grounds for a stern verbal warning from the HR department. There has got to be some sensible middle ground.

A canary yellow, three-wheel adult tricycle...errrr....motorcycle with an obese middle-aged rider, wearing matching full-face helmet and leather jacket garb pulled up beside Rose and smiled, motioning for her to roll the window down. Rose ignored the man, but I was curious. I opened the sunroof and popped my head out. "You hear me rolllinnnn, you hatin', patrolin' 'n' tryin' to catch me ridin' dirty, tryin' to catch me ridin' dirty" was blasting on his stereo with the bass at ear-busting levels. "What up?" I yelled. Rose tugged on my shorts and changed lanes.

"Just want your daughter's digits," I assumed the rider yelled back. In reality, I just saw his helmet move, as I couldn't make out a single word over his music and the wind noise. The rider followed Rose over into the adjacent lane. This guy had an unwarranted amount of swagger.

I sat. "I think the delusional gentleman wants your phone number, Rose," I lied, smiling broadly. Rose was not amused and displayed her displeasure with a single-digit salute to the rider. She sped up to nearly 100 MPH and aggressively switched between lanes to put distance between her and the unlikely Romeo. "It's not like I am scared of dying, but I was not planning on doing so on this day. I wore old drawers. I don't want to die in holy under britches," I said to Rose. She ignored me. Romeo was doing a remarkable job of keeping pace. He was a determined, if not well-suited, suitor for my wife. There is something to be said for persistence. And sometimes that appropriate word to be said is insanity. For Rose, this had become a pissing contest. We were in her E-350 Mercedes. It's a vehicle made for comfort and not speed. I have no idea what the hell the three-wheeler was made for...geriatric crisis, perhaps. Harley and Porsche have midlife covered. This was something else, but I am not sure exactly what. The Rock could not ride the ungainly contraption without looking like a complete and utter dork. The scene disintegrated into a made for TV movie with multiple, mostly perilous outcomes. The speedometer climbed to 115 MPH as Rose weaved in and out of traffic. The AC was on full blast, but my shirt was damp, and I was pretty sure I peed a little in my pants.

"Damn it," Rose yelled, looking in her mirror while breaking suddenly and moving to the right. I yanked my head back to locate the source of her aggravation. The warbling siren alerted me to the source of her distress even before my eyes could focus on the blue lights pulsating from the front of the yellow three-wheeler. I laughed from relief of knowing I was likely to live yet another day. Rose shot me an "eat shit and die look" suggesting she might think otherwise regarding that likelihood.

"What?" I asked. "You have to admit, that is the best undercover disguise ever." Rose pulled to the side of the road. The unmarked police three-wheeler followed. BJ in the backseat continued to play his video game, oblivious to the real world around him. Rose was a proud member of the legal profession. Those honorable members of our great society charged with applying our nation's laws in an equitable manner and ensuring the fair implementation of justice. Yeah, right. Let's just say that's what the parasitical assholes purport to do. Mind you, Rose was a Corporate Lawyer, accustomed to negotiating and reviewing tedious contracts and not defending perps in court stupid enough to get caught. Nevertheless, she had that argumentative nature and holier-than-thou attitude toward police officers about the law that annoyed the living shit out of cops. It is generally my practice to shun lawyer types as typically they are slimy, unethical, assholes that deal in half-truths for profit and are to be avoided…at least, the ones that make any real money. A bit of a paradox, I know, but Rose was hot and thus awarded an exemption for her chosen profession.

"This is entrapment," she noted.

I looked at Rose and shook my head; "Good luck with that. I think you may have broken a couple dozen traffic laws, some likely felonies. We are going to be a tad late."

Rose unbuttoned the top button of her sweater and checked her makeup in the mirror. "Don't underestimate my considerable powers of persuasion."

"Your tits?" I asked and was rewarded with a punch in the arm. "Ouch." Her tits were an excellent accessory for sure, but I wasn't so certain the cop would be inclined to give her the hot exemption for both reckless driving and being a dick-headed lawyer. One or the other maybe, but both was going to be a stretch.

The officer awkwardly dismounted the three-wheeler. On closer inspection, it was evident the officer frequented the occasional donut shop in the course of each day. An even closer inspection revealed he was a she with an unfortunate body shape; an ass the size of a planet with nonexistent tits and an overcompensating belly. A masculine-looking and mannered she with a short haircut, but still a she, nonetheless. I started to suggest the tatas would not be of benefit, but as the officer strutted closer, I correctly assessed the tatas might well still be in play. "License and registration, Ma'am," the officer ordered in a remarkable baritone with that annoying official police voice.

I think some cops should smoke more dope. Just chill a bit. Better yet, it scares me silly personally knowing a handful of the high-strung mental midgets with a serious case of short-asshole disease that are currently on the force. Any person that wants to risk their life for the miserable pay and working conditions just to tote a gun probably should not be allowed to do so. When I get to be Dictator, I am instituting a cop draft forcing those that don't want to be cops to be cops. Then I am going to pay the shit out of the good ones to get them to stay after their constriction period expires. Conscience's objectors can be school crossing guards. Just who do you want to take shit from…soccer moms in minivans with their over-indulged children or thugs in Escalades with leased spinners? I choose thugs. In Florida at least, you can shoot their ass with some measure of impunity. Clearly I watched too much television. Cops scares the living crap out of me…you know the show, "what you gonna do when they come for you. Bad boys, bad boys." These guys take curious joy when they bust some poor saggy-britches, toothless sap for less than a full joint of marijuana. "We took this bad boy off the mean streets, making our community a safer place." Meanwhile, three ax murderers, two rapists, a carjacker, and a gang of bank robbers stained head to toe with blue ink and disguised as the Three Stooges pass by unchallenged. Priorities, Dudes.

True fricking story…Rose and I witnessed no less than four Jax Beach police cruisers surround and tase an obese, double-amputee in a wheelchair for reasons I can't explain, while two teenagers snatched an old woman's purse and shoved her to the ground just a few feet away in the McDonald's parking lot. I'm just saying...readjust your priorities and/or smoke some more of that confiscated dope. To be clear, most cops are great guys/gals that risk personal safety for shit pay. But it doesn't take many bad apples in that barrel to make a disaster of Old Testament biblical proportions.

Rose's smile disappeared and near instantly reappeared as she completed the mental math on the situation. "Hello, Officer Johnson." Rose said and smiled, handing over the requested documents. "Was I driving a tad too fast?" She was trying the honey approach first.

Officer Johnson pulled down her dark-mirrored shades, stared at Rose, glancing down and lingering for a moment silently at the offered eye candy before responding, "A tad, Ma'am? I'm a little unclear as to the precise Webster definition of tad but relatively certain 114 MPH in a 65 MPH zone falls outside of the published definition." I laughed, only to receive yet another "eat shit and die" look from Rose. She wisely refrained from committing her second act of assault on my person for the day due solely to the close proximity of the law enforcement officer. Officer Johnson smiled before continuing, "Step out of the car, Ma'am."

Rose ignored the polite order and instead handed the officer her business card identifying her as a lawyer. "I am pretty sure this is entrapment. I know my rights, Officer." Now there is a sentence every police officer has heard uttered before. I was waiting for Rose to add she "paid taxes." The officer took an aggressive stance, placing her right hand on her Glock and backed slightly away from the car in the blind spot just behind the car door.

"Step out of the car, Ma'am," she said, a little more fiercely this time, in a voice one octave higher. I am thinking it is pretty much time to comply and step out of the car. Rose being more a non-linear thinker, and a dick-headed lawyer to boot, disagreed. Rose reached for her cell phone. Officer Johnson pulled her service pistol. BJ, lost in his own world, never looked up. "Ma'am, put down your phone and step out of the car." I moved to step out of the car to defuse the situation. Officer Johnson subsequently swung the pistol in my direction, aiming center mass. "Stay in the car, Sir, and place your hands on the dash." Maybe it was my day to die after all. The Officer radioed for back-up while I, in the meantime, added a tad of additional pee to my pants.

Rose finished dialing and put the phone on speaker before finally stepping out of the car. Officer Johnson holstered the pistol and reached for her handcuffs. Steve answered the phone, "Lt. Denver. What the hell is up, Rose? You're late." Fortunately, Steve was still very popular on the force among the rank and file officers, at least. He was elevated to legendary hero status the day he turned in his two word resignation letter to the very unpopular Sheriff; "Fuck off." The desk jockeys and senior administration assholes despised him, but everyone else worshiped the man.

Officer Johnson spoke up, "Hi, Steve. Rose, Mrs. Foster, here was driving a 'tad' too fast and I pulled her over."

Steve laughed. "Well, can you expedite the process? I need her and Zeke over at my fundraiser at the ball park right away."

"Yes, Sir," she replied, hanging up Rose's cell.

"A tad," Rose commented, tilting her head and smirking. She really needed to work on shutting the hell up. When one achieves the desired result, it is best to sit down and shut up. Nothing good can come with sustained lip-flapping. Officer Johnson began to respond, thought better of it, and wordlessly returned to her three-wheeler and rode away.

"Told you," Rose irrationally bragged as she got back in the car. I began to respond, thought better of it, and wordlessly watched as Rose recklessly merged with traffic. Given the state of my soiled pants I strongly suggested to Rose we return home for a change of clothes and a quick shower. Rose, not surprisingly, declined my urgent request, as this would make us late.   "All my fault?" I asked and was, now sans a uniformed officer of the law as a witness, assaulted for the second time in one day.

I dropped Rose and BJ off at the ballpark and returned home for a quick change of clothes. An hour late, I returned to the park and joined Rose at Lt. Denver's fundraiser. BJ had abandoned his alternate world for the real one and was deep in conversation with a lovely uniformed black police officer. I raised my eyebrow toward BJ. She was a bit old for him and clearly interested in BJ for reasons less than suitable, given his tender years. Based on his noticeably erect posture, he did not agree with my assessment.

Rose motioned me over to where she was standing with Steve and a couple of his supporters under a muted TV playing Fox News. Quick introductions all around. I was distracted, as there was beer and it was calling my name. "Nice to meet you...blah, blah, blah..."   I needed a frosty beer and did not process any of the offered information. It's not that I forget names so much as I never hear them to begin with. I would make a for-shit salesperson. My brain is cluttered enough with multiple realities to waste precious brain cells on remembering the name of someone unremarkable and/or would likely never see again. Not being rude...just efficiently using finite, waning, precious, memory space. Heidi Klum...see, I can remember remarkable names.

BJ was still engaged with the police officer. She was a toucher and kept placing her hand on his arm, shoulder, bicep, and even face. BJ was digging the attention and I feared if I did not intervene shortly, he might be really digging it, but with less clothing. I grabbed a beer and interrupted the conversation. "Hi, I am BJ's Uncle..." not really, "...Zeke." I extended my hand. She removed her hand off BJ's shoulder and shook it but never took her eye of BJ.

"He is really cute," she replied.

"And he is really 15," I replied.

"I'm 17 and standing right here," BJ answered. "Zeke," I noticed he left off the fictional, yet customary, Uncle title, "this is L' Vern."

"Lavern?" I asked.

"No. L' Vern," she replied. "There's no 'A.'" Rose motioned for me to come back over to where she was standing. I pointed two fingers into my eyes then toward L' Vern in the universal "I'm watching you" pose. Not on my watch, L minus the A Vern. Steve was saying something to me but I was distracted by the muted TV set. The news crawl line reported the State of Texas Legislature had passed a bill out of committee that if passed by both houses and signed by the Governor, would have Texas secede from the Union.

"Secede," I mumbled. It was another powerful déjà vu moment and I uttered without realizing, "Son of a bitch."

"Excuse me." Steve said.

Washington, D.C.; September 2016: The Jefferson Alert reported today that Louisiana's Governor has called for a hostile takeover of the United States. "I can sense right now a rebellion brewing amongst these United States." This comes on the heels of both houses of the Texas Legislature passing a bill to secede from the Union. Texas Governor, Rick Bush, has vowed to veto the bill, but in a statement released earlier today, strongly cautioned the White House "to put an immediate end to the flagrant, wanton disregard to the U.S. Constitution." Sources close to Bush cite increasing statewide momentum and building pressure for the Governor to support secession. A well-financed, statewide media campaign by a group calling itself Pedras Negras, sharply critical of the President's record use of Executive Order, is encouraging Texans to recall Governor Bush should he not sign the secession bill. Bush blasted the group he claims is funded largely from sources outside the United States. A White House spokesperson issued a single-word statement, "Nuts."

Alongside Global News

CHAPTER TWELVE

Rose was employed full-time, well, really more like double-time, as a corporate attorney for an evil international chemical company. I didn't think they were evil, the trolls paid for my beer after all, but the tree huggers did. The irony of it all, the huggers purchased the malevolent company's baby diapers, along with about half the other products they consumed on a daily basis from this very company they so publicly loathed. Its one thing to hold evil corporate America in public disdain, but considerably more inconvenient to change one's consumption patterns. There is chemical shit in just about everything. Read a label or two. Hey, but that's the America we live in today. Rosie O'Donnell, a staunch anti-gun advocate, defended her personal bodyguard carrying a weapon. "That's different. It's me. I am famous." Okay, not an exact quote there, but pretty damn close. Gore, Nobel Prize winner, self-proclaimed Internet inventor, and author of the "we are destroying the planet" book and movie, An Inconvenient Truth, reportedly has a residential power bill of over $2,000 a month and jets around in a private plane giving eloquent, impassioned speeches on how mankind is destroying the planet due to its use of carbon fuels. Al Sharpton, race-baiter, champion of wealth redistribution and higher taxes on the wealthy, owed nearly $5 million in back state and federal taxes in 2014. We are most certainly not of the "what is good for the goose…" generation anymore.

Where did we go so horribly wrong? Somewhere along our nascent journey as a nation, we have collectively abandoned all semblance of logic and the common sense God gave us and the very principals that made this country strong. For instance, on one hand we swear that mankind's very existence is killing the planet. Yet the same people that think you are a moronic imbecile if you disagree with this premise, promulgate laws, programs, and rules to encourage population growth. And just who is the fucking imbecile? Oh, I get it. People vote, and people that depend on the government for well, just about everything, are pretty damn sure to vote for the party that will promise them even more. It's damn easy to assume the moral high ground on the shoulders of others. Ain't that right, "Reverend"?

Personal responsibility is suddenly out of vogue, as well. You stupid, not your fault; poor, not your fault; nuts, not your fault; addicted to drugs, not your fault; fat, not your fault; lazy, not your fault; uncoordinated, not your fault. The proverbial "Man" is at fault. Just who is the evil bastard that makes us such poor, fat, lazy, stupid, crazy, spastic, drug-addled losers? I wanna kick his ass, if only I could just find him. Forget food and healthcare, cable TV, high-speed internet, and cell phones are a God-given entitlement in this peculiar dimension we call our current reality. We have tragically morphed from the great land of opportunity to an abhorrent, unsustainable land of entitlement and political correctness. We give trophies to kids for participation should we hurt their precious self-esteem for failing miserably at any given task. We change the name of sports teams, schools, roads, buildings…less we offer even minor offense to anyone. Words, we are told, are as powerful and dangerous as hand grenades and, as such, must be regulated to ensure proper civil usage. And having witnessed firsthand the irreparable destructive power of a hand grenade on a young, human body, I find this comparison grossly inaccurate and downright offensive. My generation was taught a simple rhyme, "Sticks and stones can break my bones but words will never hurt me." Mom assured me, no matter what she did, others would use words in an attempt to offend me. As such, she gave me a valuable tool for my defense. "Don't give anyone the power to use words that describe you, to hurt you, even when those words were intended to be injurious." The universal truth Mom understood is that she could never control the behavior and comments of others. To believe you can insulate your child from the realities of the world, while noble, is simply delusional. Mom could only equip me to not let those words hurt, or at least hurt a little bit less. "Embrace who you are," she taught me, "and if you want to change the opinions of others about yourself, change your actions." Maybe Bill said it best, "A rose is a rose..." No matter what set of ordered letters we assemble to describe a rose, it is still a damn rose. Marginally less eloquently than Bill; a pile of shit is a pile of shit and no matter what set of letters we use to name it, eventually that set of letters will come to mean a sticky brown pile of smelly excrement. I'm just saying. Quite the rant. Forgive me as I step down from my soapbox.

Back to the beginning and perhaps a glimpse of insight regarding my rant. Rose worked full-time and, consequently, I am assigned some of the typical housewife duties. Not complaining. Just stating facts. Today was grocery day. I shopped at the Publix off Beach Boulevard. It's located adjacent to the section eight housing at the beach. A 300-pound black woman, with long multi-colored nails, an impressive weave, ten fingers of shiny jewelry, and wearing a colorful Mumu entered the store just in front of me. She paused, blocking the entrance, to talk on her cell phone. "Honey, you know this Obama phone don't give me no internet access," she emphatically stated into her cell.

"Excuse me," I said, trying to maneuver around her considerable girth.

"What wrong with you, Cracker?" she aggressively motioned toward the other (exit) door. "Cracker," meant as a disparaging term holds no injury to me. I am an old, white, Southern man. I am good with that. Yet, even for a moment had I deigned to use a similarly disparaging racial word toward her, I would likely have been jailed. Her kids joined her in the store vestibule area. One, about 18, shirtless and shoeless, was pushing another, about two years of age, in a plastic stroller. He placed the toddler in the basket of an electric cart reserved for the handicap and the stroller he laid across his lap. Now both doors were blocked. Where was Serge when I needed him?

Rose left me a grocery list, penned on a sticky note, with the items helpfully ordered by aisle. She draws a few adorable emoticons placed randomly in the margin. Rose's exterior is tough as nails and she claims not to be a girly-girl. Deep down, though, there is that little girl in her that sneaks out on occasion from beneath her carefully donned armor. I cherished those glimpses of vulnerability. She hated them. The grocery list is most helpful only if I follow a specific pattern navigating the modern-day equivalent of both the hunting and gathering task within the walls of the sterile, air-conditioned, florescent-lit aisles of Publix. My, times have changed. Granted, I could probably manage to locate the essentials, Jalapeño Cheetos and Bud Lite beer, if forced to shop in a random pattern, but that would be just chaos. I needed calm order in my life. It's confusing enough to sort the wheat from the chaff in my disturbed, cluttered brain box on a calm and windless day. Consequently, I found myself in lock step with the obese, Mumu-wearing woman and her shirtless, motorized entourage. The teenager seemed to take great joy in knocking assorted items off the shelves. The toddler squealed with delight, which only encouraged the teenager's bedlam. Obese Mumu seemed not to notice the unruly behavior or my growing irritation as she snacked on doughnuts from the bakery aisle on her leisurely, destructive stroll through the store.

Fortunately, I lost the annoying trio in the vegetable aisle and was able to navigate a few aisles without their interference. I did, however, have to navigate the resultant carnage from the teenager's purposeful reckless driving along with several empty containers of powdered donuts, BBQ chips, and juice boxes. Seemed as if they required a snack in order to maintain appropriate energy levels. Eventually we reunited at the checkout area where there was but a single cashier on duty in the regular checkout lane. Sometimes I overestimated my importance in the universe and think God took a singular pleasure in annoying the hell out of me.

Naturally, Mumu and entourage miraculously managed to be in front of me. Mumu's cart was overflowing with brand name

Pop-Tarts, beer, pops, chips, cheeses, steaks, and assorted bakery items. She added a National Enquirer, a handful of gum packs, and an armful of candy bars at the checkout lane. Caloric consumption, at the massive levels necessitated to maintain her impressive body mass and shape, must be a horrific, time, and money-consuming burden. Her total was $437. Unfortunately, her Obama food stamp debit card was limited to a paltry $250 of other people's hard-earned money. She cursed Paul Ryan for being a cheap-ass Cracker. "How the hell a family of four 'pose to eat off of $250 a month?" I was suitably impressed she knew the name of the Speaker of the House. An ardent viewer of MSNBC and Reverend Al, no doubt.

I started to offer my version of helpful budget advice; chicken instead of steak, ditch the chips, beer, and donuts, obtain employment for herself and her teenager…but it quickly dawned on me this was a question of the rhetorical variety not even directed to this old Cracker and, if answered truthfully, I was likely to get said Cracker cut. I didn't think I could take her. Hell, I am old. The toddler could give me a serious run for my money.

The bagger, a kid of no more than 17, was a miniature, pre-steroid version of Derek Jeter, with a lightly-freckled face. He moved Mumu's buggy to the side and asked for her first name. Mumu replied, "La' Sunjalal." I, for the record, am not making this shit up. That was her name. I think her parents must have employed the Scrabble tile technique in deciding what to name their little princess. You know, toss a handful of Scrabble tiles into the air and assemble the lettered tiles that land face up into a facsimile of a name. I'm not judging…okay, maybe a little. And, after all, with my unusual Old Testament moniker, I know a thing or two about growing up with a peculiar name. Parents, don't name your kids bizarre names. Imagine just how helpful the moniker "La' Sunjalal" is on a resume. I know "Betty" is a boring label, but picture the old, white guy making a hiring decision choosing between two equally qualified candidates. You think he chooses "La' Sunjalal" or "Betty?" La' Sunjalal makes a damn fine stripper name but is that really your long term aspiration for your newborn princess? I know, the old white guy should not make a judgment based on the peculiarity of the applicant's given name. But he will. Control what is within your control. Don't handicap your offspring for the sake of originality and style points. Sure you have the right to name your kid anything you choose. Not arguing that point. But just for a minute, weigh the risk versus reward.

Bored, the shirtless teenager took to doing high-speed laps around the store with the infant squealing loudly in the front basket. The bagger, upon hearing her name, smiled broadly against his will and his coffee-colored face turned a crimson red. "Can you spell that for me please, Ma'am?" he asked. La' Sunjalal was clearly not amused by his request, although I strongly expect she had been asked to spell her name on more than a few occasions throughout her highly productive life.

She began in an agitated voice, "L-A-'postrophe…" An unfortunate, audible giggle escaped from the bagger's mouth as he silently mouthed "of course" after La' Sunjalal inserted the apostrophe in the spelling of her name. Dear sweet, innocent, ignorant boy, I thought. He sorely misjudged La' Sunjalal and her propensity for violence on even the slightest of provocation. She exploded and began yelling in his face, mixing a highly creative string of obscenities and threats, sprinkled amongst spittle blended with donut and potato chip leavings. The bagger weighed in at less than a third of La' Sunjalal's suitably impressive mass and was unaccustomed to confrontation, particularly with individuals in the alleged possession of the correct pre-assigned lady parts. He looked to be about to piss his pants and cry.

Being no one else seemed to be inclined to step in and save the poor boy, I foolishly decided to intervene. I would undoubtedly get my ass kicked, but I had lived a good life. The poor kid was just working after school to likely earn a few dollars to help him buy a new skateboard. He didn't deserve this shit and this was not my first rodeo dealing with crazy.

"Ma'am," I said, almost whispering, squeezing in between La' Sunjalal and the bagger. I have found a soft voice, unlike logic, a viable weapon in my tool box in the defense of crazy. She stopped yelling and backed off a few inches, but eyed me with unguarded revulsion in her eyes. I offered my very best sweet smile and continued, speaking just above a whisper, "The boy is just trying to get the spelling of your name correct. That's all, Ma'am."

"Shut up, Cracker. Ain't nobody be talking to your wrinkly ole ass." She tried to maneuver around me to get at the bag boy but discovered the boy had wisely used my diversion to retreat from the scene.

I used my go-to line in dealing with a crazy, unwinnable argument, "I hear you. Let me see what I can do."

"You disrespecting me, Cracker? Don't think I won't cut an old white man." The Manager, alerted by the commotion, finally left the safety of his office and joined the escalating fray. He quickly diffused the situation by offering La' Sunjalal's entire $437 of groceries for free. Likely not his first rodeo either. She started to continue to press the argument but thought better of it, changed direction, and yelled at her teenage son to ditch the toddler and go fill up the handicap cart's basket with steak. I just shook my head in silent, abject wonder. Our reality is unbalanced and has reached a critical tipping point. We reward those that don't work and are critical and judgmental of those that do. "Greedy bastards don't share enough." Even bad behavior is either ignored or rewarded. This, no matter how popular with the masses, is not a sustainable model. And now I found myself with time to kill in the checkout lane, waiting for La' Sunjalal's son to return with the additional free groceries he procured on his white-flag, high-speed lap. I noticed Brittany had put on a few pounds again. God, she was a train wreck. She had gone from cute little girl, to smoking hot mess to fluffy mess in such a short period. I get time is a cruel bitch, but good Lord, her clock was running at an exceptionally high rate of speed. Clooney was finally getting hitched. Tom

Cruise still had his boyish good looks, along with a heaping dose of crazy. And Kanye, he remained stateside, in the company of his Armenian pseudo-celebrity, big-assed bride, in the face of his promise to leave the racist U.S. behind. It was good that some things remained unchanged.

Babylon, Persia; September 2016: Brothers of Islam, The New Black Panthers Party (NBPP), and the Prime Minister of Mexico held a highly unusual, joint news conference today announcing the signing of a Mutual Defense Treaty between the three "nations." A spokesperson for the Brothers of Islam, Mohammed Ghazi, promised its full resources in defense of the NBPP and Mexico against their common enemy, the Zionist and their Western Allies. A spokesperson for the State Department noted the agreement was "peculiar." The Department of Defense Secretary called the agreement "preposterous and within striking distance of a declaration of war."

Alongside Global News

CHAPTER THIRTEEN

Simply no spoken words in our American English vocabulary says, "Hello, Asshole, what the hell are you doing in my house uninvited," more emphatically than the distinctive sound of chambering a 3-inch shell in a 12-gauge, pump-action, shotgun in anger. Perhaps the Italian vocabulary has the appropriate word. The wind, and my occasional failure to properly secure the top door lock, caused our alarm to go off periodically in the middle of the night. The combination of Jack and the relentless passage of time created diminishing brain capability and an increase in the frequency of this inconvenient scenario, requiring the house to be cleared of potential boogie men, feral animals, trolls, Progressive Democrats, and rabid ferrets. I assumed this was one of those incidents. False alarm or not, I racked the pistol grip 12-gauge and nudged Rose awake. She mumbled something utterly unintelligible and rolled over, pulling the pillow over her head. I patted her ass and whispered for her to stay put which was a total unnecessary comment. She clearly planned on sitting this fire drill out. I pulled on some gym shorts lying next to the bed. Having lost a few pounds, the pants were loose-fitting. I made my way down the stairs as I heard someone or something rummaging around. The rabid ferret was the leading scenario. I loudly whispered to Rose, "Wake up," before continuing down the stairs. This was no false alarm. Rose moaned angrily at my continued interruption of her beauty rest but did not deign to stir.

At the landing, I turned the corner of the stairs and made out a brief glimpse of the shirtless teenager doing high speed laps around our bottom floor in the handicap electric grocery cart. I quickly drew a bead on him but hesitated. The toddler was in the cart's basket. I am a strong believer in protecting my castle and I assume, should an intruder break in while I am at home, the individual is intent on violence. I have no problem ending a life in this scenario without further debating the intent, race, religion, sexual orientation, political affiliation, food allergies, or gender of the intruder. I do, however, befittingly draw the line at killing innocent toddlers. Even us old Crackers have lines. I lowered the shotgun and my shorts fell to my ankles, leaving me taking the final few steps down the stairs buck-ass naked. A sight better left unseen. Even more so from the business side of the 12 gauge. I turned the corner into the kitchen and was confronted with La' Sunjalal silhouetted by the light from the open refrigerator, plundering leftovers. "Bitch! That's my fried chicken," I thought to myself. I pinched myself hard on the inside of my thigh and there was no pain. "I am dreaming," I silently mouthed, but was none the less unable to end the nightmare.

La' Sunjalal, hearing my unspoken comment, turned to confront me. Still wearing her colorful Mumu, she was holding a box cutter. "I tol' you I would cut an ole Cracker." She lunged toward me. I reached out to block her attack but found only vacant space. She vanished, leaving me staring into the open refrigerator. A Boxer with leopard spots sat on the lighted shelf. The Boxer disappeared and was replaced with a stream of numbers. Ones and zeroes, zeroes and ones, ones and zeroes…a never-ending, seemingly random series of ones and zeroes poured from within the open refrigerator, covered it's shelves, ones and zeroes, zeroes and ones, consumed the space all about me.

Rose, finally awakened by all the commotion, called out something from the top of the stairs. "Call 911," I mumbled.

A ghostly vision of me appeared within the space of the refrigerator amidst the ones and zeroes. I was standing in the checkout line at Publix reading the headlines of the Enquirer. "Texas Rancher Spots UFO." The picture accompanying the headline was of a middle-aged man in cowboy garb riding a horse. My apparition faded and the ones and zeroes reformed and surrounded the rancher's words that now appeared within the refrigerator. "I observed from a distant hilltop a whirlwind coming from the north, a great cloud with a fire folding in on itself. The cloud was bright and was the color of amber. Out of the cloud, I saw four creatures that looked like men but each one appeared to have four faces: man, eagle, ox, and lion."

Rose yelled "Stop!" I registered her voice, but not her words. I was captivated by the ones and zeroes, zeroes and ones, circling, twisting, spinning, dancing, and consuming every surface and the space in every direction. Quietly now I could hear Rose whispering my name over and over and then calmly she said, "It's okay, Zeke. You're dreaming. Put the gun down."

I remained mesmerized by the digital vision pouring from the refrigerator. Light slithered out in numbers, ones and zeroes, zeroes and ones. Nothing escaped but ones and zeroes, zeroes and ones. And with the numbers, darkness fell about me, heavy and damp. The darkness seemingly embraced, cajoled, nudged. Tears hot and wet, streaked from my eyes without effort, remorse, or apparent meaning. My breath was labored and chest leaden. My legs fidgeted uncontrollably. My toes splayed stiffly. Life seemingly ebbed like the falling tide. Death's cool, quiet darkness sweetly beckoned, its nectar promised a short, comfortable, downhill path through eternity. Destiny be damned. Peace, tranquility, ultimate freedom, and the sweet, loving embrace of the cold, damp earth beckoned. We are born. We suffer. We perish. With darkness peace comes. Hurry, suffering. Rose furtively grabbed my finger and pulled it off the shotgun's trigger. "Its okay, Zeke," she whispered, over and over. Ones and zeroes, zeroes and ones. She gently removed the barrel of the shotgun from my mouth…ones and zeroes, zeroes and ones, and pulled the shotgun from my grip.

***

Bikers, skaters, rollerbladers, cruisers, walkers, strollers, boogie-boarders, skimmers, shark-tooth hunters, sun-bathers, shell collectors, dog walkers, volleyball players, Frisbee tossers, day-drinkers, bocce ball players, vagrants, hand holders, voyeurs, surfers, waders, guitar players, swimmers, football throwers, thieves, hula hoopers, fishermen, lovers, sand castle builders, fornicators, kite boarders, parachute flyers, and garden variety perverts all share the wide beach by our house. I watched in semi-catatonic wonder from beneath the shade of rainbow-colored umbrella as the world slowly drifted by. The ocean was flat and emerald green with only a subtle hint of a gentle, offshore breeze. A second and third vacant chair stood empty under the partial shade of the umbrella. I was uncertain how long I had been on the beach, but based on the empty cans, at least for seven beers. A cool one was in my hands, damp from condensation. And, not for the first time, I am utterly confused by my surroundings. It was busy out and somewhere behind me, I heard voices in familiar, whispered tones. The conversation traveled on the westerly breeze sufficiently for me to overhear and just barely understand.

"Darkness abides in that boy. It runs deep in the murky currents of an unchartered river that he can only see." The breeze brings with it a familiar smell, both repugnant and inexplicably comforting.

A second whispered voice, equally familiar and female whispered urgently, "Cut the poetic bullshit. Why are you here? You're the one that makes him bat shit crazy?" Rose continued, "He told me about Jonas."

Hobo responded, "Yes, I know Jonas. A very good man indeed, but unfortunately a weak one. Zeke is much stronger."

"It was you he warned Zeke of!"

Jonas was a Baptist missionary in a Peruvian Village surrounding Lake Titicaca. In my youth, Jonas had spoken at my church. He was an odd little fellow, poorly dressed, and a clumsy speaker. Yet he had touched something deep inside of me and warned me, it felt, just me, even though he had spoken to the entire congregation of our small, rural church. He warned me to not seek out certain paths and to leave some doors unopened. He spoke of other worlds of both good and horrific evil. Then he spoke of apocalyptic dreams that were eerily similar to my own. A few months later, Jonas was found mysteriously dead in the bathtub of his psychiatric hospital room. Rose knew my Jonas story and she too had been similarly warned by her Grams to avoid certain enigmatic paths.

Hobo chuckled. "No, Rose. It is not me he was warned of."

"But you seem to be intractably entwined with his madness. Can't you just leave him be?"

"I cannot. I need him to chart the river that even I can't see. It is his destiny."

"Again with the flowery prose asshole. Zeke was standing buck-naked staring into the refrigerator with the barrel of a shotgun in his mouth, Hobo. That's his destiny…blow his brains out over the kitchen cabinets? You have to stop this… whatever magic shit you are doing to my husband, now!"

Startled into awareness by the urgency and desperation in Rose's voice, I turned in my chair to face them. There were only the dunes behind me and the soft, gentle sounds of the sea oats blown by the summer breeze. I turned again to face the Atlantic as BJ walked out of the surf with his boogie board. "You good, Uncle Zeke?" I nodded in the affirmative. BJ plopped down beside me. I must have still had a confused look on my face. BJ took the beer from my hand and fished a water from the cooler. "Give the beer a rest for a bit," he said in a southern drawl. BJ, unlike his adoptive parents Sam and Flo, was unmistakably Asian by race. The drawl and his Southern manners seemed ill-fitting, yet somehow exceedingly charming. BJ had grown into a handsome young man. A series of scantily clad teenage girls seemed strolled by in a never ending procession once he was seated by me. They went unnoticed by BJ as he fished his iPhone from his bag and began checking his messages. "You sure you are good, Uncle Zeke?" I nodded again and sipped on the offered cool bottled water. I was in still a bit of a haze, Rose had supplied suitable pharmaceuticals further enhanced by alcohol consumption in order to encourage my continued mellow state. "Gotta leave you by yourself for a bit 'til Sam gets back. Going to a friend's house." His phone chirped. BJ laughed as he read the message. "What the hell?" He started typing as he spoke. "My buddy rented us two movies to watch tonight." He explained to me. "Not a date, Dude," he said aloud as he thumbed the message back to his friend. I managed a chuckle through my beer and pharmaceutical haze.

Sam plopped down in the third chair before BJ left. He brought a resupply of beer with him. Perfectly tanned and toned twins, likely no more than 17, wearing swimwear dangerously close to indiscernible strolled by, displaying perfect asses and offering warm identical smiles to BJ. BJ flashed red as Sam eagerly returned their smiles. "And you are spending the night over at some dude's house tonight?" Sam rhetorically asked BJ then turned to me for validation. "Where did I go wrong with this boy?"

"I'm not gay, Sam," BJ explained. BJ was Sam's stepson and the adopted son of Sam's wife, Flo, from a previous marriage. Sam had raised him since he was about six and they had a solid relationship. Not perfect, but then again, what parental relationship with a teenager is perfect?

"I know that. You're just stupid. I'd tap that hot little ass in a heartbeat." Sam looked at me again for validation.

"I choose a life out of jail and with my penis intact," I said. BJ laughed.

"Pussy." Sam offered to me.

"Mom would be so proud," BJ added as he walked away to join the twins who had loitered just a few feet down the beach.

Sam took notice. "Now that's my boy!"

Rose walked up and bumped my chair with her shapely hip. "Hope this pervert isn't influencing you."

"What?" Sam exclaimed. "Can't a man appreciate the beauty of a woman's body without being called a pervert?"

"Not when they're 12-years-old, Asshole." Rose tended to exaggerate. But she had a bit of a point, given these girls' relative tender age to ours, although, quite frankly, she would have just as likely not approved, had they been age appropriate hot chicks. Women. Go figure.

Sam wisely moved the conversation to safer grounds, "Texas is gonna do it."

"Do what?" I asked.

"Frigging secede."

"Succeed at what?" I mistakenly asked.

"S-e-c-e-d-e." Sam spelled out then added, "Dumbass...as in leave these here United States of Merikah."

I looked down and counted the empty Bud Light Lime "bitch beers" to see if Sam was perhaps over-served. I started to insist he was nuts but Rose spoke up, "Yeah. I saw that on the news. The state is pretty pissed off at the Feds. They seem to be picking on Texas. The Feds are importing illegal immigrants from other states and setting up massive refugee camps in Texas, promising an easy path to citizenship. Before the big election, I expect. The President's Justice Department filed suit to overturn the state's voter ID law; not even a thinly-veiled, vote buying scheme in the largely Republican state."

"Well he is from Chicago, the city of vote early, vote often, vote dead," I added.

"True that and he keeps piling on. Now The Department of Interior is seizing ranch land due to some endangered species of mouse or other and even closing off oil leases. I think Texas might just have had their fill of the President's bullshit."

"And if any state can pull this off, it's Texas. They have energy, agriculture, manufacturing, and access to international seaports. But the Governor is still trying to block it. Says it will tear the country apart and lead to a second Civil War," Sam added.

All I could see was the impossibly large Silver Airstream trailer, a peculiar glimpse into Hobo's mind, lined with newspaper clippings, crossed with lines, and annotated in the center with but a single word "Succession". I pinched myself and, even though thoroughly medicated, I felt the pain. "Not again," I thought.

CHAPTER FOURTEEN

Rose's big day was the coming Saturday. Still smoking hot, the old girl was finally turning forty. Our age gap was still substantial but, thanks to the magic of arithmetic, the percentage was shrinking to a more acceptable level, and this somehow made me feel just a tiny bit less of a dirty old man…at least in my own mind. Our age difference now fell neatly into the acceptable age differential formula; divide by two plus seven. A crevice more so than a canyon. Celebrate the small victories.

It was theoretically a surprise party, but keeping a surprise from Rose was difficult, if not downright painful. At the first hint of mystery, Rose demanded to be filled in on the details. Then Rose being, well, Rose pretty much planned her own surprise party. Again, not complaining…just stating facts. Rose hated surprises. Really more like they drove her frigging crazy and Rose, being of the sharing nature, drove everyone within a comfortable earshot nuts as well until the nature of the surprise was ultimately revealed.

Ardy, over Rose's considerable protest, was "temporarily" living in our pool room, sleeping on an inflatable mattress and downloading massive amounts of porn on my "work" computer. I planned to burn it when he moved out. It being the computer, the mattress, and the computer chair. Unlike the IRS and Hillary "losing" data, I somehow expected the data on my PC could magically be recovered by even the dullest of local law enforcement agencies. The motive for the destruction of the chair and mattress should be self-evident. It would be a very hot fire.

Ruth and her husband Mario made the trip down from New York and were staying in the blue bedroom; the one furthest away from ours. I really did not want to hear the two of them in the middle of a passionate chess play. Ruth was still using her last name and Mario's family kept giving excuses to postpone the

Mormon ceremony. Normally I would say both signs of cracks in their marriage. All such thoughts were dismissed on seeing the two together. For whatever peculiar reason, this marriage of opposites appeared to work. I was happy for Ruth. More importantly, Mom was happy.

Iris, Rose's half-sister and Iris's girlfriend Angel were staying in the guest bedroom turned office/library upstairs. The room was lined with bookshelves filled with our favorite authors. The shelves were packed tightly with an eclectic mix from the classics of Hemingway, Steinbeck, Bronte, Dumas, Tolstoy, Machiavelli, and Dante to modern day popular fiction of Brown, Grisham, King, Follett, Koontz, Dorsey, Conroy, McMillan, and Hiaasen. A Murphy bed shared a wall with our bedroom and provided a modicum of comfort for overflow guests. Some days I napped in the room just to be surrounded by and to absorb the remarkable genius and creativity stored on its shelves. Unfortunately my tactic of enlightenment via osmosis proved fruitless. The girls were not gay lovers, although often confused as such. The two were just best friends since they fled separate wombs almost simultaneously at Jax NAS Hospital. The office had a private bathroom. This was an important feature, as we planned to get Iris hammered. Angel wasn't too happy with the plan as she would, as usual, be the caretaker for the drunken and disorderly Iris. More than once she had held Iris's hair through the wee hours of the morning. There were certain inalienable house rules for our parties, the most important being it just wasn't a party until someone was puking or swimming half-naked in the pool with a one-armed man in his whitie-tighties. Life without rules is chaos and I needed order. Angel was reluctantly kind enough to be of assistance in the provision of said order. That girl is a frigging rock.

Iris reminded me more than just a bit of my sister Ruth. If I didn't know better, I would swear they shared at least one set of DNA. Unlike Ruth, though, she did have boundaries, although, they were a bit flexible and unconventional ones, particularly when mixed with copious amounts of alcohol. And tonight there was sure to be considerable alcohol. Of average height and weight, she was an exotic blend of Cuban and Italian descent with dark, curly hair and large, blue eyes. However, her most conspicuous feature was a massive pair of double xx boobs. I mean, those things could have served as flotation devices for the entire crew and passengers for the SS Titanic. One could only ponder the lives she could have spared if Iris and her tits were passengers on that fateful journey. And to her Grams never-ending disquiet, Iris was inclined to place on exhibit a considerable portion of her God-given, massive, flotation devices. Her constant companion, Angel, was her polar opposite; tall, thin, and conservative in action and dress. Go figure. They lived together in central Florida and worked at the adult hellhole commonly referred to as Disney. Iris was a photographer and Angel currently played Ariel for the theme park, moonlighting in the "borrowed" costume at privileged, over-indulged kid's birthday parties.

We were becoming a nation of polarized opposites. Our children were either over-indulged, spoiled, over-parented, insulated from reality, brats of the privileged, or the ignored, discarded, self-entitled, angry, offspring of the perpetual poor. The middle, the foundation of our country, simply stopped having kids. This is cause for concern, as it is not a sustainable model for humanity as a whole.

The brown bedroom was across the hall from our bedroom and shared a bathroom with the blue bedroom. Esther and Morris traveled down from Tifton and were staying in that room. Fortunately, the two of them had previous experience at Ruth's Belizean wedding with the craziness that often accompanies our get-togethers. I was reasonably confident they could handle one night of insanity after the full week of it in Belize. Little did I know they would be a part of the insanity. Mom was not feeling it and had stayed at home with Mary. All in all, this was a good thing, as I don't think she had enough soap and energy to scrub the filth our guests, and her offspring, would likely exhibit.

Creepy Uncle Frank and Annie Ruth traveled down from Enigma together. Annie Ruth drove her '67 Beetle Convertible while Frank slept. Rose had me inflate a second mattress to place in the pool room with Ardy. It was a tight fit, but Frank and Ardy "deserved each other" according to Rose and Annie Ruth, given her diminutive stature, could sleep on the futon.

The rest of the guests lived locally, more or less. The remainder of Rose's family, our mutual friends, and a bunch of Rose's co-workers were set to attend. Rose worked for an international firm and, as such, we would have several European guests. Rose was a bit concerned about the outcome of mixing our lovingly eccentric family and friends with her co-workers, but acquiesced once she considered the sheer entertainment value, and after receiving my fervent, yet insincere, assurances Hobo was not on the invite list. I think her words were, "you only live once." And like I had any control of where the crazy bastard Hobo showed up…but, on second thought, I may have left that detail out. I kind of wanted him to make an appearance. Crazy likes company.

Saturday morning, I started running errands to get ready for the party. Ruth took charge of Rose on her milestone day and took her to get her toes, fingers, and face done at the local Vietnamese owned and operated day spa. These people amazed me. Two short generations after coming to the States and it seems as if the entire lot of the Vietnamese War refugees had achieved middle class. Guess we are the land of opportunity for those willing to bust their ass and make personal sacrifices.

Iris offered to come with me to run errands. Ardy first attempted to head out with Ruth and Rose but was quickly and firmly denied the opportunity by Rose. "Hell to the no!" He still had a major crush on Ruth and despite, among a host of other reasons, her recent nuptials, maintained wildly delusional plans of bedding my sister. So Ardy, seeing large, attractively displayed boobs, quickly devised a suitable plan B. My sister Esther took care of the decorations and Uncle Frank volunteered to handle securing a keg and icing down the beer. I immediately regretted putting Frank in charge of the beer.

I had included Ardy into our conspiracy to get Iris hammered. Naturally he was on board, as I think his plan B now included knowledge of Iris and her incredible breast in the Old Testament Biblical sense. Yet another of Ardy's delusional fantasies. In the face of a google of reasons to sway him otherwise, he was a man not lacking in self-confidence. I made a mental note to double check the mirrors in the pool room for functionality. Yet, in spite of Ardy's self-denied shortcomings, he remained, to Rose's chagrin, my closest and most loyal friend.

Each and every day we are faced with innumerable, seemingly inconsequential choices. We select A versus B with little thought, yet even the tiniest of those infinite subconscious decisions we make can be life-impacting. Paralysis would ensue if our conscious self did not ignore the weight, the seriousness, the infinite variety of outcomes. Ardy's subconscious auto selector was tragically locked on foolish. He held no evil intent. Never did he purposefully choose stupid or make a conscious decision to do harm. It was the subtle subconscious selections that typically nudged him down his tragic path.

Our first stop was Cinotti's to get the cake. Cinotti's is on Penman Road, not far from the house. It's a decades old Italian family bakery. Rose and I love family businesses and try to support them at every opportunity. The big box retail assholes are killing the eclectic diversity small, family-owned retail stores provide. Damn, I sounded like a Democrat for a moment. Rose naturally picked out her own surprise birthday cake. It was in the shape of a giant monkey. The monkey's beat red ass was inexplicably anatomically correct. I thought this an unsuitable detail better ignored on a birthday cake. Iris dipped her finger into the monkey's ass and offered Ardy a lick. She had a curious practice of sticking her finger in people's asses. Apparently the practice conveyed to cake monkeys, as well. "Don't encourage him," I warned her. Ardy smiled as Iris struggled to remove her finger from Ardy's mouth.

Our next stop was at Angie's Sub Shop. Ed owned Angie's and had adopted a derivative of the Hooters Wings' business model for his sandwich shop, sans the stupid orange shorts and old women's opaque hosiery. He employed a bunch of hot young girls and kept the thermostat set on 78 degrees. In this manner, he could insist he did not encourage them to dress in the barest minimum of clothing…they just conveniently chose to. Whatever his tactics, it worked for him and his sub shop had been successful for decades at the Beach. It didn't hurt business that Angie's also served pretty damn good food, but that was a side benefit. Realistically, do people (and when I say people, I mean men) really go to Hooters for the food? Given the skin show, I instructed Ardy to wait in the car with the cake. I didn't want to make an afternoon at Angie's. Ed greeted us as Iris and I entered the store. Ardy caught a glimpse of one of the scantily clad waitresses, quickly abandoned his assigned post and joined us. "Perfect," I mumbled. Ed poured us each a shot of Patron Silver from a bottle not so discreetly hidden under the counter. Angie's did not have a liquor license. Ed was a Libertarian, though, and resented most forms of government intervention. Smart man, that Ed. Ardy pounded his shot and went trolling. Iris tossed her shot back like the seasoned drinking pro she was. I pushed mine over to Iris. "Pussy," she said as she threw back her second shot of the afternoon. It would not be her last.

"Impressive," Ed said.

"Yup that one…" I nodded toward Iris, "…can drink with the big boys."

Ed looked at me as if I was nuts. "The tits, dumbass." I had grown somewhat accustomed to her massive, nearly-exposed breasts and tended to forget the considerable impression they make on first sight. Ed turned to Iris and offered," You need a job, honey?" I immediately understood his hiring practices.

"No, but I will take another shot."

Ed complied, pouring her a double shot. Iris tossed it back. "How much you make?"

Iris replied, "About $85,000 a year at Disney and another $25,000 or so on the side taking soul-crushing portraits at weddings, birthday parties, graduations, and the sort."

Ed was duly impressed and abandoned his efforts to add Iris's considerable assets to his portfolio. The sandwich platters were ready. I paid for them and Iris went and gathered up Ardy from the bar, overlooking the servers' preparation table which offered an unobstructed view of Angie's pleasant nubile scenery. It was thoughtful of Ed to provide a view into the kitchen area. Very modern and highbrow, I thought.

Our last stop was Publix. After my episode with La' Sunjalal at the Section 8 Publix location, I thought it best to travel the few extra miles over to the store off of Marsh Landing located just inside the ultra-posh community of Ponte Vedra. Only a few miles separated the two stores but they were worlds apart. I found a corner parking spot under a tree to keep the car cool and hopefully scratch and dent free from little soccer brats opening car doors or their moms leaving carts rolling unattended about the lot. It's like people have suddenly become completely self-centered. I don't think they necessarily choose to be assholes, they are just utterly oblivious to others.

We fortunately had a short list: veggie trays, chips, bottled water, cookies, and ice. Lots of ice. It was a hot day and ice would be at a premium. Hopefully we could be in and out before the monkey's ass bled into the leather seats. I delegated tasks to that end and sent Ardy to get water and Iris chips. We agreed to meet in the produce aisle. After grabbing the cookies from the bakery, I located and selected a couple suitable veggie trays before spotting Ardy tailing Iris up the produce aisle. Ardy's smile conveyed mischief. The frowns of the other shoppers conveyed in order: shock, distress, loathing, violence. "What the hell, Ardy?" Iris dropped the chips in the cart and astutely continued walking.

Ardy replied unnecessarily, "I just crop-dusted the produce aisle." I shook my head, there were no words, and made a speedy bee-line for the checkout lane, correctly ascertaining distance to be my best ally from the recently desecrated mob.

I love Publix for a number of reasons. One of which is they employ the otherwise unemployable as grocery baggers. This can make for some interesting, inconvenient, embarrassing, and sometimes even unpleasant scenarios, but I admired and appreciated their effort and community spirit. And given the steep downhill path to crazy I seemed to have stumbled back onto, it was likely I would be applying all too soon for gainful employment. We still needed ice. Publix is community-minded, not stupid, and as such, the cashiers are of a slightly different, let's just say, more cerebral category than the baggers. It is one thing to handle bagging the groceries and something entirely different to handle cash. The cashier was a young man in his late teens or early twenties. He was physically and mentally sound and very likely, given certain distinct universally recognized mannerisms, gay. Somehow, the obvious detail of the cashier's likely proclivity to the same sex detail was unfortunately lost on Iris. Our bagger was an 87-year-old frail woman suffering, from all appearances, a recent, massive stroke. "I need two ten-pound bags of ice, please," I said after the cashier thoughtfully asked if there was anything else I needed. Iris subsequently inserted her index finger up my ass as I failed to immediately respond in the affirmative.

The cashier turned to the tiny, frail, aged, semi-catatonic bagger, still struggling to collect and bag our meager collection of groceries, and instructed, "Go grab a couple ten-pound bags of ice from the freezer." A teenage girl's giggle escaped my lips. I'm not sure what planet the cashier was currently residing but here on earth, the bagger struggled to even lift the bag of chips. A ten pound bag of ice was not a possibility. Ardy literally doubled over from laughter. Iris managed to keep it somewhat together but had turned crimson red from embarrassment as the bagger shuffled over to the freezer and returned struggling to manage but a single five-pound bag of ice. I was duly impressed. It was an awkward moment, to say the least, and made even more comical by the cashier's complete oblivion to the absurdity of his request... and of course the tequila.

"Looks like you're having a party," the cashier said, nervously trying to break the awkward moment, but succeeding only to send both Ardy and I both into another uncontrollable round of laughter.

I'm unsure why we found the scenario so hilarious, but Iris was sufficiently embarrassed by our behavior and replied curiously, "Yeah." She pointed at me. "It's Zeke's coming out party."

"What the hell?" I exclaimed, looking at Iris with a puzzled look on my face.

"Sounds like your party would be a blast," the cashier flashed me a smile.

Ardy returned to fits of laughter. Iris magically produced one of my business cards which included my cell phone number, street, and e-mail address and handed it to the cashier. "Come by about eight." Ardy fell to the floor and pissed himself. Iris seized the cart, damn near shoving me to the store's exit, and abandoned Ardy in a pool of his own making to fend for himself.

The cashier reached for the store's intercom and stoically announced, "Clean up, checkout lane six." The store catered to several area assisted-living facilities. Not his first incontinent rodeo. I speculated silently that I would be returning to the section 8 Publix for future grocery provisions. Maybe I should rethink Winn Dixie.

We ultimately made it home safely but sans any remaining dignity. Esther had been busy. She had hung an entire village of sock monkeys throughout the house. One hung perilously from the chandelier over the kitchen table, artfully entangled with a series of flashing miniature red solo cups. Another sock monkey, wearing a cowboy hat lifted from Woody, rode the overhead fan. (Baby Sam would likely take notice and offer energetic protest.)

Several others, tied from nearly invisible sections of fishing line, hung from the ceiling at varying heights, establishing a challenging maze to navigate for anyone exceeding Esther's diminutive stature. The little poop-tossing bastards were everywhere. Pink helium balloons occupied every corner of the room, weighed down with sand-filled aluminum foil, artfully folded to look like chrome-covered piles of poo. The hand rails on the stairs were dangerously adorned in pink and blue crepe paper and cardboard monkey faces hung from adhesive strips from virtually every door strategically located at eye level.

Frank tripled up on the beer order, taking my explicit instructions as more guidelines than directions. He ordered three kegs: Bud Heavy, Bud Light, and Bud Light Lime. Frank insisted on purchasing American beer. He was a patriot at heart. Frank would even rise from his duct-tape-repaired, imitation-vinyl recliner to stand at arthritic attention with his weathered hand reverently placed over his artery clogged heart when Francis Scott Key's anthem was played prior to the start of every NASCAR race. He also stood in silent reverence on the rare occasion Dixie was played in public. (Revisionist historians had successfully painted the Confederacy as a home-grown terrorist organization. Symbols associated with the Confederacy were despised much on the same level as the Swastika.) I didn't have the heart to tell him Budweiser was now owned by a Belgium/Brazilian beverage company. That and I was fearful he would empty the kegs on the back lawn and purchase additional ones. Or worse yet, Frank might hunt down the last remaining members of the Anheuser-Busch family in order to secure their malicious, anti-patriotic, motives utilizing escalating means of torture. Frank also ordered a margarita and daiquiri machine which had been delivered and installed in the pool room after deflating and stowing the air mattresses to make sufficient space in the room. Frank converted the pool room's bath tub into a giant porcelain hooch basin. Based on the discarded contextual clues, the hooch consisted of a toxic assortment of cheap liquor and expensive fruit. I would not be sampling his recipe for an assortment of hygienic motives. The kegs were all tapped and sufficiently iced and Frank appeared to be several deep into the sampling and quality assurance process. Annie Ruth was digging the daiquiris and dangerously close to taking an unscheduled nap. I guided her to the relative safety of the sofa.

We carried our booty in from the car and Esther took charge in placing the items in the appropriate reserved locations. She and Frank were cut from the same cloth and both took their assigned duties with needless vigor. It was five PM, two full hours before the party was scheduled to even begin, when the first guest arrived: my fishing buddy Austin. He had been out fishing at the jetties and just off shore all day with Larry for Red Snapper. The fishing ban had finally been lifted on Snapper and the catch was awesome. Austin fired up the grill and placed several pounds of fresh filleted Snapper on the grill. Nothing approaches the taste of fish caught, grilled, and consumed in the same day. "Fresh" fish from the market is typically five or six days old. Fresh fish has very little of that worrisome fishy smell.

Ardy grabbed the Patron from the freezer and poured Iris a shot of the icy delirium. He unbuttoned his Hawaiian shirt before handing the tequila to Iris. Ardy pointed to his undershirt's inscription. It read, 'Yes, you can dance - Tequila.' I chuckled and filled the remaining shot glasses from the sink faucet and distributed them. Hide in plain sight is an effective stratagem. Iris did not take notice. Austin offered a proper Italian toast, "salut" and we all, bar Iris, tossed back our tap water.

Frank, unaware of our plan, spit out his water in the kitchen sink in disgust. "What the hell was that?" In the face of bountiful context clues, Iris remained oblivious to our fiendish intent. Given her oblivion, combined with a noticeable and considerable degradation of motor skills, it was apparent the liquor was well into lubricating her soul and accomplishing our mission. Angel shook her head with a knowing look of the coming gloom. She was in for a long, difficult night of compassionate care for a demanding and ungrateful patient.

Ruth returned with a fresh, dual-browed Rose and found us on the back porch keeping good company with the kegs while watching Austin grill the Snapper. The smell was tantalizing. The keg beer was perfectly chilled and tapped. Frank, in spite of his excesses, had done good. The liquid ambrosia flowed smoothly and tasted dangerously delightful. I needed to be careful or I would be in for a long night. Iris insisted on performing the night's first keg stand before the second outside guest had even arrived. Clothing designers fail to consider certain inalienable laws of physics. Her massive xx breast slipped forward unfettered as she went inverted over the keg with Ardy and Frank's enthusiastic assistance. Austin smiled and raised his cup. Frank spewed his half-swallowed beer onto Iris. Ardy leered. Rose growled. Ruth called "next." Fortunately, Austin declared the Snapper was prepared and we abandoned the kegs before Ruth had the opportunity to likewise mount. We sat by the pool and consumed the tasty morsels that Austin had lightly-seasoned and grilled to perfection. Angel insisted Iris eat. I thought perhaps an empty stomach would be a preferable condition for Angel's future. Recycled fish would likely be quite unpleasant for both the recycler and any unfortunate proximate bystanders. I remained silent, yielding to the responsible, experienced party's opinion on the matter.

The next couple to arrive were two of Rose's international co-workers: Carlos and Britt. Carlos was Portuguese and Britt was Dutch. They were a mid-forties married couple, both well-dressed and both displaying quiet, somewhat reserved personalities. Carlos was short in stature, dark-skinned, sporting a well-groomed goatee and handsome in the Latin sort of way. Britt was an attractive, statuesque blond that triggered in me one of those intense "don't I know you from somewhere" moments that are almost always best ignored as giving voice to the thought sounds like a cheesy pick-up line. Both spoke excellent English and, in spite of a certain reserved air, were very approachable. They sipped red wine from glasses amidst Iris pounding tequila shots, Frank guzzling draft beer from a solo cup, Ardy sucking frozen margarita through a straw, and Annie Ruth drooling and farting on the coach with a half-emptied melted daiquiri in hand. Esther and Morris cornered the pair, recognizing kindred souls. Like crazy, sanity enjoys company.

Ardy called for more shots. Iris was first in line. After a brief glimpse at Iris's assets, Ardy appeared to be doubling down on his attempt to obtain Old Testament knowledge. Rose's Aunt by marriage arrived with her Uncle. Bella was Cuban and, even when sober, wild as an untamed pony. She was not sober. Bella greeted me with a full frontal hug and a kiss square on the lips. She lingered much longer than comfort allowed before I felt the pressure of her tongue attempting to part my lips. I managed to break the embrace. Bella moved on to greener pastures and approached Ardy with an open-armed embrace. "You smell sexy, big boy." Ardy, opting for a quick dip in the pool instead of showering, actually smelled of chlorine with a faint hint of urine.

Frank, in his unique gravelly voice, interrupted the embrace. "Hell, Lady. The boy smells like piss." Bella nonplussed, went in for a second hug. Frank called next. Bella complied with a full frontal hug and a kiss on Frank's cheek. "This is what we call a target rich environment."

I mumbled "Top Gun," under my breath and cornered Rose, who apparently had played a bit of undetected catch up. She was a sneaky drunk. "Your Aunt Bella just tried to slip me tongue."

Without pausing, she replied in a nonjudgmental tone, "Keep your teeth closed."

"Thanks?"

Rose and Iris's Pop, Peter, arrived, with his second act wife. Peter was a retired naval petty officer. Italian by birth, he had a dark complexion with closely trimmed jet black hair. He had the rigid posture of a career naval man and a no-nonsense kick-ass personality of a man accustomed to and even welcoming confrontation. A stern boxing coach, the U.S. Navy and time had transformed Peter into a different man. Whether he harbored past regrets or not would be difficult to ascertain, as he was a challenging man to read and one that did not openly share his emotions. I don't think Peter was equipped with a rearview mirror. Rose had made peace with their past. Peter never openly spoke of it.

Other guests began pouring in and soon the party overflowed into the backyard and courtyard. The party split into two distinctive groups. One group, predominately headquartered around the kegs, bore a remarkable resemblance to a Quentin-Tarantino-like remake of Animal House. The second group lounged on the sofa indoors, sipping wine from glasses, bore more a likeness to some future season of Downton Abbey shortly after their final surviving servant received a pink slip. Damn income tax laws! The courtyard became the party's unofficial demilitarized zone where new arriving guests could make a fact-based determination as to which party to join and the two disparate groups could briefly interact on peaceful terms for at least long enough to retrieve a frozen adult treat from the pool room, or for those truly fool hearty souls, brave a generous sample of Frank's lethal bathtub hooch. Few from the Abbey group selected the latter.

Ardy continued his delusional pursuit of Iris, having accurately gauged the single Iris a more realistic target of opportunity than a married and accompanied Ruth. His odds easily doubled from one in a million to two, maybe even two and a half, in a million. The odds of Ardy being suffocated by Rose in his sleep likewise increased in tandem, but at a logarithmic rate. Ardy, although a touch delusional, was a determined man and not at all stupid.

Never underestimate the value of determination. Ardy had a working theory. Ask 100 women for sex and all that is required is a paltry one percent success rate to get laid. The key, Ardy explained, is to find a central location with 100 single (as in no adjacent male) women (preferably drunk) and quickly and efficiently ascertain their inclination to go horizontal on the premises. It's not like you are looking for a wife...hell, even a date. We are talking "You wanna have sex with me in the parking lot?" or some derivative thereof being his standard, albeit crude, pick-up line. I have seen his theory in action and can attest to both his unlikely but inevitable success and to the redness of his face after being slapped some 99 times. Again, determination is a powerful variable in the formula for success.

Unfortunately for Ardy, 100 unattached females were not in attendance at Rose's birthday party. Nevertheless, he increased his odds by formulating a Plan C: Bella. Plan C had a reasonable statistical chance of success. Although, currently Bella was kneeled over the bathtub sucking lethal amounts of Frank's hooch through a giant straw. The sex with Bella option needed to be initiated sooner rather than later, assuming it was conscious and still breathing female form Ardy required. And then there was the competition. Frank was currently cheering Bella on and I believe also tracking Bella with similar plans of illicit, drunken copulation. She came up for air. Frank seized the moment and planted his lips on hers. Bella's gag reflex engaged from some combination of his tongue down her throat and a gallon of mystery brew and Bella disgorged into the hooch much of what she had just drank along with healthy chunks of what appeared to be Gram's spaghetti with meatballs. Perversely, I thought Ardy's chances, if not his appetite, just improved.

"I got $20 says you and your tits won't fit through the doggie door," Ardy challenged Iris. The previous owners of our house had a pair of Boxers and had installed a medium-sized doggie door in the wall of the pool room. My money was on Ardy. No way in hell those tits would make it through.

"Whip it out, fat ass," Iris responded, speaking of the wagered money. Ardy, either oblivious to the contextual clues or choosing to ignore them, started to yank his baby snake out of his pants. Rose, ever watchful for Ardy's shenanigans, bumped him into the pool with a discreet hip before he could unleash his pet snake. The commotion woke Annie Ruth. She cannonballed into the pool, making a pint-sized splash. Ruth, Iris, Bella, and Ivy followed her in. Annie Ruth flashed a toothy, ethereal grin. Her personal Nirvana realized; young vagina paradise. Frank, always prepared for this very contingency, whipped out several sets of pocket-sized numerical cards. He distributed the scoring cards. I wisely handed mine off to some unidentified twenty-something-year-old guy with a beer in his hands. Frank lead the judging of the impromptu wet t-shirt contest holding up the appropriate numbered card as each woman in turn stepped out of the pool, shirts clinging tightly to their upper body. I remained mystified as to the standards for judging. Rose's brother Giuseppe, being an internet site certified scorekeeper, was appointed as such. After tallying the votes, Giuseppe declared Annie Ruth the unlikely winner by a slim margin over Iris. Ardy followed a distant, but quite respectable third. A contestant filed a complaint with Giuseppe demanding a recount. Giuseppe dismissed her request citing rule 27-a (iii). "Judge's rulings are final and not subject to appeal."

Ardy approached Iris for a conciliatory hug he did not receive. "Whip it out, Asshole." This time Ardy wisely pulled $20 from his water-logged wallet. He handed the damp money over to Giuseppe. Giuseppe held a certification in banking, as well, and was a registered financial advisor in several Central American countries. Iris, to the delight of most of the male guests, slipped off her t-shirt and knelt on all fours in front of the doggie door. The unidentified twenty-year-old male guest fainted from a lack of blood to the brain. No one moved to assist. Iris's arms exited the far side followed by her curly, damp hair. Then, one at time, each massive boob squeezed through before her entire body almost effortlessly made its way through the door. Giuseppe handed her the $20.

"Double or nothing I can squeeze through the door," Ardy foolishly offered.

"Bank," said Iris and about ten other guests. Giuseppe collected the bets and held some $300 in cash, all betting against

Ardy. Ardy covered the bets and stripped, to the guest's horror, into his whitie-tighties splashing water from the pool onto his body for lubrication. The resultant translucent effect was deeply disturbing. Fortunately, the Downton Abbey group remained indoors and, consequently, insulated to this unraveling, slow-moving disaster. Ardy followed Iris's lead and sent his arms first through the door. His bald head appeared shortly thereafter.

Unfortunately, unlike Iris's breasts, Ardy's gut was a single, sizable object. He managed to get halfway through before getting wedged. Ardy, after struggling unsuccessfully to escape, called for help. Judge Giuseppe noted that any outside assistance would forfeit the wager. "Rule 19-j." Ardy reasoned out loud he could piss and thus remove some of his bulk, making his escape more attainable and save himself serious bank. Judge Giuseppe noted the technique while disgusting and crude was within the published rules. Rose promised Ardy a slow and painful death if he peed on her floor. Ardy always with secondary and tertiary plans, foolishly reasoned time was an ally and he would eventually lose enough weight to squeeze through. An accurate, if not practical, assumption. Judge Giuseppe noted no clock had been specified for the event.

Frank yelled his second Top Gun rip off of the evening to Ardy, "Come on Mav, do some of that pilot shit." Ardy had no pilot shit in him and the party quickly grew bored with the immobile mass that was Ardy and moved to the back porch, abandoning the securely wedged, drunken, half-naked Ardy within the confines of the doggie door. Iris's father, Peter, knelt beside Ardy as he walked by and softly spoke to him before moving on to join the Animal House group by the kegs. Perhaps now was the suitable time for Ardy to abandon Plan B and move on to plan C.

I stopped in to mingle with the Downton Abbey tea party group before moving out to the back porch. I felt mysteriously out of place in my own home with my plastic cup filled with draft beer in hand. This faction of attendees was better dressed, better behaved, quieter…in other words, a bit mundane. Or, at least, so I thought. I did observe that both Carlos and Britt were touchers. Any time they spoke to anyone in the group of either sex, they would touch them; arm, shoulder, even sometimes the face. I wrote it off as a difference in culture. I like my personal space and am highly uncomfortable when anyone, even a hot chick violates that space without my invitation. On a related note, Rose is particularly annoyed when it is a hot chick, but otherwise doesn't give a rat's proverbial ass who violates my personal space. She loves me.

The intellectual conversation turned to immigration. My brother-in-law Morris and Carlos were in agreement on our country's nonsensical immigration laws. Carlos and Britt, both well-educated contributing members to our economy would have to leave the country after three years. In the interim, a few million illegals, uneducated, often disease-riddled, occasionally gang associated, and almost always homeless were being welcomed, hell, invited, across our country's southern border. And rumor had it the President planned on inviting hundreds of thousands of Muslim "refugees" into the country as well. "Orphans and children," he said. "Your president says your country has a moral obligation to help anyone that needs help," Britt noted.

Morris replied, "It's great to be liberal, you always get to claim the moral high ground. And liberals don't necessarily require an effective policy…just an attractive one. Failures can always be assigned on the policy's flawed implementation due to conservative interference. Let me ask you this. You're a bit young but I still bet you are familiar with the story of the ill-fated Titanic?" Morris asked Britt. She sipped her wine and nodded in the affirmative. "Some 2,300 passengers and crew members were aboard the ship when it ran into the iceberg and began to sink. There were lifeboats available with only space for a little over 700 people," Morris paused.

"Yes, I'm familiar with the story, but I don't see your point?"

"If our president had been the Titanic's Captain, do you suppose he would have still held that moral obligation to help everyone that needed help?"

"I believe he would have still felt the moral obligation, but given the circumstances, it would have been impossible to help everyone that required assistance," Britt replied, moving even closer to Morris as she rested her perfectly manicured hand on his arm.

"And that is my very point. Our country doesn't have the resources to help everyone. If we tell all the passengers to jump in the lifeboat, there will be no survivors. The lifeboats will just sink to the bottom of the icy Atlantic from the added weight, killing everyone. We can do only what we can do. Attempting more than is possible will lead to even more disastrous results."

Carlos jumped in, "But it is the Christian, compassionate thing to do. Help those that need help, yes?"

Esther replied "Riddle me this, Senor Carlos…how are you exercising Christian fundamentals by providing help using someone else's dinero?" Esther had mistaken Carlos to be of Spanish origin. Close, but no cigar. Portugal stole Spain's coastline centuries before Florida followed suit, cheating Alabama out of its oceanfront real estate. "You want to be heroic…risk your own life, not your neighbor's life. You want to be charitable…give your own money, not your neighbor's money." Normally reserved around strangers, Esther was on a roll tonight. Their quarterly tax bill must have been higher than normal. She was pretty much a teetotaler, but made the rare exceptions. Tonight was one of those. She had drank almost a half of glass of Riesling. She must have been shit-faced. She continued "And perhaps compassion…" she added air quotes "…is not our beloved President's primary motive."

Carlos took the bait. "So then, what is his motivation?" He wasn't being argumentative. Most of our country's news sources have a decidedly liberal bias and it is no surprise newcomers to our country can't even conceive there are others that might possess an opposing view.

"Giving amnesty and citizenship to a few million illegals might be an inexpensive way to secure votes. Concentrate the new voters in red states, let's say Texas, and the 'compassionate' strategy might turn the state blue. I mean, the president's Justice Department fights all attempts by the states to implement voter ID laws. Why do you suppose that is? You need an ID to go see an R-rated movie, by a beer, a pack of cigarettes, board a plane, but requiring an ID to vote is somehow racist!?" Esther continued her rant, "Heck no, it's not racist…its common sense. The President and his minions toss out the race card whenever their argument doesn't hold any water."

"Amen, sister." I spoke up and raised my cup in a sympathetic salute. Esther and Morris did not get out much. In fact, neither had ever as much as set foot in one of the aluminum-skinned, bacteria-recirculating, modern miracles of aviation. (I simply don't care how many physics teachers attempted to illuminate the science of aerodynamics to me. I'm just not buying it. It's a damn miracle, I tell you, a frigging miracle.) A few cruises in the Caribbean and a dozen or so trips to Disney and the beaches of LA (Lower Alabama…AKA, Florida's cleverly acquired panhandle) with the grandkids was the extent of their travel log entries. Both were well-educated, well-read, and highly intelligent. With the lack of overseas travel and living in a small, rural, southern Georgia town, neither had cause to come in contact with many foreigners, absent Mexican migrant workers, much less had they had opportunity to engage in a spirited conversation with intelligent, well-educated aliens. Most of their outside chats and interactions were in fact limited to the under nine years old crowd. They were the kind of grandparents every kid and grandkid fantasized about, devoting almost all their time, energy, and resources to the health, education, and entertainment of the latest repackaged iteration of themselves. Consequently, neither were overly skilled in the social graces department with adults, at least.

Not judging here, just stating facts. And what is really important in life, anyway; the mastery of pairing wines with fine food or the ability to educate, stimulate, protect, and amuse future generations?

Morris and Esther were in heaven, trading and exploring ideas with a diverse and articulate source, not to mention, pleasant to look at pair like Carlos and Britt. They moved on to the sustainability of the Eurozone. I excused myself and moved on to more entertaining pastures before all the intellectual conversation ruined my hard-earned buzz.

I walked out the back door to the chorus of "...57, 58, 59, 60..." The Animal House assemblage was surrounding the keg, obscuring its view. All I could see above their heads was a pair of pale, slender, well-defined female legs and bare feet with colorfully painted toes pointed perfectly skyward. Someone was doing an impressive, unassisted keg stand. "...71, 72, 73..."

"Remarkable," Sam said. "You know this chick?" He pointed toward the shapely, inverted legs on the keg.

I wedged my way into the crowd surrounding the keg just as Aja curled her legs behind her back until her legs were perfectly parallel to the ground "...80, 81, 82." She dismounted the keg with a front summersault, jumping over the spectators two rows deep. The Animal House faction, aptly impressed by her athleticism, toned, generously-exposed body and drinking skills, broke into spontaneous and enthusiastic applause.

"I don't really know for sure." I honestly replied and pinched myself. It hurt.

"You know her or you don't. Kinda a yes or no question, Zeke."

"You would think," I replied.

Sam took the cup from my hand. "Maybe you need to take a break and drink a little water, buddy." I get that a lot. People tend to assume I am either a drunk or a lunatic. I'm not sure which I prefer but the truth, I believe, lies somewhere in between.

Ruth had replaced Aja on the keg but required assistance to maintain verticality and would fall woefully short of Aja's damn near 90 second record. And severely short on style points, as well. Ruth was a lot of remarkable things; highly coordinated was not one of them. Ruth dismounted and Austin took an even less graceful turn on the keg as his pants slid down his ass.

"What the hell? Commando dude?" I asked of no one. "Excuse me I mumbled, "I need to go see a man about a dog." I walked through the house to the mostly deserted courtyard. It was well past midnight and the party was thinning out a bit. Ardy lay unconscious, still wedged in the doggie door with his dirty drawers down around his knees. Thankfully, his mid-section and junk were trapped inside the door and safe from view. I walked into the pool room, being careful not to wake the beastly troll, in order to retrieve a frozen margarita.

Back in the day, (those four simple words initiated considerable dread in my kids as they knew them to be code for "here comes another boring, likely fictional, story from Dad's childhood"), girls were required to wear dresses or skirts to school. Pants were strictly forbidden. This led to an early fascination with white cotton panties and the dark mysteries that lay just beyond that thin, soft layer of natural fabric. Unfortunately, my sisters' Barbies and my older cousin's Playboys offered precious little enlightenment regarding the female anatomy just south of the Mason-Dixon Line. And with Gore's greatest accomplishment, internet porn yet a distant fantasy, I spent the first 17 years of my life on the outside of that enchanted cotton boundary, conjuring absurd possibilities as to what may lay beyond. Sometime early in my high school years, before my first carnal enlightenment, the school board revised the dress code, permitting female students to wear pants. The boys were roundly displeased, considering the new policy a permanent and unjust end to "squirrel season." Riots nearly ensued. What next? A smoking ban in the bathrooms?! Maybe we should have started looting and burning cop cars, convenience stores, and barbershops in our community over the injustice. I have since learned that nothing adequately communicates, "We have been unjustly wronged and demand justice," like looting and burning your own house to its foundation. Seems counterintuitive, but what the hell do I know? I drink too much. Walking into the room, I was greeted by Annie Ruth on the futon snoring loudly with her legs parted, widely offering an ancient and undesirable white cotton view. In the tortured blink of an eye, that childhood fascination with illicit cotton was severely aggrieved.

Rhythmic noises and heavy breathing from the bathroom caught my attention. I knocked on the door. Frank, in his unmistakable gravelly voice replied, "Occupado." The distinctive, rhythmic sound of sex returned, accompanied by the soft, peculiarly sensual moans of Bella and disquieting, animalistic, gravelly grunts of Uncle Frank. I knocked again. "I said occupado, Asshole," Frank angrily replied.

I started to knock once again but Annie Ruth spoke up without opening her eyes. "Don't be such a cock block, Zeke," she said as she dug inside her bra to collect and adjust her ancient breast. The frequency, pitch, and volume of the sounds increased until the sound approached what one might imagine was the sound of a feral pussy cat being ass-raped by an arthritic Great Dane on his final hurrah. I shook my head in disgust and walked out sans margarita. Annie Ruth farted.

Ardy roused and looked up at me with pleading eyes; "Can you scratch my ass?"

"You should ask Bella once Frank's dick gets out of her mouth," I suggested. Ardy listened quietly for a moment, digested the assembled context clues, and uttered an audible sigh of disappointment before nodding off to sleep again. I turned toward the pool lit from underneath by soft light subtly shifting from various shades of blue and green to see the distinctive form of Hobo's bare, lily white ass swimming in the pool buck-naked. The cacophony of sounds from the bathroom grew even louder. Annie Ruth farted. Hobo smiled. I hurled. Maybe too much to drink.

179

More likely some lethal combo of booze and disquieting sights, smells, and sounds. And it was not just a dainty little upchuck, either. I made Linda Blair my bitch. I hurled volumes directly onto Ardy's upper torso and head. He raised his head, licked his lips, and smeared the puke off his face before plopping his head back onto the stone pavers fast asleep.

Hobo stepped out of the pool, thankfully wrapping himself in a pink Hello Kitty beach towel. His hair had grown out long again and his damp, red curls dangled to below his shoulders. Water still dripped from his overgrown, flaming orange beard. His skin was freckled, darkened by the sun and leathery. Yet, as always, his eyes remained his most remarkable feature. Tonight they radiated a crystal blue, seemingly illuminating the courtyard. "Need a towel, Ezekiel?" His hand was playfully poised above the towel wrapped around his narrow hips.

"Not that one, Asshole."

"Language, Ezekiel," Hobo scolded. "Vulgar language is offensive and a crutch employed by the ignorant, incapable of otherwise effectively communicating."

"Then I must be a moron." I pinched myself and yelped from the pain. It hurt.

Hobo laughed. "You think that little trick of yours really tells you anything, Ezekiel?"

Aja and Ruth ran screaming in delight around the far corner of the house, both stripping the remainder of their tops before friskily pushing Hobo into the water, dislodging his towel. The girls fell in behind, splashing and giggling. Iris attempted to follow, but, given toxic levels of tequila, much less gracefully, as she slipped on the wet poolside tile and landed face first on the pavers with only one leg succeeding to find its intended watery target. She looked up from the pavers with a large, snaggle tooth smile and a mouth filled with blood. A stream of hurl laced with partially digested chunks of grilled and lightly-seasoned red snapper choked off her attempt to adequately rally to yell, "Shots!" And in that tortured blink of an eye, my enthusiasm for grilled snapper was likewise severely aggrieved. My favorite things were toppling like dominoes that night. Angel lifted Iris by her armpits onto the adjacent chaise lounge, officially marking the commencement of her long night's chore.

Ardy, startled by the commotion, inexplicably managed to dislodge himself from the doggie door, leaving his drawers regrettably trapped between its magnetic vinyl flaps. "Shots. I'm in, bitches!" he yelled, as he cannonballed into the pool naked, his white ass reflecting the gentle blue hues of the pool light.

Giuseppe declared Ardy the winner of the bet, placing his considerable, yet improbable winnings on the chair adjacent to Iris before hurriedly exiting the courtyard for the clothing obligatory indoor environment of the few remaining Downton Abbey muted revelers. Bella, her appetite yet sated, likewise cannonballed topless into the pool's now frothy waters. "I guess it's officially a party now," I said to no one in particular, thinking at the same time of Mom's frequent reminder to "be careful for what I wish for." Sage words those were. I walked back into the pool room bath to wash my face and rinse my mouth of vomit. The door remained shut. Annoyed, I knocked loudly. "Damn it, Frank. What the hell you still doing in there?"

"Pretty takes time," he replied calmly through the still closed door. Annie Ruth handed me a kerchief from her purse before stripping to her cotton panties and underwire bra and cannonballing into the now crowded pool.

I returned to the pool area and laid on the vacant chaise lounge by Iris. Angel had adequately stemmed the flow of blood. The broken teeth were beyond her scope of repair. Iris offered a warm, yet disquieting smile. Angel offered a sarcastic, evil smile accompanied by a solitary finger. I shrugged. Austin, Ivy, Larry, Sam, Flo, and Bertie all jumped into the pool in varying stages of undress. A siren sounded outside on the street and the unmistakable reflection of police lights were reflected through the glass front doors. Two policemen burst into the courtyard to what must have appeared as some peculiar mixture of an AARP fight club, homeless orgy, and a special needs zombie attack.

Through all the confusion, Hobo locked his eyes with mine and, in the barest of whispers, his voice resonated in my head, "The last time, 600,000 died." He shook his head from side to side in sadness and continued softly, the words screaming in my ears, "This time ten...maybe twenty times more." Darkness fell.

CHAPTER FIFTEEN

The courtyard to our house is U-shaped with a three-story stucco wall on the east, north, and south sides. The west side of the courtyard has a low, earth tone, stucco-faced fence, punctuated with a fountain, giving life to the pool, and backed by four majestic Queen Palm trees. A series of dark blue porcelain planters crown the fence, holding an assortment of flowers that gracefully fall across the wall, providing an explosion of color and a hint of fragrance. The parabolic shape to the courtyard inadvertently amplifies and focuses sound westward toward our long-suffering neighbor's home. The design subsequently masks the sun's appearance until shortly after noon in the summer and even later in the winter months.

I woke myself up with an epic fart. We are talking a fart worthy of an of Old Testament plague. Blood, frogs, boils, locust, lice had nothing on this one. It smelled of rotting eggs, festering gangrenous wounds and a not so recently deceased litter of maggot infested puppies. Rose was snuggled into the crook of my arm on the chaise lounge, snoring away, and drooling on my chest. She stirred and screwed her nose up in disgust from my noxious gift.

"You farted in your sleep, baby," I lied to her. It was a smelly, white lie.

"I'm sorry, baby. I'm so disgusting," she said as she nuzzled back into the crook of my arm. I didn't know how long I had been in the same position for certain, but at least long enough for my arm to lose all feeling. I propped myself up gently, moving Rose to one side of the chaise lounge. I spotted Frank spooning Ardy, both naked, sharing the same float in the pool and fast asleep, surrounded by assorted flotsam. A small pool of puke laced with bits of fish was surrounded by a swarm of flies, a battalion of ants, and a hairless cat. A canary yellow police summons was duct-taped to the adjacent stucco wall citing Rose for disorderly conduct and a noise violation. The glass to the pool room door was broken and shards of glass littered the pool deck. Annie Ruth was curled up in her slip on the Futon with a topless Bella. Ivy and Ruth shared the adjacent chaise lounge covered with a Hello Kitty beach towel. Mario, Esther, and Morris were walking amongst the litter of cups, bottles, clothes, puke, and cigarette butts, making an attempt to begin restoring order to the chaos.

Two notes were carefully pinned to my shirt. The first from Iris' caretaker Angel suggesting I reevaluate the limits of my home insurance liability policy and verify it to be paid in full. She added a crude drawing of what I took to be her index finger and the words "and the horse you rode in on." She further explained she had taken Iris to the emergency room. The second note was on a pink post-it. It contained the number 600,000 and nothing else.

"Good morning, brother," Esther greeted me.

"Stop yelling," I replied. "What time is it?" I asked.

"Almost noon."

"Damn." Rose said. "Can you two stop with all the racket?" She looked around for a moment as she woke up, taking in the carnage before silently laying back down with the crook of her arm covering her eyes. I nudged her. She sighed in disgust, "Please, God, tell me that is not Frank and Ardy naked in my pool."

I complied; "I am not God but I will do my best impression." I began in my finest James Earl Jones voice, which is not very good, believing his voice analogous to that of our Creator,

"That is not Frank and Ardy laying naked in your pool." Rose cracked an eye and wordlessly punched me.

"What was that for?"

"You lied."

"Excuse me, but I did exactly as instructed," I accurately noted, wondering if it is still a lie when you have been specifically instructed to utter said lie to the one and the same individual that gave the instruction.

Ruth stirred. "Good morning, Bride." Mario said.

"Shut the fuck up, Husband," Ruth replied. Mario grinned as if she had paid him the highest of compliments. Theirs was a most peculiar relationship.

Ivy cracked an eye. "Drugs. I need drugs," she said, pulling the towel around her, exposing the topless Ruth laying on her stomach. Her Viracocha tattoo had been embellished with a pair of remarkably blue eyes. Mario produced a towel and covered his wife's nakedness.

Ardy mumbled, "Damn." He was distracted from his current predicament peeking at Ivy and Ruth's wares with one eye open, hoping for a frontal view. And in an instant, fully comprehending his current compromising position, yelled "Damn" and jumped off the float, waking Frank in the process. "I ain't no homo," Ardy yelled at Frank.

"What's the matter with you, boy? I went yard with Bella last night. I ain't all queer for your fat ass," Frank replied.

"Die, please. Just die, the whole lot of you." Rose said, with her eyes still covered.

The note and the tattoo had a disquieting effect combined with the remaining alcohol and sleep-fueled fog. I felt anxious, agitated, and confused. "I'm going for a walk," I told Rose.

"Not until you get those naked creeps out of my pool."

Despite Rose's stern warning, I left without banishing the two creepy, naked dudes from the pool. After all, they may well be creepy old guys, but they were my creepy old guys. And it wasn't like her friends were saints. I found my way through the dunes to the wide beach. It was after Labor Day and as such, season was over; not that Jax Beach ever really has a tourist season. Only a handful of hotels front the beach and this far south, the beach is lined mostly with single family homes. Certainly one of the charms of our undiscovered slice of paradise is its uncrowded beaches. I walked south toward Ponte Vedra, as the majority of the sparse hotels, high rise condos, and public parking lay north. The ocean seemed exceptionally angry and the waves assaulted the beach, producing large sums of unappealing brown sea foam flung airborne in the stiff breeze. Rose calls it sea cum which explains a lot. Dozens of surfers and boogie boarders took benefit of the sea's rare tantrum and rode the unusually high waves with varying degrees of success. The Atlantic Coast is typically gentle and the surfers have precious little experience with navigating the forceful product of an angry ocean. I sat in the sand just out of reach of the sea cum to watch one surfer that seemed particularly skilled. His motions were graceful and fluid as he caught wave after wave, breaking only to paddle out effortlessly against the strong current. He had an uncanny grace about him that seemed oddly familiar and disquieting.

After nearly an hour, I got up to leave. The surfer locked eyes as I stood and waved like Forest Gump greeting Lieutenant Dan on the shrimp docks of Louisiana for the first time. His speedos and lithe, pre-pubescent teenage girl figure should have alerted me to his identity. Hobo caught a final wave all the way into shore, stepping off the board elegantly in just a few inches of water. He shook his entire body like a dog and wiped the salty water from his beard and hair. "Afternoon, Ezekiel. Good to see you survived the evening's festivities," he spoke and placed his board a few feet further up the beach away from the surf before plopping down beside me. "Where is my beer?" he asked.

"Really?" I responded. "Really" is the second most versatile word in the English vocabulary. It's meaning, based on tone, context clues, facial expression, and body language can run the gauntlet. Hobo never seemed to understand sarcasm. I think it is because sarcasm is akin to a lie and out of his ability to fully grasp.

"Really, Ezekiel. Why would I ask you a question I did not want you to answer?" Again, you can't fight crazy. Well, you can fight it, but it is like a toy poodle fighting a Mastiff. The winner is preordained. I deflected.

"Where is Aja?"

"Who?"

I shut my eyes and bowed my head in defeat. "You're kidding me, right?"

"Yeah. Just messing with you, buddy," Hobo said, grinning with over-whitened teeth. He continued, "See, I get sarcasm. I just choose to ignore it."

"You're real, right?" I asked.

Hobo pinched himself and squealed like a girl. "Darn, that hurt. Appears as such, based on your litmus test for reality. Problem is Ezekiel, you keep asking the wrong questions."

"Then what is the right question?"

"Do I look like the pompous Canadian Asshole Alex Trebek? See…sarcasm…I can use it in a sentence and include a pop culture reference."

"Really? You want a chocolate or something?" Not that Alex really qualified as current pop culture.

Hobo inquired, "Dark or milk? I don't like white chocolate. And is white chocolate even chocolate? Uhhh…Do you have candy-covered milk chocolate? M&M's I think you call them. Yum."

I just sighed, closed my eyes in disbelief, and nodded my head. Again, you simply cannot argue with crazy.

A pod of dolphins cut through the surf a few feet off shore with the same effortless grace of Hobo surfing. A seagull dove into the water just behind them, capturing a small mullet for lunch. A group of surfers jogged up behind us. One yelled back to a second group further down the beach, "Found your board, dude." He grabbed the board Hobo had borrowed and jogged off to meet him. I just shook my head.

After several minutes of silence, Hobo continued unprompted, "I can't give you the questions, just the answers to the right questions."

"I did attend South Georgia public schools, so forgive me when I ask what the hell are you talking about? You make no sense at all."

Hobo laughed. "That you did, buddy."

"I don't see your scrawny ass for years. Now all of sudden you pop back into my life. Why now?"

"Good question, Ezekiel. 'Cause I need you," Hobo replied.

"For what?"

"Look at you. On a roll. Two good questions in a row."

"Then answer it, Asshole."

"Always with the language. Your mother would wash your mouth out if she heard your filthy mouth."

"I am a crazy, ignorant asshole. We have established those facts, so save me the lecture and answer the damn question." I was already annoyed and Hobo was not helping.

"Your dreams, Ezekiel. I need to see your dreams."

I sighed. "My dreams make me crazy. I lock those away."

"You are not crazy, Ezekiel." He paused for a moment as if to consider the appropriate response and then continued; "Okay…you might slide just inside that definition, should one define crazy as the polar opposite of normal. But I prefer to think of you more as…let's call it special."

"You mean like short bus special."

Hobo smiled. "I see what you are doing. You're making a futile attempt at inappropriate humor to deflect your real feelings. I just don't understand your reference. But I mean special in that you can see things even I can't see. So dream, buddy, dream."

"Why?" I asked.

"Asked and answered, Counselor." Hobo chuckled at himself, using one of my lines on Rose when she persistently asked the same question in slightly varying forms, like a prosecuting attorney interrogating a hostile witness in order to get the desired answer. I do hate attorneys and attempt to avoid them at all costs, yet I married one. Rose played the extraordinarily hot card to get an exception.

"You see, Hobo, I can't tell the difference between my dreams and reality. Everything blurs."

"What makes you think there is a difference?"

"Junior High School physics class," I answered.

"The one you slept through and cheated off of Cathy Carter's paper to pass?"

I looked at him, puzzled. Hobo knew way too much about my life. Even things I had long since forgotten. "Yeah, that one," I replied.

"Perhaps then you should have paid more attention to Mr. Barnhill and less attention to Cathy's lovely white cotton panties."

REVELATION

"The great dragon was hurled down-that ancient serpent called the evil, or Satan, who leads the whole world astray. He was hurled to the earth, and his angels with him."

Revelation 12:9

CHAPTER SIXTEEN

At first it was a gentle, almost imperceptible flutter, just enough disturbance to cause me to stir in my sleep and shift from my right to left side. Easily dismissed, I farted, wiped the drool from the corner of my mouth and fell soundly back to sleep. The vibrations returned, but this time with enough force to jolt me fully awake. "What the hell?" I said to no one, simultaneously vaulting out of bed, assuming the innate defense posture more fitting for protection against ancient four-legged, long-tooth, predators than any likely modern threat scenario. We humans prefer to dismiss our animalistic programming. Yet, we are hardwired with specific instincts, desires, responses, emotions that, despite what we yearn to believe, live within us all. We are carnivores by birth and, at our very core, programmed to kill in order to defend what is ours and to take what we need to survive. Civility, charity, and sharing are learned responses and murderous rage lies within us all, even the self-righteous, lactose intolerant vegans among us.

Rose had already left for work but the sun had yet to fully illuminate the morning sky. The vibrations returned, persistent and deep. The sound resonated through the house, the bed, even the light cotton sheets appeared demon possessed by the vibrations. Northeast Florida is not generally prone to earthquakes. Massive sinkholes, big foot sightings, swamp fires, cataract impaired tour bus drivers, Yugo sized sharks, hurricanes, floods, gaily adorned mouse costumed adults, horrific lightning storms...yes...earthquakes, not so much.

The windows rattled powerfully against the unseen force in some curious but weighty effort to escape their frames. I was wide awake now. I went out on the balcony overlooking the backyard. A flat-gray U.S. Navy Seahawk flew directly overhead, seemingly mere feet above the metal roof. I ducked reflexively before another and another and another helicopter flew by in total darkness, all well below the normal 1,000-foot Navy imposed floor for training flight operations. I saw before I heard a pair of F18s banking hard and screaming bone-chilling-thunder as they turned west, easily overtaking the lumbering flight of Seahawks. The front windows shattered as both planes simultaneously engaged afterburners and broke through the sound barrier on completing their turns, creating a rare sonic boom over land. "What the hell?" I repeated from the instinctive crouched position I had assumed on the balcony.

Sirens filled the air, a discordant blend of car alarms activated by the pressure from the sonic boom and first responders urgently traveling to an unseen series of waiting emergences, each terrible in its own rights, but inconsequential to the coming gloom. I returned inside to catch the news. The power was off. I grabbed my cell. An "all circuits are busy" message greeted me. I tried the cell phone's web browser feature with similar but written results. I repeated what would become the question de jour; "What the hell?"

A growing cacophony of sounds assailed me as I walked downstairs and outside to the street. Dogs barked incessantly, sirens wailed, helicopters roared, people mumbled. Seemingly the entire neighborhood had walked outside and stood in varying stages of dress, looking up at the sky dumbfounded, speaking to each other in the whispered, frightened tone of dreadful ignorance. Another pair of F18s screamed off the ocean just over tree top level, bending the upper branches violently in their wake. We saw the war planes, quiet and deadly, full seconds before their sound fell over us with a powerful, thunderous rumble, causing several neighbors to squeal effeminately. Startled onlookers dropped ceramic coffee cups shattering mutely against the sun-cracked asphalt pavement. "What the hell?" This time I directed my question to Sam, although not really expecting a cognizant response based on his dumfounded expression. He was in his driveway, still in gym shorts and a wife beater freshly stained from spilled coffee and breakfast remnants. He shrugged. Sam's midgets (AKA his two youngest kids) Baby Sam and Lucy, not so small anymore, came running out of the house and jumped into his arms, causing him to drop his second cup of coffee in order to secure them within the pseudo safety of his loving arms.

"Endeavor to persevere."

I looked over to find Hobo standing beside us in Sam's driveway. He was sipping from an oversized mug with "Coffee makes me poop" in large brown letters on its side. Coffee mugs tell no lies. He was wearing a pink cotton terry cloth robe that looked disturbingly familiar and pink sock monkey bedroom slippers, also of a familiar ilk. His flaming orange hair was in contrasting pink curlers and his face, not covered by his unruly beard, was covered in a green, mud-like substance. I gave him my very best "you got to be frigging kidding me" look. "What the hell?"

Hobo responded, "I said 'endeavor to persevere.'"

"I heard what you said."

"Then why did you ask me what I said?" He looked at me, puzzled. Hobo can be an insufferable twit yet I have learned, after excruciating experience, not attempt to argue with crazy. Said endeavor is always a painful, losing proposition. Without adequate words, I sat silent for a moment. Sam put the midgets down and they scampered back inside to Flo, double-locking the door securely behind them in a futile attempt to keep the chaos at bay, or at least, out-of-doors. Sam had his forefinger and thumb resting on his chin stubble with eyes cast absent skyward in the classic thinker's posture.

"The Outlaw Josie Wales," Sam spurted out once his brain accessed the correct file. Playing the movie quote game seemed ill-fitting, given the ensuing chaos the morning's events presented.

"Bingo," Hobo said, with an approving smile and a subtle nod in Sam's direction.

"You are both bat-shit crazy," I responded.

"Language, Ezekiel," Hobo admonished. "Vulgarity is the crutch of the ignorant." Sam tried to Google the quote on his cell but with no success, as the internet remained inoperable. "The

Indian in the classic Clint Eastwood Western film, Ezekiel," Hobo offered as a scant explanation.

"So…"

Hobo shrugged like I was a complete idiot for not understanding his obscure movie reference. Sam's eyes lit up as he managed to access his extensive movie database and eagerly filled in the missing blanks for me. "Lone something or another was the Indian's name. He, the Indian, was telling The Outlaw Josie Wales what the Federal government had said to the Indians' complaint regarding the government's numerous treaty violations; 'Endeavor to persevere' the Indians were instructed."

"What the hell does that mean, anyway?" I asked.

"Exactly. What does that mean," Hobo repeated, articulating each syllable slowly, "En-dea-vor-to-per-sev-ere." He looked at my blank face and then at Sam. "Enlighten Ezekiel for me, Samuel."

"The rest of the quote from the Indian fellow was something like, 'and when we thought about it long enough, we declared war on the Union.'"

Hobo nodded again at Sam approvingly before directing his powerful gaze at me; "600,000, Ezekiel…600,000."

A blinding flash lit up the eastern sky as the sun broke the cloudless horizon. I was on the beach laying in the sand with nothing but an empty bottle of Jack keeping me company. "God damn dreams," I mumbled to no one.

***

Hobo was back in my life and with him, demons crept and slithered from the secure lockboxes of my carefully ordered mind. My cousin had long ago taught me a method to control my dreams. Well, actually, he taught me how to control my hiccups. It just so happened the same technique worked on my dreams and, as such, likely saved my life as a teenager. I had looked over the dark abyss a few times and found considerable favor in its dark, quiet comfort.

Kenny, my cousin, taught me to visualize each individual hiccup as a tangible object. If I recall correctly at the time, it was a steaming dog turd in his front yard he originally used as an example. Once I transferred the hiccup to something tangible with mass, I would wrap the object in old newspaper. Why newspaper is beyond me. Perhaps that was just the handy wrapping material of the times. (Author's note: A long, long time ago, news, along with a healthy dose of advertising, was printed on paper made from the pulp of pine trees and delivered to the front door by adolescent boys riding Schwinn bicycles. These archaic items were known to the natives as newspapers.) Regardless, once wrapped, I placed the object in a sturdy lockbox and placed the box on a shelf in a room I built specifically for storage in my mind. Sounds nuts, but I swear it worked like a charm for curing hiccups. With a little practice, I could control my hiccups after I noticed the very first one. And fortunately, the same method worked for my dreams…most of the time.

On more than one occasion in my life, I had to rebuild the storage room, add shelving, and fortifying the lockboxes to secure the ever-strengthening demons. Dreams for me can have the substance, weight, and feel of reality. Rose shared my dreams. It was likely this very commonality that served as the glue to our relationship. The initial attraction, at least on my part, was all physical. She was, is, smoking hot. But given our age gap, we would likely not have survived without this powerful and improbable commonality. Rose's Grams taught her a very similar method to capture and control her dreams. She was much better at it than I. Out of control, my dreams can creep into waking hours and reality blurs into a series of highly confusing, parallel, impossible possibilities.

I had come to the irrational conclusion that Hobo intentionally short-circuited my dream control mechanism for some bizarre, self-serving purpose. He says he needs to see them. For what reason is unclear but to fight Hobo is to swim against a powerful rip current. I need to swim parallel. Otherwise I will no doubt be washed out to sea or drown attempting to fight the invisible current.

Austin, Texas; October 2016: As promised, Texas Governor Bush vetoed the State Legislature Bill to secede from the Union. "The Bill, at a minimum, is unlawful and at its worst would lead to disastrous consequences," Bush stated. The Governor went on to warn the President to "back off." Unnamed high level sources within the Governor's administration report the Governor is very concerned his veto will be overridden.

The Political Action Committee known as Pedras Negras is funding a well-organized campaign encouraging the State's secession and the repeal of Governor Bush. It remains unclear as to the identity of the financial backers of the PAC. There is however growing speculation the Latin American drug cartel known as Los Zetas is involved with the PAC.

Bush has instructed the Secretary of State to enforce the new state law requiring voter ID and blocking the newly minted 2 million aliens granted amnesty from voting. The U.S. Justice Department received an injunction from the Fifth Circuit Court of appeals blocking the voter ID law. The Administration has threatened to send in Federal troops if necessary to enforce the injunction and oversee elections.

Alongside Global News

CHAPTER SEVENTEEN

"Don't poke the bear," Sam arbitrarily spewed out as peculiar a greeting as ever uttered, plopping down inelegantly into the beach chair beside me. He twisted the cap off the morning's first beer. Clearly he had something on his mind.

"Don't pee into the wind," I responded, thinking random tired clichés were in order.

Sam asked, "Do you ever watch the news?"

"Let sleeping dogs lie," I ignored his question, continuing to play tired clichés instead.

"Seriously, Dude. Do you ever watch the news?"

"A bird in hand…" I was on a roll.

"Really?"

"The early bird…"

"Dude!"

"Not unless Rose insists," I finally answered his asked question. "When did you grow your balls back and reclaim the remote from Baby Sam? And for Christ's sake, don't call me Dude."

Sam laughed. "The midgets slept over at your house, dumbass. Dumbass a more agreeable moniker?" Sam asked. I nodded in the affirmative. He continued, "Flo had a migraine, so I watched Big Lebowski last night for the fifth time. Top ten comedy and seriously under appreciated work of Jeff Bridges and the Coen Brothers. But, no really, crazy shit this is. The President is going to send federal troops into Texas. Federal troops!" He repeated for emphasis. "Not since Eisenhower sent the 101st Airborne into Arkansas to force integration on that state's public school system has a president deployed Federal troops against his own country. Big fucking deal!" he added, unnecessarily.

I'm a good Southern boy. You don't have to tell me deploying Federal Troops against your own people is a big deal.

"And the Black Panthers have mobilized some 3,000 members to bus into Texas to ensure Black and Latino voters aren't disenfranchised." I had been watching the news and Sam was right. Crazy shit. "Just what the hell does disenfranchised mean, anyway?" I asked Sam.

"Funny you ask. I looked it up. It means the revocation of the right to vote, according to Wikipedia. Interesting associated trivia... Women didn't get the right to vote until a full 50 years after Blacks were given that right just after the Civil War. And it was some four years later before all Native Americans were allowed to vote. Speaking of disenfranchised. We really screwed the Indians over."

"Speak for yourself. I have personally sent several Native Americans' children through college and financed a couple BMWs for their dads." I thought for a second, then added, "As a matter of record, I have not screwed an Indian, of the Native American variety at least, literally nor figuratively." There was this cute India Indian girl that worked at her family's convenience store back home. Sam looked at me, puzzled. "Casinos, Dumbass." He laughed. I continued, "And I thought 'disenfranchised' was some word Jessie Jackson invented in a futile effort to appear less imbecilic. And can't anyone post to Wikipedia as a source."

"Truth. Real word. I double-checked with Webster."

"Well since I guess you did not poke Flo, headache and all, who is poking who?"

"The President is poking Texas," Sam responded, ignoring my not so subtle dig. "And that there bear be big and ugly. Best not poke it unless you want to fight it. And best not fight it unless you plan to destroy it."

"Dude. You can't call your wife big and ugly."

"The bear, Dumbass, the bear."

A pair of F18s streaked across the sky, creating an eerie feeling of disquiet as I recalled my dream. Steve walked through the dunes in a business suit and black sneakers with white socks. I had forgotten I had asked him to meet me at the beach. Fortunately,

I had brought a third chair in case Hobo made an unscheduled appearance. I grabbed the chair out of the wagon and unfolded it on the sand. "Want a beer?" I asked Steve.

"Dude, it's illegal to drink on the beach." I shrugged. He pulled his jacket back, displaying a 9mm and a shiny, official badge. "Come on, Dude. I'm running for Sheriff."

"Remind me. Didn't you quit the force? What's that shiny tin badge on your belt there, hombre? A Cracker Jacks prize? And don't call me 'Dude'."

"I watched Big Lebowski last night. Under appreciated work by the Coen brothers."

Sam injected, "I know." I rolled my eyes.

"Pedro insists I wear the damn badge. The gun, I got a permit for."

I put our beers in red solo cups and placed the bottles in my backpack. Steve sat. "So, what do you need?" Steve pulled his chair into the shade under the umbrella, uncomfortably close to mine. I looked at him, puzzled. He offered, "I burn easy."

"You're black," I noted accurately.

Steve yanked the sleeve to his jacket back and looked at his arms in shock. "You don't say?"

I had spent much of the last few days trying to make sense of my crazy dreams and Hobo's cryptic clues. He was such an insufferable twit. He could just tell me what he wanted from me or at least be a bit clearer in which direction to search. Instead, Hobo tortured me with random tidbits of information from multiple sources, unleashed my inner demons to torment me with dreams, and then seemingly sat back to enjoy the show. I was his human Petri dish. Keep adding variables to the mixture and observe and document my subsequent reaction.

My fifth grade teacher, Mrs. Royal, was a great teacher. She taught me my multiplication tables, the secrets to unlocking word problems, the importance of common denominators, and that some women prefer tacos over sausage. Key lessons all. For word problems, Mrs. Royal had me write down what I knew and then what I wanted to know. Her system made it easier to organize my thoughts and, on occasion, come to the correct answer. Beauty is this technique, along with the critical importance of locating the common denominator, had proved helpful in solving most any kind of problem, math or otherwise. Even her proclivity to vagina taught me a valuable life-long lesson. Everything does not always fit neatly into a box. I knew Hobo was referencing the War of Northern Aggression. Damn Yankees like to call it the Civil War, but let's call it what it was. In the War, some 600,000 Americans lost their lives, which is more dead Americans than just about every other war combined in our history.

Secession was the common theme and the likely candidate for that secession was most certainly Sam's bear - Texas. Ardy had spotted El Frio Lobo, key money man for a Mexican drug cartel, in Belize and then again here in Jacksonville, with a possible front man from the Black Panthers. Outside money was pouring into Texas encouraging secession. The President was seriously messing with Texas, even threatening to send in the 3rd ID from Ft. Stewart to oversee "fair" elections. I randomly thought it was too bad Jimmy Carter had passed; he could have accomplished the task single-handedly. And the damn dream, it spoke for itself. So much for what I knew. What I wanted to know was how to get Hobo out of my head so I might sleep again without those freaky nightmares. Otherwise, I really did not know what I was solving for, as I was missing one critical half of the equation.

Earlier I had e-mailed Steve to see what he could dig up on El Frio Lobo and any likely connection he might have to the Blank Panthers. Maybe a closer inspection as to what I knew, or at least thought I knew, might lead me somewhere. Steve wasn't on the force anymore, but he remained very popular with the Sheriff's Department and he had FBI connections, as well. I was banking I could tweak his curiosity and harvest some useful intel. "You know you are crazy, right?" Steve asked. Sam and I both nodded in agreement. Steve stood, ducking under the umbrella and removed his jacket. Sweat was forming on his brow. "How is it you know this Frio Lobo dude?"

"Long story."

"Enlighten me."

I could tell he wasn't sharing unless I did some serious explaining. My problem was how to tell him what he needed to know without telling him the truth and sounding even crazier. "My buddy Ardy shared a cell with him overnight in a Belizean prison." Steve raised an eyebrow but remained silent. This was his interrogation technique. Remain silent and the other person becomes uncomfortable and feels compelled to fill in the silence with useful information. It's a great technique, particularly when the interrogator doesn't know squat, even enough to ask the right questions of the suspect. Suspect...That was how he was treating me. I didn't like that. I waited him out.

"What was your buddy doing in a Belizean prison?"

"He was charged with bestiality and soliciting a tranny prostitute at Ruth's wedding," I said, truthfully.

Steve had been around the block, but even so, his face showed a bit of shock. "Ardy? The Elmer Fudd looking dude?"

"That's the one."

Steve returned to his time honored strategy of silent interrogation. Advantage Zeke. I am an old, retired fart. I had all day, was more suitably attired to deal with the heat, and had access to a plentiful supply of icy-cold, refreshing beer. Supply chain management was my strong suit. His shirt was soaked through with sweat. Unfortunately for me, the silence was too painfully awkward for Sam, and he felt the need to fill the silent void with a fluid narration in its entirety of Ruth's wedding escapades. Advantage Steve.

Perversely, most of the story Sam knew only second-hand, as Flo had kept him safely locked away from the madness. I let him spew the always embarrassing, occasionally hurtful, yet spot on accurate details. Sam had good sources and an astonishing recall.

When Sam finished the colorful narrative, Steve looked at me with his head cocked to one side in a state of shocked disbelief and said, marking each point on his stubby fingers, "So let me get this straight…tranny, three-legged dog, shark attack, numerous incidents of bestiality, Mormons, little people dressed as court jesters, feces hurling monkeys, crocodiles, illegal sales of pirated Chinese made NFL merchandise, and a 100-year-old woman entered a wet t-shirt contest. All of this occurring during Ruth's wedding?" I was happy he had only ten fingers.

"Well, yeah, more or less," I mused before continuing, "but to be clear, not during the ceremony itself. And she won the wet t-shirt contest. Not just entered."

"What?" Steve asked.

"The one-hundred-year-old woman, Annie Ruth. She won the wet t-shirt contest," I helpfully explained. Not an important detail, but at least I had given him some information. Maybe it would provide me a few brownie points later when I omitted a few material facts. Steve slowly shook his massive, oversized head. If he were a dog breed, he would be a mastiff.

Cops, like doctors, are trained to avoid giving the appearance of judgment, irrespective of just how distasteful the actual circumstances. Even at times, proper interrogation procedure mandated the display of false empathy when only moral outrage and loathing are the germane reactions. "I see you stabbed your child bride 72 times for weeping profusely after receiving anal sex on your wedding night. All that crying just had to be annoying, right?" Or, for the Emergency Room Doctor, "I see you got your penis twisted off by a Black and Decker drill-powered masturbatory device. Was that the battery or AC operated model?" Just get to the facts and facts are better discovered without a hint of judgment, shock, or disapproval. Empathy, understanding, and camaraderie or the necessary and sometimes repulsive tools to uncover the ugly truth, no matter how revolting. Steve was struggling on the nonjudgmental account.

"You have one freaky family, Zeke."

"You don't know the half of it, Steve," I said. Sam shook his head in all too eager agreement.

"Still doesn't explain how you know El Frio Lobo."

"That a question?" I asked. Steve narrowed his dark, intelligent eyes. He was a friend, a good friend, but the cop in him was coming out and he could tell I was not "coming clean" with him. I decided to try a tiny bit of the truth as otherwise he was not going to help me. I sent Sam to get more beer to get Steve alone and, well, to get more beer. We were running low. Kanban, man. All that Business School bullshit was really starting to pay real world dividends. I was highly-qualified and quite capable to diagram the ethical business decision process utilized with the skills learned at college and I knew the rules of bowling and badminton. Money and time well spent. And we wonder why Asian countries are kicking our ass. They take advanced physics and calculus classes while our kids are getting schooled on pop culture, cultural studies, art appreciation, basketball, fashion, beer brewing, cultural sensitivity, gender neutral speak and advanced pet grooming.

"Look, Steve," I began and paused to gather my thoughts.

"I am all ears," Steve said. I started to make a smart ass remark regarding the massive size of his head, not his ears, but rightfully chose to let it pass. A reckless smart ass lived inside me. He, the smart ass, was there to help keep me sane, but I needed to let him, the smart ass, rest on occasion. This was said occasion.

"We have established I'm crazy." He nodded in the affirmative, absent the courtesy of a smile. "Since I was a kid, I have had these bizarre dreams. Really more akin to visions than dreams. And sometimes they blur with reality. Make sense?"

Steve was a man accustomed to dealing with cold, hard facts and with the artful liars that always attempted to distort those facts for their own self-preservation and benefit. He replied, without humor, "Not in the least."

I looked around the beach for a middle-aged woman. They rarely travel sans purse, replete with compact lipstick and mirror.

Not judging, just stating facts. A few feet down and back from us were two well-toned ladies, a bit on the downhill side of prime practicing the time honored ritual of solar-powered skin ruination. At least the sunbathers on the beach were utilizing a green renewable energy source. (Note to self. Get rich schemes number 87. Invent solar clothes dryer. Tree huggers will embrace as giant step forward in green energy.) I jumped up. "I'll be right back."

I feigned something in my eye as a plausible excuse to interrupt their sun worship and to ask to borrow a mirror. "Oh, honey, let me take a look." I had failed to properly consider all the possible outcomes of my strategy. Damn those infallible laws of unintended consequence. The ladies, not all together unattractive sorts, were a few sheets into the wind. Their inebriated condition had rendered me magically handsome, despite the superb lighting conditions, and consequently flirt worthy. Sam, damn his Michelangelo's David looking self, apparently made the cut without the benefit of beer goggles. "Your handsome friend coming back any time soon?" I wondered if they had flipped a Susan B. Anthony to see who had the unfortunate wingman obligation and was stuck with me. Their infatuation with Sam did however give birth to a new approach to my immediate dilemma.

"Yes he is. I'll send him back over with the mirror." I gave an exaggerated wink. "He is a bit shy so you're gonna have to work a bit for it. Inside tip…he's a boob man."

My strategy proved effective. The lady breast equipped eagerly surrendered her compact. She extended a perfectly manicured hand introducing herself. "Hi, there. I am Martha, Martha Perdue." There it was again. That intense feeling of déjà vu. I did a double take. She looked familiar, but for the life of me I could not place her. "You see a ghost, honey?" Martha asked.

"Yes…I mean, no. Sorry. It's just, you look familiar. Do you live around here?"

Martha pointed back toward the dune crossing at a large, Cape Cod style home overlooking the ocean. "I used to live right there. I downsized and moved across the ditch when my daughter went off to college." Locals referred to the Intracoastal Waterway separating the beaches of Jacksonville from Jacksonville proper, as the Ditch. She fished a business card out of a canvas bag with what appeared to be a wine bottle in the background and offered the card. "I'm a professional masseuse. Feel free to call me if you ever need my services. I give great hand." Martha winked. Her friend laughed. The more she talked, the more familiar she seemed. Perhaps I had met her on the beach before. I started walking away. Martha called out. "Hey, Tiger. Don't forget to send your friend back over." Martha winked again and pointed her finger at me like a pistol. I stopped dead in my tracks.

"How is your husband?"

"Dead," she offered nothing else and put her ear buds in, closed her eyes, and laid back onto her towel.

I walked back to Steve, who by now was sweating profusely in the shade of the multi-colored umbrella. One would think those of African descent more tolerant of tropical climates. One would think wrong, at least in Steve's case. Was that racist? I have never quite grasped why an honest observation of a seemingly self-evident, non-judgmental, fact can be offensive and, consequently, racist. But I drink a lot.

Hobo had demonstrated a little trick with a mirror on two separate occasions. I tried the illusion on Steve. I held the mirror out about arm's length and asked Steve what he saw in the mirror's reflective surface. He impatiently wrinkled his deep-furrowed brow. "Humor me," I requested.

Steve reluctantly began, "A couple little girls building a poorly designed, asymmetrical sand castle, a pink stucco house just over the dunes in dire need of a paint job, and two sunburnt middle-aged white women adjusting oversized manufactured breasts in their undersized, brightly-colored swim tops."

"Well that was all in all a bit judgmental," I noted. Without moving the mirror, I said, "Okay, my turn. I can't see but one of the sand castle girls. And I kind of admire the chaos in their design. Yup, there is Martha and her friend. Damn, those tits appear even larger in the mirror." I editorialized. "And I see an unleashed black lab with a jacked up jaw taking a massive dump."

"Get to the point, Zeke."

Still holding the mirror stationary, "Now move three feet to the left and tell me what you see." Reluctantly, he did as instructed and left the shade of the umbrella. Steve described an entirely different scene in a bored, somewhat annoyed, monotone. Steve moved back to the relative coolness of the shade. "Still don't get your point."

"A single surface, in this case Martha's make-up mirror, can reflect multiple, divergent images, all simultaneously. Each imagine is unique and relative to the observer's point of view."

"And?"

"You are the dense one. What is in that big head of yours, a massive vacuum? Is it possible that there are multiple images, realities if you will, occupying this same space..." I waved my arms around the beach "... at this very moment with each reality, independent of the others and dependent on the observer's point of view?"

"Like I said. You are crazy."

"Not arguing that point. Let's just assume my little mirror theory of reality is correct and somehow I have the ability to catch glimpses of those different realities."

"Again, crazy."

"Again, not arguing."

"And still doesn't explain how you know El Frio Lobo."

"Yeah it does. I have seen the bastard in my dreams." I omitted the middle age sunbather Martha and the home invasion incident. A little crazy goes a long way. At least for now she was not an important part of this story.

Sam returned from his logistical resupply mission with ample beer. I twisted the top off a cold one and handed Sam the compact mirror. "Please take this back to the ample-bosomed ladies currently staring at your hot little ass," I motioned toward Martha and her friend. I am a man of my word. Sam shrugged, took the mirror, and ambled into a well-orchestrated ambush. He is the somewhat gullible, compliant sort and perhaps I harbored a smidgen of irrational jealousy.

Martha's bathing suit top was not securely fastened, no doubt a deliberate, self-inflicted sabotage in order to manufacture a timely wardrobe malfunction. I secretly wondered if she might have a smiley-face pasty affixed to her nipple. When she leaned forward to accept the compact's return, her breasts accidentally toppled out. There was no pasty. Absent requisite sunshine exposure, her breasts were pale as alabaster and smooth, a stark contrast to the remainder of her deeply-tanned and grooved skin. Once a stunning woman, she had not aged particularly well.

"I'm so sorry," she coquettishly giggled, making a half-assed attempt to cover the starkly contrasting skin. Her dark, symmetrical areola peeked out from between her fingers. Steve shook his head in mock disgust but did not avert his large, brown eyes. If I were an honest man, not frightened by the repercussions of truth, I would admit the breasts were quite unexpectedly impressive. As I am not, let's just say I did not notice. Sam tripped over the unleashed, black lab beating a hasty retreat. He fell hard onto the sand. The lab scampered away, chasing a squirrel that dared breach the dunes. Both ladies jumped up to assure their Adonis' wellbeing. Martha, in her haste, failed to securely reattach her top and, as she knelt to assist Sam, both breasts hovered fully exposed in their pale glory, only millimeters from his face. As fate would have it (Murphy's Law is, after all, a law and not a mere guideline), Flo, Sam's sometimes adoring wife, breached the sea oat covered dunes just as Martha lovingly cradled Sam's semi-conscious head in her arms. I took great solace in the knowledge that Steve was sufficiently armed.

After yelling, "See you at home, Ward," in Sam's general direction, Flo surprisingly pivoted in the sand, returning in the direction she came.

Steve looked at me, puzzled. "Sam's wife just call him Ward?"

I laughed. "Yeah. Pet name as in Ward Clever." Steve still looked puzzled. I continued, "'Cause he is always looking for Beaver?"

Sam fully regained consciousness and quickly freed himself from Martha's unwelcome embrace. "Is this your first concussion?" I asked Sam.

"Huh?"

"Exactly. Time to go home. You got some 'splaining to do, son." I was mixing my sixties TV shows.

"Huh?"

I nodded my head to the still topless Martha hovering above him. He crab-crawled away with remarkable agility and speed as if her bare breasts were his personal kryptonite. They may well be. He was in for an ass-kicking when he got home. Rose would have first kicked Martha's ass then mine. Afterwards, she would have lovingly cared for me and brought me back to good health just to kick my ass again.

Sam stood and started meandering back toward the dune crossing, clearly ignorant in the totality of the compromising critical details of the last few minutes. He paused and looked back toward us as Martha hurriedly gathered her bikini top, belongings, remaining dignity, and friend and beat a hasty exit over the dune crossing just north of us. "Deny, deny, deny. In the face of overwhelming evidence to the contrary, deny. Works for our president, surely it will work for you," I gave Sam my best advice. Steve chuckled. Sam turned and disappeared through the dunes.

Steve refocused his attention on me, narrowing his dark eyes. "So, you know El Frio Lobo from a dream?"

"Yes," I offered.

"Elaborate," Steve demanded.

"Were you good at this interrogation thing once?" I asked.

"Yeah, I was, but in my day, I could pistol whip a smart-ass like you."

"So you were the bad cop."

"Only when I won the coin toss. Quit your stalling."

209

"You recall all the brouhaha over the Mayan calendar ending back in 2012?" I began, but quickly regretted leading with the thought. Steve nodded in the affirmative but otherwise remained silent. "It's a long story, but to summarize, an unlikely group of conspirators plotted to fix the 2008 presidential election. Frio Lobo was one of the conspirators. It started out as a kind of bad thing and ended as a really bad thing. Shit went horribly wrong."

"How come I have never heard this story?"

"You not only heard it, you and the large-breasted one you were just ogling were an integral part of the story," I tried to explain. Steve in that dream investigated the home invasion in on behalf of Martha's insurance company.

"You are crazy."

"And you are not listening."

"No. I hear you, Zeke. You are just talking gibberish."

"Maybe my dreams are just dreams, or maybe..."

Steve interrupted me. "Dude, you drink a whole lot. Maybe your dreams are just drunken hallucinations."

"Maybe. Or maybe they are alcohol-lubricated glimpses into other worlds parallel to this one," I offered.

We sat in silence. I rarely shared. I knew how crazy I sounded, as it sounded pretty damn crazy to me. Finally I broke the silence. "You don't have to believe me beyond a shadow of doubt. I don't even believe myself more than..." I thought for a moment. Just how much did I believe in myself? I spilt it down the middle. "...Fifty-fifty. Just give me a tiny shred of trust. I can't explain this...this, whatever it is. Hell, I can't even name it. But it's like a strange, ravenous hunger for which I am at its mercy. I am compelled to follow a preprogramed path. When I try and turn down another path, it just leads back to where I began. If you can help shed even a tiny bit of light, it might save lives...at least one, Steve...mine."

Steve answered. "This guy, Zeke, is major league bad news. I'm talking first team, all-star varsity player for the bad guys.

Best let anything to do with the Lobo asshole alone. Let the authorities handle him. I am trying to protect you from yourself."

"But you can't. No one can. This is my fate. Just help me understand if there is a link between El Frio Loco and the Black Panthers organization. Can you do that for me?"

He seemed moved by my sudden sincerity. He was accustomed to the smart-ass version of me, not the serious one. "Against my better judgment, I will try, Zeke. I will try."

Steve rose to leave. A four-wheeled mule manned with two Citizens On Patrol pulled up in the sand just behind us. They both eyed Steve with more than a tiny bit of suspicion. He was not dressed for the beach. The younger COP, a vertically challenged woman of about 70, spoke. "Either of you two seen a black lab not on a leash?" I'm not ratting out the poor beast to the COPs…even if they were two old ladies armed only with two way radios and self-righteous indignation. I shrugged. The COP pointed her radio at me aggressively. "Son, you do know there are strict leash laws. If that is your black dog, I will write you a citation." I quickly assessed the second COP. She was pushing 80. The two of them combined weighed less than 180 pounds. I could take the old bitches and get serious street creds from the local gangs for taking down not one, but two, COPs simultaneously, assuming the newspapers were a bit sketchy on the finer details of the incident.

The smart-ass version of me returned. "I think they prefer the term African-American these days. And an African-American lab has just as much right to be on this beach as a Golden Retriever."

Steve walked off, shaking his head. The black lab ran up to me from behind the dunes and started licking my hand and began rooting around in my bags. He dumped my cooler over, spilling a dozen or so empty and full cans and bottles of beer onto the sand. The COP radioed for back up.

"What's your dog's name?" the recently arrived Animal Control Officer asked.

"Not my dog." The lab continued licking my now handcuffed hands, with an occasional full-frontal face lick. His breath smelled like shit.

"Whatever, Dude. Here's you a citation for having an unleashed animal and yet another for having a dog on the beach between 9 AM and 5 PM. You can come pick up your dog at the shelter, but do so within five days or he is subject to being put down."

"You are going to kill a dog for shitting on the beach? Seems a bit harsh."

"What do you care, Dude? Not your dog, remember?"

"Stop calling me Dude."

"Sorry, Dude. Watched Big Lebowski last night. Truly an under appreciated film."

The Cop, the real one with a gun, released my handcuffs and handed me a third ticket, this one for consuming alcohol on the beach. "I get the death penalty, as well?"

"No, but if you don't shut the hell up, I am going to let those officers tase you in the nuts," he responded, pointing toward the two elderly Citizens On Patrol resting in the shade of their mule. Both of the aged pseudo-law enforcement officers were clearly excited at the possibility of picking up serious street creds at the assisted living facility for taking down an unruly perp. My, how the tables had turned. I wisely chose to shut my mouth, clearly disappointing the two of them.

Washington, D.C.; August 2016: The Secretary of Defense announced his resignation today. The resignation came just days after reports surfaced of increased friction between the White House and the Pentagon. The Secretary was reportedly frustrated at the continued micro-managing of the Defense Department by the White House inner circle. Fox News reported The Secretary had instructed his Generals to tell the White House to "go to hell" the next time they received a call from White House personnel.

The Secretary will remain in place until the President can find a replacement. A spokesperson for the Senate Majority leader speculated the likelihood of the President receiving Senate approval for a replacement prior to the end of his term was "highly unlikely."

Alongside Global News

CHAPTER EIGHTEEN

Rose was outraged. She was by no means a dog person, but the idea of putting a helpless animal down disturbed her well-cultivated sense of justice as well as her overpriced legal education. I described the lab to Rose with his misshapen jaw and exposed canine tooth. The combination gave him a permanent resting bitch face. He was jet black but for a white hour glass patch on his chest. And not just jet black. From any angle but the front, his luxurious fur absorbed all light and he appeared only as a cut out silhouette, absent any discernible detail. From the front, the patch, I further noted to Rose, gave him the unlikely appearance of being formally dressed in a tux.

I should have been wicked pissed at the beast. The hairy bastard cost me over $300 and damn near an electrical nut shot from two power drunk old biddies. Well, I shouldn't really blame the beast for the beer. I did that. But the other two citations were all him and after I had so heroically come to defend his honor. Rose called the Duval County shelter. The dog had been transferred.

Fortunately, the dog's transfer was to a no-kill shelter called Kamp Kritter. The K's were placed backwards on the shelter's website, giving the improbable suggestion that the dogs could spell, at least phonetically, but were a touch dyslexic. Suspend disbelief. Jaws was featured on the website. No mistaking he was the dog in question. Jaws, a four-year-old black lab and indeterminable breed mix had been rescued drowning in a vat of oil in an abandoned chemical plant in the heart of Jacksonville's least delightful zip code. His misshapen jaw and exposed tooth were from unknown origins, but were reportedly from an earlier injury that had healed improperly. Seemed Jaws had been a welcomed guest at the shelter for a spell, which made his appearance on the beach a bit of a mystery. Rose e-mailed. Susan, the shelter's owner and operator, responded almost immediately.

Jaws had been placed at a home in Jax Beach near our house. Susan noted Jaws was a bit of a "fuck tard." Her words. Don't judge. Jaws had escaped the home on several occasions and the family subsequently surrendered him back to Kamp Kritter after being notified by the county animal control officer of his most recent capture. I found it interesting I had not been contacted to have the citation rescinded once the proper owners had been identified. I guess revenue is revenue unless it comes from taxes paid by married couples in possession of similar plumbing. God forbid we allow a revenue stream that permits same gendered taxpayers to enter a tax bracket dominated by the traditional family mold from the 50's. That would lead to the decline of society. But once again, I digress as I tend to do. Rose inexplicably made an appointment to meet Jaws.

"But you hate dogs." Hate was not the right word. Dogs scared her shitless.

"Not this one. He, I don't know, speaks to me."

"The wine good tonight, Love?"

"Don't be an ass. I just want to meet him."

***

Kamp Kritter is on the north side of town, located at the crossroads of I-10, I-95, and the expressway to hell. You never really expect animal shelters to be in finer gated subdivisions, but this one was located in the heart of an urban war zone. Just across the way from a homeless shelter, the street was littered with crack whores, drug dealers, convicted felons, not yet convicted felons, and interspersed with hard-working, law-abiding families trying to survive the infectious brew. I always felt a bit sorry for dudes on crack. Women inherently possess portable, marketable merchandise to trade for drugs in lieu of cash. Men, much less so.

We both packed for the occasion; Rose, her pink .38 special and me, my 9mm Glock. Serious times called for serious tools. Rose's left-handed revolver was vivid pink with its moniker "The

215

Pink Lady" engraved on it, but there was no mistaking it remained a .38 and quite capable of punching a fair-sized hole through its intended target and with the added benefit of inflicting a small dose of humiliation at being crippled by Barbie's piece. I would have taken the pump 12-gauge shotgun if I could have figured out a suitable method of concealment. We pulled into the small gravel parking lot adjacent to the shelter. Susan met us before we exited our car. Security cameras in this neighborhood were not a luxury. We walked into the front entrance of the shelter to a cacophony of barking dogs and the overpowering smells of a multitude of closely-housed animals. Noah, no doubt, farmed vegetables exclusively after deboarding the Ark.

There must have been fifty dogs of a combination of mostly mixed breeds in the joint. The predominate breed, no great surprise given the neighborhood, being some derivative of pit bull. Some were in cages, excuse me, crates, while others roamed freely about the building's cramped interior. An unmade double bed occupied the corner of the room. The area was walled off by a makeshift combination of crates, portable fences, and boxes. Three ankle biters barked incessantly from inside what appeared to be Susan's personal space. One had taking the liberty of depositing a rat-sized shit on the bed. Susan invited us into her office. We followed the meandering path through the improvised housing and storage and stepped over a kid's safety gate to enter her cluttered office. On her desk was a large, formidable looking knife, a semi-automatic pistol, and a half empty fifth of Jack Daniels...the essentials for a party on the north side. An assortment of mail order pharmaceuticals also littered her desk. She offered, as unsolicited explanation, the drugs were cheaper from India and "the exact goddamn thing." Who could argue with that logic? Although I was a bit fuzzy on the heavenly damnation. The purpose for the weapons and Jack were self-evident, requiring no further explanation. An older MAC computer sat on her desk with her Facebook page pulled up on the screen. A second computer monitor displayed the exterior views from eight security cameras.

She noticed me looking. "Nothing like watching a bunch of crack heads going through your garbage at midnight. Imagine their surprise when all they find is dog shit from fifty dogs. Tee hee." Who needs reality television when you have reality life?

Another dog of indeterminate breed was lying motionless under her desk. A wolf, or at least a hybrid wolf, standing 19 feet tall and weighing in slightly north of a metric ton ambled up to the gate and stuck its head in. I was a more than a bit frightened. Its blue eyes were suspicious of our presence. I avoided eye contact and assumed a non-threatening posture. Pretty damn sure the wolf could steal my soul or any other body part it so desired.

Susan herself was just over five foot tall with short, sandy hair. I would guess late forties perhaps early fifties, she was wiry thin. She wore a pair of old Converses, soiled jeans, and a t-shirt without the benefit of a bra. Retired Air Force military police, Susan was no nonsense and possessed a sailor's mouth and an angel's heart. Apparently they are issued for all branches of military service not just the Navy. The mouth…not the heart. Quickly it became apparent Susan lived at the shelter full time, sharing the cramped quarters with the assortment of dogs. Susan was not a cat person. We all have our boundaries.

The wolf issued a low guttural growl. Susan laughed at our discomfort and said, "Welcome to my Island of Misfit Animals." She explained she took in the hard to adopt and the downright impossible to adopt animals. She gave them a loving home, if not a luxurious one, to live out their natural lives. An odd duck Susan, yet I am most certainly unworthy to stand in judgment. Quite frankly, I am truly thankful there are those like her that walk among us mere mortals.

The doorbell rang. The dogs answered the bell with a renewed vigor of various pitch, volume, and frequency. Fingernails scratched across a chalkboard could not have made a more maddening sound. (A chalkboard is an illustrative tool utilized in classrooms by prehistoric teachers to torture their charges with unsolvable riddles of reading, writing, and

217

arithmetic.) Susan took a peek at her security monitor and said, "Ahhh. The Girl Scouts have arrived. They volunteer here every Saturday."

Susan went to answer the door, leaving the wolf to more than adequately mind her office. I looked at Rose with raised eyebrow thinking Susan was pulling our leg. Rose never took her eye off the wolf. A troop of Girl Scouts wandered into the facility, the oldest no more than twelve. "I'll be damned." I pinched my exposed forearm. It hurt. I silently wondered if the Girl Scouts had a badge for bravery. The girls, each in turn, greeted the wolf with a friendly embrace. We followed the scouts out through the back door to an enclosed area that was remarkably clean. The girls began raking what little shit was on the ground and picking up miscellaneous debris. Susan explained the girls would play with the gentle dogs once we left. It gave the dogs and the girls a bit of mutual entertainment, exercise, and pleasure. It's an odd relationship, man and dog. We can't speak but we communicate almost on a higher level…If we only listen.

Susan brought out Jaws from a metal out building, located adjacent to the main shelter. He was in full-on beast mode, and, at 75 pounds, he was a formidable beast. He immediately jumped on my chest, drawing blood through my thin t-shirt. He jumped on Rose and instead of the expected scream of abject terror, she simply giggled. Susan reminded us, "I did say he was an 'f' tard. This one is not the brightest bulb in the chandelier, but he has a sweet, sweet ancient soul." Jaws looked at Susan, almost as if to say, "Standing right here." I looked at Rose, mystified. She sat on a crudely constructed plywood stage with Jaws sitting beside her, licking her face. Rose was smitten.

"Can we adopt him?" Rose asked.

"You know he licks his balls with that tongue. And you hate dogs," I argued.

"His butt, yes…phantom balls, maybe," Susan helpfully corrected, making a snipping motion with her fingers. Women can be so damn insensitive.

"You just wanted to meet the hairy bastard. You met him. Let's go home." I peeked at my scratch. I thought rightfully it might require stitches. After a brief inspection of the wound, I concluded the bastard must be part grizzly bear.

Rose grabbed Jaws by the muzzle. "How could you leave this adorable face?" Jaws' face was seriously misshapen. One eye was slightly smaller and set lower on his face. He drooled liberally and was a noxious serial farter of the first order. His legs appeared foreshortened relative to his broad stance and unnaturally long neck. Overall, Jaws' appearance was as if a kindergartner had made a commendable, yet failed attempt to sketch a cartoon dog. Adorable certainly not the word most would use to describe the unfortunate creature.

"Kidding, right? That little asshole cost me $300 bucks." Jaws pointed his paws at himself, smiled broadly and said, "This guy." Okay…Maybe I imagined that part. But in his head, I am pretty sure it happened.

"Jaws didn't drink beer on the beach. That was all you, Husband."

I started to argue. But, like crazy, you can't argue with women. Then again, that sentence is somewhat redundant. "Okay, $150 bucks."

Rose told Susan the story. She laughed. "I'll waive the adoption fee," she offered. Clearly her shelter was seriously underfunded and she was in no position to discount the fee and turn away cash. After all, we drove to the shelter in a Benz. Yet this was a woman that truly loved animals and did everything within her limited power to make a difference, including personal sacrifices that included living a pauper's life herself. Attention self-righteous, over indulged, members of the clergy. This was what a vow of poverty looks like. I admired this remarkable woman. I had no desire to trade places with her, but my God, she was something very special. She gave a damn and did something to make a difference. You can't save the world, but you can make a difference one person, or, in her case, one misfit dog at a time.

Imagine the remarkable beauty of a world filled with Susans. Living in squalor after serving her country, she sacrificed and chose to make a difference. Color me suitably impressed.

I'm not saying Susan was a hero, even though that designation's currency has been seriously devalued. As a society, we assign the hero moniker like soccer participation trophies to this generation's coed under 11 league. A marked distinction exists between victim, casual bystander, and hero that our liberal, tree-hugging, self-indulgent, irresponsible culture has managed to blur. Dying at the hands of terrorists makes one tragically an unfortunate victim. Merely having the unfortunate luck to be present at a disaster does not elevate one to hero status. Unnecessarily risking serious bodily harm to save others makes one a hero. And watching from a safe location and calling 911 on the cell phone just makes one a bystander.

My definition of hero requires the unselfish risk of personal bodily harm in order to save another. Think front-line (insert any military branch here) medic. Risking one's life to save another. HERO. Donating even exceptionally large sums of cash does not make the hero cut, either. Bill Gates, for instance, is not a hero. There is a word for that: Philanthropist. Bill is a very good philanthropist and I expect many good things have come from his considerable contributions. He may have even saved lives through donations, but not at the risk of his own. Important distinction. Steve Jobs might suggest, should he speak from the grave, that Bill was a much better philanthropist than a software designer. But I'm just speculating here. Jobs and Gates were certainly the Edison and Tesla of our time, each revolutionizing the advancement of technology while simultaneously publicly undermining the importance of the other's work.

Just a wild, tangential thought, given the impressive advancements in computing, communications, and data storage in just the last half of my life, where will technology be in a hundred years? A wandering mind is the product of genius…or perhaps, in my case, excessive alcohol consumption. Susan was an amazing human being and likely capable of heroic actions, but not a hero…just yet, at least. And calling 911, performing CPR, returning a lost billfold to its rightful owner, giving a few bucks to the down on their luck; these actions should be intrinsic. It frightens me our society has degenerated to the point we find need to give special recognition for what should be obligatory acts of human kindness.

A familiar silhouette exited a make-shift storage room on the edge of the property. Thin, with wild hair, I was almost certain of his identity even before his familiar odd odor confirmed it. "Hello, Hobo," I greeted him. "Imagine seeing you here." He was wearing pink cowboy boots, cut-off jean shorts cut just below the knee, a pink halter top, and swim goggles. He was a slave to high fashion.

"Why would I be anywhere else? What better shelter for the beings indigenous to Canis Major?" Hobo continued, "Why are you here? Or, are you here? For that matter, the better question, is anybody really here?"

Rose took a moment from fawning over Jaws, "Cut the bullshit, Hobo." She had grown increasingly aware and weary of the effect Hobo's presence had on me.

"Language, Rose," Hobo admonished.

"Really?" I said. "Susan curses like a sailor."

"She was an airperson, not a sailor. And not in front of nine-year-old girls."

Susan pointed at the Scouts, nodding in the affirmative while mouthing, "air MAN." Susan was not PC.

"Yeah, Rose. Who the hell curses in front of little girls?" I asked.

I pulled Hobo aside while Jaws continued to woo Rose with his beastly charm. He was in full on fuck tard mode. Hobo placed his leathered hand on my chest. "That wound is going to require a few stitches. Too bad my Belizean friend is not here to take care of that for you."

"The old crone?" He was talking about the old woman that gave me the mysterious disc wrapped in a tobacco leaf in Belize. "What was the disc for, Hobo?" I had never received an explanation.

"You know, Ezekiel. It's the key to the ancient Peruvian stone door. I'm going home soon as you finish up with this mess."

It was self-evident Hobo elevated crazy to an entirely different plateau. That said, I kind of knew what he was talking about. In and around the Lake Titicaca area of South America, there is a series of mysterious gates or doors. Some believe they date back to before the Pyramids were built. Then again, some believe in Santa Clause, the Easter Bunny, the tooth fairy and honest politicians. Oddly, the massive stone gates were constructed to exacting standards, even by modern day criteria. The particular gate Hobo spoke of is at Puerta de Hayu Marka in Peru. Inside the massive gate lies a smaller, rectangular indention, shaped and sized similar to a run of the mill door. Within this indention lies a circular indention about the size of a Frisbee. Legend has it, a missing disc fits into the indention, unlocking the gate. Where the hell the gate leads is a subject of even zanier speculation.

"Done with what?" I asked.

"With what you were created to do, Ezekiel. Illuminate." Another familiar oddity came scampering out of the storage shed. The three-legged mutt Rose called Tripod jumped into Hobo's arms.

"What the hell, man?"

Tripod licked Hobo's beard until it was dripping wet and Hobo placed the three-legged Belizean mutt on the ground. "He makes for a great guard dog." Hobo answered.

"What the hell do you have to guard?" I asked. "Your collection of stolen ladies panties?"

"I see what you did there. A failed attempt at sarcasm meant to be humorous. But no, you are quiet welcome to choose any or all of my panties you care to wear. I am a sharer by nature. Senor Feliz is guarding my precious metal stash."

"You have gold in that storage shed?" I asked incredulously. This was not the neighborhood to store gold in a metal shed guarded by a miniature disabled guard dog. Then again…

Hobo's face conveyed a rare moment of confusion. "Why would I be storing gold? Senor Feliz is guarding my quicksilver."

Washington, D.C.; August 2016:   The White House Press Secretary announced today the President's intent to seek an "Enabling Act" allowing the President to pass laws outside of Congressional approval. The Press Secretary noted the President's growing frustration dealing with the Republican controlled Congress.

Speaker Ryan gave a single word comment; "Nuts."

Senate majority leader McConnell, in a more lengthy comment, echoed Ryan's sentiment; "If the President thinks he can get this Bill passed Congress, basically usurping the Constitutional powers granted to Congress... he is delusional."

Fox News White House Correspondent Ed Henry asked the Press Secretary to comment on a similar power grab by the Nazi's in 1933. The Secretary declined comment.

Alongside Global News

CHAPTER NINETEEN

The newest member of our family made himself comfortably at home on the black leather sofa. Jaws strategically located himself between Rose and me in order to receive the maximum attention. He preferred a four-handed massage. As was his custom, he began licking his phantom balls while simultaneously passing epic gas. This one was a world class charmer. Something about this hairy, black bastard was special. Don't ask me what. I could not tell you, nor could Rose. She never wanted a dog. She hated them, but this one she loved; no, something more than love. I don't have a word that adequately communicates the enormous magnitude of her feelings toward this smelly, ball-licking, clumsy, deformed, prince of a beast. And Rose did not fall gradually in love with Jaws. It was as if she fell off a steep cliff from first sight. I believe Jaws was Rose's analog for something deeply loved and lost. Remarkable.

The doorbell rang several times in rapid succession. Sam and family were coming over to grill some yard bird. Beef prices had skyrocketed with the craziness in Texas. No steak tonight. Damn that Adam Smith and his invisible hand. Jaws attempted a graceful leap off the couch to answer the persistent bell. Epic fail. His paws are enormous and his nails long and sharp. I think he may be half-black bear and half-circus clown. We have an abundance of both in Florida. Unlikely as hell, but most certainly stranger occurrences have been widely documented. Grace not being a strong suit, Jaws landed on my bare foot. I squealed. Rose laughed. Jaws farted.

Sam grabbed my shoulder and, without preamble said, "Let's go check on the progress of that lemon tree of yours."

"It died last winter from the cold." It was a crazy, frigid winter for Florida and much of the country. Damn Global Warming! I think the scientists may have had it correct back in the

1980's when they raised the alarm on the coming ice age. Even a broken clock... I initially missed Sam's covert attempt to get me outside away from Flo and Rose's prying ears. I attempted an awkward recovery, "But I planted a key lime tree. Wanna go check it out?" We had installed a fire pit in the corner of our yard and placed several citrus trees in ceramic planters around its perimeter.

"Yeah, I do," he said, a bit too eagerly. Flo frowned. Rose raised an eyebrow. Jaws farted. We walked outside. Jaws followed carrying a Frisbee in his misshapen mouth. The backyard meant play or toilet time to him. He did not need to take a dump. The door had barely shut behind us when Sam said, "That topless lady at the beach was Ms. Perdue."

Now I was puzzled. I pinched myself. It hurt.

"Why do you do that to yourself?" Sam asked.

I ignored him. Sam was part of the long, apocalyptic dream and was an involuntary participant in Hobo's staged home invasion and robbery of the Perdue's home. But that was a part of a totally different reality or at least a dream. Not this one....I think. How the hell did he know her? No sense complicating this. "How the hell do you know Ms. Perdue?" I asked Sam. At times, the best route is the direct one.

"BJ just started dating her daughter," Sam said, proudly. Like most fathers, Sam took a bit of unwarranted vicarious pride in their sons' romantic conquests. "That's my boy!" For no explainable reason, we fathers hold our daughters to a different, much higher, moral standard. Daughters remain virginal creatures in our eyes long after they have given us grandchildren and the grandchildren, great-grandchildren. No excuses, it is a double standard. That is just the way it is.

In spite of our attempted denials, we are different, men and women, and not just the obvious delightful plumbing variations. We are created with an entirely different set of hard-wired programming instructions for a specific purpose – the propagation of our species. Today's social scientist would have us believe that is not true. They purport that most of our gender-specific

226

programing is taught and not innate. We teach, according to our self-assured scientists, our daughters to be sugar and spice and consequently everything nice. I beg to differ. Sure, we typically reinforce the innate programing and most certainly aberrations exist. Our Creators gave us free will, but they also gave us a set of boot programing files that will always color the way we view our world. And that boot programing is unique for men and women, causing us to react somewhat differently when presented the same set of data. I'm just saying. You can fight Mother Nature but you will likely suffer a humiliating and painful defeat. She is a relentless bitch. And before I get tagged as a homophobe...I celebrate those aberrations to the boot file. Whether homosexuality is by birth or choice, I don't know and I really don't give a rat's ass. Likely the truth lies somewhere in between, but more importantly, I don't really care. What two consenting adults choose to do behind closed doors is none of my damn business and, for sure, none of the government's business. But what the hell do I know? I am just an old, public-educated, southern, white drunk.

"I thought I heard her mom say she went off to college."

"Kinda. She is at UNF. Really bright girl. She graduated high school a year early." University of North Florida is in Jacksonville, not much more than ten miles from where we stood beside the lime tree in my backyard. Sam continued, "That little filly be smoking hot." Sam, for reasons unknown, is not currently in favor with the Gods. Flo opened the back door just as Sam was completing his marginally inappropriate comment regarding the sexual desirability of his stepson's 17-year-old girlfriend. Well, marginally inappropriate from a man's, not the father of the subject's, point of view. From a chick's perspective, a creepy comment at best. Times two if the chick is the spouse of the speaker. Multiply by four for the mother of the subject.

"So tell me, Sam, 'What little filly be smoking hot?'" She stressed "be" in an attempt to mock his attempt at urban vernacular. "The leathery old hag with her saggy boobs in your face?"

Sam started to respond. Hopefully I had taught the boy a few things along the way and he was not going to point out her boobs were in fact kind of nice. I cut in, "Shovel down." I have learned from experience to put down the shovel whenever I find myself deep in a hole. Continuing to talk only serves to dig the hole deeper. Just put on a cute smile and shrug. This was not my first rodeo. I liked Sam and all-in-all he was a standup guy. I didn't mind imparting the wisdom I garnered from my advanced years to those worthy and he had proved himself worthy and a quick study to boot. He shrugged and smiled. Good boy.

"Thanks for the drink, Honey." He leaned in for a smooch. Flo left him hanging and his pursed lips found only air. She handed him his drink of choice, Jack on the rock. Not rocks; just one cube, thank you. Sam reflexively reached for his lower back in obvious discomfort as Flo returned indoors. "Progress, at least."

"Huh?" I asked.

"Spent a few nights on the couch since Ms. Perdue had her bare knockers in my face. Flo not buying the story. Sucks when you are in the dog house and you really did nothing wrong. And sadly, I only caught a brief glimpse of them puppies. The knockers looked pretty darn nice for a MILF."

Flo opened the door again, bringing me a beer just as Sam finished his favorable assessment of Martha's breasts and her apparent fuckability. Damn, the Gods really hated Sam. Or perhaps the Gods were just mischievous little bastards entertaining themselves from the comfort of their human hide reclining love seat. Life is not fair. It just is what it is. We have no real palatable option but to deal with life and its inherent prejudices the best we can. We must simply play the cards we are dealt. Complaining only wastes valuable time and resources in making the best use of the dealt hand. We have zero say in our beginning and, quite frankly, very little influence in our end. Our God-given free will lets us choose at least a healthy portion of the middle.

Flo slapped Sam forcefully on the back of the head. "Okay, Ward. You just punched your ticket for another week on the couch."

Sam put his drink down to rub his head. Jaws grabbed the glass in his teeth and, tossing his head back in a singular motion, slurped it up in one sip. "What the hell?" Sam asked.

"The boy has a taste for Jack", I explained. "He was raised right," I added in my best southern drawl.

BJ joined us outside by the lime tree. I don't get to see him much anymore. Teenagers, understandably, don't typically hang with us old farts. He was a cool kid. Smart, respectful, and good-looking in an Asian Justin Bieber arrogant teenage boy sort of way. He greeted me with a firm handshake, "Hey, Uncle Zeke." He was raised right, as well.

"Hey, nephew BJ." I patted him on the head. He hated that. "Looking more and more like Justin Bieber." He hated that even more, although the resemblance appeared as one of intent. "Shouldn't you be with that hot new filly Sam was telling me about?"

He rolled his eyes in mock aggravation. A sly smile played across his reddening face, betraying his true feelings. He knew he was playing in the big leagues with this chick.

"Or at least playing the latest version of Halo."

"So yesterday, Dude," BJ said, exasperated.

"Well I am more like so last week, or maybe last decade. And don't call me Dude."

"Sorry. I watched Big Lebowski last night. Seriously under appreciated Coen Brother Film."

"So I have heard."

BJ pulled out his Apple iPhone 9X. Only the best and latest technology for this kid. I mean, he was Asian after all, by birth. "Now this is what's happening in this millennia. New video game from Sony."

"Sony?" I asked. "They haven't created anything cool since the Walkman."

"Yeah, can you believe it? It's a revolutionary leap in game design. On its most basic level, it is an interactive virtual reality empire building game you play on Apple devices called Garden of Eve."

"You mean Eden," I helpfully corrected, although I should have been duly impressed he understood my Walkman reference. But then again it was likely from watching Guardians of the Universe.

"No. I mean Eve." He looked at me like I had failed third grade for the fourth time. Apparently Sam and Flo slept in on Sunday mornings. "Garden of Eve..." BJ stressed Eve to further drive home his point, "...lets you be an omniscient Creator and influence an empire you build from scratch. You can also step into an existing world at any point in time or place and begin your game, should you not have the patience to go through the terra forming and evolutionary process. Consequently, infinite levels and outcomes are possible." BJ absent-mindedly picked up a red apple from the ceramic fruit bowl Rose kept outdoors and took a large bite.

"The midgets," I mumbled.

"Uh...Lucy and Baby Sam are inside," BJ responded, puzzled by what appeared to him as a random comment.

"No. Not those midgets." I motioned inside. "The Sony midgets." I was remembering the conversations with the midgets in Belize. They were writing code for Sony on some new revolutionary video game.

"That's so racist, Uncle Zeke. Not all Japanese people are short." BJ was a bit on the short side and more than a bit sensitive. I chose to ignore his comment rather than take the time to explain.

Baby Sam, not really a baby any more, but the name stuck, walked outside. I expect it would haunt him into his teen years, at least. He was carrying a miniature donut. Jaws, ever the opportunist, took advantage of his diminutive stature and pinched the sugary treat. Baby Sam shrieked and extended his arms above his head, holding his hands at impossible angles. Baby Sam returned inside for another donut.

"You starving your dog?" Sam asked.

"Well he clearly thinks so. The hairy little black bastard has filed multiple complaints with the DFCS, EECO, NLRB, Rainbow Coalition, NAACP, The Sierra Club, Greenpeace, and the Department of Homeland Security. He plans to file suit in federal court, as well, over a violation of his civil rights. Al Sharpton has even organized a march to raise funds on his own behalf. A good crisis, after all, is the perfect opportunity to exploit and profit from the pain and suffering of others." I have a tendency to drift off onto tangents without any really good reason. But then again, life does not happen in straight lines.

Sam eyed me suspiciously, but wisely didn't argue. He, too, was learning not to argue with crazy. And besides, dogs soon enough would likely get protected status, as well as voting rights. Killing a dog would soon become a hate crime. The only murder not to be classified as a hate crime would be offing an old white guy. Seemed entirely redundant to me, murder and hate crime that is. Not many murderers commit said crime out of love, respect, and adoration. But again, what do I know?

We went inside. Flo had walked back across the street to get a peanut butter pie she had left in the fridge, interrupting a competitive game of Hide the Sock Monkey. Rose loves playing the game with the midgets. The game's rules are pretty straightforward. One player hides the sock monkey. A series of clues are presented regarding the monkey's location and the hider answers yes or no to the clues validity. Eventually, a player randomly draws a card to search for the monkey based on the relevant clues. I loathe the damn game, as I play a derivative of the game on a daily basis. Hide the car keys. Hide the wallet. Hide the tennis shoes. Hide the remote. Hide the reading glasses. Hide the cell phone. There was no joy in adding a sock monkey to this ever-growing list. A rare spat was brewing. Rose had so spoiled the midgets, I doubt she had or would ever say "no" to any of their demands, no matter how outrageous. "Aunt Rose, can we shoot Uncle Zeke?" "Okay, Honey, but only in his arm. Just do it outside and try to hit the fleshy part."

Baby Sam was beside himself. Lucy had taken the unwarranted liberty to eat the last chocolate donut, save one that had a little white powdered sugar on it. Well, technically Jaws had eaten the last chocolate donut. He was a willful bastard. Although that distinction was not particularly relevant. Baby Sam, accustomed to always getting his way at Aunt Rose's house, was not at all pleased with the current situation. He threw himself on the couch in a silent, demonstrative rage. Rose ordered, "You will eat that donut." She used a voice I was unfortunately familiar with, but had never heard directed to toward the midgets.

Apparently we had missed a key part of the story. Rose was uncharacteristically adamant. "You hear me? I said, you will eat that donut." Again, this is consequential, as Rose had never ever raised her voice to the boy nor ever forced him to so much as wipe his own butt, pick up a toy, or eat a solitary black-eyed pea. Lucy served as Baby Sam's enabler, as well. He was so darn cute, he could get away with murder. I was not sure if that trait would be a liability or asset for the boy. Time would tell. Often protecting one's children from the little evils in the world emboldens them to take ever greater risks until an evil visits the parents simply cannot fix. Baby Sam ignored her, continuing a well-practiced pose of innocent denial. Our Creators trick our minds into loving kids. Let's be honest. Kids are smelly, devious, stubborn, greedy, needy, little bastards. Without the benefit of our innate programming strongly guiding us to care for them, we would have eaten our own kids for supper by their second birthday. God made kids cute. It's their camouflage. Rose raised her voice to the next level, "You will eat that donut or you're going home."

Sam and I looked at Rose perplexed. "Rose, honey…He won't eat a donut? That's your line?"

Rose laughed at herself. "You have to draw a line somewhere. And a line drawn is a line held."

Sage advice that, Mr. President. Don't embolden your enemies with empty threats.

Atlanta, Georgia; October 2016: The New Black Panther Party (NBPP), a black separatist group, held a largely peaceful protest on the steps of the Georgia State Capitol today. The NBPP self-described prophet and spokesperson, Khalid Muhammad, is calling for Black Americans to have their own nation where they can make their own laws. Further, Muhammad is demanding that all black prisoners be released to "the lawful authorities of the Black Nation." Muhammad's final demand is that all Black Americans be paid reparations for slavery from the United States, all European countries, and "the Jews."

A White House spokesperson said the President believes the NBPP demands have merit and should be given "thoughtful consideration."

The Georgia State Patrol estimated the protestors to number approximately one hundred thousand.

Alongside Global News

CHAPTER TWENTY

"What the hell is his problem?" I motioned to BJ. He was sitting in a beach chair, staring blankly out toward the cloudless horizon where the sky melted subtly into the sea. He hadn't spoken a single word all morning. Sam got up to check his rod and motioned for me to follow.

"His hot, little filly is moving to South Carolina."

"Ohhhh," I replied. Lost love and its kissing cousin lust, suck at any age. Teenagers, the males of the species, at least (I shan't pretend to speak for the mysterious fairer sex) can't distinguish between the two.

"She received an athletic scholarship at the University of South Carolina. Leaving tomorrow," Sam explained.

"Soccer?" I asked. She didn't really fit the softball profile.

"Nah. Cheerleading," Sam explained.

"Ahhh." I forget cheerleading is a sport. Not hating. Clearly more of a sport than golf, fishing, curling, or NASCAR. "I don't get it."

"Don't get what, Zeke? That cheerleading is a sport?" He asked, a little too passionately.

"Nah. I actually get that. Pretty much gymnastics in a short skirt." I paused for a minute, studying his face. I continued, "You per chance a cheerleader in college, Sam?"

"Screw you." Not really an answer. I secretly plotted to Google his college yearbook for answers. The internet had paradoxically both severely damaged and enhanced one's ability to lie. Gore must be so proud.

"So, what is it you don't get?" Sam asked.

"Why any parent would allow, much less encourage, their daughter, or son for that matter, to be a USC cheerleader."

"How so?" Sam asked.

235

"Well…" I thought for a second how best to explain, "…the team's nickname can be viewed, perhaps by the less enlightened, as a bit racy." Sam looked at me, clearly puzzled. I continued, "The Gamecocks."

"Not following," Sam said. I think he may have swallowed a stupid pill this morning with his second cup of Joe.

I spelled it out for him. "Would you encourage your daughter Lucy to wear a pair of booty shorts with the inscription 'Go Cocks' written in large print across her buttocks, while cheering on said 'Cocks' to a predominately drunken, male crowd of sixty thousand or so live and millions more watching on national television?"

Sam laughed. "I see your point. And no…Hell, no."

Sam reeled in his surf rod. Something, likely a blue crab, had stolen his bait. He selected a couple of large shrimp from the bait cooler, re-baited his hooks, and rinsed the distinctive, unpleasant smell of days old seafood from his hands in the surf. I grabbed a beer. BJ remained near catatonic.

"The boy must of had it bad for her. He is not even playing video games."

"Yeah, he tossed his cell in the toilet when she informed him, via text, no less, she was moving. We took all his electronics away," Sam explained.

"Ouch. Harsh, Dude. Just how is that working for you?"

Sam shrugged and recast his rod into the surf.

"You forget what it was like to be a teenage boy?"

"You forget how much an iPhone 9X costs?" Sam responded.

"True that." Those invasive little instruments of advanced technology would set the normal person back a week's pay. Yet, with all its remarkable advances in technology, the device would irrevocably expire in four inches of toilet water. Being a conspiracy theorist, I believed this was by design and just another form of planned obsolescence. I mean, come on. You can store the Library of Congress on the device, project images in near 3D that look clearer than real life, communicate with anyone in the world instantaneously, process more information faster than a supercomputer was capable of just four years ago, and hold the damn thing in the palm of your hand. Yet, drop it into the toilet or onto the floor, and it was just an expensive paperweight. I am calling bullshit. I just think it damn near impossible to be that smart and that stupid, simultaneously.

"Shit happens," Sam waxed poetically.

"When you get to be my age that means two things." Given Sam's recent ingestion of a stupid pill, I held up two fingers adding a visual context clue to my intended humor. Based on his blank face, the additional clue was insufficient or I had wildly overestimated my comedic skills. "You're a Family Guy fan, right?"

"Yup, but what's your point?"

"You are going to laugh your ass off at that joke in about twenty years from now as you are finishing up your second cup of coffee and eating a large, greasy breakfast at Ellen's Kitchen. I thought for a moment about the scenario, reconsidered and continued, "Well...maybe laughter not your first response." I reached for a beer in the cooler. We were out. "What the hell, Sam? How many beers did you drink this morning?" I packed the cooler with a full 12-pack and it was barely after noon.

"I don't know. Flo got you counting my beers now?" Sam replied.

"I have had four, tops. That leaves you with the other eight. And I'm the drunk?"

"No way."

I quickly did the mental math. If my figures were accurate, the third person in our company may have stealthily imbibed a few beers. "BJ not driving anywhere anytime soon?"

"No. Why do you ask?" Sam asked. Apparently he had overdosed on stupid pills today. I just shrugged. No reason to throw the poor, lovelorn, boy any further under the bus. I texted

Rose to come join us at the beach….And if she didn't mind horribly, to bring some more beer.

"Fish on," I said, pointing to Sam's rod.

Rose crossed through the breach in the dunes with Jaws and the midgets. Jaws had his leash in his mouth pulling Rose forward. He was wearing a t-shirt that read "Black Republican." The midgets were with her, struggling to pull a wagon through the deep, soft sand up past the high tide line. Baby Sam quickly abandoned the effort. Lucy was the stubborn one. She continued to struggle with the wagon, refusing any help from Rose. Patience, I hear is a virtue. I myself wouldn't know. I wanted a beer. I got up to help Lucy pull the wagon through the sand. She shot me a "fuck you" look way beyond her tender years. She was eight, maybe nine, but she still scared the hell out of me. I wisely abandoned my offer of assistance and grabbed a beer from the cooler in the wagon. Rose laughed. Lucy glared and said menacingly in third person, "You made Lucy mad." I tried not to show fear, but I think she could smell it on me. Baby Sam ran off to his Dad as he was pulling in his catch, a nice-sized ocean catfish. Rose offered me her beautiful lips. I accepted. Rose and I abandoned the wagon to Lucy and walked off to inspect Sam's catch. Lucy was nearing meltdown mode. I had no desire to be within her kill zone perimeter.

"Meow, fishy, meow," Baby Sam said, inspecting the catfish. He reached up to touch the fish's whiskers. Sam snatched the fish out of his reach.

"Don't touch it. The fins are poisonous," Sam noted. He grabbed a knife from the tackle box and cut the line, tossing the fish, leader, hooks, and weights back into the surf.

"A bit excessive, don't you think?" I was having another one of those déjà vu moments.

"Hell, no. I am allergic to those slimy bastards."

"Yeah. And everyone is allergic to stepping on a sharp hook."

Rose and I took the two empty beach chairs. Sam stood to rig his rod. Rose looked over at BJ and greeted him. He nodded. Progress, I thought.

"What's his story?" Rose asked as Sam walked off to recast his line. "Other than being drunk."

"Shh." I brought my finger to my lips. "Girlfriend problems."

Rose raised an eyebrow. "You can't give the boy beer."

"Didn't give it. He snuck it."

Baby Sam said out of nowhere, "BJ is a little bitch."

Rose stifled a giggle before gathering Baby Sam in her arms to quiet him. You really can't say shit to a kid you don't want the world to hear. One can only imagine how much elementary teacher's know about the intimate details of the personal lives of their student's homes. Another example of our innate programming. Otherwise the kid should have been eaten for dinner years before as a convenient form of protein.

"Almost forgot. Steve called. He is on his way out."

"Aunt Rose," Baby Sam said, tugging on Rose's swimsuit cover-up incessantly. "Why is the sky blue?" he asked, pointing out to the horizon.

"Because it's God's favorite color." Not sure as to the scientific validity of her answer, I think it has something to do with reflecting the ocean, but her answer worked for Baby Sam.

"Why does the bark turn dark on a pine tree when Jaws pees on it?"

"It's one of his superhero powers."

I added, "And farting. Jaws is special. He has two superhero powers." Baby Sam giggled. I think he knew we were bull-shitting him. He grinned from ear to ear as he, like most kids and grown men, love bathroom humor. When he smiles, his entire body smiles. I think it is his super power.

Lucy had made her way through the soft sand onto the wet, hard-packed portion of the beach. Her pace was increasing but she was still 20 feet away and I needed another beer. "Should I see if she wants help?" I asked Rose.

Rose took one look at Lucy's grimaced face, "Suit yourself. Just be prepared to forfeit the remainder of your soul." Damn I wanted a beer, but a quick glance toward Lucy quickly confirmed Rose's assessment and quenched my thirst. I like my soul, tortured as it is, thank you.   Baby Sam continued his impromptu interrogation. He tugged on his faded t-shirt and pointed, "Where does the color go when it fades off my shirt?"

Rose, without pausing, answered, "God calls everything beautiful back home to him in heaven."

"When will he call you home, Aunt Rose? I don't want you to leave me." Rose teared up and pulled Baby Sam into her arms for a big hug.

Baby Sam was confused by Rose's response and pulled away from her arms. "Why are your eyes leaking?" he asked, with a mischievous smile.

"Because they are happy."

"BJ must be really happy, then." BJ was within earshot but continued staring blankly out toward the horizon.

Kids are sponges. They absorb so much more than we realize, both the good and the bad. They also are without the benefit of filters and frequently surprise and/or embarrass us with their frank observations. We take so much for granted, even that which we don't understand. Rose had given Baby Sam BS answers to all his questions but I am not sure either of us could have explained the science behind any of his questions. We just took these common, every day miracles for granted. The innocence of youth can be refreshing. Maybe that is why we don't eat them. We cherish the reminders of every day miracles.

Baby Sam posed yet another question. "If I drive my car at the speed of light, will my headlights shine in front of me?"

Rose started to answer, but BJ unexpectedly interrupted. "First off, you little monkey turd, it is not possible for a number of reasons, the least of which that you can't reach the pedals to drive.

Secondly, if it were possible, the answer is, it depends. If you are the driver of the car, the relative speed of the headlights to the car would cause the light to appear as normal. Should you be an outside observer to the car, the light would appear warped and blue. But again…It's moot. Not possible. Now shut the hell up, you little spoiled shit."

Rose replied, "Those AP Physics courses sound like they're paying off."

"Yeah. We learned about Santa Clause, the Tooth Fairy, the Easter Bunny, and true love last week."

The boy had it bad. Lucy finally made her way over and collapsed at Rose's feet. I grabbed a beer and tossed it to BJ. Rose raised an eyebrow. Baby Sam giggled. Lucy hurled.

Steve made his way through the dune breach. Uncharacteristically, he was wearing clothing, if not stylish, at least appropriate for the beach: gym shorts, tank top, floppy hat and flip flops with white tube socks. His nose was covered in zinc oxide. He was carrying a small, manila folder and a folding beach chair. I offered him a beer. He declined. Steve noticed BJ drinking a beer, frowned, and sat, pulling his chair under the shade of the umbrella. Baby Sam duly noted,   "Your skin is black."

Steve responded, "And my butt is fat." He looked at me. "The boy never seen a black man?"

"Not one as pretty as you." Most Americans of African descent have a slice of European DNA somewhere in their heritage. Steve was coal black. Any trace of a white man in his family tree was cleverly disguised. "What you got for me?" I asked, changing the subject. Lucy wandered off to play in the surf by her Dad. Baby Sam jumped into Rose's lap. He was getting a little old for lap play.

"Can you identify this man?"

I took the offered photograph. "Yeah. It's Frio Lobo."

"David Shamus O'Grady is his real name. Good Irish Catholic boy from the streets of Philly. Now the alleged chief money launderer and accountant for Los Zetas, an influential crime cartel in Central America. Reportedly has aspirations to take over the gang and make it even more profitable."

"How does a good, Irish, Catholic boy get from Philly to Central America?"

"Started out oldest kid of a large, lower middle-class Irish Catholic family; Dad was a self-employed plumber and mom ran an unlicensed daycare from the family home." Steve continued leafing through his file. "He graduated summa cum laude from his public high school where he lettered in just about every sport. Undergrad at Penn State on a football scholarship. All-American linebacker, no less."

"Pretty impressive," I noted.

"Lost his scholarship early in his senior year for selling autographed memorabilia after his Dad developed lung cancer and his Mom's daycare was shut down."

"Isn't Penn State the school where one of the coaches sexually abused all those kids over the span of a couple decades?" I asked.

Steve nodded in the affirmative.

"And he gets tossed for selling autographs to help support his family? The NCAA really needs to rethink its priorities," I said, in another one of my tangential moments.

Steve continued, "O' Grady entered the pro-draft after losing his scholarship. He had received his bachelor's degree before starting his senior year and was drafted in the seventh round by the Raiders. Broke his neck in the first pre-season game, ending his short lived football career."

"So, what is his connection to the Black Panthers?"

He ignored my question and continued his narrative, "He returned to Philly after recovering from surgery." For some reason, he wanted me to hear this guy's story. "MBA from Wharton...again, top of his class. His bad luck streak continued. Pain from the neck injury got him hooked on meds. Dad died. O'Grady started washing down the pain pills with single malt

Scotch. He was Irish but liked his whisky Scotch. Even so, he still landed a great job with KKR."

"The KKK?" I asked. Not born as racist as revisionist historians might have you believe, but still, it seemed peculiar that O' Grady would be a part of what began as General Nathan Bedford s anti-carpet-bagger organization, but regrettably morphed into a hate club for ignorant white boys.

"KKR," Steve added emphasis to the final letter. "KKR is a large, ironically Jewish, multinational, private equity firm. You might remember them from their RJR Nabisco buyout in the late 1980s."

I shook my head no.

"It was a big freaking deal."

I shrugged. I have slept since the '80s.

Steve looked at me, disappointed with my ignorance. He continued, "O' Grady managed to hide his addiction and pain and quickly moved up in the organization; Vice-President in 18 months, Senior Vice-President in 30 months. Apparently a boy genius at finance, he was a rising star within the firm. Then his mom died. O' Grady took it hard...exceptionally hard and spent a month in the bottle. KKR finally gave him an ultimatum to come back to work, resign, or face termination. Heartless bastards," he editorialized. "KKR was looking at a hostile takeover of a large transportation and logistics company based in Texas. That was O'Grady's specialty. The company turned out to be a front for a Central American gang."

"Let me guess...Los Zetas." Steve nodded yes and continued his narrative. "O'Grady traveled to Laredo, Texas to check out the company. Simply put, The Zs made him a better offer."

"Really nice story, but still not shedding any light on the Black Panther connection."

"The obvious connection would be his gang supplies product to the Panthers. Which is likely true...but Lobo would not be involved in that kind of transaction. Lobo keeps his hands relatively clean."

"Then what?" I asked.

"Don't know. Here is a kid that did just about everything right. And look where his path led him."

"Don't know or not telling me?"

"Don't know. Odd thing, though...the money is flowing backwards."

"Backwards?" I asked.

"Yeah. From Lobo to the Panthers."

"What for?"

"Really no frigging idea. I'm a street cop. Hell, the wife handles our finances. I can't balance a checkbook for the life of me. Give me a good old-fashioned bludgeoning, smash and grab, sexual assault...I'll find the perp. This high finance stuff and money laundering...beyond my pay grade. And from what I can see, I will tell you this much; the Feds know who he is, what he is, but can't figure out what he is up to or how to pin a crime on him that will stick."

"Worse yet, maybe they know and are choosing to ignore," I offered as an alternative. Steve opened his arms broadly and shrugged. I expect this possibility had not been overlooked by him but he was not confirming it. It certainly would not be the first time the Feds were in bed with the bad guys with ambiguous motives.

Steve's cell rang. He listened and grunted a few times without speaking anything intelligible before rising to leave. I grabbed his forearm. Steve was one of the brightest men I had ever met. "You know, Steve," I paused staring into his face for his tell, "I'm not that stupid."

"That..." Steve said, shaking my grip off, "...remains to be seen." He walked off toward the dunes, turning as he was about to walk out of site and said, "Zeke, just let it be, Son. There are some paths best left untaken. Some doors best left unopened. Just let it be."

"So I hear," I said to no one, "So I hear."

244

Piedras Negras, Mexico; October 2016: The Mexican president, Hugo Martinez, held a press conference today from the small border town of Piedras Negras. Martinez, called for the United States to return the State of Texas to Mexico, citing the illegal taking of the property in 1846.

A State Department spokesperson noted Mexico ceded Texas to the United States in return for $18 million.

A White House spokesperson said the president has assembled a team of advisers to consult on the matter noting the United States may have illegally annexed Texas from Mexico and the proposal should be given "thoughtful consideration."

Alongside Global News

CHAPTER TWENTY-ONE

"What the hell are you clowns supposed to be?" I asked a group of bloodied teenagers approaching us. Their skeletal bones were protruding through newly shredded clothing. Arms stiffly outstretched, they each held pillow cases. The teenagers were moving slowly, all hindered with various degrees of staged physical disability. Grunting aggressively, they continued their clumsy march toward us.

Rose offered an explanation, "I know...retarded zombies."

"Kind of redundant, don't you think?" Zombies had replaced vampires as the cool monster du jour. "And we don't use that 'R' word anymore. They are special needs zombies, if you must."

"No. Not at all redundant. Not all zombies are re..." she caught herself. We were not the PC family on the block. "...special needs," Rose pointed out, dramatically adding air quotes and rolling her lovely dark eyes. "You remember the Brad Pitt movie where they were smart and fast as hell." More of a statement rather than a question. I prefer my zombies with very limited cognitive skills, slow of foot, and without the added benefit of water born mobility, thank you. Fast, smart, zombies with mad swimming skills scare the hell out of me. I have a workable game plan for the special needs ones. Rose gave the zombies an additional cursory inspection. I stoked the fire. Sam grabbed a beer.

Late October is a beautiful time of the year in Northern Florida. Tonight with the air crisp, the sky clear, the temp dropped into the low sixties. The fire pit positioned behind us kept us suitably warm, wearing only shorts and long-sleeve shirts. Later the midgets would use the fire pit to toast marshmallows for s'mores to further enhance and extend their hard-earned sugar rush. Halloween was awesome in our neighborhood and not just for the gay dentist couple that lived on the corner of First and 37th

Streets. Hundreds of kids came by in elaborate costumes. Parents joined the younger ones with many in similarly themed costumes; some of the more desperate neighborhood moms choosing to use the occasion to dress like hookers in a futile effort to cheat time. And, to be completely accurate, a sizable number of the kids would not have been out of place at the corner brothel. Not judging…just observing. Nights like these, the neighborhood sexual predators should be required to place flashing neon signs in their front windows and razor barbed wire barriers at the driveway. "Beware, evil lives within these walls." Second thought…Not such a good idea on Halloween. Liquid adult candy was secreted within plastic cups by the majority enjoying the autumn festivities. It was a giant sugar and alcohol infused block party.

"These for sure are the ret…special needs variety," Rose pronounced, with unwarranted certainty.

The groaning increased in volume. One of the kids…uhh zombies, suspend disbelief, was foaming at the mouth in a rather convincing fashion. The teenagers had spent considerable time and effort applying theatrical makeup and shredding their brand new, store bought clothing. Sam's face flashed recognition abruptly morphing into annoyance.

"I see you are still in character, BJ." He then turned and looked at me. "Hasn't spoken a word to us since we took his electronics from him."

"Still. Wow, Dude that is seriously harsh. You're changing his reality."

"Thank you, Uncle Zeke," BJ said, momentarily stepping out of character. The assembled undead nodded in agreement and their moaning volume increased in collective disapproval of Sam's harsh punitive measures.

"And when the hell did seniors in high school start trick-or-treating? Aren't you all a little old for this shit?" Sam asked.

The Gods were seriously on the warpath with Sam. Whenever he did anything remotely wrong, it was as if Flo mystically appeared. She never caught him doing good, which was statistically improbable, at best. The man was a good man. Flo walked up with the midgets and about a dozen other elementary age kids and their moms, just as Sam said "shit" a bit louder than I expect he even realized.

"Another week…" Flo said out loud, before mouthing, "Asshole."

Sam shrugged in defeat. Baby Sam jumped in his lap. He was dressed as a fish. It was our first and only fish costume of the night. Baby Sam was not a slave to convention. He began selecting favored candies from his bag.

"You still in the doghouse?" I asked Sam. I pointed at Jaws leashed to my chair, silently observing the show with his oversized head resting on his massive paws. Rose had given him two Valiums in order to calm him enough to wrestle a XXL sized shark costume onto him. Jaws shops exclusively in the Big and Tall section. He promptly ate the costume. Jaws allowed Rose to replace his costume with a sweater Hobo had knitted for Jaws. There was a bit of an illicit love affair between those two. Nothing perverse, I just think they were kindred spirits. Hobo had stitched "Sexy Beast" onto both flanks of the sweater with pink yarn. By now, Jaws was at his two drink minimum, as well. Between the Valium and Jack, Jaws was suitably calm and indifferent to the assortment of walking night terrors and street walkers. "Jaws might share his doghouse if you ask him nicely. He will aggressively frisk you for food, though," I warned.

Rose added, "And he is a serial farter."

Jaws lifted his head off his paws and yawned. He makes an adorable sound when he yawns, akin to a teapot alerting you the water is ready. The zombies collectively stopped moaning, too.

"Ahhh. He's so cute." Jaws curled in on himself like only dogs can do and started licking his phantom balls.

"Yup, cute he is."

Noticing the attentive audience, Jaws rose to the occasion. He had a special throw pillow. We affectionately call her, the pillow, that is, Bitch. The boy had been neutered, but his innate programming to perform the sex act remained intact, phantom balls and all, in its totality. He abducted Bitch from the futon the very first night we brought him home from the shelter. Jaws tossed the pillow into his crate and aggressively humped it...ehhh...her. As soon as he was done humping, Jaws belligerently tossed Bitch out of his crate. He was not much of a cuddler, as he apparently subscribed more to the "hit it and quit it" mantra." We wisely surrendered Bitch to Jaws and placed her sisters safely out of his reach on the top of the bookcase. One defiled throw pillow per household was adequate. Jaws continued to use Bitch to satisfy his animal urges, as well as a device to overcome any feelings of impotence by demonstrating dominance when he was disciplined by Rose or me.

Jaws had managed to secret Bitch in the bushes just within his reach and, with a suitable audience in attendance, he retrieved her and went at Bitch hard. The zombies laughed. Jaws reacted by increasing the veracity of his sexual assault in a failed attempt to better communicate his message of dominance to the zombies. His display was intended to be a horror show, not a comedy. "Fear me, don't laugh at me." The midgets looked on in wide-eyed confusion bordering on fear. BJ, ever the diplomat and quick-thinker, offered a speedy explanation; "When a dog loves a pillow...."

Rose added between snorts of laughter, "They are just wrestling."

A look of comprehension crossed Baby Sam's face, "Ohhhh. Daddy wrestles Mommy sometimes, too. He must love her."

Rose cried as Sam and Flo turned a deep shade of crimson red, clearly evident despite the poor lighting conditions.

Hobo walked outside from inside our house. He was wearing my t-shirt that said "I am tired of being my wife's eye candy." He had wrapped one of Rose's pink leather belts around his narrow waist, wearing my x-large t-shirt like a dress. I had grown accustomed to his mystical entrances and curious fashion sense and didn't bother to interrogate him. His bare legs above the knee glowed in the reflection of the fire. Below the knee, his skin was dark and leathery. Hobo dropped a Louis Vuitton travel bag in the grass and reached into my cooler and pulled out a Budweiser. I had rightfully anticipated an unscheduled Hobo sighting and inventoried his preferred beer. Like I said, supply chain expert.

"Have a beer," I said, sarcastically.

"Thanks," he answered without even a trace of sarcasm. He sat in the grass, legs askew, and pulled out a pair of old-school white, cracked-leather roller skates with pink laces and a boom box from the expensive bag. BJ's zombie friends quickly scattered.

"You aren't wearing drawers, Dude." I tilted my beer toward his crotch.

"Am too." He pulled up my t-shirt, exposing a pair of pink thongs on his scrawny ass. Jaws licked his beard. Rose gagged. The midgets giggled.

I tossed a spare blanket over Hobo's lap just as another large group of kids walked up to extort sweet treats. I wanted to spare them the sight of an old man's junk wrapped in lady's underwear. More importantly, I strongly desired avoiding any further contact from law enforcement officials. Hobo was not easy to explain. This grouping of future diabetics was much younger and less scary. Cheerleaders, various superheroes, animals, assorted athletes, medical workers, Disney prince and princesses, and the most adorable two-year-old in a homemade chicken outfit. Rose gushed.

Rose had no kids of her own. Our grandkids, the midgets, and Jaws served as her children analogs and they all rightfully adored her. She was great with kids and spoiled the ever-loving shit out of them. Women are typically hard-wired to reproduce. Not just the physical plumbing and the delightful desire to copulate, but a powerful yearning to actually create another living being, have it spring forth with great difficulty and suffering from their loins and care for it to its maturity….in some cases, well past maturity. How a bowling ball squeezes out of a golf ball hole is a mystery best left to the imagination. You do not want to see that sausage made. The intense drive to reproduce is critical programing for the perpetuation of our species. Rose claimed to be missing those particular lines of code and held no desire to reproduce her own DNA coded "snot-nosed, smelly little shit machines." I questioned her colorful assertion at times like these when I saw her face light up over a small kid.

"So what are you?" I asked an eight-year-old girl from the assembled group waiting her turn at the candy troth. She appeared to be dressed as a farm animal, but I was struggling with identification of said barnyard creature. The costume seemed to me to be some eccentric hybrid of cow and alien deer. Parents rightfully spend considerable time and effort to program kids to avoid contact and conversation with adult strangers. "Stranger Danger," or some culturally appropriate derivative is universally taught in most civilized cultures. Then they go and toss the safety programing out the door on occasions like Halloween and Sunday socials after mass. The little girl was consequently conflicted and hesitated at answering my question. I was said stranger. Her rehearsed script was limited to "trick or treat" and "thank you." I had gone off script. BJ responded for her with some gibberish that sounded to me like a sneeze.

"Gesundheit," I said to BJ. I helpfully continued to the little girl, "So, you're a cow?" It was my best guess.

Her face turned red and she started tearing up. "No, I'm a..." She made the same sneezing sound as BJ.

"Gesundheit. Is it allergy season?" I asked. Rose, Sam, Flo, and BJ started giggling. I ignored them and continued, trying to salvage my dignity; "It's a really nice cow costume."

The costumed little girl stomped her foot and stood rigid with her hands held closely to her side. "I'm not a cow! I'm a..." She made the same sneezing sound again.

Rose jumped in "She's a..." Rose also made a clearly manufactured sneezing sound.

I scrunched up my face in confusion.

251

"Gesundheit?" The little girl stormed off to report me to the proper authorities. Hobo shook his head.

"Here, Uncle Zeke." BJ handed me his cell phone. "She's a Pikachu. It's a Pokémon character." He spelled out the name. The phone displayed a creature that looked similar to a hybrid between a rabbit and a cow. I was way off base on the alien deer. But then again, what does an alien deer look like?

"What the hell is that?" I asked, clearly out of touch with pop culture.

Flo grabbed BJ's cell from my hand before he could enlighten me to the genesis of the bizarre creature. I was almost certain that mind-altering drugs were involved in its fabrication. "What the hell is this?" Flo asked BJ, grabbing his elbow and pulling him across the street toward their home. She was not speaking of the acid inspired animal but the confiscated device it was displayed upon. The boy had some serious explaining to do.

Hobo laced up his roller skates over a pair of white calf-length tube socks with three horizontal pink stripes. He further accessorized his ensemble with a pink headband and attached pink pom-poms to the laces of his roller skates. As he stood, he shouldered the boom box and grabbed Jaw's leash. "Watch my bag would you? My quicksilver is in there."

"What the hell, Dude?" I asked Hobo, opening the bag revealing a large iron cylinder

"Language, Ezekiel."

"Answer, Hobo."

"Quicksilver," he said slowly. "You know mercury, Hg."

"Again, what the hell, Dude? What are you doing with mercury?"

"Ezekiel, you really should have paid a bit more attention in Physics class. Mercury is a liquid metal at room temperature. Melts most other metals... Except iron." Hobo patted the iron cylinder lovingly. "You have a mouth full of mercury amalgam in your teeth. It is a poor conductor of heat and a good conductor of electricity. At room temperature it is weakly diamagnetic. But the magic happens with mercury at about 4 degrees Kelvin."

"Magic?" I asked.

"Not really magic, science, but since your attention was focused on cotton in class…" he left his accusatory comment hanging briefly before continuing; "Mercury at 4 degrees Kelvin is a Superconductor."

Hobo placed the skate's pink rubber stopper to the paver stones as Jaws in anticipation strained against the leash. "Taking the Sexy Beast for a stroll." He turned his attention to Jaws. "Giddy up, handsome." He was not talking to me. Jaws sprinted down the street, his claws clicking loudly on the pavement, in the direction of the beach, pulling Hobo behind him at a dangerous pace, with Hobo weaving in and out artfully dodging the remaining trick or treaters. The two quickly disappeared from sight with the fading strains of "I'm too sexy for my pants…" still echoing off the neighbor's houses from Hobo's shouldered boom box.

***

The alarm siren abruptly pierced the dark quiet and startled us awake. Jaws leapt from his bed and stood by the bedroom door anxiously awaiting for me to open it. Rose grabbed the iPad and started searching the security cameras for signs of an intruder. The wee hours of Halloween night is an inopportune time for a false alarm. Rose reported the cameras were clear. Likely we had failed to secure the top lock on one of the doors and the wind had pushed one slightly ajar, subsequently triggering the alarm. It would not be the first time. But then again, this was Halloween. Jaws aggressively pawed at the door. I grabbed the shotgun and chambered a round. Rose silenced the alarm and continued monitoring the security cameras while I went downstairs to clear the bottom floor.

Jaws bounded down the stairs, taking the last three in an impressive leap, skidding to a stop on the travertine floors, and managing to stop just short of the foyer wall. "Good boy," I whispered to Jaws. I was duly impressed. The hair on his back along his spine was standing up like a frightened cat. Jaws charged into the media room growling like a dog on a mission. In the moment, I was so proud of our rescue dog. Here we had only had him a couple months and he was proving a valuable and loyal guard dog. I moved toward the back door, falsely assuming Jaws had cleared the media room as he was silent. I called for him to join me when I found the back door secure. Jaws remained silent somewhere in the media room. I continued clearing the bottom floor, occasionally calling for Jaws to join me in my task, growing a bit more concerned as every second passed. The hairy beast did not answer. I moved to the garage and likewise found nothing. I walked back into the media room, shotgun at the ready, and turned on the light to discover our fearless 90-pound dog under the loveseat cowering in fear. "Some guard dog you are, Fluffy." He had put on a few pounds since we adopted him. I coaxed him out with a treat and we returned to Rose in bed, already asleep.

"You two are a matching pair."

Jaws licked my face. Rose farted. I reset the alarm. Sleep did not come easily.

I felt myself on the cusp of sleep. I knew I was dreaming without having to pinch myself. I looked out with my eyes firmly shut and I saw the Peanut midgets from Belize: Lucy and Linus. Their eyes reflected, no, more like radiated the sapphire blue sky above them. The two silently hovered above a throne-like chair, flanking each side, as if protecting the unseen occupant clouded in a mist. Four large discs appeared beside them. Each disc mirrored the identical image: a shushing cherub, Hobo, a lion, and an eagle.

Jaws licked my face. Rose farted. The alarm sounded.

Florence, Italy; November 2016: Abdon Goldstein was found dead in his Florence hotel room earlier this week. Goldstein, the former Chief of Staff for the Pennsylvania Governor, lifeless body was found nude and shackled to the bed in his Four Seasons suite in the popular tourist destination. According to police there was no evidence the room had been broken into. Police are searching for a male prostitute known only as "The Sheik" that was seen with Goldstein earlier in the evening of his death at a popular late night Florence night club associated with drug trafficking.

Goldstein was a major fund raiser for the President in both his successful 2008 and 2012 Presidential elections. He was part of group that included the billionaire George Smith that was wildly rumored to have been involved in illegal campaign activities. No charges were ever filed against Goldstein or any of the alleged co-conspirators nicknamed by the press as "The Suits."

Alongside Global News

CHAPTER TWENTY-TWO

Routine is critical to maintain order within my chaotic mind. In the early years, school and church were my routine. My Dad was a bit of a religious zealot. If the church doors were open, my chubby little ass was in the straight back pine pew. Later, work served as my routine. Once retired, establishing a new routine was essential. To offset my less than healthy lifestyle, Rose guided me to a local gym to find routine. Daily workouts had become my new regiment. The gym is an odd place on weekday mornings, filled with us retired farts, soccer moms, as well as heavily-tatted fire and police officers. It was a beautiful, fall morning. I lowered the top of the convertible and headed north on First Street toward the gym. Jaws sat comfortably in the passenger seat with his oversized head out the window drooling on the door. Third Street, A1A, is a much faster route to the gym, but I prefer driving by the ocean. Joggers, bicyclists, and skateboarders serve to slow the pace, as well as the stop signs they all tend to hold in total disregard.

The Jacksonville Beach downtown area is full of bars, restaurants, beach and souvenir shops, open spaces, a small number of motels, and the homeless. Like most beach communities, there is never enough parking and there are a large amount of pedestrians and cyclists using the streets. It's an attractive area and great place to visit during the week. On weekends and holidays, it gets a bit crowded from townies, and the personality changes from a warm and embracing family-friendly atmosphere to dark, dangerous, and volatile.

For some inexplicable reason, the city fathers chose to frivolously spend millions upgrading the aesthetics of the area back in 2011, which in turn damn near killed all the local businesses off after blocking the streets for months on end during the construction. There was no real reason to spend the money. The area was both functional and attractive as it was. Government just likes to spend other people's money and can't be trusted to do the right thing for anyone but themselves. The new design is God awful. Worse yet, it is downright dangerous. The geniuses narrowed the road, removing the bike lanes. Did I mention this is a biking community? Further, the narrower road causes delivery vehicles to now almost completely block traffic in both directions. The designers placed roundabouts in the intersections that are much too small to safely accommodate roundabouts and, in one case, left the stop signs up, thus further confusing just about everyone on who has the right of way. The same geniuses decided planting waist-high decorative grass in the median made perfect sense. The high grass serves to adequately conceal oncoming traffic and pedestrians, making for the frequent obscene gesture exchange. The curbs were removed to better facilitate walking traffic and avoid tripping hazards which kind of makes sense, given there are countless alcohol-fueled festivals held in the area. Yet the designers randomly placed concrete planters abutting into the road and sidewalk at ankle height, creating even worse tripping hazards.

I have a working theory about traffic engineers. These are the guys that flunked out of every other engineering school and the default school for failing engineers is traffic. How hard can it be to design a road? I am not talking bridges here, just the traffic flow on roads. In all fairness, I figured it was harder than I imagined, but really? Like any profession, fifty percent of the practitioners graduated in the bottom half the class. Perhaps traffic engineers discovered a secret back door to mathematics and even a higher percentage graduated in the bottom half. I mean, if anybody screwed up something simple, traffic engineers would be my prime suspect. To begin with, the entire project was a solution in search of a problem. It did not need to be done. I expect there were some "free" federal dollars floating around and our local fathers took the attractive bait. But at the proverbial end of the day, they made the area unsafe and only marginally more aesthetic. Overall, it's an incredibly poor design that I expect will be reversed after considerable taxpayer expenses defending the first few associated lawsuits and the current group of city fathers have moved on, replaced by an equally inept new group with designs on placing their taxpayer funded stamp on history.

I took a left at the roundabout on the corner of Beach and First, nearly clipping a Joe's Crab Shack waitress jay-walking. At the second round-about, I came to a complete stop and eased my car into the intersection so I could see around the tall grass blocking the view. Moving through the intersection without incident, I pulled up to the intersection of Beach and Third, which had, in fact, been recently widened after the upgrade project narrowed it just a few months prior. This is a very busy intersection. A large group of protestors dressed in white coveralls were on each corner carrying placards. In the crotch area of each jumpsuit was a large, red stain. They carried placards saying: "It's not your dick to cut." "Foreskin is real skin." "What gives you the right to cut HIS Penis," equipped with an arrow pointing towards the guy next to him, who was holding a sign that read "Circumcision kills." I looked around for the movie cameras. There were none.

A sizable number of good causes exist to rally about. Real shit to get upset about. Like huge government waste for instance. Circumcision seemed a bit over the top for a cause. I mean...I don't really know where I stand on this. Certainly removing the foreskin of a male child is not a necessary operation and we, as a society, go all apeshit about cultures that circumcise female babies. (Although truthfully, I don't fully understand that procedure.) But I also I know in the locker room uncircumcised boys caught a lot of brutal teasing. And I hear there are more than a few chicks that opt out of those men so blessed with additional penile coverage. But really people...get a job.

In my travels, I had recently observed everyone seemed to have service dogs. Like everything the government gets involved in, the whole service dog thing has gotten out of control. Originally for the blind, well-trained dogs guided the sightless and greatly improved their mobility and freedom. Awesome. Now, pretty much any self-proclaimed quack could obtain a service dog for any old mutt for emotional support. So, why not Jaws, I thought? I am most assuredly an undiagnosed whacko and Jaws provides ample unconditional love, support, and a generous supply of short, black hairs. I just skipped a few tedious steps, including certification and training and bought a red vest saving everyone the trouble of pesky paperwork and a few trees, as well. I considered it my nod to the environment. Go green. And it is not as if we had not made ample attempt to train Jaws. We had a drawer full of participation certificates from various obedience training classes. The critical importance of preserving self-esteem transferred across species. Rose cross-stitched "Blind Service Dog" to both flanks to the vest. I added a cool pair of dark shades to his ensemble. I rarely got challenged, but when I did, I pointed out that Jaws, not me, was blind. He was not but it made for a convenient excuse when he went into fuck tard mode. "He's blind," I would say in hushed tones. People tend to assume blind and deaf are either synonymous or an emblematic pairing of disabilities. I blame Helen Keller. And who am I to upset their ignorant delusion? No one can get angry with a blind dog wearing cute sunglasses.

Jaws spent an inordinate amount of time napping. Dog owners are pretty confused about their relationship with pets. Who feeds whom, after all? Who picks up whose shit? Who pays for everything and goes to work each morning? Who walks whom? Bottom line, I am pretty sure dog owners are the subservient class in the relationship. We cheerfully delude ourselves otherwise, even as we pick up their smelly shit and fill their food bowls with overpriced premium dog food suitable for nobility. Come to think of it, I wonder if dogs aren't our Creators' silent sentinels sent to earth to spy on humanity and report back. Perhaps mankind will be judged by its Creators on how we treat the beings we foolishly consider beneath us.

Rome, 2016: Pope Francis has said that the number of conflicts being waged around the globe effectively amount to "a piecemeal Third World War." The U.S., normally the world's peacekeeper is currently distracted with its own conflict in Texas and Georgia. Others, including state sponsored terrorist organizations, have taken this opportunity to exploit the power void. The Brotherhood of Islam (BOI) had stepped up attacks throughout Europe against Christians. The White House Press Secretary stated the Administration had yet to formulate a strategy to confront the BOI's aggressive stance on the world stage but went on to emphasize the Administration's strong commitment to crush any rebellions inside its own borders with all necessary force.

Alongside Global News

CHAPTER TWENTY-THREE

The Pope reluctantly agreed. Peace was vital and if this meeting, peculiar as it seemed, could lead to peace, then so be it. Pope Francis had been a breath of fresh air for the Catholic Church. His politics were unfortunately socialist leaning, but his personal integrity, and the integrity he brought to his ethereal office was beyond reproach. He lived what he preached and, furthermore, required the previously spoiled and entitled church leadership to do so as well. Vows of poverty are empty words when one is wearing $100,000 worth of jewelry and living within the walls of gilded palaces filled with priceless art. Too much of the church's flock was more than well-situated to illustrate true poverty. And child abuse would no longer be swept under the altar. Not on His watch. I respect that. His views on man's contribution to Global warming were a bit paradoxical given the church's strong stance on contraception. Perfection is a lofty goal. In sum he was a good man.

Should God's living representative on earth, The Pope, have so little faith in his God that he requires bulletproof glass to insulate himself from his flock, it's time to move on to another God, as this one was pretty darn impotent. Pope Francis had faith in his God and strolled freely amongst his flock opting for conventional, modest, unarmored modes of transportation. He possessed a refreshing, genuine concern for the impoverished and the less fortunate. Perversely, these traits were not a prerequisite for the job.

Wars are a decidedly unhealthy undertaking for just about everyone but the munitions corporations, a handful of extremely corrupt politicians (by the very nature of the career path, all politicians are at least a little corrupt), and arms dealers. Wars were exceptionally bad for the poor. Rich people are more mobile and otherwise capable of insulating themselves from its ill-effects.

Popes long before Francis initiated a series of Crusades to fight the Muslim hordes. Not that Muslim religious leaders were without guilt, both then and now for a fair amount of innocent bloodshed in the name of their God. Problem is now both sides had traded in their horses and swords for Abrams tanks, assault rifles and IEDs. A frighteningly marked improvement in killing efficiency.

Francis naively believed in his power of persuasion and the innate goodness of all mankind. He himself would talk to the Brothers of Islam. He would not dispatch some faceless designated career statesman gifted in the art of bullshit without the authority to do anything but pretend to listen and provide circular, nonsensical feedback. Diplomacy, the art of lying in its highest most despicable state. Francis had faith. There would be no blood on this Pope's hands. Since the very dawn of religion, there had been wars, beheadings, genocide, mass murder, rapes, and pillages committed in God's name. Perhaps, Francis thought, this grand gesture, and his God could put a long overdue end to that nonsense.

The Pope and four of his key Cardinals agreed to the meeting's location at the Plaza Monumental in Barcelona, Spain. La Monumental was a massive bullfighting ring capable of holding some 19,000 spectators to witness the cruel, majestic ritual. The Catalonia Region's government outlawed bullfighting in 2012. The 100-year-old building's façade is of Moorish design. The structure had been purchased by the Emir of Qatar for the purpose of renovating the building into a massive Mosque to service the growing Spanish Muslim flock. The work was not yet complete, as the local bureaucracy, dominated by Catholics, continued to slow the permitting process. Perversely, La Monmaneta sits nearby to the still unfinished Sagrada Famila, a massive Gothic-style Catholic Church resembling a sand castle partially washed away by the incoming tide. The church is still under construction from the late 1800s. Talk about construction delays. Maybe the traditional afternoon siestas slow the construction process for all religions in Barcelona and underscores one of the origins for Spain's economic crisis.

Each dressed in traditional costume, the Pope in all white, the cardinals in red, entered the arena through a tunnel lit by a series of torches. The flickering, subtle light cast ominous shifting shadows along the roughhewn stone walls. A canvas tent covered the exposed earth, mixed with the blood, piss, and sweat of countless sacrificial animals and matadors. The arena was likewise dimly lit only by a semi-circle of torches just outside the perimeter of the canvas. A massive hand-carved wooden dais had been placed on the west side of the tent, situated opposite of the torches. In front of the dais, lay a large Persian rug with several pillows arranged in a semi-circle, facing the dais. The arena was still and deathly quiet. The only sound was that of the low hiss and occasional pop and crackle of the torches. The holy men took their seats in the offered massive wooden chairs; two to the right of the Pope, two to his left. Spoiling the symmetry, was a sixth and seventh chair placed to the right of the Pope that remained eerily vacant.

The sound of giant hooves pounding the earthen floor violently disturbed the quiet. Dust stirred and filled the tent before the rider made his ghostly appearance. Silhouetted against the torch light, the dark-colored stallion was massive. The rider was dressed in black, held an object resembling a spear, and appeared outfitted in medieval chain-link armor. The Stallion anxiously paced back and forth, foaming at the mouth, and fighting against the bit. He reared his front legs, exposing a massive pink erection. The subtle light made it difficult to make out the features of the man, but it appeared he had two horns protruding from his head gear. The spear came in clearer view as the horse continued to pace, trampling the Persian rug and coming ever closer to the holy men. The weapon was tri-pronged. The Cardinals rose to leave. The Pope motioned for them to sit. He was not one to be easily intimidated by, what he considered, theater. He assumed a well-practiced look of bored intent. A bearded man stripped bare to a loin cloth, wearing a crown of thorns, crept cautiously under the canvas of the tent, clearly frightened and bleeding from his hands, feet, side, and head. The Pope's patience with the spectacle was exhausted. He rose to leave. The rider charged the bearded man, eviscerating him with his trident. The horseman dismounted and gathered a handful of freshly-spilled bowels. He produced a curved blade and a silver chalice. The horned horseman sliced the carotid artery of the fallen man and collected his blood in the chalice. He chose the seventh chair and dined on the flesh and blood of the mock Christ.

"Please stow your tray tops and place your seats in the full, upright position as the Captain prepares his final descent into Belize City."

Rose nudged me fully awake. "What's wrong, Love?"

"Damn Hobo." I pinched myself to make certain this was not a dream within a dream. It hurt.

"You are going to leave a scar on your arm if you keep doing that."

We had sold or donated just about all our possessions and chartered a dual prop plane to Belize. The plane could hold seven severely malnourished adult passengers. I sat in the sixth seat. Jaws licked my hand from seat seven. An advantage of a charter, there were many, was that Jaws could ride in the cabin with us. He was too much of a retard to pass as a service dog on an international commercial flight. Rose had Jaws in a black sweater that Hobo had given him. The sweater, in large pink letters, read "Bitches Be Crazy." The charter, though convenient and a necessity given our circumstance, cost a small fortune. The additional and considerable "tips" to avoid legal potholes added to the expense. Then again, we were smuggling in cash, weapons, and a dog with considerable behavior challenges. We had to go through customs, but Jaws and our stuff was heading straight to the boat. At least, that was the plan. Shit happens. And, for an old guy, that means two things.

We made it straight through immigration with no problems. We had a couple small bags each, trying to look like a regular no-I'm-not-smuggling-shit-into-your-third-world-country tourists. The bags were filled with much of the cash from our drained bank accounts. We scheduled our arrival to coincide with the arrival of a commercial flight. The line to customs was impossibly long, snaking through and around the baggage carousels. We chose the nothing to declare line. Just in front of was a young, attractive, gregarious couple. Together they had two overflowing carts of mismatched baggage. Perfect, I thought. They would draw the attention away from us. Thirty minutes into the wait, we started chatting with the couple, Canadians. "Nothing to declare…ehh." I was trying to be funny. I should stop.

The man, Brad, explained his mom-in-law lived in Belize on Ambergris Caye. They were on a resupply mission "…cigarettes, camera gear, vacuum cleaner, and Cheetos."

"That's a lot of Cheetos." I was disappointed our stash did not include Cheetos. "The sacrifices we must make."

He gave me a courtesy chuckle. She fidgeted.

An armed customs agent motioned the Canadian couple out of the nothing to declare line. A look of panic crossed her face. He remained calm. They made it to the front of the line before us. A porter walked up, and immediately grabbed each item the agent removed and angrily tossed it back into the suitcase. The agent seemed aggravated, but the porter became even more aggressive. The porter spoke to the agent in the bizarre language unique to Belize. Some cross between Creole, English, and Spanish.

The customs agent yanked a brand new Dyson vacuum cleaner from the bag. "What purpose could this possible have?" I thought the device's purpose self-evident; to suck.
Brad responded calmly, "We don't have maid service," he shook the agent's hand, discretely exchanging $100 BZ…$50 US.

Our customs agent greeted us with a bored, unhurried, scripted welcome and a series of questions as to our purpose for visiting her slice of tropical paradise. She could not have been more convincing with her lack of enthusiasm. After not listening to any of our untruthful answers, she gave a cursory inspection of our customs form before wordlessly waving us through. For a country that depends on tourism for its economic health, they had serious work yet to do.

Somehow, the Canadians beat us through customs. We only had a couple bags with us. Our other shit and Jaws hopefully had made the circuitous route straight to the boat. The couple met us outside with cold Belikins in hand. They were wearing diptych t-shirts. Hers read, "I eat cake for breakfast." His, "I'm cake." We offered to let them ride with us over to the island. Not so sure why we made the offer, likely in reciprocation for the offered beer, (the southern curse of hospitality) as clearly they were smuggling, as well. Not surprisingly, most, if not all, Canadians speak English. Some of us Southerners do, as well. Phillip from Tropic Ferry met us just outside the airport's swinging doors. After a brief conversation to ensure the ferry had adequate space for the two extra passengers and their considerable baggage, I extended the offer. The Canadians initially happily accepted. They had failed to make arrangements to get over to the island and the small island hopper planes were not an option. I explained the logistics in my charming, southern drawl, "Phillip here will take us to the Oar House where we will meet the ferry."

Both looked at me puzzled, then at each other. They both shrugged and he responded unenthusiastically, "Sure what the hell?" Phillip and his son loaded the van while the Canadians huddled off to the side and conversed privately in whispered tones. The ride to the Oar House travels through a pretty destitute area of Ladyville over rough roads with potholes capable of consuming a VW in a single bite. Stray dogs, barefoot shirtless kids, bright orange iguanas, and makeshift restaurants serving BBQ and beer lined the road. The BBQ joint advertised BBQ pork or chicken with coconut rice and a cold Belikin for $9 BZ while strictly restricting weed smoking to the back porch. The Canadians seemed fidgety and a bit uncomfortable. Phillip pulled the van up to the Oar House. The Canadians started laughing uncontrollably.

"What the hell?" I asked

"We thought you said whore house?"

"And yet here you are…My peeps."

The boat is pretty noisy and conversation is difficult, at best. I drank the offered sweet rum punch, letting Jaws slurp some from the palm of my hand. It wasn't Jack, but the spoiled bastard needed to learn to make a few sacrifices, as well. Everything imported costs a fortune. And damn near everything was imported. We planned to go local as best we could and that meant chicken, fish, Belikin Beer, and Five-Barrel Rum. I laid my head down in Rose's lap while Jaws assumed a precarious position on the bench with his oversized head resting on the tops of my feet. I drifted in and out of sleep to the melodic rhythm of the boat's hull parting the nearly flat emerald green sea and the drone of the boat's powerful diesel engine. We pulled up to the resort's dock about an hour later.

The security personal slash porters met us at the dock and transported our belongings to our condo. Our new friends, the Canadians, planned to join us for the night. The porters stored the Canadians belongings overnight gladly for the offered tip. Lucy and Linus, the Sony midgets, met us at the swim up bar after we had partially unpacked. We are nesters and usually require completely unpacking and stowing our belongings in a carefully ordered fashion. We had brought with us as much as the small, private plane could hold. Our eagerness to chat with the midgets outweighed our instinct to nest. They were uncharacteristically sober.

CNN was on the bar's TV and they were broadcasting the news uninterrupted by boner pill commercials, celebrity divorces, and the overdone, tear-jerking military Dad surprise family reunions. The 3rd ID out of Ft. Stewart was turned back at the Texas border by the Texas National Guard, along with the remnants of the Federal forces that had stayed behind. Texas was a powerful state with powerful congressmen and, as such, contained several key military bases. Sadly, politics more so than military strategy is the primary determining factor of base locations. Case in point, just seventy years after the brutal lesson of Pearl Harbor, our entire Atlantic carrier fleet is currently based in Norfolk, Virginia. A single ship sunk in a strategic location of the harbor would block all access. Here I go drifting off on tangents again. It's just another problem of maturing democracies and, for that matter, human nature. We tend to look out after number one, often to the detriment of the group. And politicians were masters at looking out for number one.

Fort Hood, Sam Houston, and Bliss, as well as the strategically vital White Sands Missile Range and a handful of Naval and Air Stations, all were within the boundaries of the state. The First Calvary and 4th ID are stationed in Texas. Long story short, Texas was chock full of Federal military power. Fortunately, neither side had much of an appetite for violence against fellow Americans. And much of the Federal forces located within the state had "deserted" to join the Free Republic of Texas. Hillary, as predicted, won the election and promised a peaceful yet undisclosed solution. The President was outraged, but the cards were stacked against him. He had but a few months left in office and both Houses of Congress were firmly in Republican hands. The President wisely ignored the treasonous disobedience of his generals and the mutinous troops in Texas. Give the man credit...he, like JFK during the Cuban Missile Crisis, could spell military coup even if he could not recognize the one in Egypt a few years back. Know when to fold them, as Kenny would so sagely advise.

But The President being The President did not know when to walk away. The Black Panthers petitioned the President to grant African-Americans Atlanta as an independent city state. Conveniently, the new city state would be under the Black Panthers "temporary" control. With the power of his now infamous pen, with vocal objections by just about everyone, including most of middle-class Black America, he granted the Black Panthers both Fulton and Gwinnett Counties in Georgia. He cited the land grant as a logical extension of Monroe's support of the creation of Liberia for freed slaves in the early 1800s. Not even close. And he, the former Constitutional Professor, so abhorred the very document he once studied and taught. Let's see how that works out for him, I silently thought. He continued to promise he would not allow Texas to secede but that train was miles away from the station. Most puzzling, with just a few months left in office, he fired his VP, Joe Biden and replaced him with the Irish drug Lord I knew as Frio Lobo.

Crazy as it all was, it appeared the world had survived yet another crisis. There was no blood on the street...Well, not any more than normal, at least. And Atlanta would likely remain a part of Georgia and the U.S. Even our imperial President's pen was not that mighty. What, if any, role Hobo played in keeping this crisis from spinning out of control was beyond my meager pay grade. And why the crazy bastard needed me was just nonsensical.

Linus was wearing a muscle t-shirt that read "God...he is not dead." Lucy had a matching t-shirt but with a feminine living deity. He/she/ they live, that, I have no doubt. God's nature, His perfection, His purpose for creating us...I have no frigging clue. Nor did I know His gender, for that matter, not that I find that particularly relevant. This was a view apparently not held by the Peanuts pairing.

By now, we were all suitably drunk. The Canadians slipped out a couple times to burn one. Apparently all of their smuggled cigarettes did not contain tobacco. As such, they were a couple sheets further into the wind than the rest of us.

I turned to Linus. "You're a scientist, right?"

Linus eyed me suspiciously and ordered another round of shots before answering. "No. Not really. I'm a programmer, a Creator. I sit in front of a computer screen and write millions of lines of code. Not sure that is science...more like math."

"You two write the code for Garden of Eve?" I asked.

He nodded in the affirmative, "Salut," and tossed back his shot. "Only a small fraction of it. That program has trillions of lines of code...hell, maybe more. The programs requires next generation petaflop computing devices."

"Petaflop?"

"Yeah...computing devices utilizing superconductors capable of performing a thousand trillion operations per second. You play the Garden?" Linus asked.

I shook my head no. "Real life is good enough for me."

"The Garden is…" Linus paused and shook his head before turning up his Belikin. "Anyway, we are done. We are full-time freak flag fliers now. You?"

"What part of the Garden did you guys write?"

Linus pointed at his shirt, "God."

I ordered a round of shots. "God?"

"Yeah. Turns out religion plays a pretty damn important role in civilization." I tossed back my shot. Linus explained, "People left to their own devices are greedy, lazy, assholes. Each takes actions to help themselves, often to the detriment of the larger group. A framework with rewards, consequences, and an unambiguous ruler is required for civilization to succeed. Our Creator, let's call him God, figured out after a few millions years of watching his program run amuck that he needed to revise his program. He wrote additional code and an instruction manual, if you will."

"So, the way you see it, the Old Testament was the first software update?"

"I didn't say first. There are hundreds of ancient texts we know of, purported from one God or another, and likely tens of thousands we don't know that pre-date the Old Testament."

"Color me skeptical." Linus finished his Belikin and ordered another. Wendy, the cute Belizean bartender, brought him a glass of tap water. The infrastructure on the island is very primitive. And, like most coral islands, there is very little fresh water. The resort had its own desalination plant. Not cheap, but much cheaper than bottled water.

"Did I order water?" Linus asked. "'Cause if I did, I really must be drunk."

"No, little man. I brought you water. Finish the water and I will bring you another beer. We must stay hydrated." Linus smiled. Wendy, of Mayan descent, wasn't much taller than Linus. She was cute, though. And cute is a powerful currency. Wendy turned to serve another customer and Linus poured the water on the tile floor. Rose shook her head. Jaws lapped up the water. The Canadians slipped out for another smoke.

Linus continued, after catching Wendy's eye and pointing at his now empty glass, "Let's take your Old Testament as an example."

Wendy brought Linus another glass of tap water. This glass considerably larger. "Nice try, little man." Lucy laughed, slipped off her t-shirt and dove into the pool. I couldn't help but notice Lucy was a beautiful woman. Diminutive in stature but yet, no doubt, a full grown woman. Her arms, shoulders, and back were toned from countless hours in a gym or from priceless DNA gifted in lieu of verticality. And between her well-toned shoulders, dead center just below her neck, a tattoo caught my eye. A pair of cherubs, facing each other with chubby forefingers poised at their full lips.

Linus took her half-empty beer and chugged it. The man had a remarkable tolerance to alcohol. He continued, "The Old Testament is a marvelous framework for the successful propagation of civilization. Population was at dangerously low levels. 'Go forth, copulate, and multiply. Don't eat pork. Undercooked pork, tasty as it is, will kill your ass. Don't screw your neighbor's wife. Mind your parental units. Don't kill other people or steal their shit. Take a day off at least once a week from work. And most importantly, listen to anything else I might have to say 'cause I'm the boss of you.' Structure is key to the propagation of society. And obedience of the program to the programmer is paramount."

"Yeah, we've all seen that movie. Rarely turns out well….The creation challenging the Creator, that is."

Lucy swam back up to the bar and turned up her now empty beer bottle. She shot Linus an evil look. He shrugged. Wendy brought both of them a fresh Belikin.

After a long gulp, Linus continued, "I'm not for a minute disputing divine guidance. Our Creator wanted His creation to succeed. And anyone that created this world was, by all means, divine relative to His creation. That's a shit load of code. Like every programmer, He…"

Lucy interrupted, "She."

Linus continued, unphased "…updated His initial programing to fix bugs to ensure its continued utility. But there are the haters. Or, maybe not so much haters, but anarchists that thrive on chaos or profiteers that seek financial gain. No matter their motive, they insert viruses and worms and other devious algorithms to interrupt the program's intended mission. We might call them hackers. The Bible might call them the Devil and his demons….and, if your bank account ever got hacked, you would likely call them way worse."

"Most religions teach that one day we will meet our Creator and sit in His judgment. And I had spent way too many hours on bended knee not to believe. Faith in God is in my DNA. Not saying the God that TV evangelists portend to speak for. Religion in our world has sadly become a big business, abdicating its responsibility to help the poor in favor of gilded monuments, overpaid bullshiters, and Cadillac Escalades. To profit falsely from God, I guess, is a terrible sin. A bug in the program. But to murder innocents in his name is something much more...a malicious virus, not just a flaw in the code."

Linus nodded in agreement. "In The Garden, we insert digital robots…" he caught himself… "They insert robots that identify, root out, and eliminate malicious viruses. The robots are given a specific task but have free will to accomplish the task as they see fit. The downside is that insertion process creates a bit of a disturbance… A ripple if you will in the program." Linus paused for a minute, looked out over the sea and gulped his beer before turning back to me. "Maybe God does the same with his creation and your Bible…"

"My Bible?" I asked, tilting my head and raising my eyebrows.

Linus continued without acknowledging my interruption, "…might label these robots saints, angels or perhaps even gods based on the level of difficulty and outcome of the task at hand."

"God…huh? So you two are believers?" I asked. Lucy and Linus clinked beers and nodded in the affirmative. "Wasn't it Marx that said something like 'God is the opiate for the masses.'"

"Nope. He said religion, not God, is said opiate."

"A distinction without a difference, little man."

Linus raised an eyebrow. "Beg to differ, fat man." Okay, I deserved that. He continued, "I…

Lucy interrupted, "We."

Linus continued, "…believe in a supreme being that created our world." He made a sweeping motion with his arm, spilling Lucy's beer.

"Asshole."

"Bitch."

"That's so sweet," I noted.

Linus and Lucy both extended their index fingers in my direction. I was reminded it is never a good idea to get in the middle of a civil war. Linus continued, "Like you, we are not so certain as to God's purpose, form, or nature. But without faith, there is nothing; no purpose, no hope. Let's face it; we are born, we suffer, we die. Without faith in something unseen, without hope of some future rewards, fear of some punishment to come, the good would just commit suicide and skip the whole suffering phase and the bad would go unchecked. All that would remain would be chaos, evil, and anarchy."

Wendy brought Lucy another beer and wiped the bar top down. She shot Linus an accusatory glance. "And little assholes spilling beer on my bar."

Linus ignored her and continued, "Organized religions…those are man's creation. And quite often, religion is used by mortals with evil intent as a tool to manipulate the masses. All programs have unintended consequences, flaws in the code, that can be manipulated and back doors. And all data, even without devious intent, just decays over time. This God fellow…"

"Lady," Lucy interjected.

"He, she, what the hell ever…" Linus paused mid-sentence and gave Lucy an annoyed look, "…is something special…mysterious. I hope someday to be enlightened." "Linus to another chug and added, "just not today."

Perhaps my occasional attraction to the dark abyss was the anticipated enlightenment…to see the face of God…to understand the mysteries of our universe….the purpose of our creation…the suffering of the innocents. Not that the thought of sitting in judgment was without its considerable terror. I had been much less than a perfect man. Then again according to Paul, "We have all sinned and come short of the glory of God." And, in my case, way the hell short. My suffering was not born of innocence. My thoughts abruptly turned to Hobo. He had been absent from my life for several weeks now. Was Hobo God's antivirus?

Linus sat quietly, studying my face. He asked, "What's on your mind, big fellow?"

"An old…" I struggled how to characterize Hobo. I finally settled for "…friend."

We were beat. The mixture of tension, a long day, and copious amounts of alcohol had taken their toll on Rose, Jaws, and me. Lucy and Linus took our new Canadian acquaintances to the Palapa Bar a few hundred meters down the beach. The Canadians would be safe with the guardians. We turned in. I slept a dreamless night deep into the middle of the next day.

I joined Rose and Jaws on the balcony early afternoon. Jaws jumped in my lap, spilling my drink. He foolishly fancies himself a lap dog. Rose laughed. Jaws farted. The beer was cold. The sky melted seamlessly into the sea. This life was good.

Washington DC; December 2016: The President, in a recorded Oval Office video, resigned his office today in an unprecedented move. The resignation allows the President to begin his new role of United Nations Secretary General immediately. The President was unavailable for comment. Sources say he had left DC for his new home in Dubai immediately after recording his resignation announcement. The newly appointed Vice President David O'Grady is scheduled to be sworn in as the new President later this afternoon.

Several well respected Constitutional Lawyers noted the newly appointed Vice President had yet to be confirmed by the Congress and was not eligible for the Presidency. Speaker Ryan noted, "This is an unprecedented event and there is no clear consensus among lawmakers and the remaining eight Justices. The President has created a Constitutional crises with his departure."

Ryan commented the House's investigation into Justice Scalia's mysterious and unexpected death had not concluded. The Senate has agreed to not move forward with the Confirmation hearing for Scalia's replacement until the House concludes its investigation.

Creating further uncertainty, the Federal Grand Jury charged with reviewing the FBI's case into President-elect Clinton's mishandling of classified e-mails remains in session. A Justice Department spokesperson declined comment.

Alongside Global News

Je Suis

ACKNOWLEDGEMENTS

Like many authors, I draw from my own life's experiences. Consequently, many of the characters and stories were inspired by my friends and relatives. However, the characters in this book are a quirky blend of several different real people including ones that live only between my ears. None represent real people and all the stories are pure fiction. Never-the-less, I owe many of you a gratitude for the inspiration. Thank you.

    The lone exception is Ms. Susan Towler. She single-handily does the work of a platoon of angels as the proprietor of Kamp Kritter. The rescue shelter is home to dozens of hard to adopt or impossible to adopt animals. Susan gave us Jaws, our asymmetrical Black Lab, and my rescuer. And we are blessed by his stinky presence every day. Susan's name was used with her permission. To make a donation to the very real Kamp Kritter, please visit KampKritter.com

Jaws, Jennifer, Hobo, and I would be grateful.

    No one put up with more BS and whining than my blessed wife, Jennifer. Creating a book, while joyful, requires ripping Band-Aids off wounds yet to heal. As the first reader, she managed to give helpful advice without destroying my ego. No small task. Thank you for putting up with my shit.

    Finally, thanks to Deborah Gibbs for editing the manuscript. Grammar and spelling don't be my strong points. Bless her heart.

    Cover design by SelfPubBookCovers.com/RLSather

Ezekiel: A Novel, the Prequel to Belizean Pedicure is available at DMaloneMcMillan.com.

CPSIA information can be obtained at www.ICGtesting.com
Printed in the USA
LVOW10s0044120316

478754LV00001B/1/P